this
could
be
everything

Also by Eva Rice:

Fiction
Standing Room Only
Butterfly Sting
The Lost Art of Keeping Secrets
The Misinterpretation of Tara Jupp
Love Notes for Freddie

Non-fiction
Who's Who in Enid Blyton

eva rice

this could be everything

SIMON &
SCHUSTER

London · New York · Sydney · Toronto · New Delhi

First published in Great Britain by Simon & Schuster UK Ltd, 2023

3 5 7 9 10 8 6 4 2

Simon & Schuster UK Ltd
1st Floor
222 Gray's Inn Road
London WC1X 8HB

Simon & Schuster Australia, Sydney
Simon & Schuster India, New Delhi

www.simonandschuster.co.uk
www.simonandschuster.com.au
www.simonandschuster.co.in

A CIP catalogue record for this book is available from the British Library

Hardback ISBN: 978-1-3985-1016-6
Trade Paperback ISBN: 978-1-3985-1017-3
eBook ISBN: 978-1-3985-1018-0
Audio ISBN: 978-1-3985-2236-7

The author and publishers have made all reasonable efforts to contact
copyright-holders for permission, and apologise for any omissions or errors in the
form of credits given. Corrections may be made to future printings.

Typeset in the Bembo by M Rules
Printed and Bound in the UK using 100% Renewable
Electricity at CPI Group (UK) Ltd

For Claire Paterson Conrad.
Agent, friend, keeper of the faith.

'The canary is like a man's soul. It sees
bars around it, but instead of despairing,
it sings.'

NIKOS KAZANTZAKIS

'Live baby live
Now that the day is over'

INXS 'New Sensation'

Yellow

1

Yellow

Yesterday evening, something happened. And I don't like things happening to me, it's why I stay put, so that they *don't*. But when I walked downstairs at eight minutes past eight for a glass of water, I saw a small yellow bird standing on top of a packet of Weetabix in the corner of the kitchen.

An instinct made me look behind me, as if someone might be standing there watching me watching the bird, but there was no one; Ann had forced Robert to the theatre, and they wouldn't be back for hours. The bird took off again, and this time it flew across the room towards me, and I stepped back in alarm, then felt a wave of fury, as though the bird was mocking me for being afraid of it, and it was right, I *was* afraid. It flew onto the salad bowl in the middle of the kitchen table, and it scraped its beak against the green china edge, and then it lowered its yellow head in quick, jerky movements down into the bowl and took a bite from a lettuce leaf. Then it looked up at me with black eyes, and I heard a light buzzing in my ears, the sort that you have if you're going under an anaesthetic or you're about to faint, and I felt one of those Mexican waves of anxiety that started deep in my toes and swooshed up my body to the top of my head.

I walked around to the other side of the table so that if the bird took off again, it would fly back towards the window, and out again the way that it had come. But it didn't. Even when I flapped my arms around a bit, and tried to wave it out, it wouldn't leave. It couldn't seem to fly great distances; it was as if it didn't know what to do with all the space. It settled briefly on a tube of cling film on top of the fridge, and shook itself, seeming to take stock, like good old Dennis Rodman pulled out of a Pistons game, pausing for a moment to think. I gulped into the room. There was a tightness inside me, a vertigo, like that time on the high ropes at Casey Finch's sixth birthday party when I went up and up and up without Diana and looked down to see her crying on the ground below, and the earth had swum and sickened me.

I felt an urge to lie down in the middle of the kitchen floor with my eyes closed. I closed my eyes and strained to hear Bruno on the radio and the song coming from the stereo in my bedroom upstairs, but instead I could hear the noise of fluttering wings, primitive, frightening little wings, and I opened my eyes again. Then the bird made a sound, a *chirp*, if you will, and I drew in my breath and went still as still, because honest to God, it felt like a lion had roared.

As I lay there, I decided I would just walk away. This creature had come in; it had to be able to get out. It flew back onto the kitchen table and stood on *The Times*. My uncle had finished the crossword and he always likes to leave it out on view for us, like a child hoping for praise for a painting. The date of the paper startled me, as dates always do now.

May 18th, 1990.

It had been six months now. Six *months*. That's twenty-four chart countdowns on a Sunday night with Bruno Brookes on Radio 1. Ten number ones. Lisa Stansfield the week that it had happened in November, Adamski and Seal now in May. From upstairs I could hear the sound coming from my stereo, faint but clear.

'And it's a non-mover at number 4 for New Kids on the Block with "Cover Girl" . . .'

The cassette would click off after this song; it would need to be turned over. It *had* to be turned over. But if I moved, what would happen? The bird was back on top of the cereal boxes now; the window was still open, yet the bird wasn't interested in going back to where it had been before. Outside, fighting with the Top 40 from my bedroom, I could hear the sound of a fuzzy radio tuned to sport, as Kelvin had opened his window to let in the night air, and let out the sticky smell of spliff and black coffee. My sister had loved Kelvin. Actually, let's be honest, for loved, I actually mean *fancied*. He's very hip and magnetic as anything, and his father still shouts 'Pray for the sister!' every time my aunt Ann walks out of the front door.

The bird flew from the table towards the shelves and landed on top of a framed photograph of Ann and my mother as children. I wanted to stretch out my hand and touch Mama's face in the picture. I wanted her to talk to me, to tell me why the yellow bird had chosen this kitchen, why it had chosen *me* to find it, where it had come from, when it would go back to wherever that was and leave me alone again. Mama would know.

But Mama wasn't anywhere to tell me anything. And the yellow bird just went right on looking at me.

And the yellow bird seemed to laugh.

2

Knight of the Burning Pestle

When the telephone rang, I jumped out of my skin, and the bird flew right across the room and landed on top of a coffee jar. I raced back upstairs, four at a time, jumped into bed and pulled the covers over my head, stuck my right arm out towards my stereo, felt for eject, flipped over the cassette, pressed play, buried my arm back into the bed, and waited for the music to start again. *Breathe. Breathe.* Heart thumping, jumping in my shirt, like the song said. The ringing stopped. I drew in my breath. Still, the image of the bird on the frame downstairs. I looked at the clock beside my bed. Twenty to eleven. Ann and Robert would be back soon, and they would know what to do with yellow birds. Then the telephone started up again. Again! Now it *needed* to be answered, it was *imperative*. Something *must* have happened – but no sooner had I gathered these thoughts than a new sound joined the telephone and the Top 40. Loud, persistent singing, punctuated with trills and elaborate melody-on-melody, like a Whitney Houston outro chorus. Birdsong. It sounded like it meant something; it was trying to tell me something, I swear it. Kylie Minogue's new single struck me with previously unearned depth.

It was trying to tell me something, I swear it.

I pulled a pillow over my head and wrapped it around my ears, but it didn't work, because, like Daddy used to say, when you are truly afraid, that means you are truly alive, and there is no comfort in hiding because everything is too big to escape from. Still the telephone rang on. I had to stop it. I *had* to. I took a deep breath and ran from my bed and into Ann and Robert's room where there was a telephone beside the bed. I picked up the receiver.

'Hello?' I closed my eyes, felt my heart stamping around, awaiting fresh disaster. Something had happened. The IRA had bombed the theatre. My aunt had been mugged and knifed in Soho—

'Hello?' It was a man's voice. A policeman? A member of the fire service? It had to be.

'Is Ann with you?' I spoke with that dumb crackle in my voice that happens when I'm all keyed up. I could hear my breathlessness. 'Is she OK?'

'Er – no, she's not with me. Who am I talking to?' The voice on the other end was American. A New Yorker. I knew that much at once.

6

'This is her niece,' I said.

'Her niece! Ah! The niece from Austin, Texas! How are you?'

'I'm—' I stopped. I didn't know what to say. How I was, was hardly the point. 'I'm only half Texan,' I said quickly. 'I haven't lived there since I was nine.' Briefly I held in my mind an image of my paternal grandmother, Abigail Kingdom, shaking her head at me for denying my roots even the *tiniest* bit.

'Well. *I* can hear Texas in your voice.'

'And *I* can hear Manhattan in yours.'

'Ha! Touché!'

I swallowed hard.

'So, she's out, then?' He was persistent, that was for sure. I tried to catch up with myself, but it was hard. Answering the telephone was hard, I hadn't done it for months on end, with good bloody reason.

'She's gone to the theatre,' I said. 'I thought she might be back by now.'

'Ah. The theatre. Of course. I forgot. *Les Misérables!*' He pronounced it with the full force of French melodrama.

'She's seen it before,' I said.

'Four times, so she says. I wasn't keen on it myself. If you insist on watching musical theatre, it must be entirely lacking in sentimentality or you're dragged down, and you can't ever look yourself in the eye again.' He cleared his throat. 'Look, kid. I'm sorry to call so late – Jesus! I didn't realize it was gone ten-thirty! I'm a work colleague of Annie's.'

'You work at the school?' Somehow it felt unlikely.

'Oh yes. But just for now. Temporary. Acting head of drama.' I think he wanted me to say that I'd heard talk of him at home, but I hadn't, so I said nothing. He coughed a bit as if to give me more time to think. Still nothing from me.

'Could you leave a message for her?' he asked. I'm sure I could hear disappointment in his voice. I looked down at my pink and white feet, cold on the wooden boards of the bedroom floor.

'Yes. Sure.'

'Could you tell her that I have a copy of *The Knight of the Burning Pestle*? She was going to get it from – ah – it doesn't matter. The message is: I found it, with all my notes inside.'

I blinked into the darkness of the room. There was a pen beside the bed. When I picked it up, it felt alien in my hand.

'What was the book called again?'

'It's a *play*, dear girl, not a book. *The Knight of the* – no. Scrap that. Tell you what, kid. Just leave her a note that – uh – Gregory called, and write her that I have what she's looking for. I'll bring it into school.' He paused. 'Wow. Does Annie keep birds? I didn't know that—'

'You can hear it?' I could detect a certain reverence in my voice. It wasn't my imagination. Not only could *I* hear the bird, but the birdsong was travelling down the telephone and into the unknown space where the American was.

'Yeah. I can hear it.' He laughed.

8

'We don't have any birds. Only there's one sitting down-stairs in the kitchen. I just found it.'

'Oh?' he said. Just like that, more interested than surprised.

'I don't know what it is. Or where it came from. It's yellow all over.'

'Yellow all over, singing fit to burst, it's a canary.'

There was a pause.

Canary. *Can. Ar. Y.*

'A canary?' I repeated.

'Hush a second, kid. Let me hear it.'

I held the telephone away from my ear, out into the room. From downstairs the singing grew louder still.

'You see?' I whispered into the mouthpiece.

'I *hear*,' he said. 'Anyone keep canaries round your way?'

'How would I know?' It came out sounding rude, but I know for sure that I've forgotten how to talk to people. Any case, he just laughed.

'My cousin had a canary in New Jersey,' he said. 'I'd share a room with it when I went to stay. Used to wake me up as soon as it grew light. It's all longing, you know. My God, that song takes me back. Let me listen.'

So, we sat together, the American man I'd never met, and me, and we listened to the canary singing, like it had all been planned just for us, and all I wanted to do was ask him what he meant about longing. And to where, exactly, this longing took him back.

'It must have escaped and found its way to your kitchen.'

'I guess,' I said.

9

'You'll pass on the message?'

'Yes.' I'd said too much. I'd talked too much. I wasn't used to it.

'Thanks, kid. You can always rely on a Texan.'

I'd never heard that expression before. I reckon he'd made it up on the spot.

I put the phone down and sat still, waiting for my heart to shuffle down a few pegs from the state of high alert. It can take a while. Ann keeps a photo of my parents on her bedside table, taken in my grandparents' garden just before I was born, and most times I never look at it now, as it's just more pain on more pain. But I picked it up, and I stared right at them, and I spoke out loud, just so I'd make it truer.

'There's a canary in the kitchen.'

There he was in the picture, my daddy, Richard, a quiet, dark-haired Texan of six foot six, laughing and holding a handkerchief in one hand and his wife's hand in the other. Even in old photographs I can feel him wrestling with the complexities of Mama, with all her curious demands and her blue-eyed English beauty. Mama took to Texas like a duck to water, but Daddy had wanted to live in Oxford ever since he'd read *Brideshead Revisited* in his teens. In the end, Mama, who had grown up in Dorset and had no interest in Waugh's version of England, went along with what Daddy wanted, so when us twins were nine, they moved back to her home country. But I swear to God, the way she talked about the place, Mama would have stayed in Austin forever if she could. *Poor Lily*, my grandmother

Abby used to say to Daddy. *You married a Texan bluebonnet trapped in the body of an English rose. Why d'you wanna take her back to that place, huh?*

If Mama hadn't wanted to please Daddy so much, maybe we'd all be there still. Maybe we'd be all grown Texan, with no proper notion of England, and London, and Ann and Robert would have stayed oddities from the other side of the world, a couple we knew to be related to us, but with whom we had little else in common.

Downstairs, the bird had stopped singing. Was it still there? Damned if I knew. As I walked past the table in the hall, I deliberately avoided looking at the post, because I knew there would be envelopes with my name on, from Lisa. Lisa and her blue ink, *always* trying to contact me. Every week. But I can't open the letters. I can't see her. Not yet. Maybe not ever. She walked away, she *survived*. There in the kitchen was the bird, back on the edge of the salad bowl, eating again. It looked so ... what was it? *Cheerful.* As though it knew exactly what it was doing, as though this whole thing was part of some perfectly pitched plan that was going very well, thanks very much. Nothing about it seemed troubled. It looked up at me with those little black eyes.

'What are you doing here?' I asked.

But before it could answer me, like I knew it would if I stuck around, I ran back upstairs again, as though I were being chased.

I got into bed. I keep an old T-shirt of Diana's under my

bed, and I pulled it out, and up to my face. I closed my eyes and breathed her in, but it was the image of the bird that was imprinted on my eyelids. It was the unexpectedness of it, the brightness of it, that shot of colour, near fluorescent, like the yellow brick road in *The Wizard of Oz* when the film jumps out of black and white, cartoonish in its brightness. So, I lay still, and waited for my aunt and uncle to return, but I think that the adrenalin must have given way to sleep, in the way that it does when I get afraid on aeroplanes, and I didn't hear the two of them come back. Instead, I had one of my psychedelic dreams. I dream a lot more since everything happened, and most of the time there's strange, vague comfort in among all the weird shit that goes on. This time I dreamed about yellow birds growing to the size of polar bears. I saw the words of the note that I had written for Ann printed as a headline on the front of *The Times*.

Gregory called. He has what you've been looking for.

Just before the point that I finally woke up, my grandma Abby appeared in my sleep. She was way smaller than me – the size of an eight-year-old child – but her face was older than I'd ever known it, that of a ninety-year-old woman, and she was pressing something into my hands and smiling as though she felt sorry for me.

'Don't forget to carry a knife,' she said quietly.

'Why?' I asked her.

'To open the Weetabix,' she said. Then she laughed, and vanished again, and in the odd, bleary context of the dream, when I looked down at my hands, they were bleeding.

In the morning, when I woke up, Ann and Robert had left for work. I could hear the whirring of the washing machine coming to the end of a cycle. I took a deep breath and walked into the kitchen. The salad bowl had been washed up, and Ann's mug of tea left empty on the table. The window was shut.

The yellow bird was gone.

3

The Trench Effect

My name is February Kingdom, and although I spent the first nine years of my life in Austin, Texas, and lived for the next seven in Oxfordshire, England, I tell everyone I'm a Londoner, born and bred. I feel London in my bones, you see, and I think that's enough to make it true. I fear it, of course, like everyone with any sense does. Even the people who go around saying that they couldn't live anywhere else are mostly liars, but I've never been afraid of London for the reasons that others are – the expense, the traffic, the constant sense of something rising up, a little out of your reach that's cooler than you that you will never be a part of – that's the stuff that I *like* about it, that's the stuff I respect. No. I fear London for another reason. I fear London because it took the lives of both my parents and thirty-one others in November 1987, in a fire that started when a cigarette

14

was tossed onto the escalator at King's Cross tube station. I fear London because it didn't give a damn. It woke up the morning after this happened, sighed, dusted itself off and carried on. My sister said London was too old to care, and too young to apologize. Maybe that's true. Maybe she just knew how to say things that made me feel better somehow, and maybe because I still had my sister, I was just about all right.

According to witnesses at King's Cross, Dad had become separated from Mama and had escaped the fire to start with. Realizing she wasn't following him, he had gone back into the station to look for her. His timing was terrible. Months later, we were told what happens when a small, manageable fire is given a sudden surge of oxygen and air up an inclined surface – how it spreads violently, at breakneck speed in the blink of an eye. The people who worked these things out named it the Trench Effect, and no one stood a chance once it had roared into life that cold night in 1987. Dad and Mama were pulled from the flames and taken to hospital but couldn't be revived. There's irony in every agony. Just before they had left Oxford for London on the day that they were killed, Mama had told me that she was going to 'make the house safer', as she didn't trust the boys Diana brought home with her after school not to light cigarettes in our bedroom, and cigarettes in bedrooms might very well burn the house down. So, assuming she did what she had set out to do, Mama died in a fire, holding a shopping bag containing two smoke alarms.

The weeks following that night passed in a blur. People always say that, don't they? But I suppose they say it because it's true, and certainly I struggle to recall anything meaningful from those days, beyond a flat calm of silence pricked by moments of sudden chaos, and the smell of bacon sandwiches and the ringing of the telephone. Mama's sister, Ann, moved down to the cottage to look after us, while her husband Robert prepared for the moment that his two nieces by marriage would move into their house in North Kensington, a house we had only ever visited twice before in our lives. When we first walked through the door of St Quintin Avenue, Ann actually said things like: 'This is where you live now, girls' and 'You must treat this house like your home now, girls' – the sort of lines that feel like they belong in the opening pages of fairy tales before disaster befalls – and we just said: 'Oh. Thank you,' because what else was there to say? I remember Ann and Robert's cat wound itself around Diana's legs and she bent down to stroke it, and I remember being dimly aware of the hum of traffic on the Westway.

When we were very little, at the start of our lives in the Deep South, I would climb into bed with Diana and hug her to me like she was a teddy bear, and after the fire, when we first moved to London, I would close my eyes and beg to the Lord above that nothing bad would happen to her, that she would be safe forever, that she would live to be a hundred and three years old, and for a while, it felt like someone was listening to me. Then, whoever I was talking to must've stopped listening because two months before our nineteenth birthday, a van ploughed into the car that my sister was a passenger in. The car was being driven by Lisa, who was one of the only people Diana truly trusted besides me, but that afternoon, Lisa turned the wrong way down a one-way street. Lisa was thirty-five and walked away without a scratch. Diana was unlucky. Diana was not quite nineteen years old, and Diana – my twin sister Diana – died.

The small, manageable fire of my darkness that had burned quietly in the corner of my life was overcome all of a sudden just exactly as had happened at King's Cross. The fear, the dread, the anxiety, the horror, the guilt and the pain that had been contained since my parents had died roared suddenly up the inclined surface of my life. *Whoosh!*

So here we are. I'm nineteen and everything feels over already. The Trench Effect is efficient in its intent. I shake like a leaf most of the day. My heart bangs into my dry mouth as I lie on my bed. I am nearly sick every time the telephone rings. I dropped out of everything, and speak to only my aunt and uncle, and I am afraid of all the things that once pleased me so much. Yes. That feels about right. *I am afraid of all the things that had once pleased me so much.* I could list what it was that I had loved right here like Julie Andrews does in the song, but, if you will, just imagine all of *your* favourite things, and then imagine that they were mine too, and you'll understand what I feared, and believe me, it was everything from warm woollen mittens through to cracks on the pavement, walks in the park, the full moon, tennis balls, newly sharpened pencils and, of course, my sister.

I fear her ghost: Diana as directed by Tim Burton – a sort of see-through version of her earthly self, floating vague and Gothic-cool – on trend as hell, obviously – and wailing at me. Sometimes I would picture her in the wedding dress of Princess Diana, whom my sister had loved on the grounds that they shared a name and a romantic leaning towards the underdog, or sometimes I would picture her barefoot in pyjamas, holding her toothbrush, ready for bed. I didn't want to see her, and yet of course I *desperately* did. But like I said, everything now contained fear; all light, all happiness burned away by the wildfire of grief, leaving me only faintly aware of my aunt standing in my bedroom doorway, helpless, shattered by her own shock and sadness, but trying to work a way through mine for me. I suppose she thinks I might try to kill myself when she and Robert go to work, but these fears are quite wrong; death would have required a bit of effort, and I don't have any of that going on. Ann makes sure that the windows are locked so that you can only open them a couple of inches if strictly necessary, although once a week, she marches into the kitchen and opens them as wide as wide, and makes me come downstairs and we sit and drink Ceylon tea – black, no milk, no sugar – with her back to the open glass and the lilac-in-winter and the almost-bare plane trees, and she watches me carefully in case I might decide to run past her and jump out, which of course I never do.

But last night, something had chosen to jump *in*. To fly *in*. Now *this*. Maybe it had gone forever. Maybe it never happened at all. I guess I find it hard, these times, to know the difference between life and dreams.

4

Little Earthquakes

Since Diana died, my aunt comes home every day at lunchtime to check on me, even though it must be the most
gigantic pain in the neck for her, as the walk to and from the
school where she and Robert work is twenty minutes each
way. Westbury House is one of those private schools for girls
aged eleven to eighteen that considers itself to be enlight-
ened, but is actually full of rich white girls with names like
Claudia and Anneka, none of whom like to operate outside
Zone 1, unless they're heading for Heathrow to board flights
to Sotogrande or Vale de Lobo, where they sit by the pool
in Hunza bikinis pretending to be far stupider than they
are, laughing at jokes made by boys with names like Charles
Duckworth and Olly Bentinck-Metivier. Most of these girls
sat up a bit when Diana and I arrived at school, because we
were new kids with almost-Texan accents who emerged for

20

the sixth form only, and although there are an awful lot of clever, sporty, pretty girls at Westbury House, we at least held the ultimate trump card of being orphans.

Ann and Robert had worked in the state sector for years before they arrived at Westbury, and occasionally spoke to us with a kind of shadowy disgust at their decision to move away from the tough business of educating kids who *really* needed their help. Robert, in particular, spoke every few weeks about 'going back' to where it 'made a real difference' but then something would happen at Westbury – a charity evening, a play, a decent GCSE result from someone quite stupid – and he would be so delighted that he would kick that thought of leaving into the long grass for another term. His relief at being able to get Diana and me a place in the sixth form at Westbury House felt like a big deal. He could do this for us, after all we'd been through; he would make sure we got our exams done and made new friends. Within a week or two of our arrival, I beat everyone in the year at tennis, which really wasn't difficult – non-swanks – and half-way through week three, everyone worked out that Diana had been on the cover of *Just Seventeen*, and she knew Eric Elliot, who had modelled for Levi's and looked like River Phoenix. Eric Elliot was something else. I found it hard to talk when he was around; Diana found it hard *not* to.

We were twins too. Twins always get noticed. You can explain to people a million times that if you're non-identical, you only tend to look as alike as normal sisters might look, but that seems to disappoint everyone so much.

'I thought you were twins!'

'We *are*.'

'But you don't *look* like twins!'

'We're non-identical.'

'Yes, but you're still *twins* . . .'

In a way, I get their point. I mean, we shared a womb, but Diana launched into the world twenty minutes before me, at almost double my weight, and unlike me, was capable of feeding without a tube straight away. We were six weeks early. I swear it must have been my sister who had forced us into the world before we were fully cooked, ready for her close-up, impatient to get on with the show. Sure as anything wouldn't have been me.

What I mean is that none of the heroic effort that is associated with children who survive early birth seemed to have been in me. Most premature babies, especially girls, are gifted the spirit of Boudicca. *Oh! She was barely bigger than my hand, but from day one, she was a born fighter!* Yet I languished in an incubator for two weeks, thank you very much, unconcerned about gaining weight or the need to find a place in the actual world. Diana had a head-start over me in my mother's affection, that was for sure. I never shook the feeling that while I was lying in a plastic cot, Diana was out there in the room, holding court, and as we grew up, that feeling never really went away. It wasn't helped by the fact that her name had the credibility it did – Diana was the moon goddess, the hunter, the child-bearer – while Mama chose to name me February. When we were back in England, where there were six Lucys and four Annabels in our class at school, my name felt insane.

'*Why* did you name me February?' I would ask Mama.

'Because you were *meant* to be born on Valentine's Day.' Mama looked at me with impatience.

'But we *weren't*.'

'But you were *meant* to be.'

'But no one *likes* February. Kate Simmons' mum says it's cold and depressing.'

'Well, she would know. Anyway, it's not cold and depressing in Texas.'

'But we're not *in* Texas. The English think it's a silly name.'

'The English can go fuck themselves. *I* think it's magnificent.'

'Mama!' I wailed. I hated her swearing back then.

'Kingdom is the best surname in the world,' she said, 'and think of me and your poor aunt! Growing up Lily and Ann Bones! *Bones!* I ask you! My friends said I only married your father for his surname, and they were more than half right, I can tell you—'

'Yes, but February *Kingdom*! It's like eternal winter—'

'No,' said Mama. She looked at me with sudden urgency. 'It's eternal *spring*. Eternal *hope*. Who wants to be called Summer? You're already *there* with Summer, and in case you hadn't realized, Feb, life is very often not about the arrival, it's about the journey. Oh, God in heaven, pull those carrots off the boil, will you?'

*

At about ten past one, I usually hear Ann opening the front door, then walking slowly up the stairs and into my bedroom where she sits down on the end of the single bed. Sometimes she says nothing, sometimes she turns on lights, or tidies, or turns down the volume on the stereo. Often, she talks me through her morning. She expects no response from me, and usually she gets none, although I always thank her when she walks out again, and I think she likes that. It's a routine now, something that both of us accept but neither of us are ready to change, and there is something almost feverish in the whole thing; there's an agitation in her quietly sitting there, craving a reaction from me that rarely comes. What Ann talks about makes for uneventful listening, which is a deliberate choice on her part, because at heart she is extremely funny – far more so than my uncle Robert who doesn't really have a discernible sense of humour and is most times perplexed by her ability to scatter wit into chat about the school lunch menus, or parking suspension in Notting Hill during Carnival. Often, I pretend to be asleep, and Ann pretends to believe me. But sometimes, when she talks, I close my eyes and I hold her hand, and she squeezes my hand in hers, and she knows that it has been worth coming home to me.

The wallpaper wraps around my box-shaped bedroom in St Quintin Avenue, North Kensington, in a defiant chintz, with heavy curtains of the same pattern, so that when they are pulled closed, it's like being inside a teapot, a little enclosed world decorated with the repeat of periwinkle blue Chinese men on swings surrounded by bamboo. Ann had decorated the room imagining it might become a nursery for a baby, but then she and Robert had never been able to have children, so I suppose it languished quietly until I took it on.

'I like the repetition of it,' Ann had said when she showed me the room for the first time, reaching out and touching one of the figures on the wall. 'I thought a child would like to count their hats.' She'd laughed at the improbability of it all, as though she couldn't believe she'd ever entertained such a mad thought, but the next morning at breakfast, I'd sat down and looked at her.

'There are one hundred and forty hats. Just so you know.'

'What?'

'The wallpaper. The hats on the men on swings in the bedroom. One hundred and forty.'

'Fancy that!' Ann nodded and smiled, but then she got up from the table and I saw her wiping her eyes when she left the room.

There's a fireplace in my bedroom too, the edges decorated with original William Morris tiles of parrots, but the chimney is used now by nesting pigeons. A salmon-pink basin stands in the corner of the room, and Robert moved an Edwardian writing desk in front of the window for me, where I used to stare out onto the street below as I did my homework every evening after school. This all feels like about a hundred years ago, even though it was only last year, but the pot of pens that I used during my A level revision still sits there, along with a pile of cards and letters from people sympathizing with me after Diana died. *'Your sister was a one-off.' 'Your sister was extraordinary.' 'Your sister was so full of life.' Full of life*, I now realize, is post-death analysis for someone with too much energy who pissed people off and inspired envy in equal measures. That was Diana all right.

Beside these cards is a cardboard box containing copies of *Smash Hits* with the pages ripped out where they print song lyrics, because how else are you going to find out what Neneh Cherry is saying when she's talking in Spanish at the start of 'Kisses on the Wind', for example? Every fortnight from the age of twelve, Diana and I would buy the magazine and I would read the lyrics out, and we would memorize them like we were sitting an exam. Ann still collects *Smash Hits* for me from the newsagents even now, and when I read it, I'm back with my sister by the bus stop in the village, eating Mentos and drinking Fanta ... Except of course, I'm not. And under my bed, like I said, there's Diana's T-shirt, along with a folded copy of the *Evening Standard*, the newspaper that had recorded my sister's death in a simple paragraph and explained to anyone in London who might have cared to read it that a model called Diana Kingdom had been killed in a car crash. I never look at it, but I know it's there. I'd like to throw it away, but that would mean picking it up, and I don't think I can do that right now.

Above the bed is a poster of Brother Beyond from the centre pages of *Just Seventeen*. Nathan Moore is there in the middle, standing next to Carl Fysh and Steve Alexander, wearing a white T-shirt and pointing at the camera and smiling like he can't believe his luck. Diana stuck it up because I had once told her that I thought that Nathan was good-looking – she drew a huge heart over his head and had scribbled 'Febby 4 Nathan' inside the heart. I hadn't found it very funny at the time – I generally didn't like Diana telling me who I was in love with – but when I tried to take it down, the Blu Tack started to peel the wallpaper away, so I left it up. Now the poster feels half sacred to me.

Today Ann came into my room earlier than usual. U2 were on the stereo. I allow myself an hour on a Saturday morning when I listen to the radio in real time, not the recorded charts from Sunday before, and this hour usually coincides with Ann's arrival in my room. She opened my curtains and opened the window and breathed in.

'Good old Bono,' she said, still looking down on the street. She pronounced the long Os, so that the name rhymed with 'oh no'. 'All I Want Is You,' she said. 'This was last year, no? Peaked at number 3?'

'Number 4,' I said.

'Of course. Of *course!*' said Ann. She speaks like this sometimes – throwing sudden loud exclamations into her sentences, which feels like a kind of self-conscious, long-form torture for Robert who loathes anything stagey, and I've noticed people who are married do these sorts of things to each other, poking away at the hornet's nest then running away like kids. Ann has absorbed our obsession with chart music by osmosis, and she once told Diana and me that being able to rattle off the top five singles every week to her tutor group did wonders for her image at school, but really, Ann didn't need wonders doing. Ann had more power than other women, Mama used to say, because she was the person most like herself. It's only now that I really get what she meant by that, but as usual it's too late to say to Mama that she was right. Too late to tell her that I know what she means, and she's the clever one for working it out and putting into words what others feel and can't quite express. That was Mama's great gift, no question.

Ann pleated the embroidered rug at the end of the bed and looked out of the window.

'Feb,' she said quietly. 'Feb,' she said again. 'There's a bird downstairs in the kitchen. A canary. Do come down and look. It must have come in through the open window last night, like Peter Pan. *Do* come and look,' she said again.

I felt a jolt through me. Canary! *Can. Ar. Y.* The American on the telephone had been right. I sat up; it felt involuntary. It was still here. Ann's eyes widened in surprise.

'I saw it in the kitchen last night,' I said, my words rushed. 'I thought it had flown away again.'

'Well, it *hasn't* flown away. It's still here.' I could see that Ann was afraid that if she said the wrong thing now, this progress would be immediately undone again. I was sitting up and talking to her at lunchtime. This was not in the script. Often, I hate myself for making her work so hard. Sometimes I hate *her* for making *me* work so hard.

'I found it last night while you were out,' I said. From somewhere in the pit of my stomach, I felt a need to put my mark on this, even though I couldn't begin to say why. But *I* had found the bird. *I* had seen it. 'I went to bed and thought it might fly out of the window again, but it didn't, and then the phone started to ring and it – it – joined in. It started singing.'

Ann cleared her throat and nodded. She spoke quietly. 'Come down and have another look, Feb. It's *terribly* sweet.'

'It's not ours,' I said.

'No.' She handed me a piece of paper. I stared at it. It was a black and white flyer for a club night called Three Moon Monday at the Lovelock Arms on Ladbroke Grove that Diana used to go to with her friend Isla. I recognized the logo for the place immediately: two crescent moons either side of a full moon, all three of these celestial bodies wearing bucket hats and grinning. I looked at the date. It was for last Monday. The idea that the club could go on existing without Diana felt disgraceful to me.

'I'm not going,' I said quickly.

'No, no. That's just an old flyer. Look on the other side,' said Ann.

I turned the paper over. There was a ropey, photocopied picture of a canary in a cage, and above the photo someone had written:

LOST. URGENT. My canary is missing! If found, please contact Theo Farrah at The Pet Shop, Portobello Road. PLEASE PLEASE PLEASE contact me!!

'A lot of exclamation marks,' said Ann, who doesn't approve of them, 'and there's one of these stuck on every other tree on the road. All down Holland Park Avenue. Whoever lost their canary is very serious about getting it back again—'

'Well, we don't have it here,' I said quickly. 'The one downstairs is yellow. This one in the picture's black and white.'

Ann looked at me curiously. I gulped. I was cracking a joke, I think. Ann didn't move, as though any reaction at all might frighten me back under the covers. Instead, she patted my arm.

'Hmm,' she said.

'You can call the pet shop and tell this – this – person, whoever he is – that he can come and collect it,' I said.

'Could do. But I had another thought.' Ann stopped for a moment. I sensed that whatever this other thought was, it was coming to her as she spoke. 'I thought we could go there together. Give them the good news.'

Oh no, I thought. Oh no. I wasn't going out. I wasn't going to leave the house for the sake of this bird. This canary. I didn't like the power of it, it felt uncontrollable.

'Why?' I said. I felt creeping panic rising in me. 'We don't need to do that. We can just call the pet shop and tell them to pick it up.'

'But it's a chance to get you outside. And to do something useful. What do you think, Feb?'

'You go,' I said. I lay down again, my heart thumping. I listened to my aunt breathing. She was pacing herself, killing a bit of time. '*You* go,' I said again. Now my heart hammered. I wasn't going out. Not now.

'But *you* found the bird, after all,' said Ann. Again, a moment's rest from her. A little pause. I could hear pigeons cooing inside the fireplace. Ann opened her mouth, shook her head and closed it again. She was like Steve Davis plotting how to clear a snooker table. Don't screw this up. Don't panic her.

'I don't want to come out,' I said.

'I know, I know. But some day you *have* to, don't you, Febby?'

'No,' I said. I put my head in the pillow again.

Ann struck a bold move. 'I've decided. You're coming with me. I'll drive us up there.'

'I can't.'

'But, oh! This *isolation*, February! It's not how it has to be. It's not—'

'It's how I have to be,' I said quietly.

'No!' she said. 'This thing of keeping yourself hidden away from other people, Feb – you're too young for it. If you were an old lady, I'd say: all right. Jack it all in. You've suffered enough. You've had your time. I understand. But not *you*. Not nineteen-year-old *you*.' Now she went for the difficult shot. 'You could get back into playing tennis, you know—'

'No, never again. I'll *never* play again.'

'Oh, goodness, Feb. Take up *golf* then! All I know is that you can't be sad forever. No one can. It's almost impossible.' Ann had never sounded truly frustrated with me before, it was quite a shock. I wanted to yell that of *course* it was possible to be sad forever – look at Eeyore or Charlie Brown for

31

starters – but instead I just watched her as she walked across the room and opened my curtains.

Her blonde hair was pulled off her face in two combs, as it always is, and she was wearing her long, paisley Laura Ashley skirt and a cream blouse. On anyone else this look is instantly dismissible as nothing more than the clumsy style of a Sarah Ferguson-inspired Sloane Ranger, yet on my aunt, with her height and her model-thin frame, the whole thing gives out an almost Pre-Raphaelite atmosphere. But there's an odd, undeniable twist of punk there, too. It's in the dark green Vivienne Westwood boots that Diana and I saved up for and gave her for her birthday two years ago, and it's in the unintentional grooviness of the single gold earring she wears in the shape of a crescent moon. The earrings had been given to her by my mother – her sister – and ever since the night of the fire she's only worn one of them. The sight of the boots and the lonely moon always makes my heart wrench.

'I'm sorry I'm like I am,' I said. 'I'm sorry.'

My shoulders rocked into the bed linen. Here is who I am now, here is a sketch that we all know to be true, here are the fences she's watched me go around time and again. I become a little earthquake when I cry, a whole ecosystem of tears and snot and grief, and brief recovery, and then more tears, more earthquakes, more nose-blowing and mounds of tissues in the waste-paper basket. Round and round goes the circle, and Ann never says anything while it happens, but the smell of her Penhaligon's Duchess Rose overwhelms and comforts and depresses all at once and seems to say more than she ever could with words. Ann let her hand rest on my back for a full four and a half minutes this afternoon, and I know it was this long because I was counting the seconds. Then she passed me her white handkerchief with pink flowers embroidered in the corners, and suddenly, faintly at first and then loud, foreign, unabashed yet somehow inevitable – I could hear the singing of the yellow bird downstairs, fit to burst, as though his heart were full. Ann looked out of the window.

'The best moments in the best musicals happen when the character has to sing because there's nothing left that they can do,' she said. Ann can get away with saying these things, because the rest of the time she's teaching biology. There's something about her romantic streak that feels justified and serious, when you know that most of the day, she's wrestling Darwin and locusts and the life cycle of the average cell.

'Oh!' she said in a quiet breath. She stared at me, and a huge smile spread over her face. She didn't often smile that big; I could see all her slightly uneven white teeth. 'Isn't it lovely, the singing?' she said. '*I* think it's lovely. I shut the windows and the kitchen door and the door to the Rose room, so he can't escape again.'

'How do you know he's a boy?'

'Only the boys sing,' said Ann. She managed to deliver a lot of meaning in this sentence, but then Ann delivers meaning in the smallest of things. I looked at the flyer again. There was something agonizing in the photocopied writing. The repeat of please, please, *please*.

When I spoke, I felt detached from my own body, like

something in me had made a decision that I hadn't approved of but would have to go along with anyway.

'I'll come with you to the pet shop if we go in the car,' I said.

Ann looked at me and opened her mouth as if to say something but thought better of it. She knew she was in danger of pushing things way too far.

'Good girl,' she said. 'I'll drive.'

5

The Box

I often dreamed of cats.

Diana and I had once found a box of kittens, abandoned, on the edge of a field alongside the stream at the bottom of the village. I suppose we would have been eleven at the time, old enough to walk back from school on our own, young enough for the discovery to feel like the most exciting and important thing that had happened since we'd arrived in England a year earlier. It was I who found the box; Diana had already walked right past it, but I was a little distance behind her for once, as I had stopped to retie the laces on my plimsolls. As I had bent down, I had heard a strange sound, a mournful crying and a pitiful scratching that seemed to be coming from the end of the mud slope that led to the water. It was mid-June, there had been no rain for weeks. The stream that Diana and I played in for hours with our school skirts tucked into our knickers and little cane-stick fishing nets had dried up. The noise was eerie. I stopped, stock-still.

'Whasthat noise?' I hissed. Diana didn't hear me. 'Diana!'

She turned around. 'What is it?'

'I can hear something!'

'I can't—'

'I can. Come back here! Listen!'

Diana had been discussing why Claire Jacobs from the year above us at school had been mad to lend her new BMX to Hattie Jenks who was, in Diana's opinion, 'a sneak'. She wasn't pleased to be interrupted.

'It's coming from that box there! Down there!'

As I said it, I stepped back in alarm. I had seen *ET*.

'What box?' asked Diana.

'There's a box! There!'

The noise once more. This time she heard. *Now* I had her full attention.

'Shall we find out what it is?' asked Diana.

'No!' I hissed.

'Why not?' Diana was already edging closer to the box.

'It could be anything! It might be – *anything*!'

'Well, of course it's *something*,' said Diana scornfully. 'Everything's *something*!' She pulled off her Clarks shoes – even in the thick of an adventure Diana was savvy enough to know that our mother would take a dim view of dirty foot-wear – and stepped slowly down the slope towards the box. She stretched her arm out to it. It was a smallish cardboard box, with 'Solo' printed on the side, the name of the local supermarket. I leaned towards the action with trepidation. The smell of dried mud, river water and nettles was intensified by the sun that burned the backs of my arms. Usually I loved that smell, associating it with honey sandwiches and Just Juice on the bank. Today it felt sinister.

'Diana – *don't!*'

But Diana already had. My twin sister gently lifted the lid of the box and peered in. Knowing no fear, she stuck in her hand, just like she did when she'd paid twenty pence for a go at the lucky dip at the village fete and had pulled out a plastic harmonica wrapped up in page three of the *Sun*.

'Oh!' she said in a sort of wild rapture. 'I can feel something soft!'

I abandoned fear, and scrambled down the bank beside her and peered into the box.

'Kittens!' I said in reverence. 'Kittens! And a cat! The mother! It's two kittens and a cat! They're black and white! Oh, they're *lovely!*'

'Kittens!' said Diana in wonder as though she'd never heard of them.

'Baby cats,' I confirmed.

'I know what a kitten is, you great dope,' said Diana. 'They're so sweet!' She drew in her breath. 'They've been abandoned of course, Feb. Someone didn't want them. Maybe they wanted to drown them in the stream, but then there was no water, so they just left them here instead. To die.' Diana had a look of triumph about her, a cruelty. She liked shocking me, it furnished her with temporary power, like when Pac-Man eats the flashing cursors in the corner of the maze, and so gains brief dominance of the game.

'Who would *do* that?' I asked her in horror.

'Mean people,' she said.

'We should take them home with us,' I said. 'We should rescue them.'

Diana said something that struck me as a very Diana remark, even during childhood when such things are harder to analyse. 'I always knew something like this would happen to me,' she said. 'I always knew.'

'I heard them first,' I said quickly. 'So really it happened to me more than you.'

'Yes, but I actually wanted to find out what the noise was. You were scared.'

'I was *not* scared.'

I wanted to say to my sister that she had been talking so much that there was no way that she would have noticed the noise of the cats without my prompting, but instead I went for a compromise. I was damn good at those by then.

'Well, we *both* found them. They belong to us both now.'

I devoured Jill Murphy's books; I had visions of Mildred Hubble with her plaits and stompy boots and her very own cat called Tabby. A kitten felt like a dream, thank you very much.

It was with some difficulty that we carried the box back across two fields and down the road back home – I had a tennis racket over my shoulder and three tennis balls stuffed into my gym shorts – and we had to lift the box over two stiles. Diana started on and on about Hattie Jenks again.

'She never stops,' she huffed, 'she's so full of herself, she could strut sittin' down.' This was an expression Grandma Abby used a great deal back in Texas, and Diana usually went full Deep South when she said it too. I grinned to myself. I recall my leg being scratched by the thorns from the wild roses that knotted around the second gate; a gate I would usually have vaulted over on the way back from tennis, no problem. When we got home, our mother was standing in the garden looking down the road, smoking a cigarette with the half-anxious, half-irritated expression that she reserved for us when we were late back from school.

'What have you got there?' she asked. 'Is that your science project?'

Before I could open my mouth, or say anything, Diana had wrenched my half of the box from my hands.

'Cats!' she shouted. 'Kittens! I heard a noise by the stream, and it was coming from this box, and I found kittens inside!'

I stood back, flaming with fury at my own inability to speak up for myself, to say that *I* had heard the kittens, that *I* had drawn Diana's attention to them. Our mother peered into the box.

'How some people treat innocent creatures is beyond me,' she said. 'They'll need water, and something to eat.'

'Milk! Whiskas!' shouted Diana, whose blood was up.

'Steady on,' said Mama. 'The mother cat doesn't look in very good shape at all. We'll have to take them to Michael Seecombe tomorrow.' She nodded in satisfaction at her decision and Diana looked at me with an eye-roll that, in my fury

39

over her rewritten truth of what had happened, I ignored. Michael Seecombe was the local vet. Even aged eleven, I knew perfectly well that he had a huge crush on our mother. Now Diana had felt in the box and had picked up one of the kittens. It was tiny in her little hand.

'Can we keep them, Mummy?' she said pleadingly. I could sense her sizing up both New Pet Excitement, and the headline-grabbing capacity of the event itself once it was relayed to Hattie Jenks and the rest of the class at school. I pulled a stick of gum out of my pocket, popped it into my mouth and let her plough on; if either of us could persuade Mama to let us keep them, it was Diana in full flow.

'We can keep them for *now*,' said our mother.

'Not for now, for *ever*,' said Diana at once, keen to get the deal sealed. 'Feb, give *me* some gum.'

Mama threw her cigarette end onto the ground and crushed it with her sandal. 'And I'm sorry, girls. You can have all the fun of the kittens until they're old enough to give away, but we can't keep them.'

'Oh!' wailed Diana and I together. I was astounded; usually my sister had an immediate success rate when it came to acts of persuasion with Mama.

'Can we keep the mother cat?' I asked desperately. 'I don't think anyone will want her.'

'No! We want the kittens!' shouted Diana.

'Girls! Let's not get overexcited. *Perhaps* we can keep the mother cat. If no one else wants her.'

We would have to be content with that. Diana, I could tell, was planning her next line of attack. She wasn't done yet.

'It's funny how these things happen, isn't it?' Mama said at teatime. 'It's almost as though they were looking for you, Diana. Anyone could have walked past, but it just happened to be you.'

'And Feb,' said Diana. She grinned and I forgave her everything.

'And Feb, of course,' said our mother. But somehow, I felt that she didn't mean that bit. As far as she was concerned, this was Diana's moment of triumph. Every time that the story was told in subsequent weeks, it began the same way. 'The girls were walking home from school when Diana heard a noise coming from a box. She went to see what it was, and it turned out to be a mother cat with two kittens. I mean, you *hear* about these things, but you never think you'll be the one to find them, do you? Isn't it just so *typically* Diana? Of all the people to find a box of cats, it would have to be her.'

What I really wanted to ask my mother at this point was *Why? Why* was it typical? And I realized, after wrestling with the question for weeks afterwards, that the only reason that it was typical was because my mother had said it was typical. And that, in itself, had enough power to make it true.

In the end, the kittens were rehomed together. They went off in a basket on the back seat of the Volvo one weekend to a woman called Jenny Kaplan who worked with our father. Diana and I sobbed without ceasing for several hours. We had spent all morning using our matching Mason Pearson hairbrushes on the kittens, talking to them all the time, telling them that they had to behave in their new home. Diana had called her kitten Smudge – a name that I thought was too silly by half – but Jenny Kaplan wrote and told us that she had kept the name thinking it 'suited the little thing' due to her 'smudgy nose', but *my* kitten – whom I had named June – was rechristened Lilyanna, combining both Diana's names and my mother's, in respectful tribute to 'both the young girl who had found her, and the woman who had kindly given her away to her new home'. I cried furious tears with the injustice of it all when I heard this news, and Diana comforted me by saying – with perfect truth – that February would have been a tricky name to combine with anything much.

'She didn't have to combine it with anything!' I said furiously. 'She had a fucking name already! Her name was June!'

Diana gaped in wonder. 'You said that "F" word!' she cried in delight.

'Don't tell Daddy,' I said bitterly.

We still had the mother cat, whom I adored, but one afternoon about a year after we found her, I came home from school to find her gone. Mama was glazing a ham in the kitchen.

'I know what you're going to ask, Febby. But I never promised anything. Our lives are too busy for a cat.'

'Too busy! We're not busy! You don't do anything! You don't even have a real job!'

'That's enough.' Mama could be sharp with me in a way that she never was with Diana. 'No promises were made. The cat was never going to stay here forever.'

'She's got a name!'

Mama sighed. 'I know she has. I know. But she's gone to a lovely new home where she'll be very happy. I'm sorry, Feb, but there it is.'

'Where's she gone? Wherever it is, I'm going to get her back! I'll leave school and I'll be with her all the time!'

'You're overreacting. You can visit her, I'm sure.'

'I'm not! I'm getting her back for always! Maybe not today, but one day I'll be with her again, and I won't let her go!' I ran out of the room.

When Mama and Daddy had gone, I thought often of that day, the mother cat and her two kittens, abandoned by the river that was too dry to drown them in. Since Diana died, my dreams have been vivid with the discovery of the box. But I had been right about one thing. I *did* get to leave school and be with the cat again, albeit not in the manner that I could have predicted.

Now that cat walks around the house with me. Now it knows where to find me, in the room with the Chinese men on swings and the writing desk. The cat is the same cat that my mother gave to her sister and her new husband. I had named the cat when I was eleven years old.

The cat is called Thomasina. Meaning 'twin'.

6

Boy. London.

Ann likes a big car, she says, because it's her space, like another room in the house. The Vauxhall Astra is also the only place where she smokes. Every Thursday evening after *Top of the Pops*, she de-camps to the car for two fags and she sits in the driver's seat with the windows down and the engine running to avoid draining the battery, listening to the radio. Since Diana and I arrived, she doesn't smoke in the house because of the fire, which is kind but unnecessary, and I suspect an excuse to herself as the truth is that she likes the time on her own. *Never trust a woman with a tidy car* is a mantra she uses all the time. Robert, who likes order and insists on it in the house, has never passed his driving test, but every now and then walks out to the car like a matador at a bull-fight, and returns half an hour later, triumphant, with a black bin-bag full of her crap: empty Lilt cans, KitKat wrappers, old sandals, beach towels, CD cases, battered old textbooks, unpaid parking tickets, dried-up mascara wands, unopened mascara wands, dog-eared postcards and the little tin with Battle Abbey on the front that Ann keeps her fag-butts in, and he empties it all into the bin and returns the clean fag-butt tin to the car for her. We all squealed when he set a trap in the glove compartment and found a dead mouse the next morning, but even that wasn't enough to make Ann keep the car tidy for long. Inside the house, she keeps a tight ship, but her car is something else.

'You ready?' said Ann. 'The pet shop's not far. We'll be there and back before you know it.' She sounded stupidly up-tempo, cheerful. I shook my head.

'You can go without me,' I said. I felt the bannister in my left hand. I would run back upstairs. I didn't have to do this. Ann stretched out and put a hand over mine.

'I'll be with you. We won't be long. Just . . . come on.' She lowered her head. I could see her mouthing a frustrated 'shit' down at the floor. She'd run out of encouragement. It was all up to me now. I looked up to the top of the stairs. My bed-room door. My bed. Diana's T-shirt under my bed. Bruno. The Top 40. Nathan Moore. I couldn't do it. I couldn't. I couldn't leave them. I felt furious with Ann, and I breathed in to tell her to leave me alone, but I caught sight of the ear-ring. The lonely moon, its partner forever lost. She opened the front door, and the heat from the street hit the cool of the red and black Victorian-tiled hallway in St Quintin Avenue, and I felt as mad as Roy Neary in *Close Encounters*

45

of the Third Kind, certain as all hell that alien life's out there and being shit-scared of it all but somehow wanting to stare right into the heart of it too. I guess the shorthand is that I wanted to be sick.

'If you don't come with me, I'll ... well, I don't know what. I'll be sad.' Ann and her solo moon looked at me helplessly.

So, at 2.31pm, I got into the car for the first time since November. I sat down in the back on a pile of pamphlets called *Teenagers and Visual Media: A Guide for Schools* with a picture of two boys watching TV on the front: a white kid in a red shirt and an Asian boy with train tracks on his teeth, and the smell of the whole damn shooting range kneed me in the stomach. I breathed in cigarettes and old apple cores and sunlight on warm leather, and my God, I ached for Diana.

Ann, sitting in the driver's seat, turned the key, glanced at me in the back and laughed.

'I feel like a taxi driver,' she said, but she knew why I was in the back. I could never sit in a front passenger seat again. Not after what had happened.

'All right, love? I won't keep the meter runnin' when you're in the shop, darlin',' said Ann. She's a brilliant mimic when the occasion demands it. She grinned at me in the mirror, and when we started to move away from the house, I felt the earth swaying, and it felt like the start of a fairground ride, so I lay back and closed my eyes. Ann likes to have Radio 4 on in the car; it was a programme about growing tomatoes from seed.

'They need very careful handling, warmth and light. They need attention for best results.'

Ann looked at me in the mirror again and just nodded. I don't know what she was trying to say with that gesture, but it really didn't matter. When she started speaking, I had to lean forward to hear her. The motion of the car was nauseating.

'You spoke to Greg Arrowsmith last night?' she said.

'Who?'

'Mr Arrowsmith? You left me a message that he'd called?'

'The American,' I said. I breathed in. I knew Ann was keeping me talking to distract me. Any subject would have done, but we'd landed on him.

'Yes. The American,' she said. 'He told me you recognized that he was from Manhattan. He was impressed with that. I told him that identifying accents was only one of your great talents.' She raised a hand in amazement at a white car cutting her up on the mini-roundabout. 'Arse! Bloody BMW drivers, think they own the road! Yes. Well. Gregory's been at Westbury since January. He's covering the A level English and drama students over Nettie Foreman's maternity leave. He's got a new job as head of drama at a school back in America next term. For his sins.' She sounded contemptuous and pleased at the same time. I gripped onto the back of her seat as we turned down St Mark's Road. I wanted to turn back, I *really* couldn't do this, but Ann was ploughing on. 'I may have mentioned him to you before.'

'No,' I said. Perhaps she had. She could have mentioned

any number of things since last November that would have sailed past me, unregistered and unremarked upon, including Gregory Arrowsmith and his commitment to drama.

'What's he like?' I managed.

Ann laughed. 'He calls himself an overqualified fill-in, which is accurate enough. No. That's not true. We're very lucky to have him, even if he is just passing through. He's brilliant with everyone, in a way that dear old Nettie is not, poor thing. There's nothing like the real deal showing up to shine a light on what you were putting up with before.'

'He called late,' I said.

Ann coughed.

'Hmm. Did he? He announced in the staff room last week that he never goes to sleep before two in the morning, then gets up at six and reads Brecht for an hour before breakfast. I told him to piss off.' That was the other thing about Ann. Not afraid of swearing when she needed to, but she used expletives wisely, like Mama had, to their full effect. She seemed unwilling to stop talking, unwilling to give me a moment to think. 'You must meet him,' she said, 'you'd like him.' She paused as we turned down Chesterton Road. 'Robert thinks he's pretentious,' she said.

'Is he?'

'*C'est possible.*' She grinned at me in the rear-view mirror and shrugged.

I stared out of the back seat at the world, at the streets so alive with kids, all daft with the heat of the spring afternoon, peeling open ice lollies, dropping the wrappers onto the pavement and skipping around the cyclists and the cracks, and the dog crap on the pavements. Ann is a fast, capable driver, unfazed by London traffic, which flusters Robert when he's in the passenger seat, but impressed Diana and I who used to enjoy speed and the staggering, joyful disgrace of her car. Now, I shut my eyes, not wanting to see anything. I wasn't nearly ready for it.

'Take me back home,' I said quietly to my aunt, knowing that she wouldn't hear. I recited the charts in order. *40: down ten, 'Real Real Real' – Jesus Jones . . . 39: non-mover, 'Without You' – Mötley Crüe . . . 38: new entry, the B-52's with 'Roam' . . . 37 . . . 37 . . .* What the hell was at number 37? I felt sweat creeping on my forehead. *What was it? What was it?*

While Ann parked, I panicked. The world shimmered. *I would die here. I'd die here. I was going to die here.*

'Hang on, Robert'll kill me if I get another ticket,' said Ann. Why did it matter? Who cared? Then, she stretched her hand towards me, and even though I could see her doing it, I gasped in shock and comfort at her touch. Still holding my arm in her grasp, Ann stared outside at the parking meter, as if the combination of me and it presented to her a terrible conundrum, like that riddle where you have to get a fox, a hen and a bag of grain across a river. If she made a wrong move now, I could bolt.

'Wait here,' she said.

'I can't,' I said.

'You fucking can.'

She flushed at herself. I said nothing. I said nothing at

all because I knew that if I tried to talk it would be in an unknown language, something indecipherable. I wound down the window and breathed in the heat and the strong smell of kebabs and mint, and I closed my eyes and saw myself here for the first time. Portobello Road, with its slow-cooked undercurrent of agitation, the concrete heavy scented with other countries and hot muddle, had always represented nothing but comfort to us sisters. I thought about those first weeks after the fire. We had walked the streets of Notting Hill and North Kensington for hours every day in the wake of our parents' death, trying to make sense of something impossible to grasp, yet all around us was such life, such colour, such *fantasy* that it had been like walking into a dreamscape. *Colour, life, birth.* Oxford Gardens, Bassett Road, Lancaster Road, we had walked past the lines of grand houses built by the good old Victorians who sure as hell knew how to do flashy brickwork and ornate bay windows and couldn't have known that the twentieth century would rip London to shreds with bombs and war. Some of these houses are being restored by rich Europeans now, the kind who want basements and swimming pools and mosaics and dog walkers and alarms and Basquiat; others are crumbling into disrepair, or have been chopped carelessly into flats occupied by old ladies and musicians or addicts or students smoking weed. On Saturdays, Diana and I could feel the pulse of Jamaica in Notting Hill, that relentless immigrant beat, so unlike anything we had ever known in Austin, Texas or Oxford.

It was the rhythm of the whole thing that took our breath away. Back then, after our parents had gone, the pathway through grief had felt obvious to me and Diana. The way through was by moving, by keeping moving, by waking up and stepping onto hard pavements and walking and walking. It felt logical. Movement was a solution of sorts, a way of getting through the days.

Robert had noted how much time we were spending pounding the streets, and had offered us hour-long historical walks every day after we first arrived at St Quintin Avenue, and we had accepted out of politeness, but had come to love the routine of these outings: Robert trailing Diana and me in his wake, marching data into us in a sort of semi-contained embarrassment, his voice getting louder and louder with each street that we turned down, the information more and more intricate. If it was the only way he could think of to take our minds away from what had happened, then, what do you know? It actually *worked*.

'There's nothing more powerful than local history. Understanding how it shaped everything you see around you. I never cease to be astounded at people's wilful ignorance in this regard. Girls! Look at this!' On this occasion we were staring at the remains of a house in the middle of Holland Park. 'You know what this great Jacobean pile was called originally?'

'No.'

'Cope Castle,' said Robert with the trademark flourish of his wrist that he reserved for excellent revelations. 'The original house was built in 1604 by Sir Walter Cope, when he was Chancellor of the Exchequer.'

'Isn't there a road round here called Cope Place?' said Diana.

'Yes. Very good. *Yes!*' Robert laughed out loud, pleased.

'God, you're good,' I said to my sister.

Diana had grinned at me. Pleasing Robert had been one of her great missions once we had moved into St Quintin Avenue. My sister – fascinated by the entire male species and tending to see only good in most of them – repositioned Robert's general awkwardness and occasional abruptness as a pathological romantic melancholy, and realized that the place where he was happiest was in the past. Ideally, at least a couple of centuries in the past.

'What happened to old Walter Cope in the end?' I had asked.

'Well, there's a theory that he—' But Robert never finished answering this question. A peacock strutted its stuff in front of us, fanning its tail feathers. My sister turned and wolf-whistled.

'Isn't he sexy?' she said.

I'd rather have died than make this sort of remark in front of Robert. He raised his eyebrows, pulled off his glasses and polished them with a handkerchief from his coat pocket.

'Ridiculous affectation,' he said mildly. I didn't know if he was talking about Sir Walter Cope, Diana or the peacock, but I remember thinking that the expression worked great for all three. We often referred to Sir Walter Cope after that afternoon. His name became synonymous with the need to high-five yourself for remembering something important, but more than this, names like his became invisible strings that connected us to Robert, and the more of those we had, the safer I felt.

Now, sitting in the car, watching Ann slot ten-pence pieces into the parking meter, I whispered out loud to myself. *Portobello. Named after the capture of Puerto Bello in 1739.* Or was it 1755? Shit. I couldn't remember. And again, what was at number 37 in the charts? And who the hell was Gregory Arrowsmith anyway? My head swam.

Ann scuttled back to the car. 'Come on,' she said to me through the open window. She opened the door for me, and not knowing how I did it, I got out.

We walked into the pet shop, and a bell rang. I could feel my senses lining up in five separate boxes; I felt like I do when I walk into an airport. They were no longer part of me, they existed outside of me. *This could be the last place I ever see. This could be my last hour on earth.* I breathed in and touched the fingers of my left hand against the pulse on my left wrist. Yup. Still alive. The shop was dark and cold and smelled of sawdust and leather, and Ann and I were the only two people in the place. I hadn't been into a shop since two days before Diana had died, when we had run into Hyper Hyper on Kensington High Street to pick up a fluorescent green Hunza miniskirt. Now here I was, six months later, looking at walls of dog food and cages of hamsters. A huge tropical fish tank ran down one side of the shop, full of tiny fish, all colours: bright turquoise, pink, orange. Had they been here, swimming ignorant of everything, in that tank, all these months that I had been in the bedroom at St Quintin Avenue?

'There's no one here,' I said to Ann, and I turned around to leave, but in that moment a boy burst through the back door of the shop towards us, and I mean he *really* burst through, like someone leaping on stage to liven up Act Two of a play with a memorable cameo.

'Hello,' said Ann quickly. She grabbed my wrist and pulled me back towards her.

'Hello,' he said.

The first thing I noticed about him was that he was taller and skinnier than most boys; the second was that his left hand was dripping blood rapidly onto the floor. He was holding a tissue over the cut, but it didn't seem to be helping much.

'We're looking for Theo Farrah,' said Ann in the sort of brisk tone that she uses when she's trying to round up homework from a bunch of girls that may not have bothered with it. The boy pulled another tissue from his pocket and wrapped it around the cut.

'I'm Theo. Are you the lady who called about guinea pigs this morning? Like I said, we've got two females. Sisters. Long-haired. They might fight a bit, but if you give them enough space to run around, they'll be all right together.' His long fingers held tight on the bleeding. He was wearing a Boy London baseball cap on his semi-dreadlocked hair but his voice . . . his accent . . . he was *northern*. I don't mean

North London, but north of England. You didn't hear that accent around our way much. He followed Ann's gaze down to his bleeding hand. 'I've been out the back of the shop mending some bird cages. I sliced my hand. That's all. It's nothing, just a scratch.'

'Have you had your tetanus recently?' asked Ann, stepping forward.

'Yer wha?' He looked at her, alarmed.

'Your tetanus injection? You'll have to check. You don't want that cut getting infected, it looks nasty.'

'Yeah,' he said.

He looked at his hand again as though it were not part of his body. His eyes were huge and dark brown, the colour of Yorkshire Tea when the bag is left in too long. Even from a distance, his black eyelashes looked fake. Let me be clear: I never notice boys much beyond the absolute basics. I mean, I get the *idea* of them. I've fooled around with them a bit. But unlike me, Diana had felt the lure of the opposite sex since birth, while up until today, I have always felt pretty much immune to them. Now perhaps I was noticing this boy on behalf of my sister. Maybe *that's* what it was. In any case, I felt a surge of something running right through me, and I couldn't place it. Like I'd known him before, and this was all planned.

'Sliced my hand on a bird cage, like a twat,' said the boy, as if saying it again made it somehow truer than it had been when he first said it. He wiped the blood from his hand onto his white T-shirt. 'Can I start again? Good afternoon. Would you like to see the guinea pigs you called about?'

55

'No,' said Ann. 'We're not here for guinea pigs.' She said it so slow, so serious, like we were gangsters or something, coming to hold up the damn pet shop. Ann looked at me. She wanted *me* to say why we had come. She nodded slightly, as though I were about to throw my first line in the school play. I cleared my throat.

'We are here because we found your canary,' I said. There was a sweet taste in my mouth that I associated with a maddening return to deuce when I had played tennis. Deuce would undo me. I could fall apart at deuce, anything could happen. I felt the eyes of gremlins upon me. I had been known to lose matches from 5–1 up after panicking at deuce.

Theo Farrah looked at me properly for the first time. His whole body seemed to lean into what I had said. His eyes widened.

'You *have* him?'

'Yes,' said Ann. She pointed at me. '*She* found him. Last night.'

I coughed again. 'I walked into the kitchen and there it was. I thought that it might fly out again as the window was open, but then it didn't. So, we shut the window. He's been singing.'

'You found him?' he repeated. 'You found Yellow?'

'Yellow? Is that his name?' said Ann. She gave me an encouraging smile. I looked down at my hands.

'He was my grandad's bird,' he said. 'He bred canaries. He left Yellow to me when he – he was the only bird he had left when he died. He left him to *me*. Is he safe?'

'He's in our kitchen,' I said.

The boy took a breath in and closed his eyes. He bit his bottom lip and looked at us again. 'Thank you, thank you.' The second 'thank you' was no more than a whisper, as though he had run out of ink at the end of a letter, leaving just a scratched mark on the bottom of the page. I saw a single tear run down his cheek, and he wiped it away with the back of the hand that wasn't bleeding.

'Are you OK?' Ann asked him. But she was looking at his hand, she hadn't seen the tear.

'Yeah,' he said. 'Just – I didn't know what would happen to him.'

Outside the shop, a car honked its horn, and I could hear someone swearing at a traffic warden.

'All's well that ends well,' said Ann loudly. Theo Farrah seemed to shake himself right again.

'Has he eaten?' he asked.

'When I found him in the kitchen, he was eating,' I said.

'What was he eating?'

'Salad. Marks and Spencer's mixed salad, in a bowl.' My precision sounded ridiculous.

'He's gone up in the world,' said Theo Farrah.

'We left him water, of course,' said Ann. 'What a wonderful thing, to have bred canaries!'

I'd noticed a while back that Ann thinks that anyone who breeds anything is remarkable, as she's unable to reproduce herself. The whole process of new life feels miraculous to her in its truest, most untouchable form.

'Can I come and collect him?' asked the boy. 'I can be with you by eight.'

'That's fine,' said Ann, looking at me with caution. 'I should be back from parents' evening by then.'

'You a teacher?' he asked her.

'I am.'

'Parents' evening? On a *Saturday*?'

'Yes. They want the time with the staff to talk about their children, but some of them work so late that the weekdays became impossible. We try to accommodate our parents when we can.'

'Where I went to school, you'd have to hold the parents' night in the pub if you had it on the weekend. It'd be carnage.'

'Oh, we give them all a glass of wine,' said Ann expansively. 'It puts them at ease. I won't be back late. In any case, you can open the door to Theo, Feb.'

She looked at me as though this were a big deal, which it certainly was. I didn't want to have to open doors to this boy without Ann and Robert around, but Ann couldn't seem to see a problem. 'Shall I write down our address?' she asked him.

He looked at her curiously. 'Oh. Yeah. Sure. Thanks.'

Ann took a biro out of her bag. Theo handed her a leaflet called *Caring for Your Rodent*. 'Use the back of that,' he said.

Ann scribbled on the white stomach of a gerbil and handed it back to him.

'Thanks,' he said. He smiled at her cautiously. He had very

even, very white teeth. Briefly I thought of Lisa with her eye for physical beauty. She would have loved him. She would have asked him to come into the office for a chat, *that* was for certain. Behind Theo Farrah, pinned to a board, was a poster extolling the benefits of immunizing your cat. Suddenly, from the back of the shop, came the shriek of a parrot.

'Lord!' shouted Ann, flattening her hand on her chest in alarm, and at the same time I stepped backwards in shock into a stack of dog biscuits. Several packets fell to the floor, and I scrabbled to pick them up. Theo Farrah came forward and helped me. I looked at him, right into his eyes, like they do in films, and he gave me the smallest smile, like he was laughing at me, but I'm not used to people laughing at me, so it was hard to tell what it meant. Then he nodded at the parrot.

'That's Pierre. He's eighty-four,' he said. 'He's an African grey. He's been here since 1979.'

'Where was he for the seventy-three years before now?' said Ann, whose maths is better than mine.

'Who knows? If you ask him, he always says Berlin, but I think he just says that to be cool, you know?'

'Oh, right,' I said.

'Ha!' said Ann. She gave me a triumphant look that I couldn't quite decipher.

'He's a mess, like me,' said Theo Farrah, 'African but English at the same time, worst luck, poor fucking bird.' He pronounced 'bird' to rhyme with 'cared'.

'Where are *you* from?' asked Ann.

'My dad's Somali, my mam's from Sunderland.' He said it pat like that; I suppose he must have driven out that line many times to many people. He looked at us both and shrugged as if to say that was the best he could do, and if we had been expecting anything else, then we'd need to think again.

'Sunderland?' Ann would have had more luck picking Somalia out on a map than Sunderland, I knew that much. I wouldn't blame her. I had no clue where it was either. Despite intricate knowledge of this little pocket of West London, my geography when it comes to the rest of the country is dirt poor.

'Yeah. Long way from here. I was there until two years ago,' he said.

'Do you miss it?' I heard myself asking him, but he ignored my question, just looked at me, frowning slightly.

'You look like someone famous,' he said, 'a pop star or something. Who is it?'

My face flamed red. 'I don't know,' I said.

The door of the shop opened, and a woman and two blonde children, a boy and a girl, walked in. The boy wore a Queens Park Rangers T-shirt. *Eric*, I thought. *Eric Elliot's team.*

'I telephoned earlier,' said the woman. 'We're here about the guinea pigs.'

Ann and I didn't talk on the way back until she stopped the car outside the house. She looked at me.

'Well done,' she said quietly. 'Well done, Feb.' She

rummaged in her sleeve and pulled something out; I recognized it as the handkerchief she'd bought at the gift shop in Hampton Court with 'Divorced, Beheaded, Died, Survived' embroidered in the four corners and Henry VIII's crown in the centre. She dabbed her eyes with the word 'Beheaded', sniffed briskly, shoved it back up her sleeve again and nodded at me. 'Well done,' she said for a third time.

I didn't want congratulations. I had done something without Diana, something huge, but I couldn't quite *bear* that I had done it. It meant that I was moving on from something, didn't it? I didn't want to move on from anything.

'I'm glad he's getting the canary back,' I said. 'He seemed – nice.'

'Diana would have been all over Theo Farrah like the measles,' said Ann.

'It's the voice,' I said. 'The accent.'

Ann gave a small snort. 'Yes,' she said, 'and the rest.'

Once back upstairs, I pulled back the sheet from my bed and lay down, sticking my hand out to press play on the stereo. Bruno Brookes' voice filled the bedroom.

'It's a non-mover at number 15!'

Outside came the familiar sound of a skateboard skimming past the house, clipping over the lines in the pavement at speed. When Ann came up to check on me an hour later, she touched the Brother Beyond poster before she even looked at me. That's the thing about my superstitions. They really rub off on everyone else.

Later, Ann and Robert went off to parents' evening.

Usually, Ann calls it the longest three hours of the year, but tonight she seemed wired as all hell, and even though it was six o'clock and it was Westbury House School for Girls, she went out wearing eyeliner and she'd washed her hair. As she waited for Robert in the hall, she jittered a bit, holding her bag and her coat, impatient as a child waiting to go Trick or Treating on Halloween. On top of Duchess Rose, she smelled of Timotei, and carrot moisturizer from the Body Shop.

'Once more into the breach!' she said cheerfully. Robert sighed.

They forgot to shut the kitchen door before they left. For a moment I thought the canary had gone again, but then I saw it flittering up the stairs as though it knew just where it wanted to go.

'No!' I said out loud. I followed it up the stairs, but it had found where it wanted to be. It was in my bedroom. Sitting on top of my wardrobe, happy as you please, looking at Nathan Moore and Brother Beyond. It chirped at me as though it was all hilarious. Why was it that the bird always seemed to be laughing at me?

'It's not funny!' I said. Again, a chirp. I shut the door quietly. Holy shit! Now the boy called Theo Farrah would have to come *upstairs* to my bedroom to get the bird. I could almost hear Diana screaming with delight.

When my aunt and uncle had gone, I pulled out the *Times Atlas of the World* from Robert's study to look up Somalia, and then found the map of Durham and Sunderland from

Robert's Ordnance Survey collection in the bottom drawer of his desk, and spread the two of them out on the kitchen table. I felt nervous – like a teenage boy rooting out top-shelf magazines from under his elder brother's bed – and my heart-beat sped up as I compared the geography of the two places and considered what had happened between Theo Farrah's parents, and quite how the dust and heat from the Horn of Africa and an industrial town in the north-east of England (annual rainfall 25.6 inches) could have combined to produce someone like him. The wonder of it pressed upon me. I felt something in me that I think might be that great big enemy of grief, curiosity. Fresh and new hatched curiosity, and with it I felt a great clarity, a great calm that I knew wouldn't last, but was there for now. For that moment. Something had happened. The yellow bird had flown into the house, the house where I lived, and I had gone to the pet shop with Ann, and I had told Theo Farrah that I had his canary. Upstairs in my bedroom. The yellow bird is laughing and the yellow bird is all right. I put the maps back before Ann and Robert got back. And now they're downstairs, home from parents' evening, and the doorbell's ringing and I guess it's him.

'Feb!' shouted Ann. She wanted me to be the one to let him in. The doorbell rang again. I heard Ann climbing the stairs. She appeared in my bedroom.

'Vanessa Wilson's father spent twenty minutes question-ing her last exam paper. He kept saying "how can she have got forty-eight per cent?" I wanted to say: by cheating. She deserved no more than thirty. The girl's a menace. *I'm* not opening the door.' She grinned at me hopefully. If it was a tactic, I suppose it worked. And anyway, I didn't want to leave him outside on the doorstep, he needed to get the bird out of here. I looked up at it, sitting on top of my desk now, by the bowl of water I'd put out for it, and I stood up.

This time, when I started to count down the chart, whispering it to myself as I walked downstairs, I remembered exactly what was at number 37. The Blues Brothers with 'Everybody Needs Somebody to Love'.

7

Birds of the City

I mean, let's be clear. The doorbell ringing isn't unusual. The house in St Quintin Avenue gets its fair share of visitors, although since Diana died, I have ignored them all, for the simple reason that it feels too complicated to answer the door to anyone. I find that I have to adjust my mood, speech and personality according to who or what is on the doorstep, and that's too exhausting for me in my darkness. London crawls with eccentrics in a way that the countryside, despite what all those sketch shows might imply, never actually had.

There is no pattern to the neighbours round here, no clear line linking them all together, except for the very fact of their immediate shared geography. There's Alfie, a good-looking, cockney fishmonger who shows up twice a week to flirt and regale Ann with stories of his disastrous love life; Mr Desmond, an anxious Pakistani man in his sixties, who mends vacuum cleaners and has a wife who had an accident involving a Flymo; Patricia, the Nigerian Jehovah's Witness to whom Diana sold her Batman Swatch Watch for three pounds; the Rag and Bone man with the long grey beard, who roams the streets of North Kensington wailing 'Any old iron!' with a horse and cart like a Victorian ghost; Bob, the Old Jogger, originally from Northern Ireland, who runs up and down St Mark's Road between eight and eight-thirty every morning dressed in the Newcastle FC away kit; and Andrew Jeffries, a divorced banker who campaigns for the Tories, and lives at the end of our street with a blond son called Christian who once took Diana to Pizza Express on the King's Road but ruined his chances afterwards by insisting that they split the bill. I'm not even mentioning the clusters of school kids kicking conkers onto the road come September, and the sixth formers clogging up Mr Quennell's newsagents buying Cadbury's Caramels and illicit cigarettes; the weekend drunks, the lifetime drunks, the sometimes drunks, the doctors, the impoverished posh in paisley head-scarves and moth-eaten green sleeveless puffas with pockets full of receipts from Lidgate's the butcher and dusty packets of Polos and parking tickets, the nursery school teachers in long skirts and patterned jumpers, and the meditation group led by a fifty-year-old Indian gentleman called Hanif Whagella, who meets his devotees every Wednesday afternoon to stand under the plane tree outside number 14 with hands joined and their eyes closed. *All human life is here*, as Mama said on the one occasion that I clearly recall visiting Ann and Robert in London before she and Dad died, and there was something in the way that she said these words that implied yearning, rather than the usual whack of condescension that flared up when she was jealous of Ann. It was something that I had loved about my mother, that despite all her best intentions not to be, she was drawn to people who frightened her, and, even more than that, to chaos. Opening doors was fascinating to her, whoever was on the other side.

'I thought this was the right house.' As he said he would be, Theo Farrah was carrying a small bird cage. He had a bandage over his right hand. In the brief hours that had passed since I had seen him first, I had found him impossible to picture beyond his Boy London cap and his height. I looked down at his feet; I could see his brown skin and his skinny ankles and those big, clean white trainers, all new like he'd painted them.

'Hello,' I said. 'Do you want to come in?'

He stared at me, then suddenly slapped his hand down on his thigh. 'Hey. *That's* who it is!'

'Who what is?'

'Who you look like. It's Tracey Ullman.'

'Wh – what?'

'Tracey Ullman. You know her?'

'Well, yes. I know who you mean—'

'Tracey Ullman. That's it! It's been bothering me.' He nodded at me, satisfied.

'I don't see it myself,' I said.

'She's funny. She's *really* funny. Girls aren't usually as funny as boys, but she is.'

I gaped at him, which I guess he took to be a sign that I was offended. 'I don't mean it in a bad way,' he said. 'Girls don't get a chance to be funny. My ma says once they've had kids, they're responsible. And they're tired. And that stops them from telling jokes and stops them from *wanting* to tell jokes, so the men get to tell most of the jokes and be the funny ones. But under it all, most of the time, girls are thinking: you *twat*. They're thinking: anyone can be funny if they get enough sleep. I could've told that story much better if I didn't have a baby upstairs. And they're right.'

'That's true,' I managed.

'I grew up on English comedy. *Blackadder, Fawlty Towers*. You know what I mean, Tracey?'

'My name's not Tracey,' I said.

'My point still stands.'

Thirty–love to him. This wasn't what I had expected, I had barely time enough to return his serve. I just looked at him and said: 'Do you want to come in?'

Ann and Robert were cracking open a second bottle of red wine. Robert rarely drinks, but parents' evening usually pushes him over the edge. As headmaster, he's always the celebrity in the room, but unlike most people in power, Robert doesn't have the showing-off gene. Ann once said that Robert being an intellectual – and a sincere one at that – was deeply confusing to the parents of Westbury House, who are far more at home with the affected posturing of the deputy head who only ever writes in peacock blue ink and is friends with Nick Mason of Pink Floyd.

'Oh!' said Ann. 'Hello again. How's your hand?'

'I'll live,' said Theo.

Ann looked at Theo very strangely, I thought, almost as though she were holding herself back from bursting into song. Her eyeliner had smudged, and the hem of her skirt had come loose, and she was wearing a bracelet on her left wrist that I had never seen before, but I've come to understand that teachers at posh private schools tend to receive more gifts per week than minor royalty, so I thought nothing of it, and in any case, I was too anxious about Theo Farrah to register anything else. Robert was sitting very still and frowning slightly. He's no good at unexpected visitors, although the fact that Theo's black would have interested him more than the usual fare.

'This is Theo, the owner of the canary. He's come to take him back,' said Ann.

'Ah!' said Robert. 'What a stroke of luck that the canary found its way here.'

'Yeah, I guess so.' Theo looked uncomfortable. 'He belonged to me grandad.'

Robert blinked at Theo. 'You're *northern*,' he said with an intonation of hushed wonder.

'Yeah.'

'Where are you from?'

'Just outside Sunderland,' said Theo. He looked like he wanted to laugh, but no one ever laughed at Robert, and maybe he sensed this.

'Well!' said Robert. He glanced from Ann to me with a frown, as though one or both of us were tricking him. 'Do you follow the football?' he asked Theo.

'Course. I go home and away, when I can.'

'Gabbiadini's your man of course. *Hell* of a striker. Got you up to the first division, that's for sure.'

'Oh, yeah. Can't deny that.'

'Robert supports Liverpool,' said Ann, managing to make it sound a bit tragic.

'Oh. Congratulations.' Theo bowed his head a fraction.

'Thank you very much. We'll do it again next year, that's for certain, lad,' said Robert, but Theo laughed right at him.

'You think? You might not do it again for another thirty years.' He rubbed the side of his nose. He was so tall, so *unlikely*. Robert looked at him in amazement and laughed back at him.

'You don't think we can do it again? Ha! You want a bet on that, son?' One of Robert's eccentric features is how his voice alters to ape whoever he is talking to. He just can't help it. When we had first moved in, he had even picked up a little bit of a Texan lilt from the both of us, until Ann told him he sounded crazy. But now his accent was moving north of London with the speed of the Caledonian sleeper. I wanted to get Theo out of the room, it was embarrassing the hell out of me. For such a conventional man, it's a plain weird habit.

'The canary's upstairs,' I said to Theo.

'Upstairs? I thought you said he was in the kitchen?'

'He moved,' I said. 'He can fly. He's got wings.'

'No shit,' said Theo.

'We found him upstairs when we got back from seeing you at the pet shop. I think I left the kitchen door open.'

'Is he safe now? No windows open upstairs?'

'Not in my bedroom. Nowhere much to go in my bed-room.' I blushed like a loser. There was a short pause. I knew Ann was hanging on every word between us and I wanted to tell her to stop it.

'I bought you a bottle of wine and a book,' he said. 'To say thanks, like.'

I looked at him, astounded. He might as well have told me he had bought me a line of cocaine wrapped in an elephant's ear; it felt *that* outrageous and implausible. No boy had ever bought me *anything* before.

'Thank you,' said Ann and I at the same time. I don't think she meant to say it out loud.

'What's the book?' I asked out of embarrassment.

'Oh, just a book about birds,' he said. 'How to identify the birds you get round here. It was my grandad's. Thought you might like it. For fun, you know.'

He pulled it out of his bag and handed it to me, quite without shame, and I stared at it in my hands, a worn little paperback called *Birds of the City*. Keeping my head down, I flipped it open. I could feel Diana looking down at it too. *Nice*, she was saying.

'Thanks,' I said. 'That's so – nice.'

'Oh, you won't find a canary in there, though,' he said.

'No. I guess not.' I shut the book.

Ann came to my rescue.

'You want to go and get him, then? Take him back?'

Theo followed Ann upstairs, and I walked behind them, holding the bird book. As he walked past the table in the hall, I saw him glance down at the pile of unopened letters from Lisa, and he seemed to take a breath. Her huge, sprawling handwriting on an envelope − always with a bouncy blue line underscoring the word 'London' − had only ever induced excitement when she had sent things to us in the past: clippings from magazines that we might not have been able to find ourselves, cards for every occasion, contracts to be signed ... Now that same writing, forming the same address, meant a whole lot of different shit to me. Now it was frightening, unwelcome as a ghost. I walked behind Theo Farrah, with his long thin legs and his hair and his black Boy London cap and his Nike high-top trainers, and the whole thing looked out of whack on the carpeted staircase of the house on St Quintin Avenue, and I felt desperate, humiliated by everything: the sheer white middle-class backdrop of the scene. What was he thinking? What did he think of *me*? He stopped on the landing, in front of Robert's framed print of Kevin Keegan and Bill Shankly standing in the Kop. He laughed and I wasn't sure what he meant by the laughter, only it sounded sardonic; but then one thing I know is that people who don't support Liverpool Football Club find everything about Liverpool Football Club extremely annoying, so I guess he was making a point of some sort.

When he'd finished laughing, his attention was drawn to

72

something else outside Ann and Robert's bedroom. There were two hardbacks propped up on a little shelf against the back wall, and he picked one of them up. Ann and I looked at him nervously.

'*Little Women*,' he said. 'My grandad read it to me when I was twelve. He told me that everything you need to know about girls is in that book.' He looked at the cover. It was a copy that had belonged to Mama from the latter half of the 1960s; the drawing of the four girls on the front gave them the look of the mid-nineteenth century via a Mick Jagger-era Marianne Faithfull. When Theo opened the book up, it looked small in his long fingers; he was a priest holding a prayer book.

'Your grandfather was quite right of course,' said Ann. 'Who was your favourite of the March sisters? Which one would *you* pick?' She asked this casually enough, but there was a Shakespearian seriousness in the question, as though suddenly she'd made him Portia's suitor, choosing which casket to open.

'Oh, Meg,' he said, still looking down at the book. 'Amy's the pretty one, yeah, but Meg was the one. She had a bit of everything, you know?'

'Hmm. What about Jo?' said Ann. There was badly concealed concern in her voice.

'Nah,' said Theo, putting the book back. 'I went off her when she cut her hair.'

'Good God,' said Ann. She gave a bark of laughter and looked at me. I shrugged.

'Yeah. I know she had to do it, like,' said Theo, 'but that was that for me, I'm afraid.'

'But Jo was the most interesting to you, surely?'

'I know she's meant to be, but you know, I'm not good at seeing the inner beauty of girls, and all that. I like outward beauty. I think the inner stuff can be worked on, you know?'

Ann laughed. Theo laughed, like it was a great big joke. I wasn't at all sure that it was, but in that moment, the veil of peculiar shame for the house and its contents had lifted. I could hear Diana whooping in my ears! *Now what are you going to do, Feb? Hahaha!*

8

The Ball

The stereo in my bedroom had clicked off. Automatically, I bent down, flipped it over and pressed play.

'*Number 17 . . .*' began Bruno.

'Ghetto Heaven,' I murmured.

'*Family Stand with "Ghetto Heaven" . . .*' said Bruno.

But Theo Farrah had seen his canary.

'There he is!' he said quietly. 'It *is* him,' he said, as though there was a part of him wondering if we'd made the whole thing up.

Yellow was still there, sitting on top of my wardrobe. I felt a tug inside me at the sight of him and I suddenly knew that I didn't *want* him to leave my bedroom now. He was here for a reason. He should *stay* here. He had chosen to be here! But Theo was already moving towards the wardrobe.

'We don't want to frighten him,' he said. 'Come on, Yellow. Play the game.'

He stepped forward, and the bird flew a short distance, from the wardrobe to the top of the tall cupboard full of old books from our days in the cottage in Oxfordshire. Then off again, back to the wardrobe.

'Ah,' said Theo. 'He'll tire soon.'

'So, what do we do now?' asked Ann.

He opened his mouth to say something, but the bird took off again, and this time, he took off towards the open door of the bedroom.

'Shit!' muttered Theo Farrah.

I moved towards the door, but it was too late. The canary was now on the landing, perched on top of *Little Women*, as though to make a point. There was a window propped open with a thin piece of plywood at the end of the landing. That window was always propped open, with that same piece of wood, even in the middle of winter. Ann, like Mama, believed in a breeze blowing through a house. The gap the wood allowed between the landing and the outside world wasn't a big gap, but it would be big enough for Yellow to get out again, sure enough. The bird flew closer, landing now on the lid of a bottle of blue ink on the small table that sat directly under the window. One more movement and he would be away.

'Don't move,' said Ann. She said it as a question and an instruction in one. I think she knew as well as I did how much was riding on this bird, and I saw them all in that moment:

Diana, my parents, even old Abby, my grandmother rocking on the porch outside the house in Austin, Texas – I felt them all holding their breath and I couldn't bear it. I took a quick inward breath. Behind the door of my bedroom was a tennis ball from the original tube of three that Daddy had given to me with my first proper racket. I'd lost the other two balls from that set, but this one had made it through all my early games. Now there it was, resting sentinel on top of my chest of drawers, faded yellow. *Yellow.* I'd always felt that there had to have been a reason why I hadn't lost it. It had to be there for *something*. Suddenly, I knew what that was.

I picked up the tennis ball and felt it: hard, soft, fuzzy, gentle, in my hand. I hadn't touched a ball since Diana had gone, but for a moment I was back on the court, and I felt a rush of power, of something I thought I'd lost, something that frightened the hell out of me.

'Stand back,' I said to Ann and to the stranger called Theo Farrah.

'What are you ...?' he said. '*Whoah!*'

He dodged out of the way as I threw the ball as hard as I could at the wooden stick that held the window open. A fraction of a second later, and the stick had dislodged and fallen out of the window, and the window had slammed closed. I could hear the faint plop of the ball landing on the street below. The bird flew away again, startled, back to the bookshelf, back onto the spine of *Little Women*, and then, before anyone spoke again, as if admitting defeat, it flew back into my bedroom. Quickly, Ann shut the door.

'What did you just do?' said Theo.

'I held a tennis ball's what I did,' I whispered into my own body, and to no one else.

'You *threw* a tennis ball,' said Ann.

'I felt it in my fingers. I did. I felt it.'

In my head, I saw old Granny Abby throw back her head and roar with laughter.

'You gotta eye for the ball, girl, I tell you that much!'

'The bird's safe is the main thing,' I said.

'Ha*ha*! Thanks to *you*,' said Theo Farrah. He laughed delightedly. 'That was *great*!'

'It was indeed,' said Ann. Her cheeks were flushed red, and she was laughing too. 'Oh, Feb! I'd forgotten how *good* you are with balls! As the actress said to the bishop! Haha!' She laughed again very loudly. Theo snorted. Nothing seemed very funny to me in that moment, all told.

'It was an emergency,' I said. I wanted to know where exactly the tennis ball was and to get it back to my bedroom as quickly as I could. I wanted it back where it belonged. Now I'd done it, I was filled with dread. It should never have been used again, it wasn't meant to have been used, not for *anything*.

'Where d'you learn to throw like that?' Theo asked me.

'Austin, Texas,' I said.

'Of course,' said Theo.

'I need to find the ball,' I muttered, pushing past him.

I stayed outside looking for ten whole minutes, but I couldn't find it. Probably some kid had kicked it down the road or picked it up. I felt a panic rising in me. I was *outside* again. Not only that, but I was outside looking for a damn tennis ball. Cars came down the road like they knew I was out, like everyone wanted to take a look at me. The girl who lost her parents, then lost her twin, then lost a tennis ball. The girl who had lost her parents in the fire that they all knew about, the fire with a name. That voice. The voices. The sorry, sad voices. The shocked voices. The hum of the hospital . . .

'They've both gone, February. I'm so sorry.'

I sat down on the front step, and I put my hands over my ears and closed my eyes and I started to count down the Top 40. I could do that.

At 31, it's a big jump from 52 for Hothouse Flowers with 'Give It Up' . . .

I got all the way to Adamski before I stood up and I walked back upstairs. I wanted everyone out now. I wanted to be alone, but back upstairs, still in my bedroom, normal as you please, I could hear Theo Farrah and Ann talking about his life.

'Me grandfather was more like me dad, really,' said Theo. 'I looked after him, and that. You know. Until the end.'

'Goodness,' Ann said. 'That can't have been easy for you.'

I detoured into Robert and Ann's bathroom. I sat down on the loo and noticed that I had the spotting that indicated the start of my period. As usual, the ache for Diana intensified. Another month marked without her. Or another twenty-five days, to be exact. She and I had never managed to do that thing that sisters or best friends are meant to do of 'synching' our cycles. Hers was longer than mine, and more erratic. Always Diana would say the same thing when either of us had our period. She would quote Alfred, Lord Tennyson in the voice of a witch. 'The curse is come upon me!' I would always have to add 'cried the Lady of Shallot'. I don't remember how or why this had started, but now that Diana wasn't here, I still have to do it, only now I have to say her lines too. I looked at my reflection. I was flushed, as though I'd just won a tournament. My eyes were flashing and wide open, I could feel the life in me pulsing everywhere in my body, under my arms, in my mouth, between my legs, and it shocked me. I saw myself throwing the ball.

'The curse is come upon me!' I said loudly.

'What was that, Feb?' called Ann.

'Cried the Lady of Shallot!' I said to my mirror reflection. I put a hand into my mouth to stop myself from exploding with sudden laughter.

We caught Yellow easy enough after this. Theo put out the cage and we waited, and he hopped in, just like that, pleased as could be, and we shut the cage door, and it was all done and over, and I knew that Theo Farrah would be gone soon. He was sitting on the floor of my bedroom, his back to the wall. Diana would sit on the floor like that, her legs stuck out in front of her, talking to me while I copied out essays.

'Brother Beyond!' said Theo, looking up at the poster. 'He likes boys, you know, Nathan Moore.'

'*Does* he? Stock, Aitken and Waterman are very clever at selecting these lovely-looking lads to sing for them, aren't they?' said Ann.

'Five number 1 singles last year,' I said.

'Who?' asked Theo.

'Stock, Aitken and Waterman. The producers.'

'Oh, right. I don't know much about them. It's not my kind of thing. Kylie Minogue's good-looking, though.'

'Oh, everybody loves Kylie,' said Ann expansively.

'My sister loved her,' I said.

Now that the adrenalin had left me, I felt drugged. But he was still here. The boy was still here! I kept my eyes on Yellow in the cage. He would be going now. Leaving this house forever. Yellow would go, and Theo would go, and neither of them would really have known me. Not a version of me that made sense, anyway.

'She died,' I said.

'Wh — wha?'

'My sister died. My twin sister. She was in an accident. A car ... six months ago. November. Last year. 1989. November 1989.'

I looked out of the window. I could see Kelvin's dad talking to Lady Dorritt who lived three doors down from him on the other side of our road. He was smoking a spliff with bare feet. She was wearing a Barbour and carrying a Sainsbury's bag and her West Highland terrier was having a crap on the dusty roots of a plane tree at the end of his extendable lead. As they talked, I watched Kelvin's dad hand her the spliff. She took a few drags and handed it back to him.

'Your sister?' said Theo. There was a strange shake in his voice.

I turned back to him and nodded but found I couldn't look at his face. It was too painful, watching him take it in, but he had to know. He couldn't leave here without knowing. He couldn't.

'Jesus! That's terrible.' He looked down at his hands.

'She was my niece,' said Ann.

In that moment, I think I felt, properly for the first time, how losing Diana had been for my aunt. All she had done was stage-manage my pain; I rarely considered the completely separate agony that she must have felt too.

'So, you all live together now?' said Theo.

'My parents were killed in the King's Cross fire,' I said. Might as well get it all out now. Might as well open the fucking floodgates to the whole bloody mess of it.

Theo looked appalled. 'Both of them? Your mum *and* dad? Both of them?'

'Both.'

'I didn't know that,' he said.

'Well, why would you know any of it?' I said. It felt like an odd observation.

'So, you're *really* on your own, then.'

I had never heard it put as bluntly as that. Most people I knew had written to me when they had heard the news, and it turns out that cards and stamps certainly give folk the time to focus thoughts and plan what to say, but there was a strange desperation in the face of Theo Farrah, a real horror. I hung down my head, feeling a rush of blood in my ears.

'She's not on her own,' said Ann, a little defensive.

'I'm sorry,' he said eventually.

I shook my head, unable to say anything.

'Did people say she looked like you?' he asked me. Ann blinked at him in surprise. 'Your sister, who passed away,' he said, to clarify, 'do you think she looked like you?'

Normally I have problems when people talked of Diana 'passing away'. It lacks the necessary aggression that sudden death demands, and woah, I need the aggression. 'Passing away' seems to carry with it an acceptance – a peace and gentleness that is completely at odds with what had happened to Diana. But these words from him felt like a relief.

'We were non-identical,' I said. 'We looked nothing like each other.'

'You did, you just didn't believe you did,' Ann said. She coughed briskly, as if to say that the conversation had taken a wrong turn, and he seemed to understand her.

'I'm very sorry,' he said again.

There was a terrible silence. Ann broke it.

'Where *is* Sunderland exactly?' she asked. 'My geography's so appalling.'

It's a city twelve miles south-east of Newcastle, north of the River Wear, once the greatest shipbuilding city on earth, I thought.

'It's a long way from here,' said Theo. He sounded bleak.

'I bet you miss it terribly,' said Ann.

'I'm all right,' said Theo.

Ann straightened up her back. 'Heavens, look at the time,' she said. 'I'm going for a quick drink with some friends from the staff room. I need it after re-marking Vanessa Wilson's last essay.' Her voice sounded thick and strange. Ann never went out for drinks with staff at Westbury House. *Never.*

'Where are you going?' I asked her.

'Julie's,' said Ann. She pulled in her breath after she said the word, as though she had shocked herself a bit. 'You know.'

Oh, I knew Julie's, all right. The fairy lights, and Moroccan benches and French bread sliced in baskets on the table and little pots of olive oil and Harold Pinter and Antonia Fraser holding court in the corner. Of course, I knew Julie's. Diana and her friend Isla used to dress up and sit at the bar until they were bought drinks by demob happy bankers on a Friday night. Occasionally I would cycle past them and wave, on my way home from tennis. Julie's was considerably north of decadent by Robert's standards.

'I'm not exactly sure who will be there this evening. Tonia Spratt, who always asks how you are, Mr West – you remember him? Teaches art to the lower years – oh, and Gregory Arrowsmith.'

'The temporary drama guy?' I said.

'The temporary drama guy. Yes. You'd both like him.' I wanted to ask her what on earth it was about Gregory Arrowsmith that she supposed Theo Farrah would like when she barely knew him, but Ann was already moving towards the door. 'I won't be late back. Robert's downstairs if you need anything: a piece of burnt toast, a tour of Notting Hill's past, a degree in Japanese, that sort of thing.' She laughed. I heard her go into her bedroom, and as she stuck her head back into my room a moment later, she trailed the sweet, strident smell of a perfume that I didn't recognize.

9

Useful is God

I thought he'd go right after Ann had left us, but he didn't. We heard Ann saying goodbye to Robert, saying that she wouldn't be long. We heard her leaving the house. Theo stood up.

'Do you want a Coke?' he asked.

'I don't know,' I said slowly.

'It's not a trick question.'

He took one from his bag, and handed it to me, and I cracked it open, not without trepidation. Fizzy drinks felt too frivolous, far too bloody happy. They reminded me of sports day picnics, and Saturday mornings on Golborne Road, and adverts where girls in hot pants got the man they wanted by rollerskating along a beach in Malibu. Eric had always drunk Coke like it was water. I took a sip, and, my good God, it felt *illegal*. Yellow sang on, and the Top 40 got closer to the end of the charts.

'He's singing for someone to talk to,' said Theo. He sat down on the end of my bed and retied his left shoelace.

I took another gulp from the can and my eyes watered. Theo sat up and looked at the photograph of Diana and me on my bedside table.

'That's her, isn't it?' He nodded at the picture.

'That's her,' I said.

I waited for him to make some remark about this, or about her smile, or her eyes, but he didn't. I wanted to give him the chance to think it, to say something that would let me know that her power was still there, but instead he said: 'You look happy in that photo. You're smiling.' He was talking quietly, with a great seriousness. I wanted, very badly, for him not to make any more observations. Let that be all he needed to say.

'Tell me three things about her,' he said.

I gulped at him. 'Three things? Any things?'

'Yeah. Any three things.'

'OK.' I took a breath. 'She once met Penelope Keith in a lift. She farted during Evensong on a school trip to St Paul's Cathedral and was made to go and sit on the coach with no packed tea. She thought she had a direct connection to Princess Di, just because they had the same name. She was blind in one eye, thanks to a genetic condition on my dad's side—'

'That's four things.'

'She was good at drawing.'

'Five.'

'She liked Jackie Collins.'

'Six.'

'Her favourite film was *International Velvet*.'

'Fair play.'

'She liked singing hymns. She liked sitting in churches.'

I wanted to shout everything out into the street, to make sure that everyone knew it all, knew I'd never forget it, knew Diana was always in me. Theo Farrah looked down at his hands. A stranger in my bedroom, looking down at his hands. I could have leapt out of the window and hit the ground running.

'We used to dance in the kitchen,' I said. 'All the time. We'd learn routines, you know? For fun. For the hell and the fun of it. We'd tape the music videos off the Chart Show. We were working on Janet Jackson.' I could hear my accent becoming more Texan with every word, as it always does when my adrenalin is up.

'What was the song?' he asked me without looking up.

'"Miss You Much".' I paused. 'She liked me to tell her everything was OK. She liked to know that I thought we were all right. She needed me. I was useful.'

'Nice thing, to be useful.'

'She's here,' I heard myself saying.

'What?'

'It's OK. I know she's here. I feel her sometimes. It's fine.' I stopped. I didn't want to go on. I needed something else to say. Something away from Diana.

'Did you know that the bit between Holland Park and

Notting Hill Gate is the deepest point on the Central Line?'
I asked him.

Theo laughed at me, but it was no good. I was still there.
I remembered the last time we'd danced. She'd come back
from a casting, and she dumped a pile of property details
on the kitchen table. I was reading a copy of *Elle* that Ann
had confiscated during a biology test and had brought back
home for us.

'We're going to get our own place, me and you,' Diana said.

'Huh?'

'I've heard about a place in Earl's Court. Two bedrooms.
Airy and light with garden views.'

I responded by clicking on the cassette by the kitchen
door. Janet Jackson exploded into the room.

'We have to work out the bit where she's doing all that
crazy stuff with her hands,' I had shouted over the music.

Now Diana's ghost was standing over me, flexing her
wrists and fingers.

'You said this is the hard bit to work out,' I heard her
saying. 'I'll follow you.'

I dragged my eyes up, and she vanished again.

'The dance,' I said, 'we never finished it.'

He was looking at me strangely, like he wanted me to go
on, and wanted me to stop. I took a breath.

'You miss your grandfather,' I said to him.

Theo knocked his knuckles on the edge of his shoe. 'He
got me the job in the pet shop. He knows – he knew – the
guy who owns it. He used to come up here to buy canaries

up until the last year. He'd given them up by then. He'd had to. He couldn't catch them easy like he used to. His hands would shake, and his eyesight was going. He was afraid of hurting them. He'd given them up,' he repeated. 'Except for Yellow. He kept Yellow.' He fell silent so fast at the end of 'Yellow' that it was as though the memory of his grandfather had frightened him.

'People said things like, oh, he had a good life. A good innings. But that's not how it feels to me. The human gap's still the same, like, if you leave someone when you're eighteen or ninety-five. You know?'

'Yeah,' I said. 'It's still the same.'

'I'd have jacked everything in if it weren't for Plato,' said Theo. I thought I'd misheard him.

'Plato? The – the philosopher?'

'No. The pop star. Ha.'

'The *pop star*? Who's he?' I asked him. I could hear the surprise in my voice. I think it was the first time I'd asked a question that I really wanted the answer to since last year.

'He's not a pop star yet. But he will be. He's called A Misfit Called Plato. He's a genius. A total genius.'

He looked me right in the eye, suddenly deadly serious. He shifted position and his long fingers knotted around each other. When I said nothing, he looked down again, then up at me from under the rim of the Boy London cap. *Boy. London.*

'Right,' I said. 'Cool.'

'Two Christmases ago, I heard him singing on the Central

Line. He was off his head, but he rapped the whole of "Microphone Fiend" by Eric B and Rakim, and then sang "Where the Streets Have No Name" by U2—'

'Yes, I know who sang it,' I said quickly – come on now – I didn't need him to tell me the obvious stuff like this! He laughed at me as though I was joking, which I most certainly was not. I didn't laugh back.

'Yeah, well, he did both of those songs between Oxford Circus and Notting Hill Gate. Then from Holland Park to Shepherd's Bush he sang "Once in Royal David's City" like a choir boy. I followed him out of the station, he put me in a headlock on the Uxbridge Road. He thought I was trying to mug him.'

'Why?'

'Because he's white and I'm black, and it's London.'

I shrugged down at my feet.

'We walked back to my place and he's still there now. We live together.'

'Just like that?'

'Like I said, he's white, and I'm black and it's London.'

'I see.'

'You don't see, but that's all right. You don't have to.'

'All right. I can imagine.'

'No, you can't. Don't try to.'

'OK—'

'S'all right. Anyway, I told him I'd heard him on the underground, and I said that I had some contacts in the clubs. I didn't really. Had to find some, quick, like. He moved in with me the next day. Next thing I know, he's living with me and me mam and I'm his manager.'

'Is Meemam your flatmate?'

'No. *Wha?* No! Hahahaha!' He exploded into laugher. Thick, creamy laughter right from inside him.

'What?' I started to laugh too; it was impossible not to.

'I mean, me mam! Me *ma*!' He cleared his throat and tried again in direct imitation of Prince Charles, with the hand gestures and everything. 'My mother. The woman who gave birth to me. Hahahah!' He was off again.

I wasn't ready to show him that I even *knew* how to laugh. It felt wrong.

'What's your mother like?' I asked him.

Theo stopped laughing at that question.

'She does her best. Me dad wasn't much good, unfortunately.'

'In what sort of way?'

'In the kicking her in the head sort of way.'

'Oh. Sorry.'

'S'OK. We've got out. She was with another man before him, even worse. She's made some heavy bad choices.' There was a silence. 'All I ever wanted to do was get out. When I met Plato it was: Boom! *There* he is.' He pointed at me. '*He's* the ticket out of here, like.'

'Out of where?'

'I dunno. Everything. Poverty, weakness, boredom.' He paused and twisted the watch around his wrist. 'Averageness. S'boring, you know? It's the banality of having nothing that gets to us. The sheer fucking banality.' I sensed he had said more than he wanted to. 'You know the Happy Mondays?'

'Number 18 in the chart this week with "Step On". A fall of five places from last week. Manchester-based six-piece fronted by Shaun Ryder.'

He looked at me like I was mad, and he laughed again.

'Yeah. Well. Plato sounds like them, but better. Madder than them. Dresses like Prince, only twice the size. He's from Slough, but he spent two years in Manchester. He's got a regular gig at Three Moon Monday. They love him there. It's at the Lovelock on Ladbroke Grove—'

'My sister used to go to Three Moon Monday,' I said.

He looked at me. I could just about tell that he was deciding what to do with what I had just told him, really weighing it up. He went with: 'Well, you should come then. Next week. Not this Monday, the one after. Come with us. Come and see Plato. He's headlining. It's an important gig, I've got three record labels coming down to see him, big ones—'

'*No!*' I shouted it. I didn't mean to shout it so loud. Theo registered my reaction with great curiosity, but there was no sympathy this time.

'What were you like before all this happened? All the awful stuff?'

'Like everyone else,' I said and I could hear how defensive I sounded. Defensive and ridiculous. 'I was meant to go to university back in Texas; they offered me a place in September. I'm not going now. I can't.'

'University? You're clever, like?'

I hung my head. 'I worked hard. There's a difference.'

'Well, you got to be clever to know that working hard's a good plan.'

'Maybe.'

'No maybe about it—'

'I'm not going anyway,' I said again. 'I can't leave London.'

Yellow had jumped into his bath. I heard the sound of his feathers in the water. He ducked his head under once, twice, then shook himself and hopped out again.

'Seems mad not to go if you get the chance,' said Theo. 'I'd do it just for the nights out—'

'I can't. I couldn't do it.'

Theo stared at me.

'Well, yeah, come to think of it, why *would* you if you can stay in here with Nathan Moore and Bruno Brookes?'

'I don't like going out. Since everything happened. Agoraphobia. That's what they call it.'

'Ah. All right.'

I said nothing more.

'I should get home,' said Theo. He said it suddenly, as though he should have said it hours before, and when he stood up, where he had been sitting, there was a dip in the bed, the imprint of where his bottom and his thighs had been. On my bed. *On. My. Bed.* We stood up together in my bedroom, in the little bedroom with the Chinese men on swings, and the writing desk, and the poster of Brother Beyond.

'Ah, sod it,' he said.

'What?'

'You can keep him,' he said suddenly. He frowned at me, looking annoyed as though the decision had been made and verified by a part of him that he was resisting. 'I mean, if you want him, like,' he said. 'Keep him for a little while.'

'What do you mean?'

'Yellow. You can keep him. If you'd like him, anyways—'

'But your grandad?'

'Yeah. But he's gone now. He needs company. Yellow does. Like all of us.'

I watched the bird hop from the perch back down onto the floor of the cage.

'I'll look after him,' I said. Outside on the street, I could hear a clear and loud altercation between a woman and a child.

'You stupid girl! Don't you walk into the middle of the road! You're doing it on purpose! You could have been hit!'

'I won't be hit!'

'How do you know, you silly girl?'

I looked over at Theo.

'It's – that's very nice of you,' I said.

I could sense Diana again. She was nodding at me, a cigarette dangling between her lips. *Amen*, she said. *Amen*.

'Would you like to come back and see him in a few days?' I asked him. I felt my cheeks flaming red. 'Will you come to check on him?'

Theo hesitated.

'I'll check on *you*, Tracey, if you like. Yeah. I'll do that.'

He nodded, as though convincing himself. 'Yellow will be fine. You, on the other hand – you're just a – you're someone who needs—' He shook his head. 'I mean – who names a girl February anyway?'

'My parents.'

'They had a great sense of humour, like, your folks.'

I didn't quite know what he meant. I stared at my stereo. Bruno had reached number 1 now. Adamski. Seal.

'You should get out a bit, Tracey,' he said.

I walked him downstairs and opened the door. Through the kitchen, I could see Robert in the back garden. He bent down and picked a leaf of mint from the bush by the door and rubbed it between his fingers. Ann never stops telling us that foxes and cats piss on the mint, so not to use the lower leaves, but Robert put the leaf in his mouth and sucked it like a Polo.

'Come to the end of the street with me,' said Theo.

'It's late. Don't worry about me.'

'It's nine-thirty!'

'Why do you care?' I asked him.

'You've had a rough time.' He shrugged at me.

'My daddy used to say that the only thing that can save you from anything at all is yourself,' I said.

'Yeah. No offence to your old man, but I've always thought that idea's a load of shit.'

My voice shook when I spoke again.

'I was useful when I had my sister. I was useful as a sister, as a twin—'

'Well, you can be useful to a bird now. To Yellow.

Without you, he doesn't survive. Maybe Yellow saves you. Yeah. That's what happens.'

'My sister said that if she died, she would come back to life as a bird.'

'People say that a lot. It covers a lot of options, you know?'

'But what if—' I swallowed hard. 'What if that's true? If she's Yellow? If that's her?'

'If it helps you to think like that, then go ahead. You could be right. Who am I to say whether or not your twin sister's been reborn as a canary?'

I said nothing. On the other side of the road, Kelvin's dad waved to me and put his hands into the prayer position.

'Pray for the sister!' he shouted. He was carrying a plastic bag and a plank of wood.

'Pray for the sister!' agreed Theo loudly. He turned his prayer-hands to me and said it again, quietly. 'Pray for the sister,' he said, 'for *this* sister.'

'Why are you being nice to me? You don't even know me,' I said.

Kelvin's dad was still watching us both. Beyond him, two girls I recognized from the year below me at Westbury House slunk into view, laughing at something or other. They looked like creatures from another planet; it was impossible to imagine that I had been one of them not so long ago, with a bag of lever arch files over my shoulder and a tube of nearly finished fruit pastilles spinning silver foil and sugar into my blazer pocket.

'Me grandfather stopped wanting to live when he retired

and when he stopped breedin' the birds. Stopped feeling useful. Useful is God, you know? You lose that, and that's a hard thing. But you know, you came to the pet shop. Now you've got a bird to look after. So that's all right, don't you think?'

Useful is God. It felt like Theo Farrah had spoken a truth I had never been able to articulate. I felt a jolt of recognition run right through me. A sickness and a cure at the same time.

Theo pulled out a cigarette. 'Come on. Walk with me.'

'No. It's OK. You go.'

'You saw me cry, didn't you?' he said suddenly.

'I don't know,' I said, embarrassed, thinking of the tear I'd seen him wipe away with the back of his hand.

'Well, you did. Pathetic, eh? Grown man crying on the shop floor. Didn't mean to do tha'—'

It was odd that he talked as though he had planned how to behave ahead of knowing we would walk into the shop, and odder still that he considered himself a grown man. Even in that moment, I felt I could see him for what he really was: someone still in a state of great flux.

'That thing you did. Throwing the tennis ball and dropping the window. That was good. That was – yeah.' He looked at the ground and then back up at me and laughed. He shook his head. 'It was *great*, you know?' Great became 'gree-yat' from the lips of Theo Farrah.

'I was just doing what I had to do,' I said.

'Things don't surprise me much. Everything about you has surprised me. You didn't miss.'

'Thanks,' I said. I felt like I needed to say it.

'You don't talk much, do you?'

'I think stuff instead,' I said. 'Doesn't mean it has to come out for the whole world to hear.'

'Come and see him,' he said. 'Three Moon Monday. Week after next.'

'I don't know,' I said.

'It'd be good for yer,' he said.

I heard the click of the front door as he pulled it behind him. When he left the house, I ran to Ann and Robert's bedroom and I opened the window so that I could see him walking all the way down the street. I watched him until he turned down St Mark's Road, and when he'd vanished from view, I carried on watching people, the people who could just do it – effortless as anything. The outsiders. The people who could walk like it was second nature. Like it didn't matter.

I think I heard them before I saw them. They were some way down the street, four houses away from where Kelvin and his dad lived. The woman was walking very close to a man who put his arm around her and seemed to squeeze her closer into his side. They were walking slowly, and the sound of their voices carried to the other side of the road in such a way that made it impossible to hear *what* they were saying, but very possible to hear *how* they were saying it. They were talking softly, overlapping each other, punctuating every other word with laughter. When they reached the junction, they stopped walking, and he held her in his arms, and they kissed. I pulled in my breath. I knew Ann as I would have

known her anywhere. I double-blinked in amazement as I
noticed that she was wearing a pair of faded blue Levi's that
had belonged to Diana – I knew from the large blob of white
paint on the bottom of the left leg that had appeared when
decorators had been painting the hall in St Quintin Avenue.
What *was* this? Ann's hair, usually buoyed up in the two tortoiseshell combs, was loose over her shoulders and down her
back; there was a lot more of it than I had realized. Dressed
differently, she looked ten years – *twenty* years – younger than
forty-five, but it wasn't just the clothes. It was seeing her in
the arms of a man who wanted her like this man did. She
pulled away from him and glanced up and down the street.
Worried about being seen, but too late. I'd got it all.

Diana would have known what to say. She would understand this, she would make it all right; I imagined that the
first thing she would do would be to demand the return
of her 501s. This was what happened when people went
outside! Strange, misshapen things happened, things that
didn't happen indoors! Then Yellow started singing, singing
like his life depended on it, and he didn't stop when I was
back in my bedroom, and I turned the cassette over in the
stereo, and I lay on the bed, my heart jumping out of my
body. *Looking for a mate* because sometimes singing felt like
the only logical thing left to do. I heard Ann coming in
through the front door, and she called to me from outside
my closed door.

'Feb! I'm running a bath!' she said, with the resonance of
someone announcing that they were running for fucking

president. I'd known her voice like that only very occasionally. She was drunk.

I heard her opening her bedroom door, and I knew that
she was changing out of Diana's Levi's, and pulling her
moon-pale hair up into those old tortoiseshell combs, and
rubbing off the make-up around her eyes, and then I heard
her going back downstairs and minutes later I smelled frying
onions and garlic and right now she's set up in the kitchen
making tortillas as she said she would, and as she's cooking
she's singing too in that familiar, powerful soprano, so that
now I have the yellow bird in my bedroom adding trills and
loops to 'Opposites Attract' by Paula Abdul and the Wild
Pair, and Ann's yelling the words to 'Suddenly, Seymour'
from *Little Shop of Horrors* from the kitchen, and the house
feels comforting and terrifying, too small and too large and
full of life yet overwhelmed by death all at the same time.

10

'It'

Whether or not someone had sex appeal was something that Mama used to discuss a great deal – she was the world authority on the topic – you either had 'It' or you didn't, and if you didn't then it was a great shame, but there was simply nothing you could do to acquire It, because you were *born* with It, and that was that.

Generally, Mama said the vast majority of Texans had It merely because they happened to have been born there, and Mama was madly in love with the second-largest state in the union, but when we moved to Oxfordshire, she became much more ruthless in her assessments. Claire Peel, a crop-haired, stout-legged pixie-woman with dirty nails, had It, but Beverley Farley, the blonde, soft-eyed beauty who ran the village shop, had none whatsoever. Alan Thatcher, a former rugby coach with a broken nose, had It, and his wife

Amanda, who judged small animals and root vegetables at local shows, had even more of It than her husband. And yet — 'oh, the irony' — their only son, twenty-year-old Finlay, had 'not the slightest shred' of It. Why this was the case, I don't know. I had always thought Finlay to be fascinating on the grounds that he kept ferrets, but he'd since sold his motorbike to buy a computer and a plywood desk, so maybe Mama had a point.

We had been at home one evening, pulling bones from a roast chicken to make a stock, when Mama aired her views on my chances in this regard. Diana was lying in the bath upstairs, singing 'Too Shy' by Kajagoogoo. She'd spent months trying to style her hair like Limahl.

I had come back from school crying because Kezia Reed had told me that I had big boobs and a big bottom and was a rubbish Goal Attack. I had pretended not to hear her at the time, but the oven-to-table brutality of a twelve-year-old girl dropped from the netball team was impossible to ignore. Kezia had form with me. She had said to me the term before that Diana was 'way prettier' than I was and that her mother didn't believe we were twins. It wasn't like me to talk to Mama on the topic of such painful matters as these, it usually got me nowhere, but this time was different.

'The thing is,' Mama had responded, licking her fingers, 'Diana will *always* inspire envy in women. She has a face that every woman wants. All of them.'

'Really?' I sounded doubtful although I knew it to be true.

'Oh, it's absolutely the case, Feb. Men won't quite know

what to do with her. Not for a while, in any case. She'll be better off when she hits forty. Not just because of her face, but because of everything else. All the difficult things. You know what I mean, don't you, Feb? You're twelve, but you know what I mean?'

'I think so.'

'You have more than you think you have,' said Mama. 'The way you move is wonderful. You have beautiful arms and good timing, thanks to your tennis. You have a good speaking voice, thanks to me. You value honesty, thanks to your father.' She rolled her eyes at me. 'The way you hold yourself, your posture, the way you throw a ball. You're an athlete, February. That's quite something. And you trust –' she paused and wiped her forehead with the back of her left wrist – 'you trust *yourself*. You've had to. So much trust has been put in your ability to do the right thing since you twins were little, and that's meant that you have to trust yourself. It's a marvellous thing. It's something people strive for all their lives. And when you get to seventeen, mark my words, you'll have It. Kezia Reed, poor dear, will not.'

I was too moved to speak. Mama was not given to praising anyone unless she bloody well meant it; it's why I can remember every word of what she said and, by default, why I remember what happened immediately after she had spoken.

We were interrupted by Diana shouting from the bath that she could hear something in her bedroom that sounded like a dinosaur. Mama and I ran upstairs to find a bird flapping from one side of the room to the other. I scuttled to the window and threw up the sash. Mama waved her arms, and the bird soared out again.

'Has it gone?' called Diana.

'It's gone. It was a blackbird,' I said.

There was silence. It was then that Diana said it.

'I have dreams that I can fly. All the time. If I die, I'm going to come back to life as a bird.' *If* she died. Diana felt – as I did, and most of our friends – that death might not apply to us.

But Diana had lost interest in the bird now; she was already moving on.

'Do you think Limahl likes shy girls in real life?' she said.

'Probably not now. Probably wants someone the exact opposite of shy.'

'Yeah.' She looked at me thoughtfully. 'Can you help me with my maths homework?'

It's been a week since I left the house. A week since I was given Yellow the canary to look after. A week since I saw Ann in the street kissing another man. Doesn't take much working out to know that in two days' time, it's Monday, and on Monday night, Theo Farrah will be at the Lovelock Arms on Ladbroke Grove with the singer called Plato, hoping for a record deal and a miracle. Would he look out for me? Would I cross his mind, even for a moment? I could walk out of the house, and I could find out. I could find him. I could stand next to him again, see if his hand's OK where he sliced it on the cage in the back of the pet shop. I could tell him that I've fed his grandfather's bird, that I've given him water and food, and I've looked after him like I said I would. I could do that. But I won't. That's the thing. I know myself well enough since all this happened to know that I won't. And I can't.

Well.

I changed my mind.

We were tidying up the kitchen after supper on Monday evening. Ann cleared her throat and announced: 'Gregory – Mr Arrowsmith – wants to take the sixth form to a play at Stratford.'

'Yes, I know,' said Robert, 'he spoke to me about it last week. He's a glutton for punishment. What's the play?'

'*'Tis Pity She's a Whore*.' Ann hung with unexpected violence on the word 'whore'. She was nervous, I knew that. I gulped in my chair, behind a copy of *Q* magazine.

'I suppose you want to see it too.' Robert put his glasses on and sucked in the air, looking at the crossword. 'You don't have to ask my permission, you know.'

'I'm not,' said Ann. 'I probably won't go. It's meant to be a post–exam treat.'

'Arrowsmith has strange ideas of what constitutes a treat for girls in the sixth form,' observed Robert.

'Oh, I know,' agreed Ann.

'If it's in a couple of weekends' time, I won't be here anyway. I'm going to be in Edinburgh seeing Rory.'

For a moment Ann was very still, as though any sudden movement might alter what had just been revealed, and what had just been revealed needed to be protected at all costs. I watched her unpack what he had just said. A weekend without having to worry about her husband. Christ! Was it too good to be true?

'How *is* Rory?' she asked, and her voice seemed to tremble with too much concern.

Robert didn't answer the question; he just sighed and said, 'I haven't been in eighteen months. I feel terrible about it.'

'Don't feel terrible. He's awful,' said Ann.

'He's my brother,' said Robert.

'Doesn't stop him from being awful.'

Rory was a hypochondriac with an addiction to cigars and, since being jilted at the altar aged twenty-four, a deep loathing of women. Ann – being a woman – was never encouraged to visit him, which was, of course, a great blessing for her, and a great pain in the arse for Robert who took the train north alone once a year to sit with his brother for a weekend.

'Well, maybe I *will* go to the play then,' said Ann. 'I saw a very radical production of *'Tis Pity* when I was in the sixth form myself—'

'Five down – nine letters – what's another word for "spent?"' Robert was back in the depths of the crossword. He did this an awful lot. He would simply read out clues he couldn't get, right over whoever was talking. It had never bothered me, but it had infuriated Diana, and now I also felt a seed of fury in my stomach; fury with him for being so idiotic as not to see what was happening in front of his own eyes, and furious with Ann for letting him behave as he did. Now he and Ann spoke at the same time:

'Exhausted.'

Robert looked up to meet Ann's eye with a smile, but she didn't look at him. Instead, she stood up. 'I think I will go to the play. Gregory will need someone to take control during the interval.'

'I'm amazed he can keep his mouth shut for the duration of a two-act play,' observed Robert.

'Well, *you* employed him!' said Ann, and there was *everything* in that accusation. *You* did this! *You* decided to bring him into our lives! She let out a burst of laughter. Robert's criticism of Gregory Arrowsmith was rolling off her, water off a duck's back. It was better to talk about him and receive a negative response from Robert than not to talk about him at all. She was flooding over with the need to bring him into her life, into this kitchen, into everything she talked about!

'He's a good teacher,' said Robert. 'That doesn't make him a hero.'

'He's American,' said Ann with a loud sigh, as if that settled all the other stuff, one way or another.

Our eyes met, then Ann looked away and bit her lower lip, and I swear I saw a small smile on her face and that same look of pent-up delight that I had first noticed when she was waiting to leave the house for parents' evening. It was spilling over into everything, this new light. I wasn't at all ready for it. I felt my heart harden suddenly.

'Does he have children?' I asked. I heard my voice freighted with a cruelty that I didn't entirely understand.

'He's got a son and a daughter, I think. Don't ask me their names or exact ages.' Ann sounded quite different now, and she didn't add 'because I don't know the answers', but left it at that.

I had torn at her mood with the question, pushed her over somehow, and for five minutes she said nothing to Robert or me, but went to the sink and washed up and I could see her only from the back, and there seemed to be such despair, such disappointment in the movement of her arms as she hauled the saucepans and pots onto the drying rack, like each one represented a burden moving from one side of her heart to the other, and I wanted to hug her, and tell her I was sorry for asking. Only a moment ago, she had been high on the whole thing. Was this what falling in love had done to her? Robert noticed nothing. I wanted to shout like they do in Punch and Judy shows when the dog appears to steal the sausages. *He's behiiiind you!*

Robert stood up.

'I've got a couple of reports to write,' he said. 'Can someone put the chain on the door?'

I said nothing to Ann as she finished washing up, but I was aware of the extent to which I had taken my head into another world – a world where Ann left us all to be with Gregory Arrowsmith and the devil take the hindmost – because I almost jumped out of my skin a minute later when the telephone rang, and instead of picking it up in the hall, Ann walked quickly to her study, and shut the door.

I walked upstairs and into my bedroom, and I sat on my bed and I turned down the stereo and there was Yellow, asleep with his head down and one leg tucked into his breast, and I knew then that I would go to Three Moon Monday at the Lovelock – that I would go there to find Theo Farrah, that I would go there because the scene was moving, wobbling, jolting underneath me, and if I couldn't be safe in St Quintin Avenue then maybe I could be safe somewhere that Theo Farrah was. I was going to go out. Of my own accord. Without help. Without persuasion. *Agoraphobia.* I saw the word typed on the letter from the private doctor to Ann and Robert. The letter had begun so weirdly.

'This delightful young lady has experienced great loss . . .' How did they know I was delightful? I hadn't delighted them in the surgery. I had cried. I had been helped to the door by Ann when I had half fainted after having my blood pressure taken. I was as far from delight as it was possible to be. Now I felt the presence of the *Evening Standard* under my bed. Words typed about Diana. Words to explain to people who had never known her that she had been in a crash and had been killed. *A shame*, people would think. *A shame, poor thing. Very pretty girl. Everything to live for.* Bruno confirmed to me for the twentieth time that week that 'Red Red Wine' by UB40 was at number 15, and not knowing why I was doing it, I pulled my English A level file out from the shelf above the chest of drawers, and opened it. The last essay I'd written was shoved in the front.

This Could Be Everything

Ted Hughes' poetry is often described as bombastic, hammering home themes with . . .

I felt sick. I'd begun the essay with a quote:

There is no better way to know us
Than as two wolves, come separately to a wood . . .

Were Ann and Gregory Arrowsmith two wolves, come separately to the wood of North Kensington? I closed my eyes tight, as I always did when I went into Diana's bedroom, and I stumbled towards the back of her room with my hands out like one of the ghouls in Michael Jackson's 'Thriller', and I found her chest of drawers and I pulled out her Rifat Ozbek sequin leggings, and then I went back into my bedroom, and opened my eyes wide, and I tore *off* my jeans and I pulled the leggings *on*. I would go to Three Moon Monday at the Lovelock. I would go. I would walk out of the house, and I would go. I threw off my blue sweater, and I stood for a moment in the middle of the room in my old black sports bra, and then I pulled that off too, and my breasts in the mirror looked huge and ripe and kind of wonderful, as though defying everything I had felt in the past six months. I stared at them. It was like they weren't part of me at all, like they had their own opinions and their own vision, quite separate from my own. I could see my heartbeat pounding out of my chest and into the big scary world, too full of everything, too full. Yellow looked at me. The caged bird, who had tasted freedom. I'd walk outside for Yellow.

I found a white T-shirt and my old tennis trainers, and I stuck two silver stars on my left cheek, and I picked up my yellow Sony Sports Walkman and I put on my headphones and I walked downstairs before I could change my mind.

'I'm going out,' I shouted as I opened the front door, and I heard the sound of doors opening, and Ann saying 'Feb?' but I didn't wait for their questions and their amazement. I just kept right on walking, like I had a really good plan, after all.

11

Won't Be Long

I was playing tennis on the day that she died. I was half-way through a game with a girl who had been in the year above me at school when the club secretary came running outside calling my name. I knew in an instant. I felt it, I knew that she had gone. Maybe that's because since the fire I'd assumed all news was bad news. But I knew. I just knew.

'I've got a cab waiting to take you to St Mary's Hospital,' the secretary had said.

But I knew that when I arrived, it would be too late.

From the next day Lisa had tried to get me to talk to her. Lisa had written to me, the blue ink and her big handwriting. But no. I couldn't do it then, and I couldn't do it now. Not now. Woah. Hang on. Let's remember where we are here. Let's remember what I was doing.

I was walking outside. I was walking outside to see A Misfit

Called Plato at Three Moon Monday. It was nine-thirty at night. I was walking down the street in Diana's sequin leggings, like I knew what the hell I was doing. INXS waited for me in the plastic grip of my yellow Walkman. I pressed play. Diana had listened to the *Kick* album relentlessly: 'Devil Inside'. 'Need You Tonight'. 'Guns in the Sky'. Michael Hutchence, their singer, is just about the only man that both Diana and I adored equally. But then, who didn't think he was a god? I could walk if I had Michael Hutchence. I could walk if I had Andrew Farriss playing guitar. I could. *Diana's leggings. Michael Hutchence. Keep walking. Keep walking.* The night air was cool in the way that May evenings can be, and there was a wind up. Dust and pollen from the huge limes in Ladbroke Square flew about, there was a raging sense of new life. The birds were still going, still searching. I thought of Yellow, of Theo's grandfather's bird in my bedroom, and now that I was outside the house, the fact of it seemed so private, and intricate, a delicate thing that only he and I understood. Me and Theo Farrah. Boy. London. I said the words out loud to myself as I walked. I wondered what Eric would think if he could see me now. I wonder whether he knew I hadn't stepped out since Diana had gone.

'He's a fun-seeker,' Lisa had said about Eric. 'He's very good at being alive.' I remember being bowled over by this. Very good at being alive. Wasn't that the greatest talent on earth? I didn't want to think about Lisa, not now. Every ounce of strength I had would be put into the mere act of getting me to Ladbroke Grove. It was a game, wasn't it?

London was a game that Eric was good at. He was Super Mario jumping at coins in the Mushroom Kingdom. Wasn't that what we all were? You just had to keep going. Now I spoke out loud the singles in the Top 40.

'I'll be your shoulder. You can tell me all! Don't keep it in ya!' sang Michael Hutchence.

Number 26: Up sixteen for NWA with 'Express Yourself'. Number 25: 'Don't Wanna Fall in Love' by Jane Child. Number 24: 'The Only One I Know' by the Charlatans . . .

There was a queue outside the Lovelock, and people were being let in two at a time. I stood at the back of the line and waited, and I pulled off my headphones so that they wrapped around my neck. I needed to hear what was happening because any moment now the great swoosh of the Trench Effect would submerge me in its grip. I could feel its amazement at what I was doing. *Shit! She's gone outside! Not only that, she's gone outside at night! And to a nightclub! Who the hell . . .?* What would Diana think? I imagined her standing here now, reaching for a cigarette, her thumb with its inevitable chipped pink varnish flicking a brief flame from the plastic pastel lighters that she left stuffed into her coat pockets. Those lighters were *always* nearly empty.

I looked up the steps and back out onto the street. I'm not much moved by dark skies and stars; the jaundiced yellow of street lamps feels comforting to me, and too much darkness makes me space-sick. Texas had hummed all night long with yellow lights from backyards and business centres.

Here in London, girls in platformed clogs with four-inch heels from Red or Dead and Office and boys in high-top Reeboks and long-sleeved T-shirts stomped about in the street above, smoking and talking in loud voices. A group of girls I recognized from the year below me at school were lingering around in black lycra minidresses, bomber jackets and bare legs – white facsimiles of Neneh Cherry – debating whether to queue. Fake tan, Body Shop strawberry lip balm and Calvin Klein's Eternity jostled for the number one position on the steps to the basement. Between us, Diana and I had been able to distinguish the scent and feel of every beauty product ever sold, every cheap thrill and every luxury, from the soapy medicinal tang of Neutrogena shampoo with its claim to remove all 'build up' in your hair, through to the melancholy gloop of Elizabeth Arden's Eight Hour Cream that we stole from Ann's dressing table and inhaled deeply before rubbing on our lips and elbows when we went to bed.

'"A Misfit Called Plato,"' said a girl I'd known from school called Ella Drudge, reading the poster. She pronounced it 'plateau'. Ella Drudge always had been academically disastrous but culturally brilliant. Her greatest achievement was breaking both arms playing netball, and somehow managing to get the cast on her left arm signed by Gary Lineker and the one on the right signed by Terence Trent D'Arby – a union in plaster and felt pen that had caused a damn good uproar in the upper school lunch queue. She was glued at the hip to a blonde girl called Sophie Carter, and they'd been known as Drudge and Carter by everyone at Westbury House. Sure enough, Sophie Carter was standing a little behind her now.

'Don't you remember, we saw him here before Christmas?' she said. 'God, we were drunk! I think he fell off the stage. He *definitely* can't sing.'

'Sounds like we had a good night,' said Ella astutely.

Inside, I was hit with intense heat. A girl sat behind a table in the entrance asking people for five pounds. 'Guest list only,' she said to me.

I had no money. *I had walked out of the house with no money.*

'I think I'm on the guest list.' Diana did this all the time. I *knew* she did.

'What's your name?' said the girl.

'February Kingdom?' My rising infliction made it sound as though I were questioning the validity of my own name, which God's truth, I usually am when I'm saying it to someone new for the first time. The girl raised her eyebrows.

'Are you on Plato's list?'

'No. But I know Theo.' Did I know him? Hardly.

'The hot pet shop boy?' The girl laughed at her own description, as well she might.

'I met him when I found his canary,' I said. Too much information, I could hear Diana saying. She doesn't need to know this, for God's sake, Feb.

'By canary do you mean cannabis?'

'No. I mean canary.'

'Right. OK.' She sighed at me. 'Go on, then.' She reached out and caught my wrist in her hand. For a mad second I thought she was going to bring it up to her lips and kiss it, but instead she scribbled '3MM' on the back of my hand with a purple felt pen.

'He's around somewhere,' she said.

I walked in, trying to look cool. Was I trying to look cool? Maybe I was just trying to look like a human who could walk from one side of a room to the other. The Trench Effect was waiting. *Go back home. Go back to bed. What the hell are you doing in here?* The place was thick with cigarettes, the black walls appeared to be wet with ... what? I didn't know what they were wet with – sweat? Grease? Unicorn tears? My God, the heat of it! I had only ever imagined this space from what Diana had told me, and that as a general rule veered towards hyperbole on most topics. But for once, Diana had exaggerated nothing. *'It's so loud and so hot that you could do anything and get away with it, that's the real problem with it, and the real greatness of it.'* There was dance music playing, the sort of thing that occasionally showed up in the charts in a more watered-down form by people like Technotronic, who had taken the frantic beats of the so-called happy house scene and made them mainstream. What was playing in the Lovelock was harder, rougher, yet somehow, despite my heart beating in double-quick under my T-shirt, I under-stood it for the first time. *Happy house.* My mind flickered to Ann. Well, she was happy enough in the house now, but only because the thing that was making her happy was *outside* the house.

I stood with my back to the crowd, watching two boys in

black shorts, with gold chains around their necks, fiddling with leads and amps on the boxy little stage. I straightened up my back, just as the opening bleeps of 'Killer' cut through the end of the last track. There was an involuntary surge in the crowd. This record was number 1. The emotion of hearing it in a room with other people took my breath away, and I put a hand to my forehead and looked out into the crowd, crazy overwhelmed, because for months I had not seen anyone else reacting to any music at all, and when I recorded Bruno counting down the Top 40, it was like he was doing it just for me. Just for me. But now here we were, and other people knew this song, just like I did. Even somewhere like this, where the charts weren't cool, a song like this *meant* something. All that stuff about wanting to be free to live your life and things.

That was me, wasn't it? Difference is, I don't even know what I want my life to be now. All I know is something I didn't completely recognize had got me out of my bedroom and into that club, where I stood in my sister's leggings, watching a load of people singing a song that I thought had been written just for me. Then, just as Seal started up, I saw him. Theo Farrah in the Boy London cap.

He saw me, and he looked away, then he looked back, and frowned, and then he walked over to me.

'Hey,' he said. 'You came. Didn't think you would.'

'Yellow's fine!' I shouted.

'Huh?'

'YELLOW IS FINE.'

He looked at me with something I couldn't place, an expression that was impossible to read. It had only been a week since he had sat in my bedroom, but he looked different. He was taller, more extraordinary, more himself somehow.

'Good,' he said. 'I knew it was the right thing, giving him to you.'

What are you doing? asked the demons. *You think you're going to be OK here? Who do you think you are? Get back home! Get back to bed! Who are you?*

'Your boy Plato's very popular,' I said, 'all the cool girls from school are here.' I sounded about thirteen and as dumb as a watermelon. Theo looked at me and laughed.

'Well, as long as we're cornering the private school market, nothing else matters, pet,' he said, broad north. Any moment now and the whole place would either take off into the sky or blow up with the pounding volume of it all.

'Come with me and meet him,' he said.

'Oh no, I couldn't.'

'Why not?'

'I just . . .'

'Come on. You can't come here and not say hello to the star of the show.'

And so I followed him through the crowd to the back of the room, and people moved out of the way as we passed. I was following Theo Farrah, and he *knew* me. Diana wasn't here, I wasn't tagging along behind her. This was all me. *This was all my doing.*

Theo pushed open a heavy black door into a room that

was completely empty, except for a small table in the middle, and on the table were three bottles of Peroni, four tubes of cheese and onion Pringles and a glossy sheet of black and white negative photographs photos of a girl with crooked little teeth and wearing an Indian headdress. I paused, arrested. I *knew* that face. I'd seen her before – the girl was a friend of Diana's; they had stood in line at castings together a load of times. She was shorter than the other models and, like my sister, much younger. She'd always been nice to me when I had been waiting for Diana to be seen by some photographer with his head up his own ass. Now she grinned up at me from a table in the Lovelock Arms. Theo saw me looking at it.

'Apparently she's going to be bigger than Niki Taylor,' he said. 'Plato's mate Corinne took them. She's here some-where.' He looked around vaguely.

'Kate,' I said, suddenly remembering the girl's name, but but I don't think Theo heard me as he pushed open another door into an even smaller room with a grey carpeted floor and just a red electric guitar propped up against the wall. It was like Alice in Wonderland through the prism of peak punk; I half expected a white rabbit in Vivienne Westwood to rush past us glaring into a pocket watch.

'Where the fuck is he now?' said Theo.

He marched to the switch and flicked it on. A strip light buzzed and flickered into being, illuminating the sequins on Diana's leggings. I felt a grim self-consciousness, a renewed attack. *This delightful young lady has experienced great loss . . .*

121

Stay with it. Stay with it. Theo took a piece of crumpled paper out of his pocket and smoothed it out on the table.

'Got a pen?' he asked me.

'No. Sorry. Do you want me to go and find one?'

I might as well have suggested that I found a couple of truffles and a sailor's hat.

'Don't worry.' He smiled and looked at me vaguely, as though he suddenly couldn't quite remember what I was doing there. 'Do you have a cigarette?' he asked.

'No.'

'God, Tracey. I'd have thought that if you're going through the shit you're going through, you'd at least have the good sense to smoke.' He took a packet of Rizlas and tobacco from his back pocket.

'I can roll for you,' I said with relief.

'You can?'

'I'm not a total idiot.'

He handed the packet to me, and a nearly empty pouch of tobacco.

I had learned to roll when Diana started smoking when we were fifteen. She could never be bothered to roll properly – she was too impatient for that – but had once bought me a Deacon Blue cassette single ('Chocolate Girl', highest chart position number 43, August 1988) in exchange for me rolling her ten cigarettes to take out with her that weekend. I had taught myself to roll that week after school, trying over and over again to create those perfect, tight little smokes that I knew I would never try myself; I was too self-conscious for it perhaps. I opened the pouch of tobacco and watched Theo looking at the paper on the table.

'He's got to get it right, or he'll lose the crowd. They're very, very drunk tonight. Not drugs, it's all alcohol when Plato plays. Beer and mixers. People get off their heads on booze.'

'How many songs will he do?' I asked, not looking up from the task in hand, but before Theo could answer, the door swung open and someone walked in, a boy of about Theo's age with the sort of saloon-style swagger of a cowboy in a black and white movie. He was easily six foot five and dressed in silver trousers and a ripped pink T-shirt with a black plastic jacket over the top. Even in terrible lighting it was plain he was wearing mascara and eyeliner and there was a white line painted down his left cheek – Adam Ant gone vertical. His dark hair was long on the top and half-pulled off his face in a big green velvet scrunchy, like the best-turned-out girls at Westbury House wore when they were showing prospective parents around the school. He was holding a beer in one hand and a copy of *The Face* in the other, rolled up like he was about to kill wasps, and he was shouting.

'WHY IS THE LIGHT ON?'

He drained the rest of his pint, slammed the glass on the table, flicked off the light switch and . . . *roared*. It's hard to find another word for it, but Plato's entrance was pretty damn spectacular. I dropped my handiwork on the floor, scrabbling around in the almost-dark for a half-completed roll-up and the rest of Theo's tobacco.

'Turn the light back on!' shouted Theo. I switched the light back on. Plato glared at me.

'Who's this?'

'February Kingdom,' said Theo.

'How did you know my surname?' I said.

'I think you told me, didn't you?' said Theo.

'Did I?'

'Yeah. You must have done, Tracey.'

'Tracey?' demanded Plato. 'I thought she just said her name was February, or something mental?'

'I'm February,' I said.

'She looks like Tracey Ullman, so I call her Tracey,' said Theo.

Plato stared at me. 'No, she doesn't.'

'She does.'

Unexpectedly, Plato held out a hand in my general direction.

'Good evening, Vietnam,' he said. His hand was clammy and firm and huge.

'I gave her Grandad's canary,' said Theo.

Plato stopped and stayed very still for a moment. Something passed between him and Theo but I sure as anything couldn't tell you what it was.

'Oh?' said Plato slowly. 'He's told me about you. You're the one with the dead twin sister?'

'Er – yes.'

'Sorry. Sincerely. What a fucking fuck-up. The agony of existence never ceases to amaze me.'

'It's all right. You don't have to say anything—'

'He didn't tell me you're American,' he said accusingly. 'Which bit are you from?'

'I was born in Texas,' I said.

'Ah. Well. You're a long way from home now, baby.'

'London's my home now,' I said. Even as I spoke, it was hard to believe it completely.

'Yeah, yeah. London's good like that. Takes in all of us, the loser and the dancers and the mad Celts and the academic nutters and the bankers and the money from Europe and the refugees and the ones who can never go home again for all the dark magic they've done. London doesn't give a toss about anyone, though. Don't let it fool you. It's never given a shit.' He held out a hand to define the slogan. 'London. Not giving a shit since AD 50.'

His accent was all over the place, but it was his confidence and his clothes that arrested me. The only other boy I'd known to dress like he really meant to cause chaos was Eric, but Plato's get-up would have left Eric at the starting gates. I stared at him. 'You can pretend all you like around here, but it'll get you in the end,' went on Plato. 'You can shut all the doors in the burning house, but the smoke will always find another way to get out.'

'I like your silver trousers,' I said.

'Thanks. Made them myself.'

'Did you?'

'Yeah.'

'They look like Gucci,' I said.

'I know. I copied them.'

'Will you shut up?' said Theo. He handed him the piece of crumpled paper with the set list on, and while Plato studied it, I studied *him*, and I wondered how my mother – whose ability to describe people's looks in imaginative ways, with a side-serving of snark – would have talked about him. Certainly, he had It, although he would have fitted into one of her famous sub-sections: Has It, But Genuinely Doesn't Care. To my memory, the only other people Mama had put in this select group were Prince Philip and Richard Luton, who helped Daddy with his accounts. Every feature on Plato's face seemed huge and exaggerated. He pulled a guitar pick from his pocket. He saw me looking at his magazine. Madonna curled her lip up at me from the front cover.

'My mate shoots for the Face,' he said. 'She's got the cover next month.'

'Of course,' I said out loud without meaning to.

'You know Corinne? She's here. Wanted to take pictures of the support band tonight, who are fucking terrible, by the way.'

'She photographed my sister,' I said.

Plato looked as though he wanted to ask me something else, but the door of the little room opened, and a guy walked in carrying two pints.

'Joshy!' shouted Plato.

'It's rammed out there,' said the boy. 'I had to pretend I was in the band just to get backstage.'

'Come up on stage, why don't you?' said Plato, taking the pint from his left hand.

'No, don't, Joshy,' said Theo. He had his back to me now and was rummaging around in a guitar case. He looked up briefly and caught my eye. There was a curiosity in his expression, as though he couldn't work something out. He nodded at me, and he seemed suddenly formal.

'Won't be long,' he said.

Won't be long.

Those had been Diana's last words to me.

Grief doesn't truck along behaving itself. There's no fucking pattern to the thing. It sits there like a little dickhead, ticking out its foot at random, waiting to trip you up, just when you think you might be feeling your way out of it. I don't buy into the idea of it as something pure, something to be respected and understood, I don't like people who tell me to accept it, to embrace it. I want to throw it off the scent, to do it *my* way, but I can't, it's too cunning for that. What I mean is that I expect it to punch me in the face at times that feel logical – walking past my old school, buying new clothes, hearing certain songs on the radio – but I haven't got used to the randomness of the attacks at other times. Suddenly the room felt too small, I remembered the heavy doors between me and the outside world, and I knew I had to leave. The Trench Effect was unstoppable.

I crossed the room, and I opened the door, feeling the

old light-headed unreality that came with an impending sensation of panic. I walked out, knowing nothing except that I had to get out of this place, that I had to go, that I had no right to be here, that I was nothing to Theo Farrah, that this was never what I was meant to be doing. I needed to go home. They didn't notice me walk out. I would keep on walking until I got home. I wasn't ready. I would never be ready.

12

Three Moon Monday

I was nearly out of the door by the time he caught up with me.

'Tracey! Where are you going? I looked up and suddenly you weren't there. What are you doing?'

I shook my head and Theo rolled his eyes in frustration and grabbed my arm. I shook him off.

'Come *on*! He's on stage in two minutes!'

'I don't want to be here! It's not time! I don't like the feeling of being so close to people! I don't LIKE it! I'm not READY for it!'

'No one's ever ready for Plato, Tracey, that's the whole bloody *point*.' Theo looked at me with real urgency, as though he really cared whether I stayed or not. He opened his mouth to shout something else at me but was interrupted by a man much older than us, with dreadlocks and a gold and black baseball cap. He slapped Theo on the shoulder, and

Theo swung around as though he'd been hit, and seeing who it was, his eyes widened even more.

'Hey!' said Theo. 'You came! Thank you, thank you, I promise this won't be a repeat of what happened last time—'

'I thought you said he'd be on just before nine?'

'He's about to go on. Now. Right now. This second.'

'Fuckin' 'ell. All right. I'll stay for the first two songs. I can't wait around, man. I've got to get to Camden by ten-thirty—'

'Who are you seeing?' interrupted Theo dismally.

'I don't know. Some art school twats. Playing the Falcon. Everyone wants them, apparently. But then, don't they always, love?'

'Look,' said Theo urgently. 'You won't want to leave this place after two songs. I know you'll still be here when Plato's finished.'

The man laughed. 'It's a hundred and ten degrees in this shithole and my ex-wife's sleeping with the bassist in the support band. I can *guarantee* I won't be here, mate.' He nodded at me, deadly serious. I liked serious. I knew where I stood with serious. In any case, I could see the exit, I was nearly there—

'Tracey keeps canaries!' shouted Theo, nodding towards me.

'The support band? Is that what they're called now? I thought they were called the Spooks. The Crooks? The Arses? Ah, who cares.'

'What?'

'My ex always had a thing about bass players,' he yelled. 'I had to watch her like a hawk around Mark King and Martin Kemp back in the day—'

'No. *This* is Tracey!' yelled Theo. '*She* keeps canaries. In real life.'

The man frowned at Theo and then at me as though he might have misheard but couldn't quite face getting him to repeat the sentence for a third time.

'You look like Tracey Ullman,' he said.

'You see?' said Theo to me.

The man looked at his watch and rolled his eyes.

'Right. OK. Go and tell Plato the Great or whatever the hell he's called to hurry up. He's not fucking Stevie Wonder. Vince Power's over there. He won't stick around, either. He's got Reading Festival to run.' He slapped Theo on the back and walked off.

'Well, you've got to stay now,' said Theo to me.

'Why?'

'That was Ken Phillips, and if he sees you walking out now that's not good.'

'Who is he?'

'A badass bastard, and the best A&R man out there. Last time he came to a gig, Plato went on an hour and a half late and he'd left in a massive rage. This is our last chance with him. He won't keep showing up over and over again.'

'Why did you tell him I keep canaries? I've only got one, and it's yours by rights.'

'Because the only other facts I know about you are that

131

you don't go out much and you fancy Nathan Moore. It's not a great CV, to be honest, Tracey.'

'I do *not* fancy Nathan Moore!'

'Still got him on your wall, though, haven't you?'

'You've got posters of cats being immunized in the pet shop. Doesn't mean you've got a thing for it.'

Theo laughed again. He did that thing of laughing. It was just impossible. I felt the smile edging across my lips, and I turned my face down so that he couldn't see.

'You're smiling,' he said. He poked me in the ribs, and I yelped in surprise. 'You're smiling! Girl, YOU ARE SMILING!'

'I'm not!'

'Don't go,' he said. 'Come on. You're here now—'

Any further choice I had concerning leaving was then taken away from me, as suddenly the tiny platform stage at the back of the room erupted. There was another surge in the crowd as everyone seemed to jump forward again, and I found myself pressed into Theo.

'Close your eyes and think about Yellow!' he shouted.

'Huh?'

'*YELLOW!*'

There was a screech of noise from a guitar, and the pounding of a drum kit and everything around us blocked out the fierce flame in my cheeks, and the thwack of my heart against my chest and the dizziness and the fear were assaulted by something bigger, and Theo shouted, 'GO!' as though Plato were being chased by a bear and needed to run for his life, and I looked around and no one was looking at me, and they weren't looking at Theo, and we weren't presenting as an extraordinary sight, we were just a boy and a girl standing close together watching what was happening on a stage. For the first time since Diana had died, it felt as though the world had stopped watching me, and I wanted to scream with the relief of it. The utter relief of it.

Plato was on. Groups of kids in the crowd knew the words to the first two songs he played, and they screamed the lyrics out at him, crazy as bullbats. The drummer – a girl with a shaved head, cycling shorts, a T-shirt with 'Gaultier Is My Godfather' on the front, and a packet of Cornflakes at her feet – drowned out the lot of them, which seemed to please Plato greatly; he kept turning to her and shouting, 'YES! YES! YES!' and howling with delight. Yet he talked to the crowd between songs with an odd clarity, and while he talked, he roamed up and down the stage, asking questions that were as random as they were mad. I tried to swivel round, to work out where the door was. I needed to get home. I couldn't do this. But it was like Plato had stopped time. Even the Trench Effect was stumped. If I fainted in here, if I died, would anyone even care? Maybe that made it OK. No one was watching me. It didn't matter anymore. I couldn't leave. Not yet.

'Anyone here from Sydney, Australia? . . . When did you last fly a kite up to the highest height? . . . Do you think Paula Abdul is actually sleeping with that dancing cat? . . . Sod it. Does anyone want to come up here and vogue? I need a dancer! I need fucking Bez, girls and boys! Is that how you get a hit song? Answers on a postcard to the Pope, please . . .'

This last request was answered by a girl of about six foot three who scrambled up on stage and flung her arms around him. Her left hand was holding a half-full pint of beer; in her excitement she tossed most of it down Plato's back.

'Who wants some Cornflakes? The drummer brings cereal on stage with her. It's a fucking joke, man—'

His strange accent was still impossible to place with any geographical certainty at all.

I looked at Theo and he looked back at me and he laughed, and then I found myself laughing because I couldn't not, and there was a sudden logic in everything, from the Feeding-of-the-Five-Thousand-by-way-of-Shepherd's-Bush from Plato on stage, to the noise from the crowd that wanted chaos and order simultaneously. So there I am, standing so close to Theo Farrah in the heat of a dingy basement off Ladbroke Grove, without my sister. Without her. Sweat dripped between my tits; I wrenched off Diana's top and tied it around my waist so that I was wearing only my sports bra like half the club. I could see a man at the back of the room, dimly, a shadow behind a desk, waving at Plato, trying to attract his attention. Plato looked up at him, waved back and then ignored him.

'He needs to finish!' Theo shouted. 'If he doesn't get off, they're going to pull the plug.'

'LAST SONG!' announced Plato, holding up both hands and posing like Jim Morrison's half-cut cousin. The drummer eating Cornflakes flung the packet down and they spilled across the stage. She pounded out a beat. Theo grabbed my hand.

'This is it! This is amazing! This is the hit, Tracey! It's called "Indecisive". This is why he's going to be HUGE.' *He's already huge*, I thought. In every single way. Plato was the most unignorable person I had ever encountered. I wondered how Diana would have seemed in a room with him. Would she have shrunk to make room for him, or would his presence have only magnified hers? The man called Vince Power was looking at the stage as though he'd seen it all before, but he liked it all the same.

The place went berserk. I felt myself lifted up and down by the force of the other bodies around me. I was half laughing, half screaming with fear. The boy next to Theo crashed down heavily on my left foot. Then just as suddenly, and half-way through the song, someone pulled the plug, and the house lights came up on the stage, and some crappy old house music started up again, and I could see Plato roaring and shouting, but no sound came from him now.

'*Bastards!*' shouted Theo. 'They cut him off!' On stage, everything was being taken apart again at top speed, pieces of the drum kit hauled off sideways, guitars shoved into cases, microphones folded up at double-speed. 'For *fuck's* sake!'

By now the crowd flattened out again as though some magic had occurred that we would never be able to articulate in its fullest form to anyone who hadn't been there. Theo looked at me and laughed, and even though Plato hadn't finished his set, I could sense his elation. He was Ion Tiriac at the end of a match! He looked *that* joyous. I could just make out the figure of Ken Phillips leaving the building. Theo had been right. He had stayed till the end after all.

13

On Paper

'Come with me,' said Theo, pushing open the door back-stage again. There were some girls hanging around the door, who had seen Plato storm off. They wanted him back. They wanted more of that hit, of that good stuff.

'I need to go,' I said to Theo, 'please. I have to get back.' Plato, standing just inside the door, drenched in sweat and swigging a beer, heard me.

'Why do you need to go? Who are you? Cinderella?' He leaned back against the wall and closed his eyes. 'Since you're here now, at least tell me it was all right.'

I gulped at the oddness of someone asking me to reassure them. 'It was very all right,' I said.

'T?' Plato opened one eye and looked at Theo. 'Well?'

'You need to stop talking,' said Theo. 'You can't let them cut you off again.'

'Twats,' said Plato.

He walked over to the table and sat on the corner and pulled out a cigarette. He offered me one. I shook my head.

'T looks after me,' said Plato, sparking up a light. 'I'm gonna make him rich. I'm gonna buy a big house right here on Ladbroke Grove with aviaries for the birds and a dolphinarium or whatever he wants, and a spa for racehorses! He'll be the King of Notting Hill! All thanks to me.'

'Actually, there used to be a racetrack down Ladbroke Grove,' I heard myself saying, 'the Kensington Hippodrome. Opened in 1837, closed by 1842. It wasn't a financial triumph.' I could have done that thing that I usually did of pretending to be uncertain about the dates to cover my slight shame at the intricacy of my knowledge ('it might have been 1843 or '44, I'm not totally sure' etc.), but I didn't bother this time. I knew the facts. Robert hadn't drilled them into us for nothing. What was the point in acting as though I couldn't remember them all in exacting detail? Plato laughed as though what I had said was a huge joke.

'It wasn't a financial triumph!' he repeated. 'It wasn't a financial triumph! Oooh! What the hell *is* this?'

'I know a few things about the area. Local history and whatnot,' I muttered.

'Well, good one, Space Girl Three. You gotta feel for your roots all the time,' said Plato. 'Keep feeling for them, you know?' He crushed the can of Coke in his hand and chucked it towards a bin. It missed. Theo picked it up for him.

'Where are you from?' I asked Plato. I could barely

recognize my own voice, this bravery, this ability to ask a question of another person. Plato laughed down at his feet.

'I'm not from round here. Not originally. I've lived all over. I left home at thirteen and moved to Slough. I lived with mates. We shared a house.'

'You . . . joined a cult?' I said hesitantly.

'Kind of,' shrugged Plato. 'Depends how you think of it. It was tough, sometimes we hadn't enough to eat . . . Yeah. I used to go back home from time to time, but I'd become unknown to them, all that lot, at home. They let the baby out on his own, and when I came back, I wasn't no baby no more. When I was eighteen, I got on a train to Manchester to write my music. Then I came to London, like Dick ruddy old Whittington. Wanted to see if the streets were paved with gold discs. T found me on the tube two years later, and took me in. And now I'm gonna make it, and we're all gonna have whatever we want, and we're all gonna be happy. You know? Happy like the Rolling Stones.' It was impossible to tell whether he was serious or not.

'You brought good luck with you,' Theo said to me.

'I think it went well because you were good,' I said. It seemed unlikely that I brought good luck anywhere, least of all to Three Moon Monday at the Lovelock.

Plato pulled on a white puffa jacket, the size of a super-king duvet.

'Well. Can't sit around here like a bunch of idiots for the rest of the night,' he said.

'Where are you going?' asked Theo.

'Camden. Dublin Castle.' He glanced at me again. 'Goodbye. Come again. Or don't come again. Whatever makes you happy.' He bowed his head, chucked a Sainsbury's bag under his arm, and walked out of the room.

Theo nodded at me.

'You came. That's cool. Thank you.'

'It's hard . . .' I said, then stopped. I didn't want to say anything else. I didn't want Plato's triumph and the great unexpected thrill of standing next to Theo to be contaminated by the Trench Effect. It was coming for me, that was for sure.

'I'll go,' I said.

'Don't be mad. I'll walk with you. I'll walk you back home.'

'You really don't need to.'

'Why not? I pass your house anyway.'

The door opened again. It was Plato. 'Forgot I had this on me,' he said. He lobbed a black wallet across the room, and it hit the back wall, spilling everything out of it.

'Fuck's sake!' shouted Theo, but Plato was already out of the room again.

I bent down to help him pick it all up.

'Don't worry,' he muttered, bending down for the coins that had rolled across the floor and under an old radiator. The rest of the contents had fallen at my feet. I picked up a twenty-unit phone card, and a bank card. I glanced at it. *Mr T B Farrah*. What did B stand for? Boy, perhaps? I picked up a crumpled fiver and a travel card, then I noticed that something had fallen under the table: more coins and a folded piece of paper. I crouched down, right under the table, to reach for it all. In the club, they were playing the Stone Roses.

'Please tell me that's twenty quid down there,' said Theo. 'If it's not, he's robbed me again.'

But it wasn't the money that made it hard for me to answer. I breathed in with the shock. What had fallen out of Theo's wallet was a page from a magazine, and I knew, even though it was folded up, exactly what page it was. I knew exactly what the full picture would be when it was opened, and I saw Mama raising her eyebrows at me. *Nothing is an accident.* And Daddy: *Everybody wants to be caught.* Quickly, I unfolded the page. I needed to check. I needed to check that it was the picture I thought it was, a picture of a girl – a photo shoot on a cold beach. I stared down it. It was a picture I knew so well that I sure as all hell could have drawn a replica of it from memory. It was a picture of Diana. There she was, clear as can be, unfolded in my hands, taken from Theo Farrah's wallet. It was from a shoot for *SKY* magazine; she'd done six pages of editorial inside. In this picture, she's standing in a queue at an ice cream stand on Brighton beach, with one hand on her hip. She's wearing red and white gingham shorts and a white T-shirt and a cropped red military-style jacket with gold hoop earrings and brown sandals, but her hair's in plaits on top of her head in the style of a Swiss shepherdess – she looks like Heidi reimagined as a member of Fuzzbox. She's laughing in pink lipgloss, and under the picture it says: *Shorts: £19.99 Miss Selfridge, T-shirt: £58.99 Gaultier, Vintage Jacket: £15 Kensington Market, Shoes: £45.99 Office. Model: Diana Kingdom at Hicks Models.* The paper from the magazine felt flimsy in my fingers, the folds worn, as though it had been taken out and looked at many times. Instinct made me smell the page, and the faint scent of Exclamation! was still there, a perfume that had been promoted in that issue of *SKY* with a sample sprayed onto the page of the advertisement. I had a brief, fierce vision of Diana and me rubbing these sample pages all over our necks, mixing the scents up if we felt like one wasn't enough, rubbing in the men's fragrances too, rebelling in some way against the companies who thought that women had to smell singularly feminine. Under the Formica-topped table, I stared down at the page, as though seeing the picture for the first time. Had I put it there myself? How did it get there? I felt sudden confusion, as though I'd skipped two episodes of some TV show and no longer grasped exactly what was happening. I folded it back up quickly, and I stood up and handed it to Theo. Without glancing at it, he pressed it into his wallet.

'No,' I said. 'No, don't put it away.'

'Huh?'

'That's ... that's a picture of my sister.'

He looked startled. 'Yer *wha*?'

'There's a picture of my sister in your wallet. From *SKY* magazine.'

'Huh?'

'Open it,' I said, with impatience.

'I don't know what you mean.' Theo looked at me, frowning, and then opened the wallet and started to look through it, his long fingers on the phone card, and the bank card, and the receipts. He came to the page from the magazine, and he pulled it out, and opened it up just as I had done. The paper looked fragile in his hands, as though it were a relic from another era, not something that had been available for anyone to buy from any old newsagents, not so very long ago.

'Diana,' I said in a rush. 'That's Diana. That's my sister.' Even in this context, with my heart hammering and fear tasting sweet and dry in my mouth, I couldn't hide the pride I felt whenever I said it. There she was, gingham shorts and big smile and plaits and the writing underneath.

Model: Diana Kingdom at Hicks Models.

Theo looked at me and shook his head. He took off his cap and he pushed his fingers through his crazy hair and his eyes went wide, and he looked carefully at Diana in her shorts, with her smile and her jacket and her hair.

'I never knew she was on the other side,' he said. He looked at me in bewilderment. 'I kept it for this.' He turned the page over.

It was the Levi's advert that Eric had done. There he was, *Model: Eric Elliot*, standing next to a white fridge, pouting into the camera, huge eyes, dark brows and a denim jacket with a sheepskin lining, and blue jeans and a white T-shirt. The advert had been everywhere. I looked again at the picture, and at Theo. He looked at me strangely.

'I wanted the jacket, like everyone else. I thought it was dead nice. I pulled out the page and kept it so I could see if I could find it on sale anywhere.'

'Oh.'

'I never did find it. Not that exact one. Couldn't afford it, anyway, Tracey. I'd forgotten it was still in there. Mad tha. Mad tha your sister's on the other side.' *Your sister's on the other side*. Well, that was one way of putting it. He was telling the truth, of that I was quite certain, but there was a wariness about him now.

'Do you want to keep it?' He held the page out to me. I hesitated.

'I've got all of Diana's pictures at home,' I said, 'everything she ever did.'

'Well, maybe I'll get that jacket after all,' he said. 'If Ken signs Plato—'

'The guy wearing the jacket,' I said with sudden urgency. 'That's Eric Elliot.' I felt it, a great need to bring Eric's name into the conversation, as though talking about him might reveal something to me. Theo looked down at the picture again.

'Yeah. I know who he is. Everyone knows who he is, don't they?'

'We know him. Knew him, more like. Diana and me. I haven't seen him for a bit.' I could feel a great heat spreading all over my face. 'I never knew him well. He was just – a boy around the place.'

'Yeah? You like boys around the place?'

'As opposed to girls?' I didn't know what he meant.

'Yeah, maybe.' He laughed. 'I mean, you don't seem to like us very much.'

'My sister loved boys. I don't really.'

'Why not?'

'I like being on my own.'

'Ha. Me too.' He looked back at the picture of Eric. 'Do you like *him*?' There was a seriousness in the question, but I think he was embarrassed too. I blushed like a fool.

'He's done very well,' I said. 'There are only a few of them in the industry who really make money.' I sounded like Lisa.

'Of them?' said Theo.

'The boys. The men . . .' How could I tell Theo how I'd felt when Eric had given me a moment of his time, when he'd asked me questions about what music I liked, when he'd laughed at me, when he'd paid me attention? 'He's – he's with Lisa,' I said. 'They have a son. Charlie. Lisa was Diana's booker at the agency. She was in the car too, when Diana was killed, but she was all right. She wasn't hurt.'

I gulped at saying so much. The reveals felt as big as Dallas. I could've been handing Theo a chest x-ray for general discussion. He turned the page over to Diana, then back to Eric again. I hung my head.

'I need to go,' I said.

It was colder now. Notting Hill was sharp with menace; in gremlin mode. A waxing crescent moon sat like a clown's hat over St John's Church, as two skinny white boys in shell

145

suits crossed the road in front of us, and one of them turned to grin at me with brown teeth and dead eyes. *Fuck The Poll Tax* had been sprayed on a wall in front of a shuttered-up house on Lansdowne Road. Theo and I didn't say much as we walked. He had his hands in his pockets now. He had his hands in his pockets and a picture of my sister in his wallet.

When we got back to St Quintin Avenue, I saw the curtains move, and Ann glanced out. When she saw it was me, she stepped back into her bedroom. I'd have given her hours of worry, leaving without telling her where I was going. I never left the house, now I'd shot out without even telling her. She'd have been beside herself. I knew that much.

'Thanks,' I said to Theo.

'It's OK.'

'You didn't have to walk back with me.'

'I know.' He looked at me and did that thing again, where he hesitated and seemed to defy himself. 'I'll come back. Next week some time. To see Yellow. To see you.'

'You don't have to.'

'I know.'

He turned to go.

'The picture of Diana in your wallet,' I said quickly, 'maybe it means something. You know.'

'Like what?'

'Like . . . I don't know.'

'I kept it for the other side,' he said again.

'I know. But I found Yellow, didn't I? And now this.' I felt alarmed by the sound of my own voice. What was I saying?

'You'll be all right,' he said slowly. 'You've made a start. The picture doesn't mean anything.' Theo frowned and looked at the ground. He was distracted.

He bent down to pick something up from the lavender bushes by the front gate. It was the lost tennis ball. I held out my hand. It was a clumsy throw, but I caught it all right. I looked up at the house. The window I had thrown it through that afternoon was still open, wider than before. Another rush of blood to the head, and I stepped out of the front door, and threw the ball up, and it rocketed back into the house through the open window.

'Ah, now you're just showing off,' said Theo. My heart was thumping; it felt like a victory of sorts. 'Hey,' he said.

'Yes?'

'Don't do what you'd usually do tomorrow. Walk to the other side of the room. Stand on the bed, like.'

'What do you mean?'

'I mean, you're – you're – all right. Just try looking at everything from a different place.' He looked embarrassed. 'Ah, that's just something stupid someone said to me once.' He nodded at me quickly, and he walked off, back down the road, back to where? I didn't know any more than I ever had. But he's said he'll come back. Theo Farrah told me he'd come back.

14

Cool/Hot

It was in June 1985 that Lisa Hicks walked past a shop in Oxford called the Wendy House, where Diana, Mama and I were shopping for sunhats, and changed everything forever. We were fourteen and a half; I had braces on my teeth and spots on my chin, but Diana – who had spots too, make no mistake – had white-blonde hair, long legs, wide as hell blue eyes and straight white teeth along with the spots. I recall the heat of the afternoon and an urgency in me to get back home quickly; Wimbledon had started the day before and I planned an afternoon in front of the TV. But there we were, balancing in the window of the shop pretending to be mannequins, when a short woman with peroxide hair like Billy Idol and a lot of plastic jewellery – Pepsi, Shirley, George Michael and Andrew Ridgeley all rolled into one – walked past, glancing sidelong at us as she did so. I saw her double-take, check herself, reverse-step and pull down her sunglasses like they do in John Hughes movies, and she stared hard at both of us. Even before we knew her, it seemed obvious to me that here was someone who walked around like she had her own soundtrack, only discernible to the fully initiated. I giggled because I guess she seemed comical to me then. Diana was wearing a white sundress, and she was posing with a fixed grin and a bucket and spade. I was wearing a polka-dot rain-coat and red wellington boots so I imagine we were comical to her, too.

'Shh!' I hissed to my sister. 'Stay still!'

The woman was now walking into the shop where she smiled at my mother and her friend Janette who ran the joint, both of whom were cooing over a T-shirt with an ice cream sundae on the front and the word 'Cool!' in swirling writing. You could feel the puffy writing in your fingers, and you could reverse the T-shirt and on the other side was a hot-dog bursting out of a burger and the word 'Hot!' I had begged for it since our last visit, but Mama had held fast; I might as well have asked for the moon and stars in a wicker basket all tied up with a red bow. Mama didn't cave in easy to me.

'Sorry,' said the woman. 'I was walking past but I just had to stop. Is that your daughter in the window?'

'Yes. She's not for sale, sorry. Haha!' I had always loved the way that Mama laughed with such delight at her own jokes. From my place in the window, I snorted. The woman *roared* with laughter. Her laugh was a deep, throaty cackle that set Diana off at once. The woman turned to us and grinned.

'I'm not from this part of the world, as you can probably tell,' she said. Her accent was proper cockney, the kind that old Dick Van Dyke could only dream of achieving. 'I'm only here visi'ing a friend in a crisis, she lives in Chalfont St Giles, you know it? Well, it's all very Miss Marple around there, in fact I'm hopin' I won't be murdered tonight haha, but in normal life I run a model agency in London so I'm always on the lookout for faces, I'm never not scou'ing.'

'Excuse me?' said Mama.

'Scou'ing. For new faces.' She nodded at Diana then back to Mama. 'Would you and your daughter be interested in coming in to have a chat to us? About modelling?'

Diana, next to me, gasped and almost stumbled off the raised platform where we were posing. I grabbed her back.

'A chat about modelling?' asked Mama quickly.

The woman pulled out a card and handed it to her. 'My name's Lisa Hicks. I started Hicks Models four years ago after three years at Models 1. You know Models 1? No? Well, why should you. Anyway, I left a while back and started my own agency. We represent the very best and nothing less, which makes me sound like a proper twat, hahaha, but it's true, and I never like bombarding people when they're going abou' their day. But your daughter is a *very* remarkable-lookin' girl.' She said this bit almost sternly, as though she were trying to tell Mama something very serious that she felt sure none of us had ever quite grasped before. Diana's hand was on my arm; she squeezed me. 'How old are you?' she asked Diana.

'I'm fourteen and a half and blind in one eye!' squeaked Diana, unable to keep out of it a second longer.

'Hang on, she might not have been talking about you,' I quipped. Everyone laughed again, including me.

'Oh, but Feb's a genius,' said Mama swiftly, 'and you should see her on the tennis court!'

Lisa Hicks was no idiot. She at once turned all her focus onto me.

'Oh, I love the tennis. Are you a Martina fan?' she asked me kindly. Looking back on it, I suppose anyone would have every right to assume I was. I bloody *looked* like a Martina fan.

'No!' I squeaked, appalled. 'Chris Evert Lloyd's going to win!'

'Why's that?' she asked me.

'She's a baseline player,' I said, 'consistent, you know?'

'Ah. Well, I'll take your word for it. And who'll win the men's title?' she asked. She was humouring me, I could tell. I didn't care. I could have talked tennis with anyone, whether they gave a damn about the game or not.

'Boris Becker,' offered Diana instantly, who had been following his career for the past six months, drawn as she was to anyone offbeat whose star was in the ascent. 'He's only three years older than me,' she said, 'I could marry him one day!' She had been suggesting this to me every week for the past few months. I rolled my eyes at Mama who laughed, but Lisa Hicks didn't laugh.

'And you think a seventeen-year-old boy can win?' she asked, and she seemed to freight the question with heavy meaning, as though Diana's answer was somehow more important than she knew. Later that evening, Diana would impersonate her asking the question, and we howled with laughter. At the time, she was earnest in her response.

'Oh, *yes*. He's amazing.'

'Well, I think it's lovely that you want to marry him. Misguided, but lovely.'

'Misguided? Does that mean I'm wrong to want to?' demanded Diana.

'No. But he's not the most handsome boy out there, for starters.'

'Handsome doesn't matter to me,' said Diana.

'Well, that's a good thing.'

'It *is* a good thing!' agreed Diana solemnly. 'How awful to like someone just because of how they look! It must be a terrible, *grim* thing!'

'You're quite right of course, darlin'. But I wasn't saying you shouldn't marry him because of how he *looks*,' said Lisa.

'Well, why shouldn't I then?'

'Because brilliant young boys like him can shoot themselves in the foot without meaning to, and usually bring down several others at the same time.'

Diana and I let this sink in a bit.

'Are you married?' Diana asked slowly.

'No!' said Lisa. 'I have a boyfriend, though.'

'What's he like?'

'Handsome! Hahaha! He's a model. What am I like?' She laughed again. 'He's called Eric. He's only twenty-two.'

'How old are *you*?' I asked her.

'Thirty-one. Bit old for him really, but he's so gorgeous, I might as well enjoy it while it lasts.' She grinned at me, like she was hoping I comprehended what she was on about.

'Well done you!' said Mama, who certainly did.

'You're probably much cleverer than him,' said Diana insightfully.

'Perhaps,' said Lisa. She stopped suddenly, as though she'd said too much, and she turned back to Mama. 'I'll leave my card with you, and you can all have a li'l think about it. No pressure of course, but there's a real new wave waiting to happen; people want girls who look like real girls, not like the supermodels. They want beauty, but they want the girl-next-door version of beauty, not the impossible kind.' She hesitated. 'You don't have any photographs of Diana *on* you by any chance? In your purse? I'd return them, of course.'

'No, I don't have any,' said Mama. She stood closer to Diana, as though she were weighing up whether this had all gone a little far. We had only come in for new sunhats.

'I'm sorry,' said Lisa. 'I get ahead of myself, sometimes. It's just rare to see a girl so – *luminous*. It's those blue eyes. And the face! Gorgeous!'

She looked at Mama. 'Your daughters sound American,' she said as though Mama might not have noticed it herself.

'We used to live in Texas,' said Mama wistfully.

'Beautiful place,' said Lisa. 'I had the best three days of my life in Houston. But that's for another day.' She'd snared Mama good and true with this, whether she knew it or not.

'Anyway. Think about it. The modelling. You know. Just have a think.'

'There may be some issues—' began Mama, wrestling with what to do. 'If Diana were to get any paid work, I'd have to be there while she was being photographed. She's very young still – or Feb? If she had supervision, it mightn't be so bad. She'd need someone with her all the time, of course. The girls do everything together, you see.'

'Of course. I understand.' Lisa seemed to take in her surroundings for the first time. 'What a lovely little place this is,' she said.

'Oh, we adore it here,' said Mama quickly, casting a glance at Janette who had been following the conversation with her mouth slightly open.

'Perfect for presents for my godchildren,' said Lisa.

'Oh, yes,' agreed Mama.

'I've got six of the blighters,' said Lisa.

'*Six!*'

'I can't have kids of my own. Fibroids.' Lisa slammed the word 'fibroids' out of her mouth so that it sounded almost obscene.

'Oh, that's terrible. But they can be dealt with, surely?' said Mama blandly.

'Not mine,' said Lisa. She picked up a red-and-white pair of shoes. 'These are very sweet,' she said. Janette rallied herself.

'They're on sale,' she managed.

Lisa knew exactly what she was looking for. I'd never

seen anyone shop like they were filing papers before, with such breathtaking efficiency. Eventually, she came to the Cool/Hot T-shirt. She fingered the material and looked at the label.

'Oh, Feb loves that,' said Mama.

Lisa looked at the pile of clothes she'd placed on the counter waiting to be paid for. Janette had gone quite pink.

'Let me buy it for her,' said Lisa.

'No,' said Mama. 'It's all right. I'm buying it.'

And she did. Right there, like she had it planned all along, which I can tell you now, she certainly had *not*. We all watched her writing out the cheque.

'You've got a lovely mum,' said Lisa to Diana and me. 'My mum never spent money on new clothes for me.'

'Probably why you like clothes so much now,' I said. I was high with the thrill of what was happening. I watched Mama removing the cheque from the book with that satisfying ripping sound.

As soon as Lisa had left the shop, Mama said: 'I think I'll just run after her, have a quick word,' and she dashed out, and I watched as she talked to Lisa in the street. I knew what she was saying about Diana. I knew very well what she was explaining.

'Fibroids,' sighed Diana, and giggled, and from then on, my sister and I frequently used 'fibroids' instead of 'fuck' when we wanted to swear, and because the word was associated with our first meeting with Lisa, it carried with it a strange, exotic charm quite at odds with its true meaning.

That night as I lay in bed, I remember thinking over what Lisa had said about Diana being misguided for liking Boris Becker. *Misguided*. It carried with it a threat of something I couldn't place.

By the time Chris Evert Lloyd had lost the Wimbledon women's final to Martina, and Boris Becker had taken on Kevin Curran and won, Diana had been photographed for the front page of *Just Seventeen*. Not the editorial pages on the inside. Not the photo-story in the middle. None of that second-rate stuff. She got the front cover. No matter that she wasn't even *close* to being just seventeen. She was paid seventy-five pounds, and I had my lunch and train ticket paid for, just to be by her side all day. It was also the first time I had read *Smash Hits*, which the make-up artist handed to me to read while she was rubbing Vaseline into Diana's eyebrows.

'Do I look OK?' my sister asked me when *Just Seventeen* came out, a few weeks after this. She held it up in front of my face.

'Stop it, you're holding it the wrong way around,' I said, taking it from her.

'Oh, fibroids! You're right.' she exclaimed. She swivelled it around the other way. 'I just need to know what you think.' Always the reassurance, always needing to know what I thought.

'I still think the clothes are awful,' I said, reflecting what I had told Diana on the day, 'but you look like a film star. You look like Michelle Pfeiffer in *Grease 2*.'

Diana on the front cover of a magazine, aged fourteen and

a half, was the moment that changed everything; it was the great putting into action of her power. The outward sign of the inward, invisible grace. Diana was introduced to stylists and shakers like Corinne Day and Melanie Ward, who loved her, and photographed her as she really was. There was rarely a need for make-up, just the power of that face and those eyes. Suddenly there were magazine editors out there who wanted the purity of a young girl wearing just a vest and a pair of sawn-off jeans, laughing like she meant it, in bashed-up trainers, under grey skies. They wanted precisely what Diana could give them, not the unachievable, unearthly poses of Christy Turlington and Linda Evangelista wearing Dior, bikinis, heels and diamonds, standing next to giraffes in Kenya. And me? I thought about it often enough, how it made me feel when my sister was all over the magazines. I never wanted what Diana had, not really. Perhaps that's because it was so unachievable. It wasn't a possibility, so I didn't crave it. Diana was always looking outwards, always reaching for the next star, and I was happy where I was.

Thinking about it, I'd never really wanted anything for myself except for magazines and my music. Until now. And even now, I'm not sure what it is I want, only that something's making me want to wake up, and get up, and look out of the window, and listen for the doorbell, and think.

That's it. Something's making me want to think.

15

The Rapture: Part 1

The morning after Plato played at Three Moon Monday, I woke up with the tennis ball still beside me on the bed, and I knew, for the first time since my sister had gone, that it was a Tuesday. Since the end of last year, the days have just run into each other, unnamed and unchecked, unremarked upon, except for Sundays at 5pm when I need Bruno and the Top 40, and that's all that matters to me. But this was different. *I had been out.* I had felt Monday night in my whole body and now, logically, here was the next contender. *Tuesday.* I thought about Theo, the last words he'd said to me. *Don't do what you'd usually do.* So, I pulled out the chair from behind my desk and I sat down.

Ann knows it's always been work and school that make me think of Diana more than anything else, which is in many ways ironic since my sister had spent so much time trying to get away from these things. For months now Ann's been dropping things onto my desk: poems, books, worksheets, anything she feels will get me out of bed, in the hope that I might just have second thoughts about going to university. I did my A levels last summer; I worked myself into the ground and got three As. Ann worries that my brain might disintegrate if it's only used for Bruno Brookes and chart positions, and it's *true*, sometimes I feel everything I've learned seeping out of my head and into my pillow at night, never to be retained again, but I don't care any longer. God love Ann for trying. She knows that I had liked Ted Hughes, so she still leaves his poems around the place, in the hope that it might spur me into reading again.

'Wouldn't like to have been married to the bastard,' our English teacher, Rosi Summers, had said. She was one of those teachers who liked to shock, but with girls like Ella Drudge and Sophie Carter around, we hadn't needed that. There were my notes; the corners of some of the pages had been ripped off, probably to dispense with chewing gum. I opened the book and I read two lines into the room. I felt Diana over my shoulder as I always did when I read aloud.

> *Love struck into his life*
> *Like a hawk into a dovecote.*

I had written in large writing: *Birds. Symbol of life, love, change, the poet's concerns are given wings and claws.* I'd underlined 'claws'. Not bad, I thought, not bad for someone who at that point had never wanted to hold anyone in the dark, who had never heard the ringing of the love chord, let alone dug claws into anything but the grip of a tennis racket.

I thought of the classroom at school, of the rows of girls, all that pent-up energy and all that lethargy, all those disco-ready hormones. Chain reactions of yawns and sudden hysterics. The smell of cheap body spray – Impulse, Dove – mixing with sweat from netball and the sticky, embarrassing heat of Bodyform pads and heavy periods, and Obsession swiped from elder sisters' bedside tables. Even a week ago, the thought of it all had horrified me. Now, I picked up a pen. For the first time, it hovered over a clean page. I would just copy the poem out. That was all. Yellow looked at me with little black eyes. He *knew*.

I ended up writing for two hours without stopping. I don't know whether any of it was worth anything, but I knew that the sensation of watching the words in blue ink fill the page, and the ache in my hand, and the tip of my right forefinger starting once more to harden and callus from the pen felt like it was happening under a spell. When I had finished, I put the lid back on the pen and closed the book, and then I thought I would go to Ann's study and place what I'd written on her desk. She would be back at lunchtime to check on me. She would assume I was upstairs as usual. I never came downstairs before she came back. But I wanted her to know I'd done something.

I hardly ever step inside Ann's study, a panelled room on your right as you walk in through the front door of the house, with a fireplace and wintery lighting. As I walked down the stairs, I could hear steel drums from a couple of Rastas coming from the outside world, and I thought of Carnival. Had Theo been there? Had I walked past him, glanced at him, noticed him at all? Inside the room there's a small sofa upholstered in faded William Morris that runs up against the wall in the room closest to the street. Usually it's covered in paperwork: pages and pages that needed marking, essays, notes, programmes from shows she'd just seen. These things were *still* on the sofa, but so, unusually, for half-past eleven on a Tuesday morning, was Ann. She was lying with her eyes closed and her head resting on a stack of study guides to Photosynthesis and Plant Nutrition, and on top of *her* was the man I had seen with her in the street, the man I knew now without any doubt to be Gregory Arrowsmith. He was kissing her deeply, and she had a hand inside his jeans. Irrationally, my first thought was that the carefully handwritten essays being crumpled under my aunt's long back and tiny bottom were likely to be smudged and ruined before the minute was out; I recognized Vanessa Wilson's carefree, flamboyant scrawl on top of the pile, which gave events a good slug of irony, all things considered. My second observation was that the old record player that Robert had given Ann for their anniversary the year before had been cranked into life on the desk, and a Françoise Hardy album was playing – very quietly – as though the singer herself was actually *in* the room but had been asked to keep it all très low-key, s'il vous-plaît. The hushed, sexy French vocals fitted the scene better than 'All I Wanna Do Is Make Love to You' by Heart (non-mover at number 18) that had been playing from my stereo as I had walked downstairs. So enraptured were they by each other that they didn't notice me, and I stood, entirely inside the room, as still as a statue, wondering what on earth my options were. *People see things with their heart, not their eyes*, was something that Diana used to say to me all the time, and sure enough, they hadn't seen me; they were too far into whatever this was to see anything other than each other. Gregory Arrowsmith said something to Ann. I think it was 'you're so beautiful' and she just moaned in response. I was appalled, disgusted, captivated, unable to move. A heavily annotated copy of *Molecular Biology of the Cell* fell to the floor from where it had been balancing on the end of the sofa and I closed my eyes, waiting for them to jump, but neither of them noticed. It was dark in the room; they'd had the presence of mind to close the thick, red curtains so that the street was closed off to them, and the lights were all off, except for a small lamp that stood on the floor shining dimly under Ann's desk. Thomasina was curled up asleep on Ann's cardigan, on the floor next to the lamp, unmoved by what was happening. She hadn't noticed me any more than the lovers had.

I ducked back out of the room. I stood outside the door for a moment but there were no voices from inside, and with the door shut again, I could hear my father's voice in my head, clear as day. *People always want to be caught.* Being caught *solves* something, being caught *forces* something into the open without the inconvenience of all the hand-wringing confessional stuff that takes planning and plotting and preparation. Being caught is chaos forced into some sort of order, and to hell with the consequences after that.

I went back upstairs, and I sat down on my bed. I heard Diana's voice in my head. *Fibroids! For fibroids' sake, Feb!* What in the name of hellfire was everyone doing? Was no one capable of keeping anything down and calm and *normal*? Why would Ann do this to me? I don't know, and I wonder if I ever will. Maybe this will go on and on forever. Maybe it will all blow up tomorrow. Either way, one thing I know about myself – straight up – is that I'm no good with time-bombs. I get no thrill from dangerous edges at all. Well, *you* wouldn't if you were me.

When I got to sleep that night it was as though my dreams had been spiked. I dreamed about Theo Farrah calmly taking Diana's sequin leggings off me in front of an audience at Three Moon Monday, except it wasn't in the Lovelock, it was in Ann's study. Then he kissed me in front of the crowd and Drudge and Carter were throwing roses and ripped copies of *Smash Hits* at the stage. I dreamed of Eric Elliot, in blue Levi's, and he was laughing, and clapping, his big mouth open. When I woke the next day, I was warm, with my left hand resting on my chest like Juliet. I lifted the cloth from Yellow's cage, and the sun flooded my bedroom walls, and he sang like he'd seen everything too.

16

Valentine

I was still vibrating from the dreams three days later, and when I went downstairs, I found Ann in her long-to-the-floor white Victorian nightdress, staring out into the garden. Her nightie was unbuttoned a little too much so that her left breast was almost entirely visible in profile; it struck me only then that I had never even seen Ann's breasts before. She was wearing her house slippers from Tokyo; she and Robert had been to the Far East shortly after they were married, and Ann's wardrobe was punctuated with clothing from Asia that sat oddly with her basic aesthetic of one-size-too-big lace blouses fused with the put-upon sensuality of Polly from *Fawlty Towers*. I stood and watched her for a while; she crossed the room and started flipping through the pages of a magazine – I guess it was the latest issue of *Tatler* – Ann had an unapologetic fascination with the social pages: the

Bystander photographs of Lord such-and-such's daughter's twenty-first birthday party at Annabel's with banana daiquiris and omelettes at dawn and so forth. She was singing 'Love Shack' by the B-52's, very softly but as usual she turned it into a musical-theatre number, slowing it down so that she sounded like Julie Andrews in reflective mode, trembling vibrato over the chorus, and changing the spoken-word section to Received Pronunciation. But most noticeable – a new entry at number 1 above the visibility of left breast at number 2 and her hair still loose at number 3 – was the light that seemed to come from her, that new, palpable, quivering radiance, that I could see so blatantly that it embarrassed me. I felt like the Mother Abbess from *The Sound of Music* in her presence: prim, untouched. Ann felt more like *my* mother than she ever had before.

I opened the fridge door for something to do and Ann spun around. I pulled out a yoghurt and I jolted as Thomasina jumped up on the counter behind me, and the yoghurt slipped through my fingers, and split and splattered open, white, creamy, on the lino floor. I picked up a cloth. Ann rushed to assist me, her words tripping over themselves. This new anarchy in her, this new vibration, was altering everything.

'Oh! Feb! Take another yoghurt. Oh, that was the last one. Never mind, there's a new jar of strawberry jam and there's a croissant in the bread bin. Or there's cereal! You love cereal! How about CEREAL!' With this triumphant suggestion, she picked up a packet of Shreddies, fixed her eyes on mine and shook the box violently at me, like an auditioning percussionist. I took it from her. Her left boob slipped out of her nightdress again and she bundled it back in without apology.

I wanted to bring her back down to earth with some of my pathological practicality, to let her know that I knew, that I comprehended the danger she was shoving us all into.

'I saw you,' I said. As soon as I'd said it, I didn't want to have said it. I didn't really want to burst anything. I couldn't quite bear it.

'You saw me?' She was a rabbit in the headlights, which was unusual for Ann, who prided herself on being unshockable; but this wasn't a schoolroom at Westbury House where, a week ago, she had reported to me quite calmly that a girl in the first year called Alexandra Lopez had fainted in the lab while dissecting an unborn chicken, falling head-first into a life-size model of a human skeleton, cutting her head open on a jagged rib and ending up in a pool of blood on the floor of the science lab. Now, in the kitchen at St Quintin Avenue, she felt less powerful. This was different.

'You saw me where?' she asked.

'I saw you. I saw you walking down the street.'

'Oh. Right.' Ann's voice had gone very quiet.

I gulped. No. I couldn't do it, could I.

'Well, you – you – you were – you were – it was just that – you were wearing Diana's jeans.'

Ann's relief was disguised so badly that even if I had not known about Gregory Arrowsmith, I would now have felt sure that something was up. She let out a long sigh, as though she had stopped breathing while I had been talking and needed to gasp for air now that she knew that her secret was still safe.

'Oh! Feb! I'm so sorry. I meant to tell you. I don't usually wear jeans, as you know, but I tried them on, and they fitted me, and I asked myself what Diana would have thought, and my instinct was that she would have told me to go for it. I mean, you of all people know what Diana thought about my wardrobe,' Ann went on, warming to the subject. Anything, I supposed, to keep her off the hotter topic.

'It's OK,' I said. 'Better you to be wearing her jeans than some stranger.'

'Well, that's what I thought. I rather imagined she might have approved.'

She looked at me, her big blue eyes searching my face. Did she *know* that I knew? I didn't think so. She was an unaccomplished villain. She cleared her throat again.

'I'm so sorry you saw me wearing them, Feb. I hope you weren't upset.' Ann laughed suddenly. 'You've been so, so *brave*—' Her eyes filled up. I wasn't actually interested in bravery. I knew perfectly well that I wasn't brave. 'I didn't tell Robert about –' she paused – 'about borrowing them. I thought he might think it was a bit ... odd.'

'I won't say anything.'

She gave me that searching look once more. 'I don't want him to think I'm having some sort of – I don't know – mid-life crisis thing. Trying to be younger than I am. You know.'

The sunlight streamed through the kitchen window

showing no mercy. There were fine lines around her eyes and deeper lines on her forehead. Although her skinny little ankles and her long pale feet sticking out from the bottom of the nightie gave her a child-like impression, she looked every one of her forty-five years. Yet I had never seen anyone luminous like this. Not even Diana at her peak. She looked like she could have taken on Helen of Troy and won.

Later, in the evening, when Robert came back, all I knew was that I didn't want to see him. I didn't want to know a single thing about Ann that my uncle didn't know. He put a pile of books on the table and pulled off his tie. I looked at his tweed jacket, worn all year round, even when it's hot enough to fry eggs on the pavement. Robert liked saying that, like a stopped clock telling the right time twice a day, he came into fashion every few years without meaning to. Right now, he was as far from cool as it was possible to be.

'Thank you,' I said suddenly.

Robert raised his eyebrows at me and took a biro out of his pocket.

'Whatever for?'

'For having me. For having us.'

'Oh.' Robert looked genuinely startled. He put down his biro and his eyes widened. Upstairs, I could hear Ann singing the theme tune from *Brush Strokes*.

I thought of Theo Farrah.

'Diana thought you were —' I gulped — 'Diana thought you were so —' I paused again and looked at Robert — 'so *nice*. Nice to her. Which you were. To both of us.'

Robert looked at me as though I were speaking in code.

'Ah,' he said eventually, 'it may come as a surprise, but it wasn't at all hard to be nice to you both.'

'Yes but—'

'Well, Diana always thought I was completely mad, of course,' said Robert, 'dragging you both around the place, talking about road names and railings and—'

'She liked it very much. Railings and all.'

'I enjoyed it too,' he laughed, 'very much. You forget, I never had children of my own.'

'I don't forget that,' I said.

'Well. Ann and I felt as though we'd been given a shot at something rather wonderful.'

He'd never given us the impression that he'd found taking on Diana and me wonderful, but he'd never implied that he hadn't found it wonderful, either. He was supremely, enviably impassive most times.

'But we came along, and we interrupted your lives,' I said. I didn't want to stop talking about it now.

Robert looked puzzled. He smiled at me as though I hadn't quite worked something out.

'Isn't life just one long series of interruptions? Some good, some bad? Interruptions define a life. I'm sure John Lennon had something to say about that, didn't he? I always felt Bach did.' He smiled at me rather vaguely. *So handsome*, Mama had said of him. *Good teeth, that lovely, delicate nose. But quite devoid of It, you know . . .*

'But one day you're living your lives together, just the two of you, the next day, *we're* there . . .' I realized, as I was speaking, what the hell I was driving at. It was *our* fault that this had happened. It was because Diana and I had come along that Ann had lost her mind over the drama teacher. *That was it!*

'Well, we did have to put our plans for world domination on hold, that's true.'

Robert doesn't quite know how to do sardonic, so he delivered what was not a bad joke in a way that made him sound regretful as anything – as though the desire for conquering the universe was all truth.

'Haha,' I said uncertainly.

'We wouldn't have had it any other way,' said Robert. He flipped through the first few pages of *The Times*, trying to cover his embarrassment. 'It required no discussion between us,' he said. 'None at all. I think, if anything, we've been better with each other since you arrived.'

I looked away from him, not wanting to see his face.

'Of course, not a day goes by that we don't think of Diana and wonder if anything we could have done could have prevented—'

'It wasn't your fault,' I said quickly.

'But we promised ourselves that we'd do all we could for you both. The main objective was to keep you safe.'

'You did. You *do*.'

'Feb. You've a whole long life ahead of you . . .' Robert cleared his throat and gave me a brief nod and I waited for the next part of the sentence to be picked from the Lazy Susan of clichés that most people offered up: *everything will be all right eventually, things will get better, time will heal, what goes around comes around, because you're worth it, the sun always shines on TV, is this burning an eternal flame?* etc. etc. But instead he said: 'So, February, please. Try not to – not to – fuck it up. You know? Try not to do that.' I stared at him, not just for the cursing, which was so unlike him, but also the directness of the order. He'd tried to cover the drama of the word 'fuck' by pronouncing it with a Scots burr tagged onto it, like the word 'loch'.

'Maybe it's already too late,' I said. 'Feels like it's already fuch-ed up, most times.'

He smiled at me. 'Ha. Goodness, no. It's not too late.' He sighed in sudden agitation and stood up, and nodded at me, almost annoyed. It's like every time he shows a piece of himself to *anyone*, he slams a demerit onto his report card in disappointment.

The difference between them is that when Ann came in an hour later, she picked up the copy of *The Remains of the Day* that Robert had taken out of the library last week and started reading it right in the middle of a chapter, to 'get a flavour of it'. That would have been Mama's answer too. She liked to get flavours. She liked to smell and touch things, to pick up the fruit and squeeze it round the middle, right before she decided whether it was worth eating at all. I sat at the table, saying nothing, with Thomasina on my lap. I wanted to go upstairs. I wanted to go upstairs to be with Yellow, but I couldn't. I needed to know if I'd dreamed it. As soon as she spoke, I knew I hadn't.

'Remember we've got lunch with the Arrowsmiths tomorrow,' Ann said to Robert.

I went very still. Ann glanced at me.

'Oh, Lord,' said Robert. 'I'd forgotten. Why on earth did we agree to that on a weekend?'

'I don't know,' said Ann, 'she's French. The wife.'

'Do the French only ever entertain on weekends?' asked Robert.

Ann paused and cleared her throat. 'I don't get the impression that the marriage is particularly great,' she said, as well she might. 'Not like your mum and dad,' she added suddenly, looking at me. '*That* was a good marriage.'

I felt my head going light, and the Trench Effect laughed in the corner of my eye. *There's been a fire. Your parents have been in a fire. In a fire. The station. There's been a fire. It's all over the news.* Then I heard the sound of my feet taking me upstairs, and into Robert and Ann's bedroom.

'Feb?' Ann shouted up the stairs. 'You OK?'

'I'm OK,' I shouted back down. Funny how many times you can say those two words and mean the opposite. Funny how many times people do that in their lives. *Yeah, I'm OK. I'm fine.*

I picked up the photograph of Mama and Daddy and I'm not OK. I'm not fine. I'm as far from OK and fine as anyone can be.

*

When I was twelve years old, I discovered that my mother had almost embarked on a romantic affair with John Lewitt, a white-suited Man-from-Del-Monte figure who lived at the other end of the village from us, in a big house, with an unhappy wife and three daughters with thin red hair and pale white faces. He was billed as a friend of both our parents, and he and his wife often tried to get their three boarding school daughters to mix with us semi-American state school kids, probably because they recognized in Diana a firecracker capable of cantering over class barriers slick as a whistle, but unfortunately for good old John Lewitt, we made mincemeat of Katrina, Amelia and Susanna of whom we were really suspicious, mostly because they didn't like Michael Jackson's *Off the Wall* album. But the point was: John Lewitt was rich, which appealed to my father, as he was not rich himself and admired those who had made money from nothing, and John Lewitt was crazy good-looking to the ladies, which appealed to my mother, as she was still very beautiful, and with great beauty – I have said – comes the relentless, restless desire to know that whatever age you are, you've still got whatever it was that you had when you first started giving people sleepless nights.

It was nearly midnight towards the end of February, and the wind was howling and raging around the cottage and rain was battering the windows and hammering the early daffodils in the orchard below my bedroom, and I couldn't sleep. Daddy was away in London for two nights; he was an accountant for a firm that made parts for trains. There's just no way of putting it to make it sound more exciting; Diana and I tried to for years. There was always an unsteadiness to the very foundations of the cottage when Daddy wasn't there to keep it sensible, a sense of mayhem lurking in the wings so that in some ways I wasn't altogether surprised when I tiptoed downstairs to find Mama, and from the kitchen door I heard a man's voice I recognized at once to be that of John Lewitt.

'Lily, I don't know how I can go on. Surely you feel it too? I *know* you do. The Valentine was from you, wasn't it? The Valentine's card?'

And my mother's reply in *sotto voce*: 'A card is as far as this can ever go, John.'

And John Lewitt again: 'But you wanted to tell me how you felt, Lily. You know I feel it too.'

'Oh, John.'

I remember thinking that this was exactly how they spoke in the Mills & Boon stories that Mama read of an evening; novels that would start off slim and neat enough to slip in the back pocket of her denims, but three days later would be twice the size due to being read everywhere and treated like shit. Mama had no respect for the physicality of books – for their covers, the blurb, the paper on which they were printed – and she cracked them open like she was opening a bag of Twiglets, briskly breaking their spines, climbing into the bath with them and drying out their damp pages afterwards on the radiator in the kitchen.

Now she had John Lewitt talking like he had climbed straight out of chapter four.

'Lily, you're the most wonderful woman I've ever met. I think I'm going mad—'

From my place behind the door I gulped, then without meaning to, half screamed, and they turned in horror, and I ran back upstairs, and Mama rushed up behind me, breathlessly trying to forge an explanation as she went along, but she ended up doing a crazy thing otherwise known as Telling the Truth, for which I am, even now, only partly grateful.

'What was John Lewitt talking about?' I asked her. He was always John Lewitt, never just John, to differentiate him from John Watson, a monosyllabic work colleague of my father's with a wife called Lynne who had Lyme's disease and was known by us girls as Lynne Lyme, and John Le Carré, whom my mother had once met at a drinks party and had spoken of ever since as though she were the godmother to his children.

'I suppose he likes me,' said Mama, 'these things happen sometimes. Even for people who are married.' She sat down on my bed and knocked the seven-inch single of 'Abracadabra' by Steve Miller Band onto the floor. The record slipped out of the sleeve. She picked it up.

'Funny cover,' she said. I wasn't prepared to change the subject.

'What was the Valentine's card? You sent him a *Valentine's* card?' I knotted my fingers around a knitted blanket. I was aware that although I felt horrified, the drama of what was happening was on some level very interesting to me. I had my mother's absolute attention for once – that was for certain.

'I felt sorry for him. He's always had a little *crush* on me, and I wanted to let him know that I *recognize* that he likes me. It was a sort of thank-you card.'

175

'But you don't need to thank someone for thinking you're pretty! Everyone can see you're pretty unless they're blind as bats. And it wasn't a thank-you card! It was a Valentine's card. You send those to tell someone you love them!'

'Yes. Perhaps it was a mistake,' said Mama thoughtfully.

'Have you kissed him?' I heard myself ask. There was that voice of mine: determined, practical, *efficient*. There was a silence.

'He *wanted* to kiss me,' she said slowly. I could sense her astonishment at what she was admitting; it was as if she had no choice but to tell me, in order to clarify it with herself. 'Don't tell Dad, sweet February. Please. It's not—' She paused, fishing around for how to finish the sentence. 'It's not *worth* telling him. That's it!' She looked at me triumphantly and repeated what she had just said. 'It's not *worth* telling him.'

'But you sent him a Valentine's card!' I said again. If this exchange had happened during my English Literature course, I would probably have taken some satisfaction in pointing out to Mama that Thomas Hardy had the whole Valentine card thing sewn up a hundred years ago from around chapter twelve of *Far from the Madding Crowd*. As it happened, I lay in bed that night, eyes fixed on the ceiling, listening to Diana breathing in the bed next to me. She slept through everything, my sister.

Poor John Lewitt. Whatever he had done for my mother and her vanity, she hadn't needed it for long. In any case, I was only too happy to take my mother's advice, and not

mention what I had heard that night. John Lewitt continued
to live down the road in his big house with his unhappy wife
and his three flame-haired daughters. But he didn't come
over as often, and when he did, my mother and father were
always sitting very close together in our little sitting room
that overlooked the village green with the red telephone
box with its Childline flyers on the walls and the *David H
Wants Sex With Dogs* graffiti scratched onto the inside door,
and Mama always looked nervous and irritated, which I was
later to learn is the permanent state of one who has taken a
vanity too far, and John Lewitt always looked delighted and
miserable, which I was later to learn is the permanent state
of one who is inextricably in love with someone they know
they will never have.

Ann in love with another man felt different to how I had
felt about Mama and John Lewitt. Ann in love with another
man felt real, and dangerous and wrong and right and desperate and inevitable all at once. She walked around the place
in another world, headlined by Françoise Hardy and Gregory
Arrowsmith's Wrangler's, and Robert stood on the outside
of the inside, somehow knowing *everything* and knowing
absolutely *nothing* at all.

17

The Open Cage

The next day, at nearly noon, the two of them stood at the bottom of the stairs. Robert looked resentful, holding a bottle of white wine down at his side like he was trying to pretend he wasn't holding it. Ann looked far too considered, in a long pink and red skirt that I knew she'd bought back in Tokyo, and a white blouse. She had tied a scarf around her head, which was a mistake as it made her look eccentric, which in many ways she *was*, so better not to draw attention to the fact. I would have told her to dress sharp and more together, to present as the brilliant scientific mind with a quick wit that I knew she was, not the abstract lover of musicals, inclined to veer towards the romantic after half a glass of red wine.

'We're off,' said Robert.

'We won't be late,' clarified Ann.

'Have a good time,' I said, not really meaning it.

'We really won't be late,' said Ann again.

'Come on!' said Robert with irritation.

'It's all right, Feb, we won't be late.' She sounded as though she were losing her mind.

It was two hours later when I realized what the date was. *Smash Hits* had been out for three days, but for the first time, Ann hadn't picked it up for me. I needed it. I *had* to have it. There was no other way. I would walk to Mr Quennell's newsagents at the end of the road, and it would be all right. I would walk in, and ask for my copy, and he would give it to me, and I could come back and read it, cover to cover, and cut out the lyrics to 'Wild Women Do', and add it to the pile beside my bed. I felt for my keys. It was possible. I could do it. There was a logic here. I *needed* the magazine; I would go to find it. I put on my headphones and pressed play, but the batteries on my Walkman were running low, and it made Tracy Chapman, who's already low-voiced when the batteries are fresh, sound like Barry White, and it's sinister and wrong, but it's better than nothing because without the sound of music, I'm there, on the street, with everyone else. But on the streets I'm frightened again, and I'm small again, and I want to run back. I don't think I can do it. And even if I make it to the shop and back, where's the achievement if I feel the world closing in on me, if I feel the Trench Effect all over me, if I feel sick to my boots, as much of a coward as I've ever been? I kept on walking, but there was no Theo

179

Farrah for me now. I stopped and pulled my headphones off my ears, and I bent down and gasped at my own feet. They looked normal. Like everyone else's feet. Size 6. Inside some old trainers. I kept on bending down over them, looking at them. I put a hand to my forehead. Now what? I was stuck out here. An old woman in a headscarf looked at me strangely.

'All right, love? You all right? Been running? Got a stitch?'

'Yeah,' I said down into my feet. 'A stitch.'

There was a queue of teenagers dressed up to the nines and buying sweets and I nearly turned back and ran home, but Mr Quennell saw me, and he leaned down behind the counter, and he winked at me, and he handed over the magazine. I think I smiled at him.

'Well done,' he said. As usual, other people's kindness is the worst kind of agony. I stared down at the magazine, thin and silky in my fingers, box-fresh unopened medicine. Adamski on the front.

'How to Make a Hit Record in Your Bedroom,' said Mr Quennell, reading from the cover.

A girl in front of me dropped coins onto the floor and the lot of them all scrabbled about, giggling and pushing and picking them up.

'Nice to see you out and about,' said Mr Quennell. 'Your auntie not around?'

'She forgot,' I said. I felt disloyal.

'Not like her,' said Mr Quennell cryptically. 'I don't think much of Adamski. All that bleeping. I much prefer that Betty Boo,' he said, nodding at the cover and winking at me.

Often, Diana and I opened the new *Smash Hits* while we were still walking down the street, so that by the time we got home, we'd have absorbed roughly what was in the issue, and we'd have taken most of the contents in: the interviews, the obscure jokes, the posters and who had won the record token and tea-towel for the best communication with Black Type, the letters page. I guess it was the combination of old Tracy Chapman sounding so dead-beat on those low batteries and looking down at the magazine that meant that I didn't see where I was going, and I walked right into the pram being pushed in the opposite direction.

'Sorry!' I gasped, and I tried to walk on quickly, but whoever it was pushing the pram had stopped, and she said my name.

'Feb!'

The woman pushing the pram was Lisa.

I pressed stop. Tracy Chapman stopped. The whole *world* stopped, it seemed to me. I jolted at Lisa, then my eyes went down to the baby boy. He was asleep, wearing a light blue and white cotton hat like he needed it in the middle of summer. I had only ever seen Charlie as a newborn and now he looked too big for my memory of him; my head scrambled to update the images. Lisa was wearing an oversized black and gold Dior T-shirt and black trousers, and she'd cut her hair very short and dyed it black, with a quiff, making her more Billy Zane than Billy Idol. Big gold hoops in her ears.

Red lipstick like she meant it. She held my eyes, as though if she looked at me for long enough, she could stop me from walking away, and I looked down into the pram.

'Hello,' I said to Charlie. 'You're big.'

'Isn't he?' said Lisa. She reached out and touched my arm, but I stepped back. 'Did you get my – my letters? I – I know you don't want – I don't know what – I thought you might like to see him. I've come around St Quintin a few times – I wanted to ask if you're all right—' She stopped talking, and stepped backwards suddenly, as though she'd been pushed. She bit her lip and some of her lipstick stuck to her teeth. I'd never known Lisa lost for words. I kept on looking at Charlie – Eric in perfect miniature. Charlie, who had held my hand in New York, Charlie who made everything better.

'How've you been since—' She stopped again. She couldn't bear to say 'the funeral'. I couldn't bear to *hear* her saying it. If enough people went around not saying it, then maybe it was something that I would wake up from.

'No,' I said. 'Don't. You don't need to say anything to me.'

I crouched down to Charlie. Eric's eyelashes. Eric's mouth. And Charlie who had held my hand. Charlie who had smiled at me.

'I didn't – she – sometimes I wonder, if we'd left on time, would anything be different, could I have changed the way it turned out . . .' Lisa spoke quickly, as though she had rehearsed saying this to me in a thousand imagined situations.

'I never thought anything was your fault,' I said. '*I* was meant to be with her,' I said. '*I* always took her for the appointment. Every time. *I* wasn't there. It's nothing to do with *you*.' It came out accusatory. I heard that in my own voice. *You. You did it. You should have been more careful. You.*

'You did nothing wrong,' said Lisa. She was whispering as though she was afraid someone could hear. But who? Mr Quennell from behind the counter in his shop? The old woman who'd asked me if I had a stitch? Charlie? Who? 'But after everything you'd been through, with your mum and dad and everything . . .' she trailed off.

I looked down at Charlie again, that solid, uncompli-cated little elf, and as if he could feel that I was there, he opened his blue eyes and looked at me, unfocused, and seemed to nod at me, then he closed them again, and I could hear Diana – I could hear her over Lisa, and over Tracy Chapman. We were standing outside a house with jasmine twisting around the garden railings, and the jasmine smelled like Eternity by Calvin Klein, and I could see the advert for it on the pages of *Vogue* – Christy Turlington at peak beauty, lying on a beach in black and white – and as I stood in the street with Lisa, Diana talked to me, and I strained to hear her. Diana talked to me. My sister was there with me. She was reading from the front cover of *Smash Hits*, even though *I* always read it out to *her* on the way home, and her voice was more Texan than I knew it to be, it was her voice as a young child.

'*Bumper Poster Bonanza! Black Box, Paula Abdul, Jason, Donnie Wahlberg, the Chimes, Beats International.*' I could hear her roaring with laughter.

'How come *you're* reading?' I said to her. And I said it out loud, to Charlie, sleeping in his pram, I said it as though I were talking to my sister.

'What do you mean?' I heard Lisa asking me. 'How come he's reading what?'

Why shouldn't I? Diana said to me.

'Nothing,' I said to Lisa.

I closed my eyes tight and when I opened them again, Diana was gone. I looked at Lisa; I saw the dark rings under the layers of make-up.

'Are you OK?' she asked me. 'Feb?'

'I don't know.' I took a breath.

And then as sudden as Diana's voice, came the image of Yellow.

'Oh God. I've left his cage door open,' I said under my breath.

'What cage?'

'Yellow. My canary.'

'Canary?' she called after me, and her face was pinched in, as though she'd seen Diana too, as though something about the word 'canary' had frightened her.

I ran back, and I opened the door, and my heart was pounding like it does in dreams, and I raced up the stairs, and when I opened my bedroom door, there it was, as I had left it. *The open cage, and it was empty.* My window was open wide as I had left it. Yellow had gone.

I reached out of the window, and I shouted into the North Kensington weekend: 'YELLOW!' and Kelvin's dad looked up at me from his front porch and waved at me, but I slammed the window down again. I sat on my bed, and I could hear the sound of footsteps on the stairs. They couldn't be back already? It was only two-thirty. Robert walked into my room at speed.

'Feb? Was that you shouting?'

'Yellow's gone! I left the cage door open, and I went to pick up *Smash Hits* from Mr Quennell—'

'You went out? Again?' He sounded astonished.

'Yes. And when I came back—'

'Ah,' said Robert. 'You left the window open?'

I nodded at him. I felt flat calm now that he was in the room. *It was over.* I hadn't been able to do it, after all. Theo had given me a task, and I couldn't see it through. I had been crazy to think I would ever have been able to look after something as delicate as a songbird. Robert walked over to the window and looked out. He squinted up into the sky.

'He might come back,' he said. 'We must look for him.'

'He won't come back,' I said. 'I should never have gone out.'

'Neither should I,' said Robert. 'I said I had to finish marking some essays and left early. There's too little time on the weekend for capering around with members of staff.'

'Where's Ann?'.

'I left her there,' he said. 'I find the whole thing too much.'

'What's too much?' I felt faint, nightmarish. 'Where is he?' I whispered.

Robert hauled himself out of the hole he was in. 'Don't

give up,' he said. 'I'll take another look around. Check the kitchen again.'

I listened as Robert walked around the house, opening doors quietly, padding from bedroom to bathroom to bedroom again, and downstairs again and into the kitchen. I heard him opening Ann's study door and I wondered if he'd see anything – some grimy little clue – that might tell him what had been going on in that space between Ann and old Gregory Arrowsmith on Tuesday morning, on the sofa with Françoise Hardy. I stared around my bedroom, looking from the mirror to the top of the cupboard. I looked under the bed, I stared back out of the window and into Yellow's empty cage, and the sandpaper on the cage floor was still wet where he had flapped his wings in the bath earlier on, and his food bowl was nearly empty, but sure as all hell, he had gone.

Robert came back upstairs, slower this time. He sat down next to me on the bed.

'I'm sure this happens all the time when people keep birds. It's instinct, to fly towards the open sky. Some birds just aren't meant to be caged.'

'Yellow *was* meant to be caged,' I whispered. 'He was born in a cage. It was where he was safe. Theo said he wouldn't survive in the wild.'

'There are those who might suggest that a few hours in the wild is better than a lifetime in captivity.'

'Not for Yellow,' I said.

'Let's wait a while,' he said. 'We'll sit here. The bird might be hiding. All we can do is wait.' Robert looked at me with sudden urgency; there was an expression on his face I'd never seen before, but I don't like people speaking in code. I like *clarity*. Diana needed it, I needed it too.

'He's fallen in love with her,' said Robert suddenly. He laughed, as though in saying it out loud, he'd amazed himself with the truth of it.

'Who?' I asked, pointlessly, but wanting to offer some blessed ignorance, at least. I threw a bit of incredulity into the question, but I'm no actor.

'Arrowsmith. Gregory Arrowsmith. The temporary drama teacher. He's actually fallen in love with her.'

'How do you know?' I asked, into the floor, my face flaming. Robert answered so quickly, and there was everything in there: anger, amazement, hurt and a sort of reverence at the same time. His voice sounded an octave higher than usual.

'He can't cover it up! He hangs on her every word – it must be clear to every member of staff who sees them. Let alone the girls. Let alone his *wife*!'

'What's the wife like?' I asked, hardly daring myself to ask.

'Not my cup of tea,' said Robert. 'Beautiful, but ...'

'She doesn't have "It"?' I said.

'I'm afraid that's probably the case, yes. I can quite see what's happened.'

'Maybe he just likes Ann and thinks she's interesting,' I said faintly. 'He doesn't have to be in love with her.' *Please, Yellow. Please come back.*

'Precisely,' said Robert grimly. 'From liking someone and

thinking them interesting, all kinds of chaos emerges. Far more dangerous that way round than merely thinking someone's face or – or *body* – is agreeable. The thrill of a new face is always unsustainable. The thrill of finding fascination in what people have to say takes much longer to wear off. You don't realize this when you're young. It's all muddled up in competition and point-scoring. But by the time you're our age . . .'

I was astounded by these opinions from Robert. He only ever spoke with emotion when it was firmly enclosed in quotes from others – Shakespeare, Mark Twain, Frank Sinatra. He shook his head.

'Ah. Don't mention it to her,' said Robert. 'I shouldn't have said anything to you. You mustn't worry. I'm sorry.'

I was saved from saying anything back as there was the sound of the front door opening and I knew that Ann was back.

'Up here!' shouted Robert, pre-empting something difficult, and cutting off any further questions from me. I imagined Ann hesitating. What was he doing upstairs with me? Had he found something out? I could hear a wariness in her movement, guilt and fear treading deeper into the carpet with every step. She poked her head around the bedroom door, eyes all wide and expectant as though she'd run all the way home.

'The bird's flown away,' said Robert.

'What?' I could hear Ann's relief and dismay at the same time. She stepped into the room. 'Feb?' She looked to me and then to the open cage.

'I left the door open. And the window.'

Ann looked down at the copy of *Smash Hits* on the bed.

'I meant to collect it,' she said. There were acres of guilt in her voice. She looked out of the window, then back at the two of us, sitting on the bed, then looked away again; it was as though being in the same space as Robert, particularly when he was with me, was an agony to her, an agony that she resented with every bit of her. I guess my aunt would have loved to have had the shard of ice in her heart necessary for managing a love affair with success, but she just didn't possess it, and she was discovering this on the hoof, which was terrifying her.

'I'll look downstairs,' she said. 'Check the kitchen again. We can leave the window open overnight in case he comes back.'

'I've just checked downstairs,' said Robert.

'Well, I'll check again.'

Robert followed her out of the room.

'They thought it was strange that you left early,' I heard her saying to him.

Yellow started singing just after five-thirty the following morning. That song that I knew now, a song that I would have known had I heard the solos of a hundred other birds all singing at the same time. His voice came from the kitchen, easy as liquid, just as it had that first evening that I had found him. I gave myself no time to think, I went down to him, past *Little Women*, past Robert and Ann sleeping side by side in their marital bed. Yellow was standing centre stage, on the kitchen table, and when I walked in, he seemed to nod at me. Like he was saying, *Hey! Here we are again!* And I laughed at him, like he'd laughed at me that first time, and I think he laughed back. *My* canary! I felt a swell of something you'd be hard pushed to describe as anything other than joy, and part of me wanted to thank him for leaving, because he had come back to me, and now that he was back, I'd worked out how much I needed him. He sang on, and I stepped towards him, and I stretched out my hand to him, and I thought that perhaps he would come to me, because in the movie version of this scene that's *just* what happens, y'all, *every* time, but he didn't, because this is real life, and he's not some bluebird in *Mary Poppins*, and I admired his suspicion of me. It was correct! But for all that suspicion, he flew off again, and he flew up the stairs, like he knew the drill, and by the time I had caught up with him, he was back in his cage, scraping his little beak along the perches, and stretching out his legs, then flying down to his bath. I closed the cage door and breathed out and I lay down on my bed and slept.

When I woke up it was after ten. I turned up the volume on the stereo.

'I bumped into Lisa and Charlie,' I said to Yellow, over the middle of Was (Not Was) and their cover of 'Papa Was a Rollin' Stone'. I said it out loud, like Yellow would understand. He just looked at me and chirped, as though waiting for me to catch up with him. Then I heard the telephone ring and Ann answering it.

'Feb!' she shouted up the stairs. 'Phone for you!'

'I'm coming over later,' said Theo.

'To see Yellow?'

'Yeah.' He paused. 'I've got something for him.'

And I didn't tell Theo that I'd lost Yellow, and that he'd come back again. I didn't want him to think I'd left the cage open and gone off just to get a copy of *Smash Hits* with Adamski on the front and an interview with the Pasadenas inside. I just said that everything was fine. You know. Like you do. Because you don't always need to tell the whole story, if no one will ever know any different. And anyway, Yellow had come back. So, it *was* fine. You know?

18

Kate

When the doorbell rang, I was waiting for him.

'Hello,' I said to Theo Farrah.

'Said I'd come over, didn't I?' He wasn't wearing his cap. His hair was wild, he looked tired, but taller, braver somehow. 'Can I come in? I've got something for you. Well, for Yellow, to be exact.'

'What is it?'

He bent down and picked up a bird cage at his feet. Inside was another bird, this time so pale were the yellow feathers that they were almost white. 'A friend for him,' he said. He laughed at my expression.

'Another one?'

'Why not, Tracey?'

We walked upstairs and into my bedroom. The heat of the day oozed into the house.

'To start with, we keep them apart,' said Theo. 'They just look at each other. Realize that they're in the same room, on the same planet, that sort of thing. Only thing is, he'll stop singing now he's got her. The search is over.'

The female bird flew onto a perch and looked about with black eyes.

I felt a lump in my throat. 'Did you get her from the pet shop?'

'Yeah,' said Theo. 'She's been there a while. I felt sorry for her.' He was speaking quietly, sitting on the floor, looking up at the cage. He had his legs crossed in front of him. The smell of him filled the room, that intoxicating mix that was impossible to recall when he wasn't with me. It was candy floss and coconut and Armani and motorbike fumes, although I don't think that it was really any of these things. It was just *him*.

'Where are your uncle and aunt?' he asked me.

'Out.' I paused. 'They like you.'

It sounded like I was making a deeper point than I actually was. Theo laughed.

'That's nice. They probably like the idea of me.'

'What?'

'Well, I'm pretty sure that the only time you've ever had anyone non-white in your house was when I walked through your door the other day.'

'That's not true,' I said.

'It is true,' said Theo. 'I could tell.'

'So what if it is true? Does that make me less human than you?'

193

'Probably,' said Theo. 'Being black *and* white is like being human turned up to eleven.'

'I don't know what you mean,' I said. But I did. I knew what he meant. Why didn't I want him to think that I knew? I felt I understood him perfectly. I felt as though losing your parents and your sister turned you up to eleven too. It made you *more* of something. At least, it *should* do. There had to be something more about you, the more loss that you felt inside.

We sat there, watching the birds together. Outside the house on the opposite side of the road, a drill plunged into a pavement, splitting the road apart for new wires, new pipes, new centuries, but we didn't shut the window, it was too hot for that. I could hear the music coming from the flats next door; the smell of marijuana, new tarmac and fried chicken drifted into my room, and I felt last summer all around me. Yellow stared at the pale white stranger opposite him. He had been silenced now. He had got what he wanted, but it was almost as if he couldn't quite believe it. Maybe he wanted to talk but he couldn't think of what to say. They stared at each other through the bars.

'He just wanted company,' said Theo. 'What do we call her?'

I thought about what he'd said about Diana's friend; the model in the photos left on a table at the Lovelock.

'Kate,' I said.

'Not bad. If we put them together, you might get eggs and babies.'

'Yeah, I've heard that can happen.'

He grinned at me. 'They'd have to build a nest first.'

'What do they build a nest with?'

'We help them. We put a plastic nest in, and they make a proper nest inside it. We give them the stuff to make the nest and they do the rest. Grandad used to use my grandmother's hair, pulled out of her hairbrush. He'd lay it on the bottom of the cage, and the birds would do it all themselves. When she lays the first egg, we take it away and replace it with a dummy egg, like. A pretend egg. We keep the egg she's laid safe and warm until she's finished laying. Then we take out the dummy eggs and put the real eggs back.'

I stared at him. I wanted to be an egg, kept safe and warm by Theo Farrah. It was the way he said it – 'say-aff and wo-am' – it would make anyone feel like lying still, sleeping until the hour of rebirth.

'Why do you do that?' I asked him.

'To make sure that they all hatch at the same time. Otherwise, if there's one ahead of the game then you have one bird that's taking up too much space, one bird that's stronger than the others. If they're all born at the same time, there's less chance of that.'

'What if I mess this up?' I hadn't meant to ask the question out loud, but there it was.

'Mess what up?'

'The birds.' I paused and looked at him. 'Everything.'

'You won't,' he said. He chewed on his thumbnail then said, without looking up at me: 'Do you want to go out?'

'No. I don't think so.'

'I do. I *do* think so.'

'No. I don't want to.'

'Come on. Not far. Just with me, like. Get you out ...' He looked at my Walkman; a slice of sunshine plastic on the bed, headphones tangled up beside it, waiting for me.

'We can take that with us,' he said. 'If it makes you feel better. You know. Bruno can come too.' He laughed. I swallowed hard.

'I feel stupid,' I said. 'That's the thing. I feel like a stupid idiot.'

'Yeah,' he said. 'I'm not surprised.'

And so, we walked down Ladbroke Grove, Theo Farrah and me. People walked past us, and they saw us together, and I guess they might have thought that we knew each other better than we did. None of them knew who they were looking at, what they were seeing. He walked fast; I had no time to question it. No time to ask myself what the hell I was doing. Maybe it was the speed we were walking that made me want to say it. Then before I knew it, I *had* said it.

'My aunt's having a thing with someone.'

'Huh? A thing? What kind of thing?'

'The kind where ... I don't know.' I didn't know how to say it.

'The kind of thing where you think you're in love with someone you shouldn't think you're in love with?'

'Yeah. I guess.'

'Oh, yeah? How d'you know?'

'I saw her kissing a man who isn't my uncle.'

196

'Ah. Right. Were you shocked?'

'Partly. Partly not.'

'Ah. And does he deserve it?'

'Who?'

'The man she's married to. The Liverpool fan who's not from Liverpool. Your uncle.'

'I don't know. Perhaps it's nothing to do with him at all.' I felt relief at telling him, but also it made it real. 'Don't tell anyone,' I said. I felt foolish, as though he would mock me with the idea that anyone in his life could be interested in the idea of my aunt kissing a man who wasn't her husband. But he didn't. He just nodded at me.

'What about going to Texas?' he said suddenly.

'What do you mean?'

'You said you were thinking of going to university over there.'

'I said I used to think about it.' I felt idiotic for having told him. 'It's not something that could happen now.'

'Don't see why not,' said Theo.

The world jammed and all danced around us; the red buses hurtling down Ladbroke Grove like toys, the sun in the cherry trees, the kids and their bikes, the nannies in cotton dresses pushing prams with bottles of Aqua Libra and copies of Jilly Cooper's *Rivals* sticking out of their bags, the drunks and the aggrieved, and down the hill, down Kensington Church Street past the antique shops and the pubs and the cafés and the horse chestnut trees with their candles that seemed to throw more light out onto me and Theo Farrah as they towered behind the black railings of the private gardens. Down past St Mary Abbots Church, crossing the road to the same side as Barkers of Kensington.

'John Barker opened his shop in 1870,' I said. 'He wanted to work with William Whiteley, but Whiteley wasn't interested so he went off and did his own thing. And it's still here now.'

'He must be knackered,' said Theo.

I had walked down these roads with Robert and Diana, with Diana so close to me, talking to me, asking me questions. I had seen the looks that people gave her, and she understood that it was happening too. Her awareness of her beauty had become something of extraordinary power. Now Theo listened to me in a way that no one ever had. Diana used to say listening was the only option, the only way you could make any sense of anything, but it was more than this. Something in her soul told her things: that exams didn't matter but thank-you letters did, that make-up only worked if you wore it like you meant it, that fourteen-year-old boys preferred the girls who appeared much stupider than them, even if they were much cleverer, and that *I Capture the Castle* told you more about life than Dostoevsky. My instincts, so like my father's – work hard, keep your head down and don't expect dreams to come true – had always felt brittle by comparison.

Plato was standing next to the fountain inside the tube station at Kensington High Street, smoking. He was wearing black jeans and what looked like an orange and brown Mexican-style cloak. When he saw us, he clapped slowly. People around him turned round and stared. He didn't care.

'I've been waiting here for half an hour.' Plato looked at Theo. He nodded at me suspiciously.

'Well,' he said. He threw his cigarette butt down and crushed it with his boot. 'What did he say? What's happening?'

'And a very good afternoon to you too,' said Theo.

'Well?' said Plato.

'He still wants to sign you. But he's really into this band, Blur. He wants to sign something that sounds like them. You don't sound like them. But he likes you. He thinks—'

'Who the hell are Blur? What kind of a shit name is that?'

'You supported them once, at the Mean Fiddler? Remember?'

'No.'

'They used to be called Seymour.'

'Another awful name—'

'We had a drink with the drummer that time.'

Plato kicked the ground with his huge foot. 'Right. So, what more do they want me to do? WHAT MORE CAN I DO FOR THE LOVE OF GOD?' He roared out this last question, throwing his hands out towards us both. Several people stopped and stared. A child started to cry and was pulled away by his mother.

'Keep your hair on,' snapped Theo. 'It probably just means one more gig.'

'BLUR!' yelled Plato, undeterred by Theo.

'They're all right, actually—'

'Don't say it! shouted Plato. 'I know the type! I know exactly who they are! Imbeciles with floppy hair staring at the floor and muttering about Marx into a Marks and Spencer's sandwich. Students with rich parents, prancing around pretending they've grown up in a project town on the outskirts of Hell—'

'You told me you had the greatest weekend of your life in Hull—'

'Not Hull, Hell! Hell! I said *Hell*! Fuck me!' Plato dug in his pocket and pulled out his cigarettes, and as he did so, a Rubik's Cube dropped from his pocket onto the ground. He bent down and picked it up. He pushed a cigarette into his mouth, edged towards Theo nodding for a light, and started to assemble the Rubik's Cube at astonishing speed, barely glancing down to check his progress.

'Do you carry that with you everywhere you go?' I asked him.

'Of *course* I do!' cried Plato in great agitation. 'I can do it in thirty-one seconds!' He took a breath. 'Idiots! Clogging up the charts with their CRAP.'

He sighed heavily and looked at me. 'Well. How's the bird? You're gonna tell me it's been signed to Island Records now, I suppose.'

'He's stopped singing, actually. He doesn't need to sing anymore. We've got him a girlfriend so he's happy.'

Plato looked mutinous. 'Tweety-Pie's getting more action

than me. Right.' He clapped his hands together vigorously.
'Let's go to Sticky Fingers.'

Diana and I had been taken there for our fifteenth birthday
party. Plato looked at me and misread my expression.

'I'm a total prick when it comes to food. I like all the places
the tourists go. Pardon me for being so uncool.'

We ordered burgers. I didn't want to eat one little bit,
but Plato ordered vanilla ice cream for us all, and he started
talking about the charts, tearing up every act in the Top 40.
His knowledge was pretty good, all told; I'd never talked to
anyone apart from Diana who followed chart positions like
us. I was safe when I was talking about the charts. Plato had
opinions on everyone.

'INXS?'

'Hutchence is cool. For an Australian.' He looked at me.
'You love him, I suppose,' he said dismissively.

'Prince?' I said quickly.

'Only man I'd sleep with.'

'Madonna?'

'Only woman I *wouldn't* sleep with.'

'Happy Mondays?' I asked him.

'One good song. And it's a cover. And they got the hook
from me. I did all that twisting my melon, man, stuff.
Shaun's a thief.'

Plato stuck his hand into his back pocket and pulled out
a load of paper.

'These are flyers for the next gig,' he said. 'You could give
some out.'

'Where?' I said dumbly.

'You ever venture into Chelsea?'

'Not anymore.'

'The Chelsea crowd are a good lot to pull in. They spend money at the bar, they get wrecked and they love me. It's half-price if they show up with a flyer.'

I opened one up. There was a black and white picture of Plato dressed as a clown sitting in the middle of a field smoking, a Rubik's Cube beside him. Above the picture was written:

A MISFIT CALLED PLATO

'Because love is a grave mental disease.'

'Nice,' I said.

'Oh, he's the very spirit of positivity,' said Theo.

I folded up the flyers again.

'Diana and I used to walk to Our Price on the King's Road most weekends.'

'Get these given out there, then. Then you could walk down to the cinema and leave a few in the entrance.'

Plato leaned forward towards me and drained his beer. I could see two girls on the next table staring at us. He leaned back in his chair and frowned suddenly at the tennis racket necklace around my neck and leaned forward again and pointed at it. 'Who gave you that?'

I felt the necklace in my fingers. Under the table, my legs started shaking. 'A friend,' I said.

'Do you play tennis?' demanded Plato.

'I used to. I don't anymore.'

'Whaddya mean? You retired? How old are you now? Ninety-four?'

'She was county-level,' said Theo.

Plato stared at me. '*Were* you? Really? No shit?'

'Yes. But not now. I don't play *now*.' I felt a hammering inside me.

'She played five days a week until seven months ago,' said Theo. I wanted him to stop. I couldn't bear it.

'Why don't you play now?' Theo asked.

'I just don't,' I said. I felt the room trembling all around me. Everything looked too big. I could hear Bruno Brookes tapping on his desk impatiently. *Four-thirty!* He was waiting for me to get back! What was I doing here? I was always waiting for the show to start! It couldn't start without me. I had to be back. I couldn't sit here and talk about tennis. Plato leaned into the table and stared hard at me.

'Right. Shut up with all this bullshit about not playing. You want to play some time? *I* can play tennis. *I'm* good. I mean, *really* good. I'll give you a proper game. That's what you need, Tracey-November. A proper, good, long hard … GAME.' He leaned back again and nodded at Theo.

'I don't play anymore,' I said.

'Oh, come on! Wouldn't your sister have wanted it? If not, why the fuck not?'

'Leave me alone,' I said. 'Stop talking about it. *Stop!*' I banged a hand down on the table.

I could hear a hysterical rise in my voice. I was tipping over the edge of somewhere.

'She just wanted me to go with her to her hospital appointment. That's all.'

'Feb, it's OK,' said Theo. I saw him looking at Plato and shaking his head, like he was warning him not to say anything else. But he was too late. I was there now. They had to know now.

'She had a hospital appointment the morning of the accident,' I said. My voice was rattling like a train on a track now. I felt Grandma Abby watching me, nodding, on the porch; I felt Mama and Daddy looking at me, listening to me as though they didn't somehow know what the hell had happened that day. 'It was her regular check-up, and I always went with her. She went twice a year. Her eyes. Her eyesight was bad. Poor. Very bad. Her eyes needed to be checked. There was a chance she could lose her sight altogether if it wasn't monitored. She had a hospital appointment, and she wanted me to go with her. She went every six months, to have her eyes checked. I said I couldn't go with her. I had a tennis match. When she was away, I got used to myself, to *me*, and when she got back, it was as if it all had to go back to how it was before. Me running around after her, making sure she was all right. I didn't want to. I wanted her to understand how it had been for me all our lives. I told her I wasn't taking her. She was surprised.'

'Angry with you?' asked Plato.

'No. Not angry. Worse than that. She was just – *confused*.

I went off to the match. All I had to be was her twin. I just had that and I wasn't. And now she isn't.'

'She wouldn't want you to blame yourself,' said Theo.

'How do you *know*? You never *knew* her! You never *met* her!'

I realized as I said this, how much I'd wanted to say it to him: You didn't know her! You never met her! What can you tell me about Diana that I don't already know? He put his hand out to me.

'Feb, I . . .'

I put my hands over my ears and stared down at the table. *Concentrate on anything but tennis. Last week's Top 10. The lyrics to 'Doin' the Do' by Betty Boo . . . 'I'm bolder, c-c-cold, gettin' colder . . .'*

But it was no good. I could see myself, standing on the court, holding my racquet, waiting to serve . . . I could see myself watching the club secretary hurrying out, see her rushing onto court, holding up a hand to make sure that we stopped the game. She had tripped over as she ran towards me and fell right over like a child in the playground. I'd run to her to help her stand up again, and when I looked at her face, she was white as a sheet and she had grazed knees and palms. In my head, the conversation that Diana and I had had that morning.

'Will you come with me to hospital?'

'No. I can't.'

'What?'

'I said, no. I don't want to. I can't. I'm playing tennis.'

'But you always come with me! Every six months—'

'*Your eyes haven't got any worse, have they?*'

'*No, but—*'

'*So, I have to come with you forever? You're a grown-up, aren't you? You can take someone else with you, can't you? I can't run my life based on what you're doing all the time.*'

'*All right. All right. It's OK. Lisa can drive me. I won't be long.*'

And that puzzled look on her face. And the strange, dark little sense of triumph in me. I had refused Diana something! I had said *no*!

I stood up. The only thing that mattered now was getting back. The smell of chips and beer was making me feel sick. I *had* to get back to Bruno. I could picture Diana's face, anxious, as we hurried back to listen to the Top 40 after Mama and Daddy's funeral.

'*Come on, Feb! We can't miss it! If we miss it, something else bad might happen.*'

No one could have accused Diana of not speaking everything that was on her mind. When she feared things, she tipped them out of her head and into the space in front of her, regardless of who or what was there. Her magical thinking had overtaken her, just like it had overtaken me.

'Don't go,' said Theo.

'Diana and I used to listen every week,' I heard myself saying. 'It was our good luck thing. We couldn't afford any more bad luck in our family. We only had each other left.'

'Hate to say it, but I'm not sure the good luck thing worked out,' said Plato.

'But I missed the charts the Sunday evening before she

died. I hadn't got back from tennis on time. After the accident, I made the promise to Diana. I had promised I would listen every single week, and record it, and feel her next to me every Sunday and every day of the week after that.'

'Then you keep yourself locked up forever?' Plato had a loud voice. Several people turned and looked at us again. People had never really talked to me like Theo and Plato did. I had never known it, I had never felt the focus, the light on me, the questions, the demands. Everything had always been *for* Diana, *at* Diana, *to* Diana. I was never enough on my own. Never. I didn't like it. I *had* to leave.

'You want *everything*, Tracey,' said Theo. He leaned forward. 'I can feel it in you. In everything about you. When I first saw you, it was like seeing someone who had taken themselves captive and was trying to gnaw off their own arm to set themselves free. But you know the key's in your pocket. It always is. It's in your pocket all the time.'

'Back to the point,' said Plato. 'When do we play? What does the winner get?'

I could see Bruno in my head, putting his headphones on, pulling up his chair, gulping down a mouthful of coffee, waiting to start the countdown. I could hear him talking to me: *And we are waiting for Miss February Kingdom! What are you doing, Feb? We're all waiting! Diana's waiting. You can't be late, we have to start on time. This is the only chart that counts. What are you doing?*

'I'm sorry,' I said to Theo. 'I can't do this. It's too hard.'

I started to walk fast uphill again, and I ran, ran, ran back to St Quintin Avenue, barely stopping at the top of Notting Hill Gate, rushing over the road on red lights, and I pounded my body back towards my bedroom, back to Yellow and Kate, and to my bedroom where I was safe, and where I couldn't be tricked by the daylight pretending everything was all right when it wasn't all right. I ran as fast as double-struck lightning away from Kensington High Street, and this time, when I felt the Trench Effect assailing me, it was flooding every part of my body, it was in the energy, in the thud of my feet on the ground, it ran with me, so that with every step it felt like it was gaining power. I could see them all – Mama and Daddy trying to escape the flames at King's Cross, Mama knowing that Diana and I would be waiting for her, Daddy unable to save her and himself. I could see Diana, her face on the morning that she died, when she had walked off after I'd refused to drive her to her eye appointment, the disappointment, the confusion in her, impossible to ignore. My hand shook as I turned the key in the lock, and I raced upstairs and ripped the plastic off a new ninety-minute cassette and shoved it into the stereo. I bowed at Yellow and Kate, and they looked at me agitatedly, and I sat on the floor and watched them fly up to the perches on the top, down to the bath, up again, and they seemed uneasy, restless, like they understood. I held my hands in front of me. Sometimes when I look at my hands, I can imagine I'm looking at my sister's, they are the only parts of us that were identical. But then again, I didn't want to see Diana's hands. I pulled the sacred tennis ball off the shelf and held it out in front of me so that they became my hands again. I could come back to myself—

Well, you cut it fine! I heard Bruno saying to me, and then a moment later, he was on air introducing the chart and I felt a salty relief. I had done it; at least I hadn't broken that promise.

'*Good afternoon, it's exactly five o'clock and this is Bruno Brookes with the official UK Top 40 . . .*'

I opened the window and lay on the bed and I imagined Theo and Plato leaving Sticky Fingers and walking back to the tube together, and I wondered if they had talked about me, and I wondered if . . .

No, I thought. Not that. I can't actually *love* him.

Love is a grave mental disease.

For the first time, I understood what the hell Diana had felt when she had talked about Daniel.

19

Double A Side

Diana had fallen in love every other week since the age of about seven months old, but her most meaningful encounter with the lure of boys had been with Andrew Adamson, the only son of the folks who lived across the road from us in Austin. Andrew was just ten − a year older than we were − and looking back, I think probably knew in his own soul even then that he was as gay as the day was long, but he loved Diana for her sheet of thick, straight white-blonde hair, and he would ask us over to his house nearly every Thursday after school to play hairdressers. Our grandma Abby would walk us over there, slow as slow, in her great big red and yellow flowery dress, her ankles swollen in the heat, plodding along the hot concrete waiting to cross the road, and when we arrived she would stay for one cup of coffee and a slice of apple cake in the garden under the shade with Andrew's mother, Moira, and then she would plod slowly back home, and Diana and I would sit next to one another on high stools in the Adamsons' newly modernized kitchen, holding magazines upside down and talking gossip like real ladies we had heard in Headspace, the salon on Cut Saddle Pass down the road, and Andrew would talk to us in his unbroken, pitchy Austin drawl, while he twisted our hair into knots and plaits and buns, handing us glasses of iced water from the new fridge, and packets of tiny salted crackers shaped like fish that we tipped into our greedy little mouths in ecstasy.

One baking June afternoon, Diana asked him to cut her hair. Andrew— give the guy credit – hesitated.

'But I don't *want* long hair anymore,' Diana had said. She pouted and flipped her ponytail at us. I frowned at her. 'Go on,' she said again, looking at Andrew. 'Do it!'

'I might-could cut it,' he said hesitantly. He was hard pushed to disguise the tremor of excitement in his voice.

'No might-could about it,' said Diana. 'Just get it cut.'

'Your mama won't be pleased,' observed Andrew, who was not the brightest kid on the street but at least knew how to read a room.

'Mama won't mind,' said Diana. 'She lets me do things I want to do, long as they're good things.'

'Don't be so silly,' I said. Diana had annoyed me that afternoon by telling Missy Jackson in our math class that I would help her with her homework, and I would be happy to be paid in cherries. Diana always had to be liked, even when it meant pulling me into her plans, whereas I didn't really mind

211

whether I was liked or not. Missy Jackson was a liar more slippery than a pocketful of pudding. I didn't want to help her with her homework, cherries or no cherries.

'I think Andrew could cut my hair real pretty,' said Diana. 'I'd like to feel it short in my fingers. It's too hot for long hair in summertime. Anyway, thing about hair is it grows back, any case.'

'You're stupid,' I said.

'I'm not! *Off with my hair!*' shouted Diana. She exploded with laughter.

Andrew looked at me and I shrugged. Let him ruin her hair for all I cared! He needed no more encouragement than my silence. Hesitantly, he took the ponytail in his hand and held it up like he was holding the brush of a fox.

'I got some scissors,' he said quickly.

And lo, Andrew did her hair *so* beautiful, it looked like it had been cut by Vidal Sassoon. He copied the style from the model on the inside of a copy of *Vogue*, but Diana ended up looking better than the model. Her hair was now short as short; I wanted to ask him to cut mine too, but I was aware of how the comparisons would fall, so I said nothing, and went home with my hair still long and uneventful, while everyone around – even Grandma Abby who despised change – went mad for Diana's new look. People copied it at school, and before too long Andrew started to charge people for his services, and he sure as hell wouldn't accept cherries for haircuts. Diana fell heavily in love with him after this; he was her one great, soft landing of an unrequited love. It wasn't until right at the end that this happened to her again, and the landing wasn't soft this time. It was hard as dried mud, jarring everything out of place.

Usually, when Diana liked a boy, or more often when a boy liked her, I would hear about it every second minute, but it would be over as fast as it started. Once they fell in love with her, once they had fallen at her feet, she lost interest. The boy called Daniel was different. She started talking to me about him just before our eighteenth birthday. It was December.

'When can I meet him?' I asked her.

'Not yet,' she said.

'Why not? What's wrong with him?'

'Nothing! He's just ... nothing.'

'He sounds like he must be *something.*'

Diana sounded exasperated, truly pissed off with me. 'He's not *ready.*'

'Not ready! What does that mean? Why does he have to be *ready* to meet me? I'm not going to set him a test or something! Is he at Cardinal Vaughan?'

Cardinal Vaughan is the school a little further down the road from Westbury House. It tends to yield the cleverest boys, with the added thrill of Catholicism, which Diana admired for its heavy emphasis on incense, melodrama and self-flagellation.

'He's not at Cardinal Vaughan.'

'Oh. Holland Park? St Paul's? Has he left school altogether? Have you taken an older lover?' I laughed at her.

Most times Diana loved this sort of chat from me. But she lowered her eyes.

'Leave it, will you, Feb? I want a cigarette.'

'OK.' I paused. 'But he's nice, is he? He's nice to *you*?'

'He's perfect,' said Diana. 'That's the problem.'

'Why is it a problem?'

'Just is.'

'If I could meet him, I could tell you whether he's perfect,' I said. 'Are you ashamed of me?'

Diana raised her head and smiled at me sadly.

'Oh, Feb. The only person I'm *ever* ashamed of is myself.'

As it happened, she never introduced me to Daniel, because he ended it with her a few weeks later, at the start of 1989. People didn't end things with Diana, it wasn't what happened. She didn't seem to know what to do with the facts of the matter; she was – at first, at least – more astounded than anything else, then her astonishment turned to desperation.

'He said that we would never work in the long run,' she said to me. 'He kept talking about the long run. I'm saying to him, who cares about a long run?' We were walking through Kensington Gardens, the wind up. There was snow forecast, the sky was pewter grey so that it felt like a pillow was being held over the park, a slow, gentle suffocation, for which we should all be grateful as we were moving towards the end of the twentieth century and maybe the whole world would fall apart anyway, and gentle oblivion was better for all of us.

'How does *he* know about the long run?' I said. I felt a fury with Daniel for reducing my sister to this, but at the same

214

time, I couldn't quite eliminate a tiny degree of admiration for the guy. Who was this man who dared to dump my sister?

'He said I'm too young for something this intense, and I should be living my own life. He says it would be a mistake for us to carry on as it will only get worse.'

'God. What does that mean?'

She pushed her hair under her hood. 'He says it will only get worse,' she repeated.

We were nearly at the Serpentine. People were throwing sticks into the water for their dogs; a black Cocker Spaniel ran up to us and shook water over our legs. We had stopped in front of *Physical Energy*, the statue of a horse and rider a little in front of the lake. Robert had marched us up to the statue on one of our historical tours, and when he talked to us about it, I could have sworn there were tears in his eyes. Now Diana stretched out her arm and felt the huge bronze horse's hoof in her hands and closed her eyes.

'"A symbol of that restless human impulse to seek the still unachievable in the domain of material things,"' I said.

'How do you remember all that stuff he tells us?' Diana said.

'I don't know,' I said. 'It's the weird way my brain works.'

'Easy to be restless and seeking material things and fame and glory if you're a man,' said Diana, with sudden savagery.

'But you've made more money in the past few weeks than Daddy did in a year,' I said.

'Yeah, well. Why don't I care then? Why doesn't it mean anything to me?'

The birdsong was muted around us. In the distance I heard the wailing of a siren.

'Lisa says I should get out to New York,' said Diana. 'I got another three offers this week for work there. She says she'd come with me.'

I breathed in.

'What? Now? What about the exams?'

'We both know I'm shit at exams.'

'But you have to do them. You have to get your A levels—'

'No, *you* have to get them.'

'What do you mean by that?'

'You're the clever one. You're the sporty one. I know what everyone thinks about me. Good face, must be thick as mince. Why should I do the exams, and prove them all right?'

'You're not thick. You just don't care. There's a difference.'

'Chicken and egg, Feb. I don't care because I'm thick. Or I'm thick because I don't care.'

I stared at her, trying to work out if she was serious. She looked at me and smiled sadly. I knew then, she'd already decided.

'It's probably the right time to go,' she said.

'What will Ann and Robert say?'

'They'll try to tell me I'm making a mistake, obviously. And don't go telling me that Mama and Daddy would be disappointed.'

I thought about it. Mama had quite liked Diana's success as a model – perhaps because having a daughter every-one wanted to photograph somehow validated her own beauty – but for Mama the whole thing only worked so long as I was there, balancing out the whole thing with good results at school. Daddy would have been horrified at the idea of Diana quitting before she'd finished.

'They'd have been proud of you whatever,' I said doubtfully.

'Yeah,' said Diana. 'Easy to say that, I guess.'

'What'll I do without you, though?' This wasn't sentiment. It wasn't a kind remark, designed to make someone feel as though they will be missed; it was plain and simple concern for myself.

'It'll go fast,' said my sister. 'Truth is, I can't be in this city knowing he's here.'

'Really?' I looked at her in disbelief. *'Really?'*

She smoothed her hands over the horse's hoof again, and I knew what she was thinking. She was thinking that I was ludicrous, but that it wasn't even worth trying to tell me why because I had never felt it. I had never known how it felt, and the expression on her face made me feel like maybe I never would. I started singing 'Angel of Harlem' by U2 to distract us both.

She left for New York at the end of March. Lisa came to collect her from St Quintin Avenue. When I hugged her into my arms before she stepped into the car, my sister felt brief, fragile as a little girl.

'Keep listening to Bruno,' she said. I didn't talk for fear of wanting to drag her back into the house and tell her not to be crazy, how could she leave me, *how could she?*

217

'Keep working, Feb,' said Lisa to me. 'I wish I'd got better exam results.'

I looked at the boot of the car taking them both to the airport – Lisa's suitcases covered with stickers from around the globe, Diana's coat – Vivienne Westwood, given to her free after she'd walked in her show – and Lisa's remark felt truly silly.

'No two people could be a worse advertisement for sticking with school,' I said as brightly as I could. Ann came out and handed Diana a warm tortilla wrapped in kitchen roll. The hot oil was seeping through the tissue.

'For the journey,' she said. Diana took a great bite, and a red pepper dropped onto the lap of her jeans.

'Oh,' she said, looking down at them.

Ann looked at Lisa. 'You'd better look after this one,' she said. What was unspoken was everything else in that sentence. *You'd better look after this one because she's everything to us. She's made a life for herself in London. She likes it here! She shouldn't be going anywhere. Where the hell is she going? This really shouldn't be happening . . .*

Lisa nodded.

'Call me anytime,' she said, 'fuck the time difference.' To my amazement she marched up to Ann and pulled her into a quick, effective embrace. Ann emerged, stunned, her cheeks red, trying not to split her face into a huge grin. It was typical of Lisa to do this; like Diana, her power could be abrupt. Unlike Diana, she used it only at unexpected times.

'She's still a baby, really,' gasped Ann.

'I know,' said Lisa. 'Jeez, I know.'

It struck me that Ann could have been talking about herself, and about Lisa, about me – about all of us. But they were off, in the dark blue Mercedes, heading for the airport.

'Well,' said Ann. She put her arm around my heaving shoulders. 'Five months is nothing really, Feb. We'll be all right, won't we?' I said I supposed we would, but I wondered how the hell I'd let this happen. For the rest of the day, thanks to their parting embrace, Ann smelled, disturbingly, of Lisa's Chanel No. 5.

I had quite a lot of sex after Diana left, which was a great surprise to everyone, most of all me. I mean, when I say a lot, I mean a lot compared to never having done it before, and when I say it was a great surprise to everyone, I mean it surprised Ann, who didn't think I'd ever thought about it in my life. To be honest, I still didn't much like boys, but sex was all right because it provided me with something to talk to Diana about when she called, something to imply that I was all right without her. One evening I called Diana to tell her about Sam, a boy with a mouth like a letterbox who had a spontaneous nose-bleed when I introduced him to Robert. Another time I told her about Quintin, I boy I had slept with simply because . . . well, you can imagine why.

'Did you fall in love?' Diana asked me every time, and I would laugh because as far as I could tell, there was no connection between the tragi-comic-semi-naked bedroom antics that happened between me and these boys and the serious, implausible choice to love someone for their actual soul like she seemed to love Daniel.

'No,' I would say. 'I'm *fairly* certain I'm not in love. How do you know?'

'You know because you're miserable,' said Diana.

'I'm not miserable.'

'Well you're not in love then.'

'Didn't think I was.'

'Make sure you always use a condom,' Diana would say, prim as you like on the other side of the Atlantic, and I would try to picture her walking the streets without me, her twin, but with Lisa, and sometimes it would disturb me so much that I didn't know what to do with myself.

Then one afternoon just a couple of weeks into their stay, Diana called to tell me that Lisa had discovered that she was pregnant.

'WHAT!' I had never known someone I knew well to be pregnant.

'She's already five months into it,' said Diana.

'How is that *possible*?'

'Well, even *you* know the basic criteria for how babies are made, Feb—'

'I thought Lisa could never have babies?' I said.

'Turns out she can,' said Diana, 'but she didn't think she could, so she didn't believe it until it was confirmed.' Diana sounded odd and formal. 'She's terrified something will go wrong. Her blood pressure's shot up so she's off work for a few weeks, taking it easy.'

'Gosh. Well. *Fibroids!*' I used the word as an exclamation as usual, but Diana didn't laugh. I felt an unexpected surge of envy for Lisa and her unborn child. 'Eric's going to be a father,' I said, realizing it as I spoke the words.

'He's not being very grown up about it. He keeps saying he's not ready,' said Diana.

'Oh, he'll be good at it,' I said.

'Oh, Feb. Always thinking the best of him. You're so silly.'

'Why am I silly?'

The lag on the telephone, as her voice crossed the Atlantic down the wires to find me in North Kensington, gave gravitas to every question asked, as though we were weighing up our responses to one another in a way that we'd never bothered to do before.

'Eric's like a pop star,' said Diana. 'He's Nathan Moore and Marti Pellow and Michael Hutchence. You like the idea of him because he's pretty and he's impossible.'

'Not for Lisa, he isn't,' I said. 'She's having his baby!'

'And she'll make it work, for her and the baby, whether or not he sticks around,' said Diana. She sounded convincing and serious and not like my sister at all.

When I put down the telephone, every one of the three and a half thousand miles between us yawned open and huge, and something shifted beneath my feet that I couldn't explain and could never change back.

20

Kick

All right.

Check me out.

It took me six days to get the courage to leave the house and be useful for Theo. It was Saturday when I stepped out of the house again and walked to Our Price on the King's Road. Be useful. *Useful is God.* I had stuffed the flyers for Plato's next gig into the bag over my shoulder and I walked to Chelsea, like I said I would. One foot in front of another. Walkman playing Aztec Camera's *Love* album. Roddy Frame's voice would get me there. I took a route through Earl's Court. Robert had only walked up this way with Diana and me once, but I remembered it well enough because we stopped at McDonald's on the way back and Robert had eaten his bi-annual Big Mac, fries and large Coke with the reverence of one of the apostles tucking into the bread and wine at the

Last Supper. Now, I walked past a cul–du–sac where a group of kids were playing football.

'Childs Place,' I said out loud to myself. Robert had talked about this. Samuel Childs started his wax business here in 1825. Or was it 1835? Some drunk guy staggered out of the doorway of the tube station and knocked into me. My heart sped up again. I could just turn around. I could get back to St Quintin Avenue quickly if I ran. I didn't *have* to do this. But I *needed* to. I needed to be useful to Theo Farrah. *Useful is God.*

On the King's Road, the streets were heaving with Saturday afternoon shoppers and show-offs, and boarding school kids out for half-term, smoking Silk Cut Menthol and walking four abreast along the pavement in black suede boots from Shellys and fluorescent Lycra from The Garage. I stood in a queue holding 'Better the Devil You Know' on CD single. I needed to buy it; I wanted some proof that I had been into a shop, that I'd walked into Our Price, King's Road, like an actual human being. I liked being in there. The music was loud in record shops, and people dressed like they were all experiencing their own crunchy little anxiety attacks: the Goths in black with their blanked-out faces and stylized doom; twenty-somethings with high hair, cropped tops and strong body odour from the worry of whether their boyfriends would show up in their meeting spot in the New Releases section; ordinary white men galloping towards mid–life reaching for Simon and Garfunkel albums; tourists with bum–bags and baseball caps and plum-red lip-liner; teenage girls wondering if anyone would know they touched themselves when they listened to Prince's *Purple*

Rain album; and teenage boys wondering the same thing. I was safe here. The girl ahead of me in the queue was paying for a twelve-inch single of 'World in Motion'. Where would she take it to play it? Whose house? Would she listen to it with friends, all of them joining in with John Barnes rapping? When I stepped up to the counter, she glanced at what I was buying and smirked.

It wasn't until I was back outside, just reaching into my bag for the flyers, when I saw him. Wait. He needs a new paragraph. He *always* should have one of those.

It was Michael Hutchence.

He had appeared outside the shop, standing like he was waiting for someone, wearing sunglasses and a green and black patterned shirt and checked trousers.

'Oh my *God*,' I said out loud, and I turned around and walked straight back in again. I put out my hand to steady myself on a rack dedicated to Whitney Houston's last two albums. I felt searing pain in the ends of my fingers, and I felt Diana's presence surge right through me, cartoonish.

Woah! You're not going to let him walk off without talking to him, are you, Feb?

A group of girls sauntered past him, nudging each other and giggling. He lit a cigarette. I stepped back outside. Took a breath. Turned to him. I would do it. I would talk to him because – well, because what other choice had I?

'Hello,' I said. 'Sorry to disturb you—' I took another breath in.

'Hey,' he said. His looks and clothes were so utterly

modern. I felt everything heightened, every sense sharp as a needle, sharp for this moment, for the woah-hard truth of it: Michael Hutchence under damp skies in June on the King's Road in 1990.

'I think *Kick* is the greatest album of the past ten years,' I stammered.

'Thank you very much,' he said. His Australian accent was soft. He bowed his head towards me and grinned. 'What did you buy?' he asked, looking at the thin red and white plastic bag in my hands. Cringing, I pulled out the Kylie CD single.

'Perfect,' said Michael. He nodded at me and laughed down at his feet, shaking his head slightly. He looked up at me again. 'It's her best record so far in my view,' he said. He looked down at the case of the single.

'My sister played "New Sensation" every morning before school,' I said.

He dragged his eyes from Kylie and looked up at me. 'Ha. That's sweet.' He glanced down at his watch. 'Shall I sign something for you? You got a pen?'

'Oh, um—' I plunged my hands into the pockets of my jeans. 'Can I run and get one?'

'Sure.'

I bombed back into Our Price, barging past a man buying *Sonic Temple* by the Cult on vinyl, and up to the counter.

'Can I borrow a pen? And a bit of paper? *Anything*.'

The girl behind the desk looked at me without sympathy. She was wearing a black crop top over gigantic boobs. She sucked in air through her teeth.

'Who's outside?' she asked me, holding the biro tantalizingly just out of reach.

I paused. 'Michael Hutchence,' I muttered.

Her eyes widened. 'Holy shit. Are you sure?'

'Yes.'

She called out to the guy stacking shelves. 'Cover for me for a minute, will you, Nick?'

'Oh please,' I begged her. 'Give me two minutes with him on my own. Please.'

She looked me up and down. 'He's going out with Kylie Minogue. You do *know* that?'

'Yes. Of course I *know* that. But it's a sign. Me seeing him today. It's a sign.'

'Oh yeah? Who from?'

'My dead twin.' There was a silence between us. I glared at her.

She snorted, but she handed me the biro, sure enough. 'Yeah,' she said. 'That's what they all say.'

I handed Michael Hutchence one of Plato's flyers to write on. He turned it over without even looking at the picture of the clown.

'What's your name?' he asked.

'February? Um. You can just put Feb,' I muttered.

'Great name,' he said. 'Hot in Australia in February. Damn hot.' He scribbled: *To February. Love Michael Hutchence.* He hesitated, then drew a heart with an arrow through it.

'Do you have another piece of paper? What's your sister's name?' he asked.

'Oh, she's—'

And *this* is what I mean about that little fucker, grief. Like I was being suffocated, thrown under a bus, like some nightmare was closing in on me, suddenly I could say nothing. I couldn't speak. I could feel Diana looking at me sadly, wanting everything to go back to how it was before, knowing that everything had changed forever. All the times that I had blurted out what had happened to her, all those times I had been desperate for people to know, so that they knew what I was carrying around, so that they could comprehend it for themselves . . . now I couldn't talk.

'Are you OK?' asked Michael.

I looked down at the ground, mute, shocked. My shoulders shook. It was as sudden an assailment as I have ever known, it winded my chest, rendered me dumb. I felt a wave of adrenalin and dread run right through me, that most physical of responses to the sudden onset of anxiety; my heart pounded. The man I had barged in front of in the queue to pay walked out of the shop, and suddenly all I could hear in my head was the Cult.

'My sister was killed in a car accident last year,' I said.

'Jesus.'

I looked up at him slowly. He looked horrified. 'Jesus, sweetheart. I'm so sorry.'

'She was my twin. She was called Diana. She was a model.' I told him this for something to say, to rescue the singer of INXS from this shit-show. I opened up my purse and pulled out the passport photo of Diana taken before she went to New York, before she left me, and held it out in my palm, like a strange, torturous offering to him. I saw us from above, a rock star and a nineteen-year-old girl, looking at a photograph of my twin sister, one of us unable to breathe. In minutes, this would be over; in moments, Michael Hutchence would walk off again, but right now, he was there, in the thick of it, poor guy, whether he wanted to be or not.

'Beautiful girl,' said Michael, looking at the photo. 'You must have been very proud of her.'

I jammed my mouth together, my lip wobbled, I strained every inch of myself to prevent it from flooding out of me, but I couldn't hold it. Tears chucked themselves merrily onto the pavement.

'Oh, my God. You little angel. Don't cry, sweetheart.' He pulled me towards him.

With a series of staccato in-breaths, I bit down on my lip and cried, silent, violent tears, and he held me tight into his shirt, tight into the warmth of his chest, and I was appalled with myself, but unable to wrench myself away from him. I could see nothing but our shoes, so close together on the pavement, my scuffed-to-shit Wayne Hemingway black suede loafers from Red or Dead and his bashed-up black biker boots, and I felt as though Jesus himself was holding me: I was standing in the River Jordan, cleansed by Jesus – Christ himself, Jesus with shades and a girlfriend at number 6 in the charts, Jesus smelling of cigarettes and Yves Saint Laurent's Jazz, telling me that I was all right. When I opened my eyes, I saw, through a blur of saltwater, the girl behind the counter stepping outside the shop, lipstick reapplied and tits pushed up so they were practically under her chin. She baulked in shock at the sight of me in the arms of Christ, stooped low in reverence and reversed back into the shop still bowing.

'I'm sorry,' I said at last.

He looked at me. 'Why sorry? There's no need to say sorry.' He shook his head. 'Funny, I'm seeing a friend called Diana this evening. I'm walking to her place now. Thought I'd go through the parks. She's going through a tricky time at the moment.' He said nothing more, but he wrote something on the second flyer and handed it back to me.

'Thank you,' I said. 'Thank you so much.'

'You OK now? What are you doing now? Are you going home? Do you need a taxi? Shall I get you a cab?'

'Oh, I'm OK. I'm meeting my – I'm OK.'

'You're sure?'

'Yes.'

'Look after yourself. No. Forget that. That's not easy. Let someone look after *you*.'

I felt spacey and high now, high in the way that you can only feel after grief's messed with you, high on the aftershock of the Trench Effect, high on something indefinable but emphatic. High on existence after a funeral, high on feeling shit. Feeling *shit*! *Feeling*! Shit! I opened the piece of paper he'd signed his name on. His handwriting was exactly how it should have been. Intimidating and intimate at the same time. I turned the paper over. He'd written one of his own lyrics for me. He'd written a line from 'New Sensation'.

Cry baby cry, when you've got to let it out!

When I got home, I called Theo at the pet shop. I wanted to tell him, at once.

'I gave out some flyers, like you asked,' I said. 'I went to Our Price on the King's Road.'

'You did? Tracey, that's very, *very* good. Thank you. Saved me a job. And people are more likely to pay attention to you than me, anyway.'

'Why's that?'

'Girls usually have more luck. You know. Being girls, and everything.'

I tried to compute the compliment. I felt the truth of me being interesting simply because I was a girl run liquid down the telephone receiver, and into my body like a shot of something delicious and shocking.

'Ha,' I said uncertainly. Theo had moved on.

'So, anyone say they'd come?'

I'll never know why I didn't tell him about Michael Hutchence that afternoon. All I knew is that I suddenly wanted to keep it to myself. The only person I told was Kate. And before you ask, Yellow was asleep.

Before bed that night, I went to Diana's bedroom and found her hairbrush. It was the old Mason Pearson brush with 'D' painted on the back that Diana had used on the kittens we had as children, only the 'D' had rubbed off so that the letter just looked like a swirl of chipped green paint on the white plastic back. The brush was full of her blonde hair. I breathed it in; there was a vague scent of the Body Shop – banana conditioner and ice blue shampoo that Diana had got through by the metric ton. I'd been thinking about this ever since Theo had told me about his grandfather and his canaries and their nests; I pulled out the ball of her hair and I placed it on my bedside table. Then I padded to Ann's room and took the hair from her brush – finer, thinner, more delicate than Diana's, strands of pure silver mixed in with the blonde. Finally, I found my own brush – the one that matched Diana's except that my letter 'F' was still clearly visible in turquoise – and my brush smelled of Ann's Timotei. I pulled the hair out, and I put it with Diana and Ann's hair and then I placed the big ball of it all on the floor of the cage for the birds. I placed Diana's brush in the top drawer of my desk. I felt witch-like, as though what I had done had its roots in something ritualistic, as if I were playing with something far more powerful than I realized. Maybe that makes what happened moments later all the more insane.

I went back into Ann and Robert's bathroom to put her hairbrush back, and as I shut the door of the cabinet above the sink, something fell off the top of the cupboard and onto the floor. I picked it up, and I jolted and dropped it onto the floor again, almost as though it were red hot to the touch. Bending down, I picked it up and looked at it, turning it over in my hands. There could be no doubting what it was. Two lines. One strong blue line, another very faint one crossing, forming a shadowy plus sign.

I stared at my reflection in the bathroom mirror, and Diana was there, clear as the long day. She nodded.

I've just heard her come in. Now, are you gonna ask her about it, or shall I?

21

Faint Lines

I know about pregnancy tests. I'd once coaxed a Westbury girl through pissing on a stick during a Wednesday lunch break, after she'd slept with some guy at a party and had been too drunk to remember whether he'd used a condom, and too ashamed to ask him the next day. There had been one line only for Leonie, and she had bounced back into Double English happy as anything. But the test I was holding now was a test that meant business.

'Ann!' I called down the stairs.

'Feb?' I heard her hurrying up to me. 'Are you all right? I was about to ask you if you wanted something to eat—'

'Is Robert downstairs?'

'Not yet. What is it?'

'I've found something,' I muttered, more to myself than to

Ann. She stepped into the bathroom, and Diana was gone. She saw what I was holding, and she went very still.

'What's that you've got?'

'This just fell off the top of the cupboard,' I said to her.

I handed it to her. She took it between her fingers.

'Yes,' she said, and she tossed it into the bin under the sink with a clatter. 'I'm sorry you had to see that. I feel ashamed. Just thought I should be cautious, you know. Thank God it was you who found it.' She had gone pale. 'I meant to throw it out. I took it last week. Not that it matters. I suppose I thought for a moment that there would be a certain poetic irony in me conceiving a baby with him. At my age. With him married and everything.'

It was the first time she'd admitted it properly to me. She knew that I knew; there was no point pretending any longer. It was out there. There was a certain defiance in her voice.

'You're married too.' I couldn't help pointing it out.

'Yes, yes. But he's the one with the children. I didn't tell him I'd taken it. I just did it alone. You know. However silly it was.' She reached into the bin again. 'It needs destroying before Robert finds it,' she said.

Ann hadn't grasped what was happening here. 'But it's positive,' I said.

'No. It's only positive if there's a cross, Feb. A plus sign. Two lines, one across the other. There's no cross.'

'Yes. There *is* a cross. A faint one, but it's a cross all right.'

'No there's not. There's no crossed line.'

'I can see a plus sign. It's there. A cross.' How many other words were there for what I was looking at?

'There's no cross.'

'Have a look. Hold it under the light.'

I watched her stare down at the test again. She pulled it up to look closer, then she cleared her throat, and blinked at me.

'Oh.'

For a whole minute and a half, she sat on the bed, staring down at the test, saying nothing. I know it was that long because I counted the seconds, for something to do to keep me from hitting her and hugging her and hating her. Then she pulled a tissue from her sleeve and blew her nose.

'Do you – do you feel . . .?' Even the asking of the question felt crackers.

'I – I – my boobs are sore.'

'Classic,' I heard myself saying.

'I feel sick, and I've had these headaches—'

'So, yes. Yes, you do feel like you're pregnant, then.'

I wanted to scream at her, to shake her, to tell her I'd never loved her more, or as little as I did right now. I bit my bottom lip. She looked at me.

'I'm so sorry,' she said. 'I was meant to be the one who stayed steady for you girls. That was the only thing I had to do. Look at me. I've gone stark staring mad.'

Yes, you have. You're forty-five and you're pregnant with the child of a man who isn't your husband.

'Don't say sorry,' I said, and as I spoke, I thought of

235

Michael Hutchence saying the same words to me outside Our Price on the King's Road, and I knew that we were doubles partners, Ann and me. Whatever was happening now, I needed to back her.

'Perhaps this happens sometimes,' she said. She was talking to herself rather than talking to me, I could tell. 'I thought it was negative. I certainly didn't see another line. I thought I'd chucked it out.' Her teeth started to clatter up and down, her whole body shook. 'Jesus,' she said. 'That's why I've been so – that's why—' She squinted at the test again. She stood, looking out into the garden. 'This is how it feels,' she said. 'This is it. This is how it feels when you know. I thought I'd never feel it. This is how it feels, Feb! I thought I'd never know! Now, whatever happens, I know. It's happened to me. It *has*. I was a few days late, but my dates have been muddled,' she was half whispering now, and with the repetition she favoured when she was trying to understand things, it sounded like she was casting a spell under her breath, like she was chanting something barely comprehensible to anyone else. 'I haven't kept an eye on dates. Why should I? Why *should* I at my age? I think I took the test because I felt like I still had the right to. No one could tell me not to. So, I went to Boots on Kensington High Street and I bought the test, and the lady behind the counter said: "Do you want a bag, love?" and I said: "Yes, please" and I wanted to shout: no, not really, actually. I want to walk down the street holding the test out in front of me like a . . . like a . . . ring on a cushion on the way to a palace, to show everyone that it's still plausible. That it's still *possible*. Just. That I'm not so old for it to be totally unreasonable behaviour. That was it really. The buying of the test was ... was everything. The last hurrah. I drank a pint of water before bed, and in the morning, I woke up, and I pissed on the stick, and I felt like a stupid old idiot. And I waited for the result, and when I looked at it, I thought it was negative. I wasn't surprised. I *knew* it would be. Negative because I'm old. Negative because time ran out.' She stretched her arms out towards me in a gesture of child-like helplessness. 'Then I walked out of the bathroom. I forgot to take the test out with me. Because maybe I'm senile, too.'

'But it *wasn't* negative,' I said.

We let my words sit between us. My voice sounded more Texan than I had done in ages, like I always do when I'm shocked.

'Feb. I've slept with a man who isn't my husband, and now I'm pregnant. I'm that woman. My God. *I'm that woman!*' She stared down at the test. 'I am that woman,' she repeated.

'Are you all right?' I didn't know what else to say, but I sure as hell know that the only thing that mattered was Ann being all right, whatever was going on inside her body.

She was still staring at the line. 'I must be no more than six and a half weeks. Six weeks, six days? No, maybe seven days. Six weeks and seven days.'

'Six weeks, seven days is the same as seven weeks, sure as I know it,' I said. Maybe she *was* losing her mind.

'Yes. Seven weeks. I'll miscarry. Of course I will. I'm too old not to.'

'You might not. You've got this far.'

'I'm forty-five, for God's sake.' She looked up at me. 'How many successful pregnancies happen to women of forty-five?'

'You tell *me*. You're the biology teacher.'

Ann cleared her throat and reached out and took my hand in hers. She was whispering between tears, so that hearing everything she said was difficult, but she had the facts all right, and hearing them spoken so quietly, between jagged in-breaths, made every part of them sound fantastical, impossible – beautiful even, certainly godlike. She talked so softly, I had to strain to hear her. I could feel her womb listening too, so still, so alive.

'Every single female baby is born with every egg that she'll ever have. In utero, a female foetus can have anything between one and two million eggs. By birth, this number drops dramatically, and after this, it carries on dropping.' She unravelled the toilet roll and blew her nose. 'No one quite knows why this is what happens,' she whispered, 'what the method or logic is behind it all, but the one thing that's certain is that no new eggs are made during our lifetime. Not *one*. This egg has been inside me for forty-five years! Hahaha!' Her sudden burst of outraged laughter was the sort that happens when you're flung into the air on a fairground ride when you're all geared up for the stomach-flipping, but at the same time, you're never ready for how it actually feels when it happens.

'Hell of a time to be hanging around waiting for the action,' I said.

Ann swallowed hard and blew her nose again. 'What do I tell Robert? Oh, I'm pregnant, by the way. No, it's not your baby, but not to worry, we'll muddle through . . .'

'And Gregory,' I said, 'should he know?'

Ann pulled her hand from mine and stood up. She looked down at the test again.

'I can't tell him. Let me wait. I should wait to see if – I'll wait for another week. No point in saying anything just yet.' She looked up at me. 'You won't tell him, will you, Feb?'

'I can keep secrets,' I said.

'My head,' she said. 'I need to lie down.'

When Robert came home, I told him that Ann had a headache and had gone to bed early. What had actually happened was that I had put her to bed, tucked a sheet around her like she was a child. Her eyes closed. Her hand rested somewhere close to her womb, somewhere near where those mad cells had divided to start new life, like little warriors.

'Don't tell him, will you?' Ann had said again. 'Not yet. I need a week with this on my own. Robert can't know. Gregory can't know. He's coming here next weekend, remember. Robert's away until Tuesday. We've got the weekend together.' It was clear that these few days without Robert, the weekend in which Ann had Gregory to herself, had taken on such significance in my aunt's love-crazy head that its preservation mattered more to her than anything else.

For the rest of the weekend, I stayed close to Ann. I was afraid of her because I didn't know what she would do; I couldn't see or feel how it was making *her* see or feel. The wonder of pregnancy had combined with the threat of her age, and the knowledge that the truth was coming thundering down the tracks towards all of us in St Quintin Avenue and it felt like being drunk and sick at the same time. Robert spent the weekend looking into the possibilities of taking the lower sixth on a trip to Spain to complement a term's worth of work on Lorca. There was something surreal about the conversations I heard him having on the phone with the travel agency:

'We'll be with twenty-three sixteen-year-old girls . . . We'd like to take a train from Madrid to the University of Granada if possible . . .'

After Ann left the house on Monday, I was restless. I walked around the house, alone as I'd ever been, my head full of it. My head full of Ann and Robert and Gregory. I sat at my desk, and I watched Yellow and Kate. *Love struck into his life like a hawk into a dovecote . . .* I watched Yellow and Kate, and Bruno talked between songs like he knew they were listening too. *'And it's a new entry at number 21 for Luciano Pavarotti with "Nessun Dorma" . . .'* If Yellow flew from his bath to the floor by the end of this song, I would call Theo. I would call him and tell him about Ann. I would call him because it was too much to keep stuffed inside me. It was too much. So I jacked up the volume on my stereo, and I sat as still as I could, and I listened to Pavarotti doing it for good old Puccini, who sure as can be wouldn't have known he was writing a song for English football, far less that he was writing a song that would sit in the charts next to Bobby Brown's 'Freestyle Mega-Mix', and I watched Yellow and something came into my head, and I remembered what Ann had shown me, way back when we first moved into St Quintin Avenue, which feels like yesterday and a century ago. She had shown me a book.

Robert had been collecting Diana from a casting in Shoreditch when Ann had come into my room and had held it out to me, like it was a present.

'Look,' she said. There was a strange, high colour to her cheeks, the sort you have when you're running a slight fever. 'Isn't it pretty?'

I took it from her cautiously. I didn't want it to be something that had belonged to my parents, something she'd now decided I should keep in their memory. People had sent Diana and me a ton of stuff after the fire – nothing had helped a single jot. I didn't need to keep things in Mama and Daddy's memory, I just wanted *them* back, thanks very much.

'What is it?' I asked Ann. It was small, a worn red hardback with Asian lettering on the front.

'It's Robert's,' she said. She looked at me expectantly.

'Is there a reason you want me to see it?' I asked her slowly. Ann did this a bit; she handed you things for general remark almost like she was testing you. I think it was part of being a teacher – 'look at this and pass it on to the next person'.

'He keeps it hidden,' she offered cryptically.

'What do you mean?' I flipped through the incomprehensible pages. 'You want me to tell you what it says?' I remember I laughed out loud.

Ann took it back. She looked almost offended.

'No,' she said. 'No. It's silly. It doesn't matter. It just makes me think. You know. I wonder where he got it from. I wonder who gave it to him?'

'Why don't you ask him?'

'I can't. He ... he told me he'd thrown it away. But here it is, you see.'

'Do you think it's something ...' I didn't know how to finish the sentence.

'It's a silly thing. I found it just after he asked me to marry him. We were having a chuck-out, just before we moved here. I found it in a bag, and he took it from me – almost snatched it out of my hands – and threw it on top of a pile of books for charity. But the thing is, he *hasn't* thrown it away, has he? It's still here.'

I looked at her. 'Does it matter?'

'I don't know,' she said. 'I don't think so. Everyone needs a secret, don't they?'

I watched her put the book away again. 'All I can say in Japanese is "what have you done with the scissors?"' she said.

'Useful and accusatory,' I said. 'I like it.' I think I remember her laughing at this.

'I let Robert do the talking when we were out there.'

'Well, I guess it's not the easiest language to pick up.'

'No,' said Ann. 'And not the easiest to let go of, either. There's writing in the front,' she said.

'In Japanese,' I said, staring down at the odd shapes.

'Yes,' said Ann. 'So I suppose we'll never know.'

I don't know why she used the word 'we' as though I were now part of this intrigue.

'You could ask someone to—'

'God, no. No. I couldn't do that. It would be wrong.'

We'd heard the sound of the front door opening, and Diana shouted up the stairs that they'd picked up burgers from Tootsies.

Just before Pavarotti got to that big top note, Yellow flew down to his bath and splashed in. I watched him shaking his feathers in the water. *You don't need to wait for him*, I heard Diana saying. *Theo. You can just get on and call him anyway.*

When he answered the telephone at the pet shop, I could hear that old parrot squawking away in the background.

'Can I come and find you, after work?' I heard myself saying. 'Something's happened.'

'What's happened?'

'Something at home.'

'Something good?'

'Er . . .' I was temporarily stunned by his assumption that impending news was *ever* good news. 'Something odd,' I said.

'Are the birds OK?'

'It's not the birds. It's something else.' There was a pause.

I guess he thought I might tell him over the phone, but what was the point in that? I didn't trust the phone.

'You Texans trade in mystery, huh?' he said.

'I don't mean to,' I said. 'And I'm not just Texan. I'm a Londoner.'

'Yeah,' said Theo. 'Me fucking too.' He laughed. 'I finish at six.'

So, I pulled on my Walkman, and I ran all the way down to Portobello, and as I crossed Bassett Road, a man I could have sworn was Eric Elliot drove past me, windows down on a clapped-out Golf, stereo blasting 'The Only Rhyme That Bites'. But it couldn't have been Eric, because back then, whenever I saw him, my heart would flip over, but this time there was nothing. Nothing at all.

22

Variations on a Theme

He was locking up when I arrived. When he walked out
of the shop and saw me, there was a flicker of something I
couldn't place, like he wanted me to be there and didn't at
the same time. *I don't know you*, I thought. *I don't know you at
all, but here I am, running down the streets of W11 towards you,
just to tell you stuff about my life that you don't need to know.* I
looked back up the street. I could run back. I could race back
to my bedroom and back to the birds, but the temperature
was dropping, and the wind was picking up and the leaves on
the plane trees shuffled around like they were full of ghosts.
I didn't want to be alone again. I was here, wasn't I?

'Hello, Tracey,' said Theo.

The shock of seeing him again was arresting. He was
always taller than I remembered him, and every time his face
was more complicated, though I couldn't say why.

'I'm sorry,' I said.

'What you sorry for?'

There was a crack of thunder.

'Shit!' said Theo. He laughed.

The rain bounced off the dry pavement. Wipers swiped windscreens double speed like a video game, and Theo chucked me his coat.

'Shall we run for it?'

We ran, skidding in the rain and the dust. Diana and I had been to all the pubs in Notting Hill with Lisa: Diana's favourites had been the Prince Bonaparte on Chepstow Road, full of old geezers and record company owners escaping their wives and children, and the Ladbroke Arms with its non-stop sport on the greasy TV screens above the entrance, and its floppy-haired poshos, drinking warm pints in the front garden in boat shoes and pink chinos. Lisa liked the Warwick Castle on Ladbroke Grove, always jammed full of locals and musicians, Wendy James and Mick Jones, school kids pretending to be older, actors from the 1960s pretending to be younger. Theo pushed open the door.

'Get a table,' he said. 'Plato'll be here in nine minutes.'

'How do you know?'

'I'm meeting him here. And he's always on time.'

I sat down, watching people watching the rain. My legs were wet, soaking into the sticky wood of the stool, and my trainers stuck to the floor. There was an unemptied ashtray in the middle of the table; I breathed in stale smoke and wrecked leather. The juke box played something old – the Kinks or the Lovin' Spoonful or something like that – and I thought of Ann, lying in her bed, and Robert downstairs in St Quintin Avenue, and Yellow and Kate, knowing everything and saying nothing, and the time felt so short, so borrowed. This place would empty out soon enough, and the next day would come, and then the end of the year, and it was all so uncertain, so fucking unfixed! I thought of the times when I had trembled in Eric Elliot's presence, and how impossible that was to feel now. Like it had been switched off at the source. Theo looked at me from the bar, and he nodded and smiled. I was here with him. I was warm, and he was buying me cider, and I was here with *him*.

He came and sat down again, opposite me.

'We've got five minutes, and counting,' he said. 'So, what did you want to—'

'It's Ann,' I said. 'She's pregnant.'

Theo lit a cigarette and leaned into me. 'Woah. The American drama teacher?'

'Yes.'

'He doesn't know?'

'No. She thinks she'll miscarry because she's forty-five.' I paused, waiting for him to say something else but he didn't so I talked on. 'I thought I'd tell you because – well, because you're new. So, you don't know me before everything happened. You can see it for what it is now, rather than what it was then. You don't ... I don't know ...'

'Haven't you got any friends to talk to?' he asked. There

247

was a gentleness in his voice, as though he were treading carefully. I felt a flame of shame.

'I have friends,' I said. I sounded hot with the worry of the question. 'I *had* friends. People from school. Girls from school. People. You know. Friends. Yes. I have friends. They wouldn't know what to say. They're too full of pity. I frighten them, I think.' I looked at him, and the newness of him struck me again. 'You're not frightened of me,' I said. 'You don't see me the same way that anyone else does. You didn't know me before.'

'No,' he said. 'I didn't.'

He looked at his watch and then at the door.

'Do you want me to say something to make you feel better, Tracey?' He looked at me with some urgency.

'Yes. I think I do.'

'All right.' He took a drag on his cigarette and leaned back. 'It's all out of your hands. The whole thing. Isn't that great?'

Gree-yat.

'What do you mean?'

'Your aunt and her thing for the American. Your uncle and whether or not he'll find out. You're not the manager in that band, you're not even the lead singer. You're the bassist, at best. It's not your choice what happens.'

'But she might leave. Or *he* might leave. Then what?'

'It's not up to you. *That's* what.'

For a moment neither of us said anything. I gulped at the cider. I was warm now; I felt drugged by it, and by the rain outside, and by having Theo Farrah's attention in the

Warwick Castle. *The Warwick Castle, built 1853.* Or was it much earlier than that? Robert had given us a quiz one night on the dates of pubs. My mind scrambled.

'Two minutes now,' said Theo. 'How else can I make you feel better?'

'She's having him over for dinner when Robert's away. She's asked me to be there. She says she needs me to be there.'

'I'll come too. Next.' He said it right away, like it was the most obvious thing in the world.

'You . . . you will?'

'Yeah. One minute thirty seconds. Come on.'

'Will I be all right?' I asked him. I laughed down at my hands on the table. I shook my head. This was madness, for sure.

'Only you can answer that. But I'd say, signs point to yes. You'll be all right.'

'How – how do you know?'

He stretched out his hand, hesitated for a split second, then put his palm over mine.

Everything stopped.

All I could feel was his hand. He was so warm! I breathed in, like the moment required more oxygen. Theo's face seemed to open up, his beauty and his newness and his hands, and the kick of the unknown all joined up together. I put my hand up to his cheek, and he took it and held it close, and he nodded at me, like he understood everything.

'I'll be all right,' I said to no one, and to everyone.

'Ten seconds,' he whispered.

Plato swung open the door of the pub like Wyatt Earp,

and whatever crazy magic had happened those moments before splintered and scattered off again. Theo sat back against the wall. Plato stood in the door, and shook himself like a Labrador, and as if on cue, the volume rose on the juke box, but then the volume rose everywhere that Plato went. He saw us and marched over. Theo looked at me and nodded fractionally. Plato stood over us. He ran a hand through his hair and looked right at me. 'Ah,' he said. 'How are you?'

Theo stood up and walked off to the bar. Plato sat down where he had been, taking up so much more of everything, not just around the table, but in the whole room. He was too big to be contained, his contradictions and opinions spilled over into everything, even when he wasn't speaking. I didn't want to be ambushed by him. Part of me was still very frightened of him.

'I'm going,' I said. 'I just needed to talk to Theo about something.'

'You don't have to justify sitting in a pub, for God's sake.' He sat back and frowned at me, a half-smile on his face. 'Anyway, it's all right. It's cool. You're here because you needed to be near him.'

'What?'

Plato raised his eyebrows at me. He leaned forward.

'He's a pro when it comes to damaged goods. People like you and me. You with all your tragic past, me who can't exist without self-sabotage. Some people are drawn to people like us. The damaged survivors. They work their own shit out through us because we've come through. You know. We give them hope. They like themselves when they're around us. We make them feel good.'

I wanted to say I didn't know what he was talking about, but I did. I knew exactly.

Plato's eyes were on Theo at the bar, leaning in, his hand around a five-pound note.

'He's adorable, no?' He laughed out loud as though he'd tried the word out for the first time and found it rather thrilling. 'He's adorable and you love him because you think he's rescuing you, and anyway, you can't help who you fall for, can you? Anyone will tell you that. Bob Dylan and Stock, Aitken and Waterman and Sylvia Plath, it's all just variations on a fucking theme, isn't it? I should be so lucky, lucky, lucky, lucky and all that.' He lit a cigarette. 'Save yourself some time. You'll never win with the guys who feel sorry for you, who want to make sure you're all right. It's too uneven. They lose interest eventually.'

'What are you trying to say?'

'Tell me this. Why aren't you doing what you're good at? Your body works, right? You can run? You can throw? You can hit? Why aren't you playing tennis?'

'I . . . can't.' I looked away from him, but I could feel his eyes on me, wanting answers.

'The way I see it, you think someone's great, you show them the bits of you that make you stand out from the rest.'

'No one likes someone more just because they're good at tennis.'

'Bullshit. I do.'

251

I scraped my nail along the edge of the table and picked at the wood.

'What you really want to know is one thing, and one thing only.' He looked at me and raised his eyebrows.

'What is it?'

'All you want to know is: Does he think about me when the lights are off?'

I looked down at the table. 'Maybe that's what *you're* thinking,' I said slowly.

Plato laughed. He leaned in closer towards me and put his cigarette up to his big mouth. 'Maybe,' he said.

He sang at me. He sang INXS like he knew how much those songs meant, like he was taunting me just because he could. There was a cruelty in it. I wanted to shake him. I wanted to shout at him that me being here, me sitting down at a table in a pub, was about as mad a thing as I could have imagined not so long ago. I wanted him to know that I couldn't have stepped one foot outside of the house without Yellow. Without Theo. Without Three Moon Monday. Without him. But I said nothing, just watched him singing 'Need You Tonight' like he'd written it. He banged his hands down on the table. Two girls at the table next to us grinned at him; one of them even joined in with him on the word 'sweat'. Theo glanced over from the bar and Plato stopped singing, leaving the girls hanging. He leaned back again and sighed and reached for a cigarette.

'All good songwriting is prophecy, isn't it, February Kingdom?'

Theo walked back to us and put the drinks on the table.

'I need to get home,' I said to him.

Plato raised his pint to me and grinned at me.

'She's gonna play,' he said.

'I'm not,' I said.

Theo walked me outside. A branch had come down across the road; some kids were climbing over it, and a car had parked right up in front of it, unable to get past. The rain had stopped as quickly as it had arrived, and the stunned sun was blinking its way out again. *What was all that about? I go out for ten minutes and all hell breaks loose ...* The fresh-drenched road smelled of hot greenhouses and tomatoes and tarmac and warm earth.

'I used to talk to Lisa when I needed help,' I said to him, but I don't think he heard.

I don't know why I mentioned Lisa. I wondered if there would be something more from him, some recognition of the noiseless thunderbolt that had passed between us before Plato had walked in. But Theo had in him some strange flicker of something I couldn't unwrap.

'Don't worry,' said Theo. He said it like he meant it, like it was an instruction that didn't merit disobeying. He stopped in the street.

'You should write to Texas,' he said.

'What do you mean, write to Texas?'

'To the place you want to go to. The university. Just write to them. Say you're still thinking about it.'

'But I'm not.'

'You should be.'

'But I don't want to go now.'

Theo blew the air out of his cheeks. 'No harm in just writing, is there?'

I made my way back to St Quintin Avenue slowly, and I walked back past 192, the restaurant that I kept in my head as the place that I'd had my longest exchange with Eric Elliot, on a freezing December evening in 1988. It had been snowing that evening, and everything was transformed, pure fairyland, and even several years after the heat of Texas, Diana and I were still imbeciles over the cold white stuff. We had looked through the window.

'We'd be mad not to go in for red wine,' Diana had said to me. 'Watch everything going Narnia?'

'I've no money left on my card,' I had pointed out.

'Fibroids,' sighed Diana lightly. She nodded at the crowd inside, 'but *they* do.'

She walked in ahead of me. Three men were sitting at the bar talking in fascinating riddles.

'Yeah, but the production's only worth something if she's in it, but she's drinking so much now, she couldn't remember how she got to work the other day. Spent the whole weekend at Julie's with Wayne Sleep and David Gower. She got locked in. She wasn't discovered until the next morning when the cleaners opened up.'

'We got Hockney to say he'd come.'

'It's worth half a million more than she said, but I'm telling you, that area is going to go up and up and up . . .'

Suddenly the three of them had looked up and noticed

us with great interest, especially directed at Diana of course, who was wearing a full-length fake fur coat she had bought from the market the week before and a pair of white moon boots.

'Come in, girls,' said one of the men. 'Hey! Are you waiting for Angelo?'

'Probably,' said Diana, grinning at them.

'Come and have a drink, it's freezing out there! Close the door! Are you having dinner? Wow! You've got moon boots on! Is it snowing?' At the back of the restaurant, in the corner, I could see Eric sitting with a group of boys. He hadn't seen us come in. I remember thinking how lucky Lisa was, that she got to lie down every night next to him. How lucky she was that he had chosen her over anyone else.

'Eric's over there,' I muttered to Diana.

'*You* go and say hello,' she said. She turned back to the men. 'I'd love a glass of red wine,' she said. I hardly heard their replies, but I guess they were falling over themselves to make that happen for her. I could only see Eric now. I walked over to him, idiotic.

'Hey!' He stood up and kissed me on both cheeks. My face flamed. What to say to him?

'We're just passing,' I said.

'We're just passing out,' said Eric. He looked at my Walkman and grinned. 'Whatcha listening to?'

'Oh, nothing—'

'C'mon!' He took it from me and ejected the tape.

'I borrowed it to see what it's like,' I mumbled.

'Brother Beyond. *Get Even*,' said Eric. He raised his eye-brows at me. Why on *earth* had I taken De La Soul out of my Walkman that afternoon? I could have wept.

'I just think their singles are quite fun,' I said.

'I know Nathan a bit,' said Eric. 'Nice guy.' He broke into a perfect chorus of 'The Harder I Try'. I laughed, but I was as embarrassed as hell.

'I really prefer Wet Wet Wet,' I said.

Eric smiled. I remember thinking how weird it must be to be as good-looking as he was, how it distracted from everything else about him. He spat out a stone from an olive and placed it in the ashtray, a gesture that felt acutely sexual. Seeing him without Lisa made me see him for how young he really was. Only seven years older than Diana and me. Twenty-five. It was his voice that was so wonderful, so *London*, so lazy, so perfect for the TV ads he was starting to be asked to shoot. You could have fallen in love with him over the telephone without even looking at him, without even seeing him on the pages of a magazine. I could feel myself blushing hard. I scrunched up my toes.

'Well, we're off, anyway,' I said.

'A great shame, my darlin',' said Eric. He looked over at Diana, laughing with the guys who were waiting for Angelo. 'What's your sister doing over there talking to those oafs?'

'You know them?'

'Maybe.'

'She's got a new boyfriend, so she doesn't want to stick around,' I said. 'He's calling her later.'

'Ah.' Eric nodded slowly.

'He's called Daniel,' I said, offering information he hadn't asked for. 'She's mad about him.' I was saying too much, but I wanted Eric to see Diana and me as adults, capable of going out with boys and breaking hearts.

'Well, for God's sake, tell her to be careful,' said Eric.

Now I stood outside 192 once more, and the rain had soaked through my trainers and I felt Diana next to me, looking through the same window.

Tell her to be careful, she said slowly.

When I got back to my room, I could still feel her. I pulled off my wet shoes and I lay on my bed and pressed play on my stereo, and then, feeling as sure of change as I've ever felt, I looked into the nest. A little egg lay perfect, Fabergé-precious in the beautiful nest, and the birds stood on the edge of the bath together like there was nothing about each other that they didn't know.

23

We Always Hang in a Buffalo Stance

Robert packed his bag on Friday morning. He was missing the day at school to arrive at Edinburgh Waverley just after lunch, where he would get in a cab to his brother's flat. Robert was quiet and furious before he left, which made sense because his brother's crazy as a bullbat, and no one could head for his company feeling anything other than half mad themselves. When he walked out of the door, he pulled Ann towards him and held her in his arms as though he were going off to fight a war. She pulled back from him.

'Don't do anything I wouldn't do,' he said with a cheery laugh that veered towards irony.

'Bloody hell,' said Ann with an ironic laugh that veered towards cheeriness. She kissed him on the forehead, but he seemed like he didn't want to be kissed. I wished I hadn't seen it. They looked like children.

'Don't forget your sandwiches,' said Ann. At breakfast, she had offered to make him something for the train. Robert liked rolls with two inches of butter and cheese and lettuce and salt and pepper – he was snobbish about these things – and I suppose Ann thought that making sandwiches how he liked them was an easy win for her, but this time she had simply spread a thick layer of Stork margarine and honey inside a hastily defrosted bun. Her head was filled with Gregory Arrowsmith. Some part of her must have anticipated Robert opening that tin foil package on the train and staring at it in astonishment. Some part of her was really *quite* into that idea.

As soon as Robert left, Ann started to tidy up, to shift things, to alter the mood of the house – a house that's dominated by Robert's intellect, and by his traditional, tasteful desire for order. She spread a red silk scarf that she had bought in Seville on the back of the plain cream sofa in the little sitting room and wrapped a gold muslin around the base of the white lamp that Robert used to illuminate his paper when he did the crossword. We both stood back to look at it. It was as though the sofa and lamp were in the process of being seduced and were not entirely sure whether seduction was a thing that they were keen to buy into right now.

'Just wanted to make it look like I've got a life worth living,' said Ann.

'You *have* got a life worth living,' I said.

'Thank you,' she said. 'I know ... You think I'm terrible for all this, don't you? An awful woman who's only thinking about herself. I can see why you'd think that. *I* would think that.'

'I can't work out what I think,' I said.

'Gregory and I could go off somewhere on our own this evening. We don't have to be here with you if it makes you feel ... weird.'

'Of course it's going to make me feel weird!'

'Oh,' said Ann. She looked dejected.

'But I want to understand it. I have to meet him.'

'Oh, forget that. You won't understand it,' said Ann. She sighed. 'I thought I'd get my eyelashes dyed.'

When she got back later, she was weighed down with food. She'd gone all-out, and there were bags of champagne, white wine and beer from Nicolas, the new off-licence on Holland Park Avenue, and two bags of things from Mr Christian's on Elgin Crescent overflowing with hard and soft cheeses, Italian hams, chilli jams, jars of wholegrain mustard and mayonnaise, bread sticks flavoured with caraway seeds, raspberry macaroons, and chocolate brownies full of pieces of white marshmallow and pecan. As she unloaded the bags, she made vague, half-hearted attempts to justify it all, but she needn't have bothered. Her new black eyelashes were startling, opening up her eyes even wider. She'd also bought herself new underwear – I only knew this because I went into her bedroom to borrow sun cream and found a bag from Rigby & Peller half hidden under her nightie on the chair beside the bath, and I looked inside. Whatever she had bought was extremely small and wrapped in pink tissue paper with a black ribbon. The whole thing reminded me of Grandma Abby before a party day. *We'll paint the town and the front porch, and we'll hallelujah the country!* Only it felt like Ann was strapping into a handcart to hell at the same time: I'm going down, but I might as well do it in good knickers.

In my bedroom were two more eggs. I took them out, and I replaced them with the dummy eggs. Careful as I could, I put the real eggs in cotton wool in the drawer beside my bed.

Theo and I had the kitchen to ourselves, because Gregory Arrowsmith wasn't due to arrive until seven-thirty, and Ann had shut herself away claiming she was marking essays, but no one marks essays in a bath stuffed full of remedy salts from Neal's Yard, singing 'Eternal Flame' at top volume. Theo studied a piece of paper with the recipe on.

'Good handwriting,' I said.

'It's Plato's.'

'He's used an ink pen?'

'Yeah. He collects stationery,' said Theo.

I wanted to tell him what Plato had said to me, but I was too afraid of it being the truth. That odd strand of lightning between us felt buried again.

'He's still going on about your tennis match,' said Theo. 'He's found some woman on Ladbroke Square with access to a private court. God knows how.'

'How?'

Theo looked at me.

'He won't stop until you say you'll do it. I once said I'd

never read Charles Dickens. He took it upon himself to read the whole of *Great Expectations* to me over the course of six months. Not out of generosity, mind. He just had a total obsessive need to know what I thought of it. He kept appearing with it in his hands. Backstage before gigs, in the pub, on trains . . .'

'And?'

'Greatest book of all time, obviously.'

Theo was crushing garlic and spices into a cereal bowl when the telephone rang. I picked it up and it was Robert. He sounded a million miles away. I could hear the strident wailing of seagulls overhead.

'All I'm calling to say is that she knows how to get hold of me, if she needs me,' he said.

Not a chance, I thought, thinking of Rigby & Peller and dyed eyelashes and jars of expensive chilli jam that would have to be hidden somewhere before he returned. *Not a bloody chance.*

We carried the table outside into the garden and covered it in a white lace tablecloth found in a bottom drawer of the kitchen cabinet. We filled empty jam jars with roses from the garden and put tea-lights that Ann had bought by each place.

The neighbours had a sprinkler going in their garden, and their two children shrieked as they ran under it in their school shorts. These kids went to the prep school Norland Place, one of the schools that sent a ton of girls on to Westbury House. Norland Place enjoyed an annual burst of satire by holding their sports day on the athletics track by Wormwood Scrubs prison, and the kids' blue aertex shirts were decorated with coloured ribbons.

'I got more than you!' yelled the little girl to her sister.

'That's because you cheated in the three-legged race!' yelled her sister, pushing her over into the paddling pool with some violence.

Be nice, I wanted to shout. *A sister's worth a million ribbons.*

Instead, I waved at them, and they waved back, embarrassed that I'd seen them fighting, but steely with the will to carry on.

At eight, the doorbell rang. Ann was still upstairs, although I suspected this was all part of the act. Theo was picking almonds out of a packet of mixed nuts. He chewed with his mouth open.

'That'll be the bastard now,' he said. I stared at him. He laughed. 'Go on, then. Answer it.'

When I opened the door, Gregory Arrowsmith was standing looking out onto the street, so that he had to swing around to see me when he heard the door opening. He was carrying a bunch of sweet peas and wearing a pale blue shirt and a blue and white woollen tie, and he looked as though he was searching for the right words to start a long speech. The vibe was of a lone actor stepping in front of the curtain at the start of Act Two and hoping the audience have warmed up a bit. I was almost knocked sideways by Polo by Ralph Lauren, an aftershave that Daddy had always worn at Christmas. That smell I associated so directly with winter, and my father, felt kind of at odds with Gregory Arrowsmith, standing on the hot pavement of St Quintin Avenue, come to fuck my aunt. Still. I smiled at him.

'Hello!' he said. He stuck out a hand to me. 'You must be February. How wonderful to put a face to the voice on the end of the telephone! February Kingdom. What a name! Although I have a friend with a son in New York State called September Leaf McBride, so really, you've got off lightly, I'd say.' That Manhattan accent was deceptive; made me want to like him, and I sure knew I didn't *want* to like him. Close up he was even taller than I thought he would be – although to be fair, the last time I had seen him he had been horizontal – and he had the standard death-pale skin that I so associated with the competitive academia that blighted friends of Ann and Robert, but his nose was sprinkled with freckles that made him look younger than I had imagined he was. His dark hair was just starting to thin on top, but for now it served him well, and fell forward, and combined with his jacket, shirt and tie gave him the look of a malnourished undergraduate. Robert, who had turned down the chance to model for a Scottish cashmere company in his early twenties, would have wiped the floor with him in terms of man-on-the-street good looks.

'Most people call me Feb,' I offered.

'Feb. Feb. Of course. Well, Feb. Ann told me about your sister,' he said. His accent lingered on 'sister', keeping it in the atmosphere far longer than usual. He didn't bother lowering his voice, as most people did when they remarked

upon Diana. 'What an unbelievable – an unbelievable tragedy. A *tragedy*,' he confirmed. He shook his head in a sort
of wonder.

'It hasn't been easy,' I said.

'Ah. But should it be? I don't think so. It *shouldn't* be easy.
You would never have – have – uh – wanted it to be easy.'
He spoke very quickly, and as he was speaking, he glanced
around sharply behind him like a thief mid-sentence, but
then I imagine thieves become very easy to relate to for those
having sex with another man's wife. A couple of old women
were struggling along the road carrying bags of shopping.
'These streets,' he said, turning back to me, 'what have they
seen? Who was standing here on your doorstep fifty years
ago? What of *their* lives? Where did *that* go?' I stepped aside to
let him into the house, and he took off his glasses and looked
at me with determined kindness.

'Come in,' I said.

He smiled at me, and with the instinct of an unusually tall
person, he ducked as he walked through the door. 'These
houses are wonderful,' he said.

'They'd like more of a garden, I think. My uncle talks
about selling some day,' I said. Neither fact was strictly true.
He looked at me, confused.

'Ah. Well. What do I know?' It was a good question. What
did he know? 'I think she'd be mad to sell in a hurry. Oh, I'm
so sorry. I'm the most gruesome kind of – uh – American.
The kind who can't stop saying what they're thinking all
the time, regardless of circumstance. Awful. Just awful. Oh

God. Will you forgive me? No, you won't, will you? And
who could blame you?'

He looked at me with wide blue eyes. His eyelashes were
longer than Ann's; no wonder she'd had to do some work in
that area. He grinned at me. 'I bore myself sometimes. You
have to tell me to stop talking.'

'Only the very interesting get to say such things,' I said.

'Well. Maybe. That's a nice compliment I think, isn't it?'
Again, the anxious look of someone treading on uncertain ground.

'Ann's upstairs,' I said. I thought he'd walk through to
the kitchen with me, but he gave me a half-regretful smile
and nodded so that his hair fell forward again, and then he
walked up the stairs, slowly at first, then two, then *three* at a
time until he was outside Ann's bedroom. I struggled for a
moment to work out who he looked like, and then realized
that if you squinted and were feeling *real* generous, Gregory
Arrowsmith could pass for an older, less hip Bryan Ferry,
and if you closed your eyes completely, his hurried, self-
consciously stuttering speech made him sound exactly like
Jeff Goldblum in *Earth Girls Are Easy*, a film I'd seen with
my friend Emma twice in the cinema. I heard the sound of
him knocking on the bedroom door.

'Feb?' called Ann from inside.

'No – uh – it's me,' said Gregory Arrowsmith.

The door opened. He tried to keep his voice down, but I
could hear every word.

'God, you're so beautiful, Annie, my darling,' he said.

'Outstanding. Baby. Outstanding. That dress. Baby. My darling. I'm a mess. I'm an absolute – oh, my darling . . .'

Nobody *ever* called Ann Annie. It was as though he were
addressing a different woman altogether. And she *was* a different woman. *I didn't know her.* I thought of Robert sitting
with his lunatic brother at a table eight hundred miles north
of where we were, completing the crossword, an unnamed
rage in his heart. Nope. No time for that. I squashed it all
out of my head and walked back to Theo in the kitchen.
He was holding a cigarette in one hand and trying to chop
coriander with the other.

'Where's Dr Feelgood?' he asked me.

'Upstairs. He bolted up there like he couldn't wait.'

Theo handed me the cigarette like he was offering me a
magic wand. I took it and our fingers touched, but he didn't
look at me. 'The chicken's all right, you know. But the question is, Tracey, will anyone *care?*'

'Open a bottle of something,' I said. It was the sort of
comment that my mother would have made, I thought.
Open a bottle. It showed authority. *I* didn't care about the
chicken. I wouldn't have cared if Theo had told me that
he had chucked everything out of the window, and that
we were starting again with baked beans on toast washed
down with orange squash. Upstairs were the birds – our
birds – with the pale blue mini-eggs waiting to be placed
back in the nest made of hair. I could be losing Ann to this
American stranger, and who would I live with then? What
of my bedroom, and cold croissants consumed straight from

the packet in the morning, and the lilac in the garden, and the wallpaper with the Chinese men on swings, and St Quintin Avenue itself? What of Bruno on my stereo by my bed? Would the whole street evaporate without her? Would Robert and I wait here for her to come back? I suddenly saw myself aged fifty, sixty – eighty. Ageless, ancient, modern all at once.

'What if she really loves him?' I said.

'Maybe she does,' said Theo. 'What can you do? Just keep on doing what you're doing. You're doing OK.'

'You think so?'

'Yeah, I think so.'

For nearly an hour we drank Peroni and waited for the lovers to come downstairs. Afterwards, I wanted to write it all down, everything we'd talked about, like I was writing a scene in a play, just to know that it had happened like it had. Theo talked to me about Plato, and about growing up in Sunderland, and I told him about Texas, and about school in Oxfordshire, and playing tennis, and Westbury House, and I found that once I'd started to talk, I couldn't stop. It was as though something had been untied in me. He was here because he wanted to be. Because he liked me enough to be here. I could hear myself answering his questions – laughing, understanding, absorbing, *responding* like a real live human being – and my voice was clear, and interested, articulate as hell! When I thought of it later, it was like I was taking each new sentence and each new thought out of a box, tearing the wrapping off them at speed, and offering them to Theo

Farrah as fast as I could. *Feb never draws breath.* I was talking like I hadn't talked since the accident.

Ann and Gregory walked into the kitchen together, like they were arriving for dinner on holiday. Theo had put a bootleg cassette of *Raw Like Sushi* in the stereo on the kitchen counter, and when he held out his hand for Gregory to shake in greeting, the up-tempo scratchy first few moments of 'Buffalo Stance' blasted out and it looked for a moment like Theo was asking him to dance. Gregory looked at him, then at me, then cleared his throat and rapped the first line of the song, lyric perfect, acting every word:

'Who – who – who – who – who – who's that gigolo on the street?
With his hands in his pockets and his crocodile feet?'

Ann had told me that he was very funny, but I hadn't really believed her. She and Robert didn't tend to have friends who were funny; they might be quick-witted, sharp, but rarely truly hilarious. But this was. This was how I knew that Ann was lost to him – because on top of the side-order of him being a New Yorker, and therefore on some level exotic and thrilling, and on top of him knowing about the theatre, and being able to quote ancient poets and Neneh Cherry, he was funny. Theo laughed and clapped. I knew him well enough by now to know that he only did this when he *really* meant it. I grinned because I just couldn't help it, it was so unexpected. Ann looked between Theo and me and Gregory, watchful and nervous, as though she had orchestrated the whole thing and was finally witnessing something coming together exactly as planned.

'Ah, I don't know the rest of the words,' said Gregory. He went red and laughed.

'Number 3, January 1989,' I said under my breath.

Gregory pulled Ann beside him and kissed her on the forehead. 'She's so wonderful, this one,' he said. He looked at Theo and me as though challenging us to respond. What was he doing? Ann looked down at the floor; she was mortified and bursting with pride at the same time. She was wearing a dress I'd never seen before, floor-length and black and gold, like something one of the Rolling Stones' girlfriends might have worn in 1971. The neckline was as low as low, so that I could clearly see the tiny, perfect red lace Rigby & Peller bra on her white skin underneath, and under the red lace, the darker sight of her swollen little nipples. She literally throbbed with needing to be touched, it would have been impossible not to feel it. The pregnancy seemed to imbue her with even more sexuality; it was as if the secrecy of it had given her even more clout. I couldn't believe that Theo didn't feel it too. My God, there was indescribable power in the female liberated – it banged the eye and the heart towards its centre and held those looking on fascinated.

Theo handed Gregory a glass of wine. 'So how long have you been a fan of Neneh Cherry?' he asked him.

24

The World According to Gregory Arrowsmith

We ate outside. The food was really far too hot because Theo had added more and more chilli. The heat felt necessary for Ann somehow; nothing about the evening could be background, it was foreground all the way, bring *everything* to the front! She was a great consumer of spicy food, having lived in Asia for those sacred six months with Robert, and didn't mind it one bit, and it was obvious to me that her ability to eat hot, combined with her extreme brand of English Rose, enhanced her appeal even further. Gregory Arrowsmith couldn't cope with it as successfully and kept wiping his watering eyes with his napkin and laughing and saying things like 'Christ in Heaven! This is delicious but are you trying to kill me?' and pouring himself more water. I had added sliced cucumber to the water jug like they did in Tom's on Westbourne Grove, which Gregory picked out with his fingers and chewed up, gasping a bit. Theo apologized. Gregory waved the apology away. I was quite still.

Gregory's approach during the evening was quite different to what I had expected. I had imagined that there would be a necessary secrecy in what was happening between him and Ann, that the immutable facts of the situation – that he had a wife and she a husband – would have stopped them from touching each other in front of us. But as soon as he had shown his hand, Ann fell into his arms, entirely succumbing to the truth of it. The evening darkened, and she sat so close to him, her hand on his. The candles flickered in the middle of the table, watching us. Occasionally a warm breeze took one of them out, and Theo reached forward and lit it again. I could feel Diana in their faltering light. Who would have imagined this? Ann sitting in a red lace bra next to her American lover. This is what happens when you look away, I wanted to say to her. This is what happens if you take your eye off the ball. This kind of chaos. And yet Theo was listening to me. He was there for me.

I pulled some vanilla ice cream from the freezer and Ann took all the exciting things she'd got from Portobello out of the bag, her face thrilled as though she were opening a Christmas stocking. We opened packets of biscuits, of cheese and chocolate, nougat, caramelized figs, strawberries in tiny punnets, cream from Devon, each one with a whoop of triumph. Ann was an entirely new person, more brilliant and vivid, far, far more complex than I had ever imagined her, as though she were suddenly speaking a different language, and speaking it faster, louder. It was as if everything that I had known of her before was suddenly revealed to have been only the visible part of the iceberg, and now I was able to see the full two thirds beneath.

'I've wanted to meet you for so long, February,' Gregory said, 'I've heard more about you from Annie than anyone else. Of course, we talked the very night that you found the canary.' He made it sound as though he were personally responsible. I looked at Theo.

'Yes,' I said.

'How I love that song. It's like nothing else! And it turns out to be the bird of the beautiful boy from the pet shop.' Theo snorted in vague protest, but Gregory waved it away. 'I'm stating the facts, kid. No, you're lucky. Don't go all bashful, all shy, it's meaningless. Anyway, Annie told me everything.' He turned his attention to Theo, swivelling around in his chair so it looked as though he were about to interview him. 'You look after a – a – musician of some kind? A pop singer, I hear?'

'He's promised me he's going to make me rich,' said Theo.

'He's full of shit,' I said, thinking of how Plato had spoken to me in the pub.

Theo looked at me and laughed.

'Well, *all* singers and actors are full of shit, aren't they?' Gregory raised his hands up to heaven in a gesture like the ones that Plato threw around so often. 'So, you lose your grandfather's canary, and it shows up in the house of a girl who looks like the goddess that is Tracey Ullman, and now – uh – it's – uh – *perfection!* The beauty of youth in the city!' His eyes were wide open and searching. 'What I'd do to be your age again and living in Notting Hill.' He pronounced it 'Nadding Hill'. 'How is it,' he asked Theo, 'being a black kid in this bit of town?'

Theo breathed in quickly. I never asked him things like this.

'Maybe the same as it is for you being an American, only with an eighty per cent higher chance of being knifed,' he said.

Gregory snorted. 'That's what *you* think,' he said. 'You know, I got on a bus the other day, and I asked the guy next to me for the time. He said: "Are you American?" I said: "Yes". He said: "Fuck you!" Just that. That was it, there was no other – no other word – not another word between us. We both sat there in silence for forty minutes. And you know what he was reading? *The Bonfire of the Vanities!* I mean, you gotta hand it to the guy. That's *some* nerve.'

'This is London,' said Theo.

'Ha. Yes. Quite right. But you know, I just wanted to be *nice*. That's my problem. Needing to be liked. I wanted to be an actor – uh – you know – like everyone does when they've watched too many cowboy movies and like showing off after dinner. But I ended up a drama teacher. Same old story, no new twists.' He dragged slowly on his cigarette and grinned at us. 'I always dreamed about going to Europe, so I moved to France to teach at the American School. Stayed there for – uh – for four years. Taught English and drama to kids. Didn't much care for the French parents. Or the American ones, actually. Kept being told that in London the streets were paved with gold—'

'You married a French woman,' observed Ann.

'Yeah. Yeah, I did,' conceded Gregory. He squeezed Ann's hand tightly. 'I applied for a job in a big private school in England. A boarding school. The most famous school in the world, I guess,' he shrugged modestly. 'I got the job.'

'How was it?' asked Theo, who had huge curiosity for the notion of paying to go to school.

'It's bracing. It's wonderful. I threw everything into it. We lived in Windsor, opposite the castle.'

'You had children,' said Ann.

'I did. Two girls. Life is simultaneously ruined and exulted.'

Ann looked at me. Mama would have said the same thing about her life once Diana and I had arrived. *Ruined and exulted.* That was exactly it for her.

'I was at Eton for twenty years. Planned to return to New York in the fall – uh – you know, back to the Big Apple. I wanted to have some time off before then, write a book, or something – then, on a whim I applied for the temporary post of head of drama at an all-girls' day school in West London.'

'What about your book?' I asked. He waved my question away.

'Shush, I'm just getting to the good bit. I get to Westbury House School for the first time, think "I hate it, I want

the boys back. I want to teach boys. Where are the *boys*?"
Anyway, I decided to stay for the interview, and that's when
everything changes. I meet Annie. She's like – like the part
of me I've been searching for all my life. She's the missing
part of my soul.'

If I hadn't been drunk, I would have been a little disappointed with this; the delivery of the story had been flawless,
but the romantic descriptive work from a man who taught
great literature was kind of below average. He was still
going. 'From the moment I left the school that day, she's
become all kinds of things to me. Unstoppable things. She's
Anna Karenina, she's Hedda, she's Titania. She's Juliet, she's
Cinderella,' he ticked off the names on his fingers with relish,
'she's – an – uh – an *uncomfortable*, wonderful thing. I walked
into the staff room on day one, and there she is. Even more
astonishing than she was when I first saw her. I fall in love
for the first time in my life. Of that there can be no – uh –
no doubt.' Ann was looking down at their entwined fingers
now. She was too embarrassed to look at me, but I know that
she wanted him to go on. How much easier for their story
to come from him than her.

'Did she fall in love too?' I asked.

'You'll need to ask her,' said Gregory.

Ann looked dejected. Theo suddenly put his hand over
hers. She smiled at him with infinite gratitude.

'It's painful,' she said. She looked up and spoke directly to
Theo, not to me. 'When we went for lunch the other day . . .
I talked to his wife and she . . . she talked about Italy, where

they take a house every year in August. I couldn't bear it.'
Ann said 'take a house' with such bitterness, imbuing the
phrase with chronic disdain, and there was such *energy* in the
disdain, such motivation in the dislike for the two of them
for having a holiday in Italy in August, that it hit Gregory
with some force, and he stepped in, to level the playing field.

'*I* couldn't bear it either,' he said. '*I* couldn't bear *her* sadness, and I couldn't bear her lying every night next to a man
who didn't understand her, who took her for granted, who
couldn't see what he had in front of him—'

This was too much for me.

'He knows what he has,' I said. 'Robert knows.'

This took the wind out of Gregory's sails for a few
moments. He said nothing, just dragged on his cigarette.

'I hate myself for this,' said Ann simply.

'Ah,' said Gregory, 'we can all hate ourselves. It's the easiest thing in the world to trade in dislike for yourself.'

I said nothing. It was like sitting next to the canaries; I
didn't want to make any sudden movements. But it was too
late for that – Ann got up as the telephone was ringing. It
would be Robert, no doubt about it, and I think something
in her wanted to leave us to Gregory for a bit, on our own.

'I won't be long,' she said, and she stumbled slightly on the
way back into the house. I looked at her departing back in
the black and gold dress and felt a great surge of love for her.

Gregory Arrowsmith leaned back in his chair. He let out a
deep breath and looked up at the moon. It was a great piece
of theatre, all told. I felt as though this was something he had

spent a lifetime doing, making a stage of wherever he was and whomever he was with; it was as though everything became a prop or a backdrop: the garden, the bottle of wine, the very evening sky, like it was the only way he could operate, and these speeches, these proclamations were really all about the performance. He somehow succeeded in giving away very little about what was really going on from a practical point of view: was he going to leave his wife, what of his children, and that sort of thing. He also had an instinct for where our thoughts were going.

'I love my children. I *adore* them. What I wouldn't do for them! My God! They burn me up with how much I love 'em. But until I met Annie, I'd never had anything close to the stuff that I'd read about in great literature, or seen in those shitty, dirty seventies B-movies that I snuck outta school to watch with my best friend when we were fifteen, or experienced when I saw how people kissed outside subway stations late at night. What I'd had was an odd version of love that was like an artist's impression of it, but nothing to do with the actual real thing.'

He sensed that he hadn't much time until Ann returned to the table, so he spoke even faster, and with even more of the stammering and dramatic hand movements.

'I'd never believed in it before, this great religion of love for another – another – human being that was drummed into me from the moment I understood the facts of life. It felt phoney to me. And can you imagine! What a fraud I was! A drama teacher – uh – a *drama* teacher who had never really understood it all before! The second I'd met Annie, I wanted to go back into every rehearsal room, every school hall, every stage I'd ever been near and slash a pen through every word of advice I'd ever given anyone. It rewrote everything for me. It's everything. It's unstoppable, and it's *everything*.'

'My mum thought it was everything when she met her last boyfriend,' said Theo, 'then she said, one day she woke up and it wasn't anymore.'

'It wasn't what?' asked Gregory.

'It wasn't everything. It was everything for a bit, then it wasn't.'

Gregory chose not to remark upon what Theo had said. Instead, he just nodded and went on. 'The love that you have when you're our age is very different to the sex you're having when you're nineteen. And my God! What a relief!' He rose to his feet and raised his glass heavenwards. '"Godlike is the man who sits at her side, who watches and catches that laughter which softly tears me to tatters! Nothing is left of me each time I see her!" That's Catullus, of course,' said Gregory.

'I thought it was Bon Jovi,' said Theo.

I could see into the house from where I was sitting and could see that Ann was no longer on the telephone. She was looking at herself in the mirror above the fireplace. I could see her lips moving; she was talking to herself. What was she saying? Go for it, you deserve to be with him tonight? Or: How could you do this to your husband? Was she telling herself that she was pregnant, saying it out loud to frighten herself into something?

'What do you do about it, when you're both married to someone else?' I asked Gregory.

He laughed sadly. 'What you do, is you live every day as if it's your last. You sit outside and you thank God you're alive. You take these God-given weekends, and you lie in the arms of the one you love, and you think: yeah. Yeah! All those sonnets, all that poetry, all those words! Suddenly they mean something. And nothing can take that away. Not even if she walked out of my life tomorrow. I would have *loved*.'

He looked pleased and relieved that the end of this speech coincided with Ann walking back out to us. Ann sat down.

'I've been boring these two, I fear,' he said. 'For God's sake, I'm such an old bore. When can I see these glorious songbirds I've heard so much about?'

He was a strange man, but there could be no doubt in my mind that his great talent lay not as an actor, but in something much more prosaic yet way more admirable – in his ability to *teach*. When he talked, he was impossible not to listen to; his manner, his movements, his style of talking, detouring casually from the central thread of his conversation to topics as varied as Aristotle's first pupils through to Steffi Graf's serve. If channelled the right way, this would surely have a mesmerizing effect on a class of teenagers of either sex; there was no slack in his rope. I could feel it even after a short time in his company.

Ann was wild, and in her I saw Diana and my mother. It was a strange new delight and agony, Ann in this new form, like a Greatest Hits compilation of all the women that I had loved in my life. Theo sat beside me, and I burned beside him. Burned like a planet, unable to help it. Then I thought of Robert, of Diana and I walking the streets after our parents had been taken from us. I thought of Robert and how he had done this for us, and suddenly I needed to hear his voice. I got up and I walked back into the house from the garden, and up the stairs into Ann and Robert's bedroom. *Their bedroom.* The telephone number in Edinburgh was written in biro on a scrap of paper beside the lamp. I picked up the phone and dialled the number. Robert answered immediately.

'Hullo?'

I said nothing.

'Hullo?' he said again.

'It's – it's me. Feb.'

'Feb! What's happened?'

'Nothing. I was just checking you were OK.'

'I just spoke to Ann. Aren't you with her?'

'Yes. Sorry. I am.' I put a hand to my forehead. 'I just wanted to make sure you'd arrived and you're all right. You know.'

'Oh, I've arrived. I'm here.'

'You'll be back soon, won't you?'

'Good God, I don't want to stay here a second longer than I have to.'

'It's not the same without you,' I said.

I could hear Robert's surprise in the silence.

The door opened. It was Ann.

'Who are you talking to?' she asked me. She looked horrified.

'Is that Ann?' asked Robert down the line.

'Yes,' I said.

'Can I talk to him again?' asked Ann.

I handed her the phone. 'Is everything all right?' she asked him.

I walked out of the room. Let her feel it. Let her know he's still there. When she came downstairs five minutes later, she'd pulled her hair up off her face like she wears it for school. I don't know if this was an act of rebellion or one of contrition.

When I got back downstairs, Theo was standing on the doorstep, waiting to go.

'Thanks for coming tonight,' I said. 'You didn't have to. I don't know why you did.'

Theo put his cigarettes into his pocket. 'I don't know either, Tracey. Maybe it's Yellow. Kate. The eggs. The saga of your aunt and the drama teacher.' He paused. 'You,' he said. 'Aren't you enough?' He picked up his keys and did one of his classic shrugs. The ones that remind me of Michael J. Fox in *Back to the Future*.

I lay on the bed, but I couldn't sleep. Where was she? Where was my sister to help me with this? Where was she to talk me through this knot inside me, this tight fear of losing Ann and Robert, this great awful ache of knowing it might not always be this way? But more than that, more than all of that, where was she for me to tell her about Theo? In agitation, I walked to my desk, and I sat down. I pulled out a piece of paper. Write to Texas. Tell them you'd still like to come. In the end, it took me half an hour. When I had finished, I put the letter into an envelope. I don't know if I'll send it, but I sure as hell don't think there's ever going to be another night that I could have written it.

At three in the morning, I peeled off Diana's sequin leggings and they lay on the floor beside my bed, still glinting in the dark and I thought of Lisa. Lisa, who had given Diana the leggings, on our fifteenth birthday. Lisa, who had taken us both out for dinner that same night, with Eric. Eric, so very beautiful – so South London, so hip. Eric, with his friends called things like Bruiser and Alessandro sitting there so damn cool, wearing a gold necklace and smudged black eyeliner from a shoot earlier that day. Eric, who had been in campaigns for Gucci and Louis Vuitton. Eric, who smelled of white towels and the crisp pages of a newsstand-fresh copy of *Vogue*, and the sour Nicorette gum that he chewed incessantly. That's gone now. All of those evenings, those fantasy nights, those dance routines under the lights in the kitchen at St Quintin Avenue, those vague watercolours of hope I'd painted around the life that I thought I could have when we'd both left school. Now there were canaries in a cage under a sheet in my bedroom, and there were three eggs in a drawer beside my bed waiting to be put back into their nest. There were letters of condolence by my copies of *Smash Hits*, and Ann lay in the room next door to me, in the arms of another man.

But there was Theo. He'd come to see me, to help me, to cook, to talk to me just because I was enough. I guess it's up to me now, whether to believe him or not. I was enough. I *am* enough. I was *enough*.

25

Charlie

When I walked into the kitchen the next morning, Ann and Gregory were sitting at the table drinking coffee and eating breakfast; they looked almost formal. Gregory seemed relieved to see me. Ann was flicking through an old copy of the *Radio Times* with Ruby Wax on the front cover. I sensed an odd, calm resolve in her, a self-containment that had been entirely absent the night before. She was wearing a plain red skirt and a white shirt; she looked pale but efficient and confident, as though she could have led a Duke of Edinburgh expedition without breaking a sweat. For a weird moment I wondered whether I had imagined everything, and that perhaps Gregory and she were just friends after all, that everything that had happened the night before had all been a chilli-inspired fantasy, that she wasn't pregnant.

'How did you sleep?' Gregory asked me. Just like that, as though he lived with us and everything was perfectly normal!

'Fine, thank you,' I said.

'Where's the beautiful Theo?'

'He left last night. He's at work.'

'The pet store must be busy on the weekends,' he observed. He smiled at me. Did he *really* care? Did it matter to him that I liked him because he was planning a life with Ann? Or was this just all for display purposes only?

'Plato has a gig later, so he needs to leave work on time,' I said.

'Ah! The Misfit Named Plato!' proclaimed Gregory.

'*Called* Plato,' corrected Ann.

'Do you think he's familiar with Ancient Greek or is it all a great pretension?'

'Hard to tell,' I said.

Gregory gulped his coffee and through a mouthful of toast he said: '"Nothing beautiful without struggle."' He looked at Ann and raised his eyebrows. 'Where's he performing?'

'The Lovelock on Ladbroke Grove. He won't be on until after ten.'

I suppose I was hoping this might put him off.

Gregory looked at Ann. 'Well, why don't we go after dinner?'

Ann hesitated. 'We could . . .'

'Wonderful!' said Gregory. He looked truly thrilled with the whole business. 'My God! Last rock concert I went to was – uh – Tina Turner, Madison Square Garden, New York City!' Gregory sighed and put a hand over Ann's.

'There will be similarities,' I said, looking away.

'You ever been to New York, February Kingdom?'

I looked at Ann. 'No,' I said. 'Never.' I was lying.

Diana had been in New York for several months before I made a plan to visit her. I wanted to go to New York, not just because I missed Diana, but because I liked the idea of shocking her by doing something that she would never have imagined me doing. I'd never been spontaneous, and I hated flying. We'd said goodbye that morning, when Lisa had hugged Ann into her chest, and both my sister and I had assumed that we wouldn't be together again for five months. But I wanted to shock her and thrill her, and I wanted to be in on the ground floor with Lisa and her baby who had come early; no one I knew had a newborn child. I couldn't stop thinking about it, the newness of it, the idea of Lisa as a mother. Perhaps there was something else too: I wanted to make Diana feel that there was some part of me that she couldn't predict, some part of me that was unknown. And so I kept my trip to myself, swearing Ann to secrecy.

'It'll be very hot,' she kept saying to me, as though I hadn't spent a childhood in the Lone Star state, where the humidity bombed you out like you were living on Venus half the year round.

'I'll be fine,' I said.

'You're sure you don't want to tell her you're coming?'

'Sure. I've got the address. I'll get a taxi there.'

'What if they're not in?'

I hadn't thought of this.

Ann wrote an address on the back of a Marks and Spencer's receipt and handed it to me.

'What's this?'

'Peter Brown's number.'

'Who's he?'

'I've known Peter for years. He used to look after the Beatles. You can always call him.'

'How do you know *him*?'

'Just do.'

I pretended to my aunt that she was overreacting, but I memorized that number proper. I listened to *Revolver* on repeat for the duration of the flight, and I drank four whiskies to get through the horror of two hours of bumps through clear blue skies, and by the time we landed, I felt like a pop star and a cowboy and a wreck, but I was going to see my sister again. I was going to meet Lisa's baby. The cab rattled over the Hudson and into Manhattan, and I could hear Paul Simon in my head. *Ba da ba da ba, feelin' grooovy* . . .

'From England, are you?' asked the cab driver.

'Uh, kinda. My dad was Texan.'

'Yeah? You sound English to me . . .'

Lisa opened the front door of the apartment block a fraction, then when she saw me standing on the other side, she shut it again in my face.

'Feb!' she shouted through the door. 'Holy crap, baby! What are you doing here?'

'I missed you! I wanted to see you both!' I wanted to laugh out loud.

Lisa opened the door again and looked at me.

'You could have *told* us!'

'I wanted to surprise Diana,' I said.

In the gloom and cool of the hall, it had taken a moment for my eyes to become accustomed to the sight of Lisa. When they did, I noticed the bundle in her arms.

'Oh! The baby!' I whispered.

'The baby indeed. This is Charlie.' Lisa was wearing denim shorts and a white cardigan over a black bra. She still looked like the coolest girl in the upper sixth, but I'd never seen her like this. No make-up. Bare feet on the dirty stairs. Knots in her hair. Caught out. Vulnerable. In that instant, I regretted my decision. I shouldn't have come over without telling her. But Lisa hesitated, then she smiled, and gently handed the blanket and the baby to me.

'Oh!' I said. 'I don't know how to hold a baby.'

'Neither did I. Turns out it's really a matter of common sense. You know. Just don't drop them and you're more or less OK.' She looked at me anxiously, then seemed to soften.

'Come up, Febby, my darlin'. Come up.'

I had followed her feet and their chipped pink toenails up the stairs. The landings were rough as shit; there was a trap containing a dead rat under a chair on the third floor, and Peter Gabriel blasted out of a door on the fourth floor, to the accompaniment of the heavy smell of rotting fruit and old flowers and spliff. On the fifth floor, Lisa unlocked a door.

'Ta-dah!' she said.

I stood there gawping for a bit, still holding the sleeping baby bundle tight to my chest. Her flat was small, but light, and because Lisa was living there it was brilliantly well thought-out, every bit of space utilized — there were books piled on the floor in stylish towers, copies of US *Vogue* and modelling cards were stacked like giant playing cards one side of a desk, and on the other side there was a spotty towel and a neat pile of nappies ready to be used. Bottles for the baby were washed up by the sink in the kitchen where there was a big chrome and red fridge with heavy doors like everyone had in Austin when I was little. I thought briefly of Andrew Adamson and his mother in their new kitchen back when he'd cut Diana's hair off. He'd have loved all this.

'It's so tidy,' I said.

'Yeah, well. You know me. If I'd known you were coming, I'd have trashed the place.'

I grinned at her, feeling that perfect point in the graph where jet lag is merely making you high, not yet at the point where it overtakes the thrill of being somewhere different and makes you crash into the furniture.

'Look at your baby,' I said. 'He's so *nice*.' I laughed at my own words and looked down at him. Lisa's baby. *Eric's* baby. There was something powerful about holding Charlie, a piece of Eric, a helpless little offshoot from the Levi's boy.

Lisa bit her lip.

290

'Are you OK? Did I say something?' I said.

'No. No, it's just very special, Febby. You, meeting him.'

He was so tiny, so perfect, so unaware of who I was. 'He's brilliant,' I said. 'He's so *cool*.' I laughed again at myself, at the absurdity of my own language.

'He's doing his best, that's the main thing,' said Lisa.

'Is Diana working?' I peered around the corner, expecting my sister to walk into the room.

'Oh, Feb. Yeah. She's not here, baby girl.'

'When will she be back?'

'Darlin'.' Lisa looked at me with big regretful eyes. 'She left two days ago. She's in Los Angeles until the end of the week. That casting she kept getting called back to? She got it.'

I stared at her. 'The Calvin Klein?'

Lisa nodded. 'She won't be back here until Sunday.'

Thousands of girls had gone for that job.

'Woah,' I said again.

'The girl's unstoppable. Funny thing is, she doesn't even have to try. Once you start riding the wave, you can just lie back and let it take you. You should be proud of her. And of yourself. No way she'd be doing any of this without you.'

'Without *you*, more like,' I said.

'Nah,' said Lisa. 'I just happened to be in the right place at the right time. She'd have been grabbed by another agency within seconds if she'd set foot in London before I met you both in that funny little shop in Oxford.'

'Why didn't she tell me she was going to Los Angeles?'

'She wanted to surprise you. She knew you'd ring at the

end of the week – she wanted to tell you over the phone. She was going to get them to send some Polaroids to St Quintin Avenue, that sort of thing. Shit. She'll blow up if I tell her that you came out here without her knowing.'

'We can call her together,' I said.

Lisa looked worried. Really worried, like this was something too big for her to work out. She spoke to me slowly, and she really looked into my eyes like she wanted me to understand something difficult.

'Oh, Febby, no. No. She's sensitive at the moment. It'll put her off her stride, I think. Knowing you're here and she's missed you. Darlin', I think we shouldn't tell her.'

'But how can I hide it from her?'

'I just think she'll find it too hard. And this campaign's the most important of her career. Let her do it without worrying.'

'Seriously? I've come all the way here to pretend I'm *not* here?'

'She's a brilliant, brilliant model. She says work's the only thing getting her through the days.'

'*I* could get her through the days!' I couldn't hide the hurt in my voice.

'Of course you bloody could, Febby. But if you're here with me and she's there, she'll want to come back. She's capable of that sort of thing. Throwing a job for you. You know her.'

'*Couldn't* she come back? Could they change the dates?' I said, knowing the answer.

Lisa handed me a sheet of paper. It was the contract for the job.

'Is that right? I whispered. 'Is that what she's being paid?'

'Yeah,' said Lisa.

'*Fibroids!*' I exclaimed, unthinkingly. I don't think Lisa knew that Diana and I had taken her use of the word to such a new place. I went red. Lisa looked at me as though she'd misheard.

'These big jobs don't muck around. They're looking after her properly. She's got someone with her all the time, making sure she's OK. She's talking about buying her own place. With you. For the both of you.'

'Where?' I said, suddenly uncertain. 'Because I don't think I could leave London.'

'London makes her sad at the moment,' said Lisa.

I felt a wave of nausea, like I was still on the flight. I closed my eyes.

'Daniel,' I said. 'This is all about him, isn't it? The worry and everything. It's about him.' Lisa looked at the baby and said nothing. 'Has she heard from him?' I asked her.

'No. He's hurt her, Febby. Really *really* hurt her.' She pulled the blanket over the baby's feet. Perfect little feet, feet that had never yet stood on the ground. Unused little pink and white things, currently for decorative purposes only, so small they made you want to laugh and weep at the same time.

'I thought she'd come over here and get over it. She will, won't she?' I wanted Lisa to tell me that Diana's unhappiness

had an end, that broken hearts never lasted more than a des-
ignated amount of time.

'Yeah, she'll get over it. She's eighteen. You bounce at that
age.' But she didn't look sure of this. Not at all.

'Do you?'

She hesitated for a moment, then handed Charlie to me
again. He felt like a live toy, something fascinating, ingen-
iously put-together, well considered, perfectly engineered.
It was the warmth of him that I couldn't get over, as though
Lisa's kindness and open heart was being handed to me
wrapped in that blanket. Outside, I was aware of New York
behaving like a hangover from a twenty-first birthday party,
pouting and horn-blowing and shouting in the heat and
smoke, but inside that little apartment, the world was all
cotton wool.

'Where's Eric?' I asked Lisa. 'He has his eyelashes.'

'He has his mother's eyes,' said Lisa. She sounded so sad in
that moment. *He has his mother's eyes.* I looked at her.

'Isn't he here?'

'He's still in London for the moment.'

'What? You've just had a baby . . . '

'He's getting used to the idea. He's so bloody young, Feb.
I mean, don't get me wrong. You're young. Diana's young.
I work with people of your age all the time. But Eric . . .
he's a baby himself, but he's a dangerous baby because he
convinces you that he's a proper grown-up in the world
when actually . . . If you don't mind, Feb, I don't really want
to talk about him,' said Lisa. But she started right up again.

'Thing is about Eric is that even though he's young, he's had plenty of girlfriends. I thought he was a good bet because he'd already been around the houses. I thought even though he was young, he might just be all right with responsibility. But it doesn't always work that way.'

I thought of Mama. 'So maybe the people who've been around the houses are still thinking about the houses even when they should have walked away from the houses,' I said.

Lisa laughed. 'Yeah. I guess he's still thinking about the houses.'

Had I ever been a house for Eric? A thought? A possibility?

'For what it's worth, I think he'll be really good at being a daddy,' I said. 'In the end.'

Lisa stared at me. 'Jeez, Feb. London's going to bed. I need to call the office, Vivienne Westwood have asked for three models with blonde hair for a show, and one of our moronic lot has just dyed her hair black and cut it all off. She looks like Manuel from *Fawlty Towers*. Hold the baby for five minutes, won't you?'

So, I never told Diana I had been to New York to see Lisa and Charlie. Never. I think maybe I had planned that one day I would tell her, maybe a year from now. She'd laugh and scream and say *WHAT?!* And I would say that I'd known she was working and miserable about the boy called Daniel, and Lisa thought that she might decide to jack in the job and come back and find me if she'd known I'd flown over as a surprise. I would have told her how Lisa and I had sat and laughed for three days, and I'd shopped for her and she'd cooked, and we'd watch the lights come up over Manhattan with the television on in the background showing the first-ever episodes of *Seinfeld*, and I'd told her about Mama and Daddy, about growing up in Austin and about how it felt to be a twin and she'd talked about work and the madness of the fashion industry, throwing several famous designers under a bus every time she opened her mouth.

'They're all awful,' she said cheerfully. 'Apart from Kenzo of course. He's my man. I bloody *love* the Japanese.'

Indeed, one afternoon she had been distracted by the sight of a scrappy little Asian girl with plaited hair wearing a kilt and DM boots on the street below handing out flyers to some concert, and she made me go down and ask if she was already with an agency. The girl said no, and by the time I boarded the plane home, she was in a casting for L'Oréal. That was Lisa's great gift. She understood what people wanted to see in advertisements, she knew what people wanted to buy into. She was so forward-looking, it was sometimes like being in the company of a mystic. Yet with baby Charlie, she turned in on herself, became someone else entirely. I'd never known deep feelings of love for a baby before, but I couldn't get enough of that good stuff. Imagining how Lisa must have loved him was too much for me.

I'd planned to tell Diana all of this, you see. But it turns out that it's another one of those things that I never got to say to my sister. Another secret I'm holding onto, without wanting to at all.

26

Pop!

Theo was pleased that Ann and Gregory were coming to see Plato, but I think only because the more people there were, the fuller the place looked and the better the impact on Ken Phillips and his record company. I was worried that Theo might think it uncool that they were so much older than the rest of the crowd, but he couldn't have cared less. Plato was his great discovery; his desire to make it happen, to pull it off, was so strong.

'Come on,' he said. He held out his hand and led me towards Plato's door, and I felt Diana behind me, and the crowd parting, and I put my left hand out behind me, like I always did for her.

Like I *always* had done.

Plato was in a mood, pacing around with his Rubik's Cube, his hair huge. He was wearing a pair of pin-striped suit trousers, shredded at the ends, a ripped green T-shirt, and a white blazer spattered with pink paint. He'd streaked the shots of fluorescent colour down his cheeks again, and his eyelashes were thick with mascara. Far from the overexcited retriever that he had been last time he played, he now looked menacing, a hulk, too big for the room, too big for the stage, a giant who had robbed someone on the way back from the beach. He picked up a guitar and grimaced at it, then held it down in front of him like a bat, and swiped the air, taking on an imaginary ball in a reverse sweep.

'I miss cricket,' he said. He looked as though he wanted to stamp his feet. 'Why am I even *here*?'

'You're a cricketer as *well* as a tennis champion?' I asked him, not without sarcasm. I was fed up with Plato's domination of everything.

'Yeah,' he said. He grinned at me. 'I used to play all the time, growing up. With the boys.'

'Go on stage like Gower, then,' said Theo quickly. 'Treat tonight like trench warfare. You can do this.'

'Oh, I know I *can* do it,' said Plato. 'The question is, whether I *want* to do it. Whether I *will* do it. Whether I can be *arsed* to do it. Whether the whole thing will have been worthwhile.'

'Don't be such a child,' said Theo. His Geordie accent became more pronounced when he was anxious. 'Ken's already here. He's with the entire A&R team from JumpJam.'

'Hmm.' Plato sat down and stared at his black fingernails.

'Not to mention the fact that Tracey's aunt's lover is showing up to watch you,' said Theo.

'Much more interesting,' said Plato. He meant that, too, I thought. People in chaos and flux were way more interesting to Plato than anyone who had a grip on their lives. We were interrupted by Angie the drummer walking into the room carrying a cymbal case and a bag of fruit.

'Don't want this to be a late one,' she said to Theo. 'I've got an exam tomorrow.'

'What in?' I asked her.

'Hotel management,' she said. 'I can't stick around forever waiting for this showboat to get unleashed into the charts. I've got kids, you know.'

'Kids?'

'I'm thirty-six next week.'

Ann and Gregory arrived late and stood right at the back of the room; they craned their necks over the crowd and waved to us with no intention of moving any closer to the stage. There was no hope of either of them getting a good view, although you could have heard the band in Texas. Plato's mood had lifted when he walked out in front of the crowd.

'Anyone for tennis?' he shouted at one point and, taking an orange from the bag beside the drummer's feet, he used the guitar to serve it into the crowd. It hit a boy in the back of the room on the forehead. *Not a bad action*, I thought. *Nice continental grip.* But even something as far removed from the game as seeing Plato hitting a piece of fruit into a crowd of teenagers made me feel edgy with the idea of playing the game again. Ken Phillips caught my eye and raised his pint glass at me. The boy who had been hit with the orange

299

picked it up off the floor and threw it back to Plato, who caught it and handed it back to the drummer, who took two more oranges out from the bag and juggled with them behind the kit before throwing one orange down but keeping two in the air as she started banging out the beat for the next song with her free hand. It was freewheeling circus-stuff, it was spontaneous and witty and crazy as the day was long, like Plato himself. It was unlike anything else I had seen; this was something at the beginning, something feeling its way, and all the more thrilling for it.

It was even more high-energy than the last time I had seen him, and the venue erupted at the end of Plato's set – he could very well have been Tina Turner; certainly his hair was as big and his swagger as intense.

'I think he's done it,' said Theo to me. He looked shattered, as though he had been on stage with him. 'If I go and find Ken, you promise you won't run off?'

'I promise,' I said.

'Go and find Ann and Gregory,' said Theo. 'Bring them both back to say hello to Plato.'

They were standing by the bar, ordering another drink. Ann was wearing a lot of make-up, and Gregory looked older than the night before, but he was buoyed up on love and the implausible thrill of the Lovelock.

'What did you think?' I asked them.

'Oh, wonderful!' shouted Ann. 'We couldn't really see anything, but everyone loved it, didn't they? He sounds a bit like Prince, doesn't he? I liked the girl playing the drums.'

'He's a superstar!' shouted Gregory, handing Ann another beer. 'Reminds me of the early punk scene. Lovely stuff. Wonderful. A Misfit Named Plato—'

'*Called* Plato,' corrected Ann.

'A Misfit *Called* Plato!' said Gregory. 'And on that stage he showed all the bravery of the man himself! Not that we could see his face from back here. But who was his Aristotle, I wonder? Who taught him all he knows? It's all very Greek, isn't it? Thank you for uh, for uh, for inviting us.' He bowed his head at me. The way that Gregory spoke was exhilarating and exhausting, like almost-brilliant fringe theatre. It was as though he was continually reviewing his own performance as it happened, while mentally demanding the same thing of whoever he was talking to. Ann squeezed my arm.

'Diana would have loved this,' she said.

For a moment Ann held my eyes in hers. My hand behind my back felt for Diana's again.

'Come and say hello to him,' I said quickly.

'Oh! Backstage!' said Gregory gleefully.

'Can we finish our drinks? We'll come and find you afterwards,' said Ann. Like him, she didn't want to break whatever the spell was. She needed to stay with Gregory for as long as she could without other people. Her mascara had smudged under her eyes, and close up she looked older again too, tired, as though she'd been at a mad clambake that had gone too far, and now she had woken in the middle of a dream to find herself twenty years on from when she had fallen asleep. I wanted to tell her that she should go home soon, and rest, and was Plato's music too loud for a pregnant woman?

I pushed open the backstage door. Through the door that led to the car park, I could see Angie the drummer loading her drums into the back of an old Renault 5.

'You were brilliant,' I said.

She stopped what she was doing and looked at me. 'Thanks. It's a mug's game. If you ever have a child, for God's sake don't let them take up the drums.' She hauled another bag into the boot. 'There's a price to pay for anything that's too fun to start with.'

The rest of the band were still on stage packing up. Theo was talking to Ken Phillips who was drinking another beer. Plato was bending down in a sort of yoga pose, his back rolled down over his ankles, his hair touching the ground. His ripped T-shirt was drenched in sweat, and he held a small pink hand-towel over his face. For the first time, it struck me how physically wearing his performance was. Right now, he had the vibe of a tennis champion. He'd be impossible to beat. Not just because he was huge and strong – that was obvious – but more than that, because it would never have occurred to him to lose. He stretched himself up to full height and took in the fact that I was in the room.

'Feb,' he sighed. 'Well. How was it?' He rubbed his eyes and actually yawned. 'Did you bring your aunt and the man she gets off with in the street?'

'They're coming in a minute,' I said.

Ken Phillips looked at me and nodded again. He was mid-conversation with Theo.

'We think that if we got him to Reading Festival, he'd break through,' Theo was saying. 'And Vince Power is the one who's brought Reading back from the dead. He loves Plato. He was here again tonight—'

'Vince was? I didn't see him. You sure?'

'Oh, yeah. He never misses a gig. He's here. At least he was here. Might have left now.'

Ken looked at Plato. 'Where you from, man? Originally?'

Plato stood up. 'I was homeless when T found me. He saved me. I'd been living in a commune in Slough for years, then I went to Manchester—'

'A commune?'

'Yeah.'

'Did you play guitar as a kid?'

'Nope. I went to gigs when I could. I liked opera. I'd dodge the fare up to London from Slough and sneak into the back of Covent Garden. Verdi blew my mind. I used to—'

The door opened, and Ann and Gregory walked in. Now, backstage in Plato's lair, they looked like two ordinary teachers, navigating a scene they knew nothing about, but Gregory adapted to new scenes very quickly.

'Come in,' said Theo.

'Oh, hello,' said Ann self-consciously.

'Hello!' said Gregory. He beamed around the room.

The expression on Plato's face had altered to one of astonishment, shock, amazement. I followed his gaze, but he was looking directly into the eyes of Gregory Arrowsmith, who in turn was standing stock-still, gazing at Plato in wonder and recognition.

'Doukas?' said Gregory Arrowsmith. 'James Doukas? Is that *you*?'

'Sir?' spluttered Plato. 'Sir!' He stared at Gregory, his huge mouth wide open.

There was a short silence in the room then Plato spoke again.

'Sir! What are you – where did? I didn't know you were – are you? – I just – are you with Tracey, Sir? I mean, February.' He stepped forward, pushing back his hair.

'What's he done to get called Sir?' said Ken, laughing loudly.

Ann laughed too, in obvious confusion. 'Do you two know each other?' she said. I was glad she was the one asking. Gregory took a great big breath. I could see that he was genuinely knocked out, but not as flabbergasted as Plato, whose face had taken on the expression of a child.

'Do we *know* one another? Well, yes! I should say we do! I taught Doukas classics for five years and directed him in *Kiss Me Kate* in B Block! He was quite wonderful!'

'B Block? You were knocked up?' asked Ken. If this were the case, then a lot about Plato suddenly made a lot more sense.

'Hahaha!' Gregory roared with laughter. 'Well, that's one way of looking at it, I suppose. No, no. I *taught* James. At school. I was his tutor!'

Theo stared at him. 'No, no. This is Plato! You just saw him on stage. He's the singer, you've just seen him—' He sounded suddenly uncertain. He looked at me and frowned as though I had somehow orchestrated the confusion. I shook my head at him dumbly.

'Well, I realize he's the singer *now*,' said Gregory, 'but as I said, from the back of the room, he was all hair.'

Again, a silence. Theo found his voice first.

'Small old world,' said Ken. 'Was this school in London?'

'Just outside,' said Plato.

'Eton,' said Gregory. 'I taught him at Eton.'

'Eton? As in, Eton?' said Ann.

Plato laughed, almost to himself, and stood up straight. He grew three inches when he put his shoulders back. I had no idea how he was going to play this. At first, he opted for defiance.

'Well, yeah,' said Plato. 'What of it?'

Theo and I actually gasped at the same time, like at the end of an episode of *Scooby Doo* when the mask is lifted.

'I left years back,' said Plato.

Gregory addressed all of us now. He could sense that this moment required someone to take hold of it and give it the time and energy it so richly deserved. He stepped forward and placed a hand on Plato's sweaty back.

'This young man was a treat to teach, a *dream* boy. Mad, difficult, brilliant — a classicist and an actor, a scholar in Japanese, no less.' Gregory stepped back as he said this and clapped his hands together and laughed in delight. 'Behold

the man! James Doukas! With a *nom de plume par excellence*!
A Misfit Named Plato!'

'Called,' said Ann and I together.

'*Called* Plato,' said Gregory. No one else seemed capable
of talking, so he carried on. 'Due to go to Oxford when
he left but ducked out just before term started, as I recall.
I heard that you were joining your father's company, but
it seems that wasn't the case. You were pursuing other
interests, and quite rightly too. You're a *born* performer.'
He turned to address Ken who was standing next to him,
his mouth slightly open, the beer tilting forward in his
hand. Gregory gulped a bit. 'You still playing – uh – what
was your sport? Cricket? Tennis? You were – uh – a golfer,
too, weren't you?' Gregory putted an imaginary ball as he
revealed this.

'Golf!' whispered Theo beside me, slack-jawed.

'Yes! And Doukas was President of Pop,' said Gregory.

'What's that mean?' asked Ann.

'Head of the cool gang,' said Gregory, tapping the side of
his nose.

Plato looked slowly from Theo to Ken, then back
to Gregory.

'President of Pop. Yeah. Still aiming for that now, Sir, in
many ways,' muttered Plato. He looked down at his feet.

'So, how about the whole growing up in Slough in a
commune?' asked Ken.

Plato looked up at him. 'I did. In a way. The first term,
I was just thirteen. I flew to Heathrow from Athens on my

own and took a train to Slough, and I did that every term after that. Nothing I've told you was a word of a lie.' For a moment he looked like he might cry. 'I never saw my parents from the start of each Half to the end,' he said. He was standing very still and so very straight. Suddenly I could picture him quite clearly in the top hat and tails, or whatever it was that the Eton boys wore, nervousness disguised by bravado. He put the bottle of Stella he was holding down on the table, and he looked Gregory in the face and grinned suddenly. 'Sir, it's great to see you,' he said. 'I would never have expected you here, but now you are, it's – great.'

He turned to Ann, Theo and me and seemed to get a grip of himself. It struck me that he had probably drunk just about enough for this to be exciting and interesting rather than embarrassing and awkward, and in any case, embarrassment and awkwardness didn't come easily to Plato. Of course, they didn't. He was an Old Etonian after all.

'This man changed my *life*,' he said. He spoke slowly, deliberately, with quiet fervour, as though he were being directed by Francis Ford Coppola. He spoke with *meaning*.

'Oh, come *on!*' said Gregory, but he smiled so wide I thought his face might crack. He shooed away Plato's words with his hand, but really the shooing away read like a beckoning on. *Come on! Tell them more! MORE!*

'You were the first to take me seriously, to see something in me.' Plato sounded faltering; his voice shook as though he were articulating truth for the first time, and he hadn't quite got used to the sound of his own voice doing so. 'Every

307

Div with you, from F Block onwards, Sir. You were the beak I actually looked forward to being taught by. Everyone loved GRA.'

'GRA?'

'My initials,' said Gregory, with a sort of bow. 'All Eton beaks are known by their initials. And before you ask, my middle name is Roald, as in Dahl.'

'Beaks?' said Theo faintly.

'Teachers,' said Gregory kindly.

'Everyone wanted you, Sir,' said Plato.

I glanced at Ann, who surely could relate to this sentence more than anyone else in the room. Her hand had found Gregory's, and he was gripping it tightly. He turned to Ann and spoke just to her this time. It was a kick-ass piece of self-direction. Relentless house music throbbed through the walls.

'I got to know James because I worked with his English beak, Angus Graham-Campbell. Brilliant man, brilliant mind. He saw potential in James as a performer and made sure that he auditioned for every play he could get to. But it wasn't until *Kate* that he landed a big part.'

Theo was staring at Plato, his mouth wide open.

'You went to Eton? All this time you've been telling me you have no money, and nowhere to go, but you went to fucking Eton?'

'Of course, Eton's a hell of a brand name. Maybe not one you want to carry around with you in the – uh – in the music business,' said Gregory, with a rare falter in his voice.

'You went to Eton College?' repeated Ken. It bore some repeating, I suppose. 'So, is this whole thing being paid for by Daddy?' he asked. I had to hand it to the guy, he was asking the right questions.

'My father pays an allowance into my account every month, but I refuse to take a single penny from him, so every time the money comes in, I give it away within twenty-four hours. I never have any cash. I don't want it.' Plato had embarked on the truth; now it felt there was no choice for him but to plough on and see what happened on the other side of it.

'Fuckin' hell!' said Ken. He let out a bark of amazed laughter.

'Good for you,' said Gregory warmly.

'Who do you give it to?' I asked.

Plato looked down at his feet, then around at all of us, then up at the ceiling. 'The church,' he said, simply. He carried on staring up at that ceiling, as though the Angel Gabriel himself might appear to validate this information in some way.

'The church?' said Theo, Ken and I together.

'Yeah. The church. What of it? They need the cash. Seemed as good a place as any to give money to.'

The stunned silence in the room meant that a dance remix of 'Real Real Real' could be heard coming from the club.

'So, you give to the *church*, but you're quite happy to take from me?' said Theo.

Ken dropped the last of his cigarette into the remains of his bottle of beer.

'It's the only way it can work,' said Plato.

'You didn't *know* any of this?' asked Ken, looking at Theo.

'I guessed he was unusual,' managed Theo.

'I've never taken anything from you,' said Plato. 'I just thought you wouldn't take me seriously if you knew where I'd been to school, and you knew about my family. I thought you'd give up on me. Ah shit. You probably will now, anyway. Everyone gives up on me in the end.'

What happened next was something that really only happens in books or films, so that when it occurs it's spoken of afterwards as though orchestrated by some sublime alignment of the stars, or by God himself, or through the power of prayer, but at that moment, the backstage door swung open, and a man walked in; a man dressed in black jeans and black boots and a black leather jacket. A man with wavy dark hair and dark glasses, Mick Jagger and Eros rolled into one, carrying a beer. It was him, all right. Unmistakably him.

It was Michael Hutchence.

27

Sweet-faced Youth

'Hello,' he said, stepping into the room. Ken, Theo, Plato, Ann and I all went very still. Ken's eyes shifted from Plato to the lead singer of INXS. He found his voice faster than the rest of us.

'Michael! Hey, man! How *are* you? Great to see you, man!' He slapped Michael on the arm.

'How are *you*, man?' Michael nodded at me. 'I saw the last three songs,' he said. 'Total chance, I happened to be walking past and I had the flyer in my pocket, so I thought I'd drop in.' He bowed at me, and his wondrous hair fell forward. Theo was looking at me in amazement.

'Thank you,' I said. 'Thank you for coming.'

'Great show,' said Michael. 'Hilarious, in fact, wasn't it? Funny and kind of amazing. A sort of pop-comedy mad-show.'

Michael looked around the room again, and his mouth twitched. I sensed he wasn't unaware that he'd walked in on something, only he wasn't quite sure what. None of us were. 'I couldn't make out your accent, man. Where are you from, originally?'

'*That's* the question,' said Theo.

Plato was buoyed up by Michael's entrance; it felt as though weight had dropped off his immense shoulders.

'*Where* am I from?' asked Plato. 'Where are *any* of us from?'

'I've just remembered!' cried Gregory. 'You were in *Comedy of Errors* in C Block, Doukas, weren't you?'

'*Comedy of Errors* is a play about mistaken identity,' said Ken suddenly. We all stared at him. 'My mum liked Shakespeare,' he said. 'Took me to Stratford-upon-Avon every year right up until she died. We'd get the National Express from Victoria. Sandwiches and chocolate cake all the way there, and she'd read me what the play was about on the way. I loved it.'

'It's a play of *doubles*,' said Gregory. 'Can anyone tell me what Shakespeare's trying to tell us about ourselves by using twins in his plays?' He looked around at us expectantly. My God. We were in a *lesson*!

'He's trying to ask us to what extent we're all one consciousness,' said Plato.

'Or, on the other hand, to what extent we are all individual souls,' said Ken.

'Where is the soul in any of us?' asked Theo. I had no idea if he was answering Gregory or not, but it was certainly a comment worth making.

'Very good,' said Gregory. He turned back to Plato.

'I remember you and I rehearsing that final scene from *Comedy* over and over,' said Gregory. 'The twins together again . . .'

The twins together again. And there she was. I could feel Diana next to me. I wasn't exactly surprised. She wasn't one to miss out on a perfectly good drama.

With cat-like agility for one so large, Plato jumped up onto the blue Formica-topped table in the middle of the room, kicking a tube of Pringles off onto the floor, and standing tall so that his head almost touched the ceiling. The table wobbled, but he held his arms open towards us, and he looked down at us. Theo, standing beside me, seemed hot with shock. Ken's mouth was wide open. Plato took a breath and pointed at Gregory Arrowsmith. When he spoke, he *acted*, unashamed, uninhibited, possessing another man's words, as convincing now as he had been on stage just minutes before.

'Methinks you are my glass, and not my brother:
I see by you I am a sweet-faced youth.'

Gregory, not to be outdone, stepped forward towards the table and raised his beer up to Plato, stepping into the role as though he'd rehearsed it all afternoon.

'Not I, sir, you are my elder.'

'That's a question, how shall we try it?' said Plato.

'We'll draw cuts for the senior, till then, lead thou first.'

Every eye moved from Plato back to Gregory, and Jesus Jones carried on pumping in from the club. Gregory held his hand up to Plato. He had inhabited the lines he was saying. I could see, in an instant, how he had influenced Plato at school. Teacher and pupil, they elevated everything in the room with that strange synchronicity.

'Nay, then, thus:
We came into the world like brother and brother
And now let's go hand in hand, not one before another.'

In one swift movement, Plato had pulled Gregory up onto the table beside him, and they stood next to each other, the rich-kid-would-be-pop-star, and the drama teacher in the steely grip of a mid-life crisis. They stood next to each other, and they looked each other straight in the eye, and they laughed. Both fakes, but both as real as real.

Michael started to clap. Gregory grinned down at us and ran a hand through his hair.

'You remember it!' he said to Plato.

'I don't forget anything,' said Plato. 'I could do the whole play, right here, right now. And all of *Kiss Me Kate*, including the dance routines.' He'd lost the fear of the situation now, it was all delight.

'So, are you an actor too?' asked Ken. 'Is this all a show? Look. I'm confused, man . . .'

Theo looked at Ken. 'So, you gonna sign him?'

Ken walked up to Plato and looked right into his face.

'How old are you? You said you left Eton years back. How *many* years, exactly?'

'Fuck it,' said Plato. He looked at Theo, who frowned and shook his head at him in a whisper of movement. *Don't tell him, for God's sake.* Plato grinned at Theo, bit his bottom lip, stepped forward, looked Ken right in the eye and laughed. 'I'll be thirty-three next week.'

Theo looked down at the floor. Ken stepped back but Plato held his ground. Kept on grinning at him.

'Shit,' said Ken.

'Same age as Jesus when he died,' said Plato unapologetically. 'Thirty-three.'

'You've been trying to make it for *fifteen* years?' said Ken.

Plato nodded slowly. 'Well, yeah.'

Ken sucked air through his teeth. Jesus Jones ended and 'The Only Way Is Up' started up in the club, that song I associated with Diana and the summer of 1988, biker shorts and big shoes and four weeks at number 1 as we stomped around Notting Hill like refugees, when just opening our mouths and talking made us tourists, and we had keys in our pockets to a house we barely knew. *Please,* I thought. *Sign him for Theo.*

'You'd better keep that to yourself,' said Ken. 'You're twenty-four again. Go home, work out your fucking dates.'

'Does this mean you're signing him?'

'Oh, yeah. I'm signing him,' said Ken. 'I was always gonna sign him.'

There was a pause. I was going to cry. Theo looked like he couldn't quite trust or compute what Ken had said, like a child being told that, most unexpectedly, his parents had decided to get him a puppy for Christmas after years of begging for one. Gregory, no surprise, was first to recover.

'Whatever you've just said, it sounds great!' he said, and

he slapped Ken on the back with some force. Ken staggered forward and frowned.

'You're in the best hands in the business,' Michael said to Plato. 'Congratulations, man! Welcome to the craziest ride of your life.'

Everyone started talking at once, and Theo rested his shaking head on my chest.

'Don't wake me up,' he said, 'and when the *hell* did you ask Michael Hutchence to come tonight?'

'He was outside Our Price on the King's Road,' I said. 'I never thought he'd come.'

'You didn't *tell* me that?'

Michael Hutchence was leaving, heading for the back route, where Angie and her Renault 5 had long since driven off. I walked up to him.

'Thank you for coming,' I said.

'I was in the neighbourhood, anyway, seeing a friend.'

'Your friend Diana?'

I could hear Plato banging on about Vince Power and the Reading Festival again.

'Maybe,' said Michael. 'She said something interesting to me this evening. She said to me that the problem with most marriages is ambivalence. The ease with which either party can convince themselves to leave, or to stay. I told her I felt the same about being a singer in a rock band.'

Plato marched up.

'We're playing tennis one day,' he said to me. 'I don't want any of your excuses.'

'You've just got a record deal, and you're *still* talking about winning a game of tennis?'

Plato started saying something about unfinished business, and finding a court for the afternoon, and a minute later, when I looked around for Michael Hutchence, he had vanished.

Ken raised a beer into the air.

'To A Misfit Called Plato!' he shouted. 'I must be outta my mind! I don't know if I'm signing bloody Shaun Ryder or Sean Connery!'

Both, I thought.

Theo, Plato and I went back into the club. People were dancing like maniacs around us, and we were dragged back under the wave again.

'Sorry about this,' shouted Theo to both of us.

'Sorry about what?' I said.

'This,' said Theo. He stepped forward and punched Plato in the stomach.

'Ooof!' Plato bent down in agony. 'What the fuck!' he managed, glaring at Theo, bent double like a hurt dog.

'Don't ever lie to me again, you absolute knob,' said Theo. 'I'll support you, I'll work my arse off for you and I'll be loyal to you to the end, but you can't hide that sort of shit from me again. Oh, and next time you get a cheque from your dad, before you file it off to God, you could pay to get the fridge door mended.'

'You're such a dick,' gasped Plato.

'Eton,' said Theo. He folded his arms. 'It explains *everything*.'

317

'Like what?' Plato straightened up.

'Your belief in your own rightness, mainly,' said Theo.

'You say that like it's a bad thing—'

Two girls came strutting up to Plato, boobs pushed out.

'Did you know Michael Hutchence was watching you?' one of them asked him.

'Yeah,' said Plato, recovering fast. 'Not an idiot, Hutchence.'

'How do you know him?'

Plato opened his mouth to spin some bullshit story to them, but he caught Theo's eye.

'He's a friend of Tracey's,' he said, nodding at me. 'She asked him here.'

'He's so sexy,' said the other girl to me. She sounded accusatory.

And on the other side of the room, I watched Michael Hutchence leave the club, and as he walked out, he turned and caught my eye and raised his beer bottle to me and nodded. And I don't know that I'll ever see him again. But that won't matter.

Tonight was enough.

28

The Deepest Point

Ann had left her coat in the club, so she left Gregory and me standing outside while she went in to find it. She glanced at us both before she walked back inside the place, with fear in her eyes, nervous as a fly round a glue-pot. I knew things that he didn't know about her. About them. She didn't want us to be alone together. Not really.

'I'll only be a minute,' she said, reassuring no one, especially not herself.

Gregory looked at me.

'What a strange night,' he said. 'Strange and quite wonderful. Doukas! I really can't get over it.'

'You have to be careful with her,' I said quickly.

He nodded at me. He got it all right.

'Oh, I am careful with her, February Kingdom. I am.' We stepped back onto the street so that a bunch of kids on bikes could get past us. Gregory reached into his pocket and pulled out his cigarettes. He lit one and inhaled deeply. 'Just so you know, in case you were in any doubt, my dear, it's killing me, this whole thing. Killing me.' He looked at me and shook his head so that his hair fell forward over his face. He was happier like that; his eyes obscured from view so that the truth of him was harder to see.

'I'm smoking *weed*, for God's sake – I haven't done that since I was sixteen years old. I'm fucking lost.'

I thought of Mama and what she'd said to me the night that I'd asked her about the Valentine and I said it right back to Gregory.

'Any old idiot can fall in love,' I said. 'It's what you do with the falling in love that matters. It's the action you take afterwards.'

'I didn't *ask* to fall in love with her,' said Gregory. 'It's not exactly been the most convenient of things. I could never have predicted this would happen. I didn't think she'd be interested in me. Not really. I'm nothing special.' As he said these words, for the first time I believed that *he* believed what he was saying about himself. I felt his amazement at the whole thing, his befuddled wonder that someone as brilliant and interesting as my aunt would want to chuck the dice into the air for someone like him. 'I'm nothing great. I'm just an actor who found he could teach.'

'But you get to know *everything*, and you keep some of it from Ann and most of it from your wife. You take away their choice! Her choice and Ann's. Gone. Because they don't know the full picture. You are the only one who knows everything from both sides.' I knew as soon I said it that this was just what had been gnawing at me; keeping secrets from people that kept them blind, looking into a strange dark mirror without truth to clear it. 'That's the most dangerous thing you can do to a person. Take away their choice.'

Gregory pushed a hand through his hair.

'We can't talk about this *now*.'

'Why not? When else? When you've left the country?'

Gregory gave a half-shouted laugh and walked slowly away from the entrance of the club, looking down at the pavement, talking into cement and stone.

'You're quite right, of course. None of it means anything when you're faced with the inescapable truth of one's own deafening cowardice. Wilde knew it, Shakespeare knew it . . .'

I put my hands over my ears.

'She doesn't *need* any more poetry, any more letters, any more words. She needs *action*. One way or another. Shakespeare knew that limbo fucks you up more than anything. *I have no spur to prick the sides of your intent*,' I said.

'God, February,' said Gregory, appalled. 'That's Macbeth plotting murder!'

'But it *is* a form of murder, isn't it? Either way. You murder your marriage, or you murder your pleasure outside of the marriage.'

'Very good, February. Very good.' He nodded, then he pointed one finger at me. 'You're cheating too, you know.'

'What?'

'*You're* cheating.'

'What are you talking about?'

'You're cheating because you're pushing away all the things that you were good at, by assuming mediocrity is enough for you now. Ah. What does it matter me saying all of this? You won't play tennis again until you have permission from your soul to do it.'

'Oh, fuck that!'

'No, no! It's true! Theo frightens you because he makes you feel things you think you shouldn't feel. Doukas frightens you because he's doing what he set out to do. You and I both came to this place as foreigners. Both of us Americans—'

'Well, I'm not American now, not really—'

'Oh, come on. It's in your skin, it's in *you*, whether you want it to be or not. The Texan way of life, the *space*. Don't kid me that you don't miss it. It's a whole different way of thinking. Once you're standing on little islands like these, all battered about by the changing weather—' The wind had picked up, and he pulled his collar up on his coat and shrugged at me.

'I'm from London now. Diana and I decided it!' I knew I sounded tearful and babyish. I choked everything down again.

'But it's not up to you to decide where your roots are. Not really. You can't dig up them up that easily. They're in the soil long before you learn to think. But there are things you *do* have a choice about. Don't throw it all away. Doukas, for example,' he said, looking up at Plato's poster outside the club. 'He's an intellectual, for God's sake! Ha! A great mind. A thinker. He'll work it out, eventually. So will you.' He nodded as though it was all so damn obvious to him. 'Play tennis again, because your bones won't be young and strong forever. Play again. Play Doukas. Play *everyone*! Take risks again. Enter public examinations again. Go to university. Your sister would expect it.'

'You never *knew* her!' I hissed at him like I couldn't bear it, but he didn't care.

'I know what sensible people want for the people they love,' he said.

'Except she *wasn't* sensible! You didn't know her!' I shouted again.

'Oh, stop it! You – you – *child*!'

I felt my eyes popping out of their sockets at him. No one talked to me like this, no one. No one questioned me when I talked about Diana.

'My God! Anyone under the age of twenty needs stringing up for their sanctimony! Their certainty that they would never behave like the broken, fallen adults they see around them. But what I'd give to have the chances you have now! Of *course* Diana would want it. Annie wants it! Make no mistake, your uncle wants it too. *Don't* cheat all of them with self-pity,' he threw his hands into the air, 'or, on the other hand, why not? It's cheap, and it's available whenever you want it. The bloody Jack Daniel's of the emotions. But holy hell, it's lonely.' On the word 'lonely', he pointed at me again, and for a second, I just wanted to run into his arms and sob. *Put me on an airplane back to America, back to the big spaces, and the roots of it all. Buy me a ticket back to Texas. Please.*

'I'm sorry,' he said. 'Jesus. I don't mean to be harsh. I've no right to be harsh. I admire you for talking to me. I really do,' he said. 'Do you forgive me?'

'I'm not a kid. I'm nineteen.'

Gregory laughed.

'Sorry. Sure, my dear. You're nineteen. I forget myself. My God. My mother was pregnant with me when she was nineteen.'

'What if Ann got pregnant? Now? What then?' I'm not sure I meant to say it out loud, but once I had, there was no stuffing it back in.

'I'm sorry?' Gregory looked at me in amazement; no question could have caught him more off-guard.

'What if you'd got Ann pregnant?' I said.

He stared at me, horror creeping into his expression. 'Are you telling me she *is*?'

'No, of course not,' I said. 'I'm just asking how you'd feel.'

'It wouldn't happen,' he said. 'She's never been able to have kids. She told me.'

'That's true,' I said.

'And she's . . .'

'Too old?'

'She's still the queen of the world as far as I'm concerned but . . . hell, this isn't a soap. We're not twenty-five anymore, you know?'

'Have you ever thought about it? Talked about it with her?'

'No!' Gregory almost laughed at me – almost. 'I'd *never* have another child,' he said, 'and she wouldn't want it either. Now? Even if she *could*? Why would she want that? She's a brilliant woman. She's never needed a baby. That's not what this was about.'

'Doesn't matter then, does it,' I said.

A girl walked out of the club and, calm as could be, she took Plato's poster off the wall and stared down at it. Gregory and I watched her.

'You liked him?' called Gregory as she walked away. She turned around.

'Yeah,' she said.

'I taught him,' he said, 'at school.'

The girl hesitated. 'Yeah? What was he like?'

'A gentleman,' said Gregory.

The girl smiled and looked from Gregory to me as though she'd understood everything about us in two seconds. Then she looked down at Plato's face on the poster again.

'He's so sexy and so gorgeous and I would go anywhere to see him.' She said it so dead-pan, I thought she might be joking, but when she looked up at us again, there was nothing but truth in her eyes. She rolled up the poster and walked off.

'Pop stars,' said Gregory, 'somewhere between ponies and boyfriends they lie in wait—' I switched off because now I could see Ann walking back up the steps of the club, emerging once more from the underworld, her coat under her arm.

'Don't jump the gun for me,' said Gregory quietly. 'It's not for you to do that. If the grown-ups around you are going to fuck it up, you have to let them do it.'

I watched Ann and Gregory as they set off down Ladbroke Grove together, his arm around her shoulders, not knowing he had his arm around not one, but two beating hearts.

Notting Hill was queasy with street lamps and the amber glow of cars. Theo and I walked past the tube station and I felt a swell of yearning for my dad, and, sensing it, like he always seemed to, Theo walked closer to me. We walked past Boots.

'Started in 1849 by John Boot, the pharmaceutical store was taken over by his son Jesse in 1860,' I began. Theo just let me talk on, like a loon. And I knew that if I didn't talk, I'd dance or I'd explode, because there it was, that energy, that hit, that chemical explosion in the air between us that meant that as soon as we walked through the front door, as soon as we were upstairs in my bedroom, it would happen. *I just knew it.* We said nothing when we got back, but we didn't need to. I walked upstairs and he followed me.

'The bit between Holland Park station and Notting Hill Gate is the deepest point on the Central Line,' I said.

'Fuck that. *You're* the deepest point on the Central Line. *You* are. *You're* the deepest point. *You* are. *You* are. *You* are.'

He held my face in his hands, and he kissed me, and I pulled at his clothes, and his grey T-shirt with 'A Carrot Frenzy' written on the front came off over his head, and I wrenched off my jeans and my knickers and then we were naked, and lying on the floor, and quickly, quickly, without me knowing how it happened, he was inside me, and moving in me, Theo Farrah was inside me, so quickly, as Jesus Jones carried on playing in my head, and on the rug on the wooden floorboards of my bedroom with the wallpaper of the Chinese men on swings, he was inside me, and it felt like we were rolling in warm earth under some blurry new star, and he covered everything about me with kisses, and he was himself multiplied by one hundred, there were one hundred Theo Farrahs and just the one of me, but I was standing on the edge of myself and right in the middle of myself, and watching every inch of my life open, open, open, and my past and all those slow seconds and those grief-struck slow-as-death nights had led me to him, everything was opened up and held out in my hands in front of me, offered to him like I was bringing something to the altar of Boy London, my Boy, London. My London, my Boy! and I felt drunk and weepy and ecstatic and shamed and glorified and his skin on mine was unknown, unfathomable, temporary and permanent, mine and not mine, and I was an immigrant and a landlord, and a queen and a match-girl, and the two canaries rested in their cage under the sheet and the house stood still and quiet in the street, and St Quintin Avenue stood still in North Kensington, and North Kensington stood still in good old London, and somewhere a dog barked and the Westway hummed low, and we were just two people, but it was all heaven because it was happening, and all hell because I didn't know what would happen tomorrow, and all purgatory because I didn't know why it mattered so much. But I think I know. It's the photo, you see. It's Diana, in her gingham shorts on a beach in Brighton, always tucked into Theo's wallet. That's what I still don't understand.

He was exhausted, there were purple smudges under his eyes. When he fell asleep on my bed, I lay down too, next to Theo, so close to Theo that I could feel his breath on my face as he slept beside me, his hair all chaos, his eyelids and his eyelashes babyish, defenceless. Being next to him, I was being lit from inside. I had never known anything like it; I felt certain he would be able to feel it in me, this burning, this quiet, traumatic flame that had kept me awake at night, hot-faced, unable to eat. The heat of it was in everything. His wallet lay on the floor, but I could feel the page from *SKY* magazine burning through it. I wanted to throw it out of the window, but I knew that I wouldn't. I knew that I would squash it down and try to forget it.

29

The Other Side of the Page

I woke up from sleeping that wasn't sleeping. I woke up from lying still, listening to him breathing. I kept my eyes half closed when he got out of my bed; I didn't want him to know I was awake. I didn't want him to think I was asleep either. I knew that I wanted him to grasp that I'd done this before with boys. Watched them get dressed and leave the room after they'd stayed the night. But this was Theo Farrah. This was him. *Boy. London.*

Once he was dressed, I thought he might leave quietly, closing the door behind him. I thought he might lie down again. I thought he might make a joke about what had happened. I thought he might feel sorry for me. I thought he might be afraid of me. But he didn't do anything. He didn't say anything; he just sat down on the end of my bed with his head in his hands. He pulled the cloth off the birds' cage. Yellow looked at me and cocked his head to one side. I stretched my hand out to Theo's back. He looked at me.

'I have to tell you something.'

No. No. No.

I felt my heart bursting out of my chest. I sat up. Here it comes, I thought. *Assume the brace position. Prepare for crash landing. This is it.*

'You look so scared, Tracey,' he said. He sounded part-sad, part-annoyed.

'I'm not scared.'

'You look scared.'

I reached down and turned the tape over in the stereo, closed my eyes and pressed play.

Bruno.

'And it's down five at number 18 for Erasure.'

There was Yellow, chucking seed out of the plastic cup on the side of the cage. *Don't take away Yellow. Don't leave me without Yellow.*

'What is it?' I said. *Tell me. Just get it over with.*

He covered his face with his hand. I sat up. Stood up. Pulled on my jeans. Be prepared. You might have to run. He's going to serve you an ace you can't return. You can't return anything unless you're prepared. Think ahead. Think. Think.

'I've hidden things from you, Feb. From *you*. From beautiful *you!*' he said.

'Don't tell me, then,' I said quietly. 'I don't want to know.' I covered my ears with my hands.

'No. It's no good.' He sat there, still as still, looking down at his hands. 'Let me talk, will you?'

Theo stood up and moved to the window, looking down onto the street. Everything about him looked *approximate* suddenly, the way he tied his trainers, his hair, the expression on his face, as though he wasn't entirely part of himself, but just trying to be the best version of something he had only ever pretended to be, a cobbled-together thing, not completely true. He looked tired, as though he'd come to the end of something, as though the road had stopped. I bit my lip, and I closed my eyes again. Erasure pounded on. Andy Bell's voice into the small bedroom with the Chinese men on swings in St Quintin Avenue, North Kensington, almost hysterical.

'One rule for us, for you another! Do unto yourself as you would see fit for your brother . . .'

It was all there in the music. I had let myself step too far ahead of myself. I was safe when I was hidden, safe when I wasn't writing, or walking, or trying, or loving. Theo sat next to me and took my hand in his. I pulled my hand away. When I opened my eyes, he had taken the page from *SKY* out of his wallet. He held it in his hands, still folded up. I could see Eric's hands and arms on the page.

'You told me you'd kept the page because you wanted the jacket. I believed you. I *wanted* to believe you,' I said into my hands. I talked with my eyes fixed on the birds. Yellow looked at me, then flew down to the bath on the bottom of the cage. He stood on the side, then he jumped in, his wings flapping,

331

and water drenched the floor of the cage and he looked like he was laughing, happy as a clam at high tide, and for a split second I wanted to open the cage door and show him the open window, because how could he be happy now when everything was falling, how could I help him anymore?

'I did want the jacket,' said Theo quietly. 'I wanted it more than anything. It's true. Look at me, Tracey, for God's sake.'

I forced my eyes up into his face and looked up at him. Still looking at me, he opened up the page and there was Eric, Eric in Levi's, and his big mouth seemed to be mocking me, Little February Kingdom, the girl who walked around listening to Brother Beyond.

'I wanted the jacket,' said Theo again.

'Just *stop* it—'

'No, no! Listen to me!' He sounded angry now. I stopped talking, shocked as hell. 'I wanted it because the guy wearing it was – *is* – my brother.'

He looked right at me now, but his voice sounded like it was coming from a part of him that I didn't know, a part of him that I had never heard speak before.

'What do you mean?' I almost heard a break of laughter in my voice. This wasn't a plausible twist. This wasn't anything real. This wasn't right.

'The model. The boy in the picture wearing the jacket,' said Theo. He handed the page to me. 'That's my brother.'

'But it's Eric.' I was suddenly uncertain of the plain facts. 'Eric Elliot. I told you that back when . . . remember? You said—'

'Yeah,' said Theo. '*Eric's* my brother.'

I felt as though I were being pushed off a cliff. I wanted to hang onto something; a vertigo hit me. It felt like the only answer was to lie down on the floor, to press myself into the earth.

'How *can* he be your brother?' I heard myself saying. 'He's *not* your brother. He doesn't—'

'Because he doesn't look like me, you mean? Because he's not black?'

I said nothing. Instinctively, my hand moved to the volume on the stereo. I needed protection. Protection could come from Andy Bell, good as it could come from anyone else.

'*Your pain is never ending! Just one psychological drama after another!*'

When Theo talked again, he spoke slowly, carefully.

'He's my half-brother to be exact. We've got the same mum. He's eight years older than me.'

'I know how old he is,' I whispered to the floor.

'Well, there you go. Twenty-seven. His dad's called Dave Elliot, he's a roofer from Mile End, so white he's almost see-through. Eric's got two white parents, so yeah, we don't have the same skin colour, doesn't mean he's not my brother.'

'Stop talking like I'm some kind of jerk. I don't—'

Theo held up a hand to stop me saying anything more.

'Listen to me, will you? When Mum got pregnant with Eric, Dave Elliot didn't stick around. He had a family already, a wife, four kids, maybe five — I don't bloody know — and he didn't want another one. Simple as that.

My mum didn't do much better with *my* dad but at least he tries to stay in touch. He's useless but he has a go at being a human being from time to time, you know? Dave Elliot's just a plain and simple bum. But Eric wasn't. Eric was everything his dad wasn't. At least, that's what I grew up thinking, like. So, I tore that page out of that magazine at the time because we were all so proud of him! *Course* I bloody wanted to look like him! *Course* I wanted the cool fucking Levi's jacket. He'd been paid a fortune, and he was my big brother. That jacket was about the best thing I'd ever seen in my life! I didn't know your sister was on the other side of the page, Tracey.'

He turned the paper over and looked at the photograph of Diana. Then as if he couldn't bear to look at her, he turned it back over again. I took the paper from his hand, and I looked at the picture of Eric again.

'All this time, you never even said that you *knew* him when I talked about him?'

'I wanted to tell you right from the start.'

'So why *didn't* you?'

'I can't do this. I just *can't* do this.'

'Tell me,' I said, 'for God's sake, just tell me.'

'Eric was in a thing with Diana,' he said.

'What do you mean, a thing?'

'A *thing*, meaning he was seeing her. They were mad for each other. It went on for six months. Lisa didn't know.'

'Shut up! Stop saying stuff! Stop making things up!'

Out of the window, a robin flew onto the fence opposite.

Free to fly wherever it wanted to fly. Not like my birds, trapped in a cage.

'I'm not. I'm really not making it up.'

'No. I'd have known. How can you say this? You didn't know her!'

The robin flew off again, into the lowest branches of the ash tree on the other side of the wall that separated our garden from next door's. 'She was crazy in love with Daniel,' I said, 'but he'd ended it with her. There's no way she'd have been in a thing with anyone after that, especially not Eric. She wouldn't have done that to Lisa. Never. She wouldn't have done it to me.'

I let him hear what I'd said, what I meant by it. She wouldn't have done it to me because I was her sister, and because she'd known how Eric Elliot had made me feel.

'Yeah. That's the thing, Tracey, that's the thing.'

'What is? I don't understand.'

'Eric and Daniel are the same person. Eric is Daniel.'

I could feel Diana in the room with me, and I saw her lowering her head.

'Eric's real name *is* Daniel,' said Theo. 'He was Daniel until he was ten. Then he started calling himself Eric because he loved Eric Cantona, and it stuck. It was a bit of a joke at first, but those sorts of joke stick around, don't they? He used the name Eric with all his college friends. No one calls him Daniel now, except our mum. And your sister. She called him Daniel. But Eric *is* Daniel. They're the same person.'

'No. You're wrong.' I could hear my voice calm, practical.

'She would have told me. She wouldn't keep this from me. She wouldn't.' But even as I spoke, I knew that she *had* kept it from me. This was shadowy, dark material, this was stuff cut from a different cloth, far outside of how Diana and I operated as sisters. This was a darkness that she didn't want to let me into. Diana and Eric. Diana and the boyfriend of her greatest ally, the boyfriend of the woman who had found her aged fourteen and a half, standing in the window of the Wendy House and had seen something in her face. Diana and Eric. The only boy who had ever kept *me* awake at night, and Diana had known that, too.

'He told me about her,' said Theo.

I breathed in. 'What did he tell you?'

'He had a weird way of telling me things.'

'In what way?'

'He told me things by *not* telling me things. He just said there was a girl who liked him and that she was a twin. He said that he was in way over his head.'

I looked down at my hands. 'Did he — did he love her? Did he love my sister?'

Theo spoke quietly, carefully, his accent stronger than ever.

'As much as he could, I guess. The thing with Eric is that he doesn't know how powerful he is. That's the trouble. When you look like Eric and your sister, weird things happen to you. People don't talk about it much, do they?' Theo looked at me, right into me. It was like looking right into the eyes of a ghost.

'Stop staring at me like that! You're scaring me!' I looked

down at his hands, then up into his eyes again and I knew. I just knew. Theo straightened his back and winced as though he were in pain.

'Go on, then,' I said. 'Say it. Tell me.'

He shook his head. 'Should've said it before. I should have told you before.'

'Say it now.'

'Now's too late.'

'Say it NOW.'

Theo swore. Then he sat next to me, hunched over, and talking down at the bed. That bed. Those sheets and pillows where I'd died a thousand times every night since Mama and Daddy and then Diana had left me, the bed where I'd kept myself hidden until Theo had found me, undone me, translated the night into another language for me and him alone. *Alone.* He looked down at the bed.

'She came to my flat,' he said.

'My sister?'

'Yeah. Your sister. She came to my flat.'

'When?' I heard myself cold.

'It was two years ago. October.' I said nothing. Let him talk. Let him say it. 'She rang the doorbell one Tuesday evening. She was in a state. A real mess. She'd come looking for Eric, but it was me who opened the door. It was *me*. Not him. I'd not met her before, but I knew exactly who she was, first moment I saw her. Eric had told me about this girl he'd got himself involved with. Another model. He'd told me she was going to be famous as she was so lovely, and he says to me that she might show up to my place, so as he can meet her there, like. So, there she is. And she says to me: "You're Daniel's little brother," then she says: "I'm a terrible person." She says it straight, just like that, like something out of a film. "I'm a terrible person." And I thought, yeah, and she believes it, like. She really believes it, poor thing. She's wearing no coat, and she looks so thin, not like one of the models Eric's usually hanging about with, and even though she's my age –' he paused and looked at me – 'even though she's *our* age, she looks like a little girl. It's raining outside. She says she hopes I don't mind but he'll be along soon to meet her. Daniel'll be along. I couldn't think who she meant at first. Then I realized she meant Eric.' He breathed in, and looked up at me. I looked right at him, and my eyes didn't move from his eyes, so that he looked down first. 'We sat in the kitchen and she told me she was Eric's lover. I remember thinking the word was dead weird. "I'm your brother's *lover*." Like it was a calling or something out of the Bible, like. She asked for a drink. I gave her a whisky.' He laughed as though looking back on it, the whisky had been an absurd gesture. 'There was a packet of Alpen on the table. She keeps eating it, pouring it into her hand and picking out the raisins first. Making a pile of them on the side of the table.' He looked at me.

'She hated raisins,' I said, and my voice cracked on the word "raisins" and it sounded so silly, so pathetic, so mad.

'Oh, don't cry,' he said. 'Please don't—'

'I'm not crying,' I said, or I might have shouted it. I *wanted* to shout it. Theo crossed the room again. Yellow jumped down from the top perch to the side of the bath. Theo kept talking, like if he didn't keep talking, he'd never be able to say it. 'She said that Eric had said they'd be safe in my place. Like they were outlaws or something. Anyway, a minute later, there's a knock on the door and there's my big brother and then he's holding her in his arms and she's crying like she's never gonna stop, and he's telling her everything's going to be fine, and I don't know what's happening.'

'And then what?'

'Eric says that he's working stuff out, and that Lisa doesn't know anything about all this. He says that Diana knows Lisa from work, and that it's all a great big mess, but that he wants me to trust him that he'll make it all right. She kept saying thank you to me, over and over, like I'd rescued her. They stayed the night. I didn't question it. I didn't question them. I just wanted to be useful to my brother. It's all I ever wanted to be. Of fucking *use*. To someone, and you know, Tracey, *anyone* would have done, but if it could be my big brother, then . . .'

'So, they stayed with you?'

'Whenever she stayed, they took my bedroom. I slept in the lounge, next to Yellow, but I didn't mind, really. I'd wake up when he started to sing in the mornings. Diana, she'd . . . she would . . . she would . . .'

'She would what?' I said.

'She would always leave me a present. Something to say thanks for having her to stay.'

'What did she give you?'

'Magazines, mainly. Not the ones she'd been in. She thought it was funny.' He laughed at the memory of it. '*Trout & Salmon, Caravan Monthly, Horse & Hound*. A magazine and a bar of chocolate, she'd leave me. I liked it.'

'You liked it because you fell in love with her too?'

'No. I didn't.'

'You expect me to believe that?'

'Well, yeah. I do. She was Daniel's. I didn't think of her like that.'

'She wasn't his!' I shouted. 'She was *mine*! She was *my* sister!'

'I know,' said Theo. 'I know.'

'How long did this go on? My sister staying at your place?'

'A couple of months. They'd stay two or three nights a week. Sometimes more. Then one evening, she shows up, and Eric never arrives. She says to me he's ended it. He's saying he can't carry on because of Lisa, but I could see past that. He's not good with the worry of things, not when the worry starts to overtake the fun of it. He'd got bored of the worry of it, so it didn't make sense to him anymore. And your sister was ... your sister was ... I suppose he broke her heart.'

'And Lisa never knew?'

'Oh yeah, Lisa knew. She told Lisa when it was all over. But Lisa forgave her.'

'What, just like that? She forgave her?'

'She's practical, is Lisa. Then the pregnancy happens, and they go off to New York and the baby's born.'

Charlie. My heart wrenched thinking about him, the smell

of him, that peaceful little animal, that puppy, that kitten, lying on my chest while the city shouted outside the window of Lisa's apartment.

'He's not a bad boy, my brother. He wants to be there for the kid.' Theo sounded defensive. 'Then after they got back, the accident happens, and Lisa shut herself away with the baby. Wouldn't see Eric. Wouldn't see anyone. Won't even talk to him. And that's how it's been ever since.'

'Lisa never *stops* trying to talk to me,' I said. 'I don't want her to. There's nothing she can say. I don't want her to keep writing to me. Tell her to stop!' I could hear a hysterical rise in my voice. I was tipping over the edge of somewhere.

'She thinks you blame her for what happened.'

'Maybe I do!'

'But it wasn't her fault. You can see that, can't you? It wasn't her fault, any more than it wasn't your fault.'

'She had . . . *me*,' I said. 'She had her sister. Why did she need *you* to talk to? Why didn't she tell me? Why did she . . .?'

'She was ashamed. They both were. You were probably the last person she'd want to know.'

'But I would have been all right! I would have helped her.'

'You were crazy about Eric,' said Theo. He nodded at me. 'It's all right. She never told me, but I added it up. And when you talked about him, I could tell.' He gave a short laugh. 'Makes sense, now I know you. You know. Nathan Moore. Marti Pellow. Michael Hutchence. Seal. Eric's like one of them, no?'

'He's just a boy,' I said. 'Eric's just a boy, and Diana's just a girl. She's just a girl!'

Theo nodded and shrugged gently. Like he knew I was using the present tense, but he understood it. He didn't mind it.

'I heard about the accident from Eric,' he said. 'He came running into the shop like he'd gone mad. Face like a ghost. He was out of his mind, like. She's gone, and he thinks it's all his fault. And he kept saying, "Feb, Feb! The twin sister. She's the most amazing woman." And you *are.*'

Christ! I was a *woman!* No one had ever called me anything but a girl before. I felt a rush of something shoot up my arms and into my fingertips, a feeling so strong that I wanted to spit it out: desire, fear, hatred, disgust, love, loneliness – the whole fucking lot of them – colliding in me at the same time and shouting at each other like kids, and suddenly Theo and I were up against the wall, and I was kissing him like I could kiss all of this out of him, like I could understand it through his body, because his body was where everything made sense, his skin was the only safe place in the world to me now. His skin was so hot, burning hot into me, and when he was inside me, he moved like it was the first time and the last time. Beautiful Theo Farrah. Boy, London. *My* boy, London. It was over in seconds. I held him tight into me, hearing him breathing, breathing him in. It felt like it might never happen again.

30

Tell Her to Be Careful

I stood up and went to the bathroom. Twenty-five days again.

The curse is come upon me! I could see my face in the bathroom mirror, high colour tinting my cheeks like I had a temperature. How could my body carry on functioning, continue to know what to do, when all of this was happening?

When I walked out, Theo was standing in my bedroom looking at the birds. He reached out his hand to me, but I didn't take it.

'Eric became obsessed with knowing how you were.'

'Knowing how *I* was?'

'He knew that you wouldn't answer Lisa's calls or letters. She'd given up coming to the house. He said that the only thing that would have mattered to your sister was knowing that you were getting through it. So he ...' He breathed in.

'So he what? Come on? What now?'

'He paid me to check on you, Feb. He paid me to spend some time making sure you were OK. So, I set Yellow free in your house.'

'You *what*?'

'I didn't know how else to talk to you.'

'You did it deliberately?'

'I thought it would force something into happening. Didn't know what. Just knew it was better than nothing.'

'Yeah,' I said. 'Well done on that.'

'I didn't know how it would work out. I went through what might happen. You could have opened the window and set him free again. I'd thought about that. But there was a chance you'd see the notices, and you'd come to find me. That way I'd know if you were all right.'

'What kind of a plan is that? Why didn't you just ring the doorbell like everyone else?'

Theo pushed his hand through his hair. 'I knew that you'd never answered Lisa's letters, even before I saw them all piled up in the hall here. I didn't think you'd answer the doorbell to a total stranger like me. So, there you have it.' Now there was defeat in his voice rather than defiance. I swallowed again. Once. Twice. Then I looked up.

'How much was I worth to Eric, then? To you? How much was knowing that I wasn't about to jump out of an open window *worth*?'

'I called him after I'd given Yellow to you to keep. I told him what I'd done and said I didn't want the money.'

344

'Oh, right. That's very very honourable of you.'

'I never wanted to be part of any of it. But once I saw you ...'

'What did you tell him? Did you tell him I was OK? A bit of a tragic figure, but still able to chuck a tennis ball at an open window if I needed to prove a point?'

'I told him you were a mess.'

'*Thanks*. Thank you *so* much.'

'I told him the truth of it. You'd not been into a shop in months, you'd not been outside, you'd shut yourself away from the world in this house, you hadn't opened any post, you weren't sleeping, listening to Bruno Brookes on repeat all hours—'

'Don't bring Bruno into this! None of this is his fault!'

'I never said it was!' Theo gave a shout of laughter. 'You know this is mad, right? Don't you? You know Bruno Brookes doesn't *know* you? You don't *know* him! It's all jumbled around in your head, the things that are real and matter, and the things that don't.'

'What about *you*? The first time we met, you'd cut your hand, and you cried on the shop floor! In front of me and Ann—'

'Yeah. And I remember watching the blood running down my arm and not even feeling it. Plato was all I had. Imagine that for a minute, will you? Plato was all I had.'

'Plato and the memory of my sister.'

'Yeah! And that! It felt like I was doing something good, you know? Doing something for someone else. Someone needed me. I didn't think for one second that it would turn out like it has. Not for one second.'

'Like what?'

Theo was shouting now. He was pushing his hands over his face, over and over. God, the palms of his hands *broke* me.

'My grandfather had just died! The only reliable man I'd ever known in my whole life! And there *you* were, this girl who'd lost – everything! And . . . and . . . and' – he flinched with frustration at the sudden stammer – 'and that was everything, including all the stuff that made you who you were. Your parents, your sister, tennis, school, hope. Some bit of me wanted you to take away the one thing that I had left after Grandad went. I know! I think to myself: What if she had Yellow? It felt like a . . . solution. I felt the weight of it, you know? What my brother had meant to your sister. Christ!' He put both hands into his hair, like he wanted to pull it all out. 'Sometimes I thought that *I* could've stopped it.'

'How?'

'I don't know! I don't fucking know!'

I thought of Eric, sitting in 192 that snowy night, so completely pretty. Talking to me about Nathan Moore and Wet Wet Wet. Hating himself for loving my sister because they both loved Lisa so much. *Tell her to be careful . . .*

'You found Yellow,' said Theo. 'You and Ann came to the shop. As soon as I saw you, I knew it was impossible to tell you all of this. You were smashed up. It scared me. *You* scared me.'

'No! *You* scared *me*!'

'Well, isn't that enough, then? We scared each other, then we bloody loved each other right after we realized that there was nothing left to be scared of, because all the scary stuff had already happened?' He stood by the window in my bedroom, with the wallpaper of the Chinese men on swings, and his profile was so sad and so lonely, I couldn't bear it. 'I really love you, you see,' he said. 'Not like people just say it, because they like the sound of it and they think it's what they *should* say. Like it's just a line from a crappy old pop song or something. But because you – you – *move* me. You *touch* me. Your sadness and the way you came to see Plato that first time even though it was so hard for you. You moved me. Right here.' He hit his fist across his chest. 'I've never felt that before. Never.'

I wanted to press myself into him and vanish forever, to become part of him, invade his body, get him to heal everything for me, because I knew he could do that for me if I allowed him to. I just knew it. It was the warmth of him I wanted. The heat of his skin. It was the only thing in the world that felt real to me. The only thing.

'Weren't you moved by my sister? Didn't she move you?'

'Ah! She was too like Eric. I can't explain it. I didn't understand her. But you move me. YOU.'

'I don't want PITY!' I shouted at him.

'It's *not* fucking PITY! It never was!'

'But all the time you were hiding all of this from me when I needed to know! How could you?'

He didn't answer at first. We just let the question hang there. He spluttered something, like a mad boy, like he didn't know how to form the words. Then he just threw his arms up in the air.

'I'm sorry,' he said at last.

I looked at the Ted Hughes poems, stacked up beside my desk.

'There is no better way to know us than as two wolves, come separately to the wood,' I said out loud.

For a moment, both of us looked out of the window. On the street below, the wind was whipping dust into the eyes of Kelvin's dad who was mending a window with the radio blasting out Transvision Vamp. I understood it all. I saw it all quite clearly.

I don't want your money, honey, I want your love . . .

I thought of Theo's face when he had looked at the Levi's advert. *Yeah, I kept it because I wanted the jacket.* He was calmer now, but he carried on talking down at his hands.

'Eric called me after the accident. He became obsessed with wanting me to check you were all right. You *weren't* all right. Then I found I couldn't walk away.'

I looked at Theo and I saw him again as I had seen him that first day in the pet shop, turned in on himself, those silent tears for a dead grandfather, and the safe return of Yellow.

'Maybe *you* weren't all right,' I said. 'Maybe it wasn't me who needed someone worrying over me. Maybe *you* wanted someone to worry over *you.*'

Now when he talked, I saw Eric's profile for the first time, and I couldn't think how I hadn't seen it in Theo before. And when I looked down at my hands, I saw my sister, and now I knew that Theo had known her too, that she was more than a spirit-girl in gingham shorts on the worn pages of a magazine, more than a ghost who had loved Theo's brother, a ghost who had loved me. He had known her to touch her, to hear her cry, to hear her talk about Daniel, to watch her sieving raisins through handfuls of Alpen. I heard myself speaking, I heard myself saying something that I didn't know whether I meant but I said it anyway.

'I don't know how I feel.'

Theo looked at me. 'Please, Tracey—'

'You *knew* all this time. You might have never told me. I feel betrayed.'

I don't know that I'd ever used that word before; for sure I hadn't ever used it in the context of my own damn life. Hearing it out loud made me understand the hugeness of the word. I felt the room lit with a new colour.

'I've told you now. You know everything now,' he said.

'Too late,' I said. 'You told me too late. And why? So late. So *late*. I'd have given you anything! I'd give you everything I've ever written, every shot I've ever played in every game of tennis from the first moment I stood on a court! I'd give you – give you – give you – every hour I've spent watching Yellow, every hour I've spent memorizing the Top 40! I'd have given you my time in the arms of Michael Hutchence outside Our Price on the King's Road! There's nothing you couldn't have!'

Theo reached his hand towards mine; I pulled my hand away. I could see Eric reaching *his* hand towards Diana, and her falling into him, every bit of her given to him. I could feel every inch of her sinking into his body, every bit of her giving herself to him, blindly. *Blindly.* Jumping off that cliff, expecting him to jump after her. Trusting nothing but that destructive old con-artist, love.

'Are you *ending* it? Is this the end?' said Theo.

'Ending what? I don't know what this is. How can you end something when you don't even know or understand what the hell it actually is? I thought it was something but it's not. It's a shape-changing thing. I can't hold it, like smoke. Like smoke.'

No fire without smoke. No smoke without fire. Smoke alarms. Alarm at the smoke. They've gone, Feb. The fire. The fire that had a name. The fire that made the headlines. They were in the fire. Both of them. Gone.

'Will we be all right? Will you let it be?' he said.

'Will I let it be?'

'Will you just try to work it out? Try to understand why I didn't tell you?'

I could feel the Trench Effect assailing me. I needed Bruno, I needed the rhythm of the chart countdown, I needed to lie down.

'I need to be on my own,' I said.

'Fuck that. You don't,' said Theo. 'You're the last one on earth who needs to be on your own. You need to *live*. Simple and as straightforward as that.'

'You knew my sister and all this time you kept it hidden. I don't *like* it!' I was aware of that deep, unsettling unrest that I had felt when Diana had her hair cut by Andrew Adamson and everyone had swooned; it was the feeling of losing a game from deuce, it was Diana claiming that she was the one who'd found the kittens, it was knowing that someone had kept something from me. It was Mama and Daddy dying in a fire while I sat at home, waiting for them to come back, not knowing a thing about it. It was an unexpectedly brilliant serve from an opponent, a cruelty, a *secret*.

'Is that it, then?' said Theo. 'You don't like it? I've told you now, haven't I?'

'But it's too late.'

'Only too late if it's you that says it is.'

'I don't like it,' I said again. This time there was a child-ishness in my voice, a fear, an aggression, all in one. I could have been nine. I could have been ninety. It was in me then, and now, and it always would be. Fear of what was around the corner, fear of what was going to jump out at me, like I was riding some mountain ghost train, opening my eyes, from time to time, through gaps in my fingers, only to screw them tight shut again when the monster jumped out. BOO! As I knew the monster would jump out. As it *always* did. Theo picked up his bag and his jacket.

'All that stuff,' he said. 'All that information you've got. All those statistics you come out with. The street names, the history of the fucking railings in Notting Hill, the charts, the quotations, the shit about the tube lines. Ted Hughes and

Bruno Brookes and what's his name ...?' Theo clicked his finger in exasperation, ' ... You know. The Holland Park guy? Walter Cope! Fuck that, Feb! Fuck it! They only make sense if you have someone to talk to about it. You know that? *None* of it matters without that. You want me to go? I'll go. But you don't come after me if I go. It's too hard. Not too hard for you this time, too hard for me. For *me*! That's it. This is it. It's gone.'

From the window, I saw him walk down the street, and I didn't know where he was going, and I didn't know where he would be tomorrow, only that he wouldn't be with me. I could feel the sting between my legs, and I could smell him on my body, the smell so strong I felt it was coming from me. I could hear his voice in my head, but he was gone now. He's gone, and like the robin, he's free to go where he wants. Maybe freedom is the only way for me and Theo Farrah now. It was the busyness of birds that we were envious of, I thought. Their purposefulness. Their confidence that whatever they were doing, like it was the only thing to be doing. Their instinct without doubt.

So I'm numb again. I'm dark again. I'm left again. And in my room, the thing that scares me most of all isn't that I've lost the past. It's that I've lost the one chance I had of a future.

31

Something Between Your Fingers

Robert came back from Edinburgh on Tuesday morning to find the house immaculate. Ann was wobbling on the edge of the earth. I don't think she'd thought the world would still be turning after the weekend, and now that Tuesday was here it felt cold. She picked up the red shawl from Seville; I could almost hear the sofa sighing with disappointment.

Robert had bought Ann a green cashmere cardigan from the Edinburgh Woollen Mill.

'Try it on!' he said.

It was far too big for Ann, who had practically stopped eating since Gregory Arrowsmith had entered her life, and who I knew to have been ravaged by morning sickness. It hung off her. I thought of her new underwear carefully hidden in tissue and boxes upstairs, and the miles of missed communication between my aunt and my uncle gaped oceanic, unquantifiable.

'Thank you,' said Ann. 'It's very nice.'

'Thought it would suit you, matches your eyes. I got medium, but it didn't look like it would be big enough in the shop. Now I see I misjudged your size.'

'I'm smaller than you think, actually,' said Ann, meaning a million things.

'I always think of you as bigger than you are,' said Robert, meaning a million things right back at her.

'Thank you,' she said again.

'Good. Well, that's good. So, how were you two?' asked Robert. 'What's happened?' Diana whispered loud in my ear – so loud I wanted to tell her to shut the hell up.

'I'm going to take my things upstairs,' he said, walking out of the room. 'I'll have a bath.'

Robert believed in frequent swift, shallow baths, like all good Englishmen. I'd only ever known Daddy to take showers; if we were somewhere without one, he would improvise with a tap in a sink turned to full throttle and soap rubbed under his arms. Ann looked at me and then at the cardigan.

'Why did he buy that for you?' I said. I couldn't help it. I wanted to shake Robert for not knowing how far wrong he'd shot with this, but then what was the point? What could he have bought her that would have made a difference now? Freedom wasn't any easier to come by in Edinburgh than it was down south.

'He's doing it to make a point,' said Ann, 'even if he doesn't know it.'

All around me, I could feel the long hours of the day ahead of me. A slow train. *He had gone. He had gone. He had gone.*

'I'm meant to be at school,' said Ann. 'I've got a meeting about the new science block.' She looked around the room. 'Is Theo around?' she asked, as though she expected him to jump out of a cupboard.

'No,' I said.

Ann looked at me. 'Everything all right?'

'He's gone,' I said.

'Gone home?'

'I don't know. He's not who I thought he was.'

'Who is?' said Ann sadly. I think she'd like to have asked me more, and questioned me more, but more than that, she wanted to get out of the house before having to face Robert again. 'We'll talk about it later,' she said.

She left the cardigan on the bottom of the stairs, and she picked up her bag, and she walked out of the house.

The front door closed behind her. Had she run away? I lifted my hands to my face and breathed in Theo again, he was there, on my hands, on the tips of my fingers, in my hair. I could feel the Trench Effect laughing in the wings. *Get upstairs. Get to Bruno. Get to the Top 40. Get into bed. He's gone. He's gone. He's gone. It was too soon for you. Maybe it will always be too soon for you. You're not capable of any of this. He knew Diana. He watched her picking raisins out of the Alpen. You weren't there. That happened without you. You can't control that. It's gone. You can't go back. What were you thinking? Going to watch bands! Walking down the street with a boy who makes you feel things? What things? Mad things! Things that don't make sense. Not for someone like you. Are you crazy?*

I stood up, but Robert walked back into the room, and I saw his face, and I knew that everything was about to change again. I had a flash of fear and strange elation together, just like I had when I'd seen Yellow in the kitchen all those weeks back. Something was happening, because it couldn't *not* happen and there was nothing you could do about it, just like there was nothing I could do about Theo being Eric's brother, and nothing I could do about what he'd chosen to do.

'Ann's left for school,' I said.

Robert nodded, and cleared his throat. 'I found this,' he said. Simple as that. He held a pregnancy test between his fingers, and towards me, holding it out like he was casting a minor spell with a magic wand. The second test. She hadn't thrown it away. Again. *There were no accidents.* This time, the cross showing the positive result was so clearly defined that I could see it from the other side of the room. There was no need to hold it up to the light for affirmation.

'What is it?' I asked, as though some part of me didn't know.

'It's one of those home pregnancy tests,' said Robert. He frowned down at it, then looked at me, and I felt Diana nudge me. *Go on. Speak. You know what you must do. Cover for her. For now. Give her time.*

'It's mine,' I said.

Robert breathed out. He put the test on the table, and

356

folded his arms, and looked at it again, then back at me, and for a split second I believed what I'd just said. Somewhere, on a parallel latitude, this had happened to me, and not to my aunt, and I would have to find Theo to tell him what had happened, else keep it all stuffed in my own head, in my own little body, just as Ann was now, until it burst out into the open and couldn't be hidden anymore.

'It's mine,' I said again.

'You're pregnant?' said Robert. There was a high flush in his left cheek only, as if only one side of him had heard or believed what I had said.

I nodded. 'I just took the test,' I said. A huge surge of adrenalin flooded up my legs so that I felt I could have stood up and taken off like an eagle. I had wings all right. This sort of lie was more than words, it was a cliff-leap, a double-dare to the flyers. I looked down at my hands, and the two of us stood for a moment in silence in St Quintin Avenue, North Kensington, this ordinary street in London full of hard-baked secrets and drunken happiness and carpet burns and truth. Outside, a bunch of kids were laughing as they passed the house, our house with this strange, huge lie set free into the room. I could feel it stretching its wings and circling me. *Well, now what?*

Robert walked over to me. 'Christ. I don't know what to say. I don't know what to think.' He looked down at the floor and said something under his breath that sounded like why isn't your mother here? 'Do you need some help?' he asked. He looked right at me. There were dark rings under his blue eyes, and his forehead was etched with new lines. New lines, new crosses. I closed my eyes. Get upstairs. Get safe. Get away. But when I spoke, I heard Diana talking through me.

'Can we go for a walk?' I asked Robert.

We didn't talk until we reached Holland House, Robert and me. A group of Italians sat on the grass behind us, eating ice creams, and a terrier started a fight with a spaniel puppy, and from some old radio somewhere I could hear Janet Jackson playing and I knew Diana would have danced.

'It had to happen one day,' said Robert. 'But it's like everything. You can imagine how it's going to feel all you like, but you'll never get close to the truth of it until it happens.'

A girl carrying a bunch of yellow tulips and wearing a T-shirt with Prince on the front rushed up to Robert like she knew him, and he swung around to her, startled.

'I'm sorry, do you have the time?' she asked.

Robert glanced at his watch. 'Eleven-thirty.'

'Shit!' said the girl, loud, and into his face. Her eyes widened at him. 'I'm late!'

She turned around and ran off, shouting thank you over her shoulder at him. Robert looked at me.

'Is that what she said to you?'

'What do you mean?'

'Is that what she said? I'm late ... just before—' He broke off and looked down at his hands.

'What do you mean?'

'When she took the test?'

'Huh?' I thought I'd misheard him. He kept right on look-ing straight at old Holland House in all its ruinous glory but his hands by his side were shaking.

'I know her too well. And I know *you* too well, too. That's been a great thing, in fact, finding out that I know you better than I thought I ever would. It doesn't happen very much in life, does it? Realizing you're one step ahead of yourself, simply through the act of investing enough time in someone else's life. It's *her* test.' He reached into his back pocket and pulled out a packet of cigarettes.

'You don't smoke!' I said, like that was the thing that mattered.

'Not usually. I save them for this sort of thing.'

'What sort of thing?'

'Oh, discovering your wife's pregnant with another man's baby. You know.'

I looked at his profile as he lit up, and suddenly I could see the melancholy poet that Diana had always insisted was in him. His face should have been grey with shock but instead it seemed shot through with a glow of something brilliant; it seemed to tilt towards a force unknown, something higher than him, another sun perhaps or Bach, Sir Walter Cope, God himself, but at the same time, the very act of putting a cigarette to his lips made him James Dean. A sudden youth flooded him, and it was like I was seeing him as he had been before he had known Ann, long before he was a headmas-ter, and an uncle. I saw him the same age as me, like a twin brother, my equal. He took a long drag, then he handed the cigarette to me. I took it from him. Sometimes just the act of holding a cigarette is a good thing, it steadies the ship. *You don't have to smoke the thing but holding something between your fingers sure as hell gives your hands something to do.* Daddy used to say that to excuse Mama's habit.

'I employed him,' he said simply. 'I didn't have to. I saw her face when he walked into the room. I left her with him. *I* did that.' He gave a shout of laughter like he had that day in my bedroom when he had admitted to me that Gregory was in love with Ann.

'What are you going to do?' I asked him.

'February. Do you know how old I am?' He took the cigarette back from me and took another long drag.

'No,' I said.

'I'm forty-five years old. Imagine that.' He looked at me sideways with a half-laugh. 'No, you can't imagine it. It's unimaginable when you're your age. Guess what? It's still unimaginable now. But here we are, and I've been around all that time, so we must conclude that it's a truth, of sorts.'

'Doesn't seem old to me,' I lied.

'I lost someone dear to me when I was nineteen,' he said suddenly. 'In Japan. I lost them, you see.'

He spoke as though he had lost them in a crowd, at a crossing, at a fun-fair, as though it had been carelessness on his part that had caused the loss. 'It was the wrong time and, as you know, everything in life comes down to timing. So, there we have it.' He kept looking right ahead at the house. 'I don't go back,' he said. Not 'I've never been back', not 'I don't want to go back', but 'I don't go back'. The phrasing was curious.

'Ann knows it,' he said. 'She knows. I met her just afterwards. She saved me. She provided an answer. A reason. That's what you need from people, isn't it? Validation. A reason to believe you've a right to be in the room. She was clever. The brightest woman in the room. She made people laugh.' He said this last fact as though it were the most important of all. *She made people laugh.* 'Sometimes I wonder whether she's ever forgiven herself for saving me,' he said.

Mama's face flashed into my head. Mama at thirty-six, sitting downstairs while John Lewitt begged to understand the meaning behind her Valentine, which he could never know or understand, because Mama herself would never know or understand it completely. Why she'd sent it, what she was trying to invoke in him, in herself, in Daddy.

'You dismiss the thoughts you had in your childhood, your *dreams*, if you'll allow me a romantic word, as almost completely pointless.' He cleared his throat and held out his hand towards Holland House. '*When I became a man, I put away childish things. For now we see in a mirror darkly, but then face to face.*' He didn't look at me but kept right on staring at the house. 'That was St Paul's first mistake. Putting away childish things and thinking that was the right idea. I'd say hold onto them for as long as you can. Your truth is in them. The very essence of your soul.'

He shook his head and looked down, and a sense of

361

regained embarrassment seemed to set him right again, and he handed me the cigarette with a puzzled look on his face, as though he couldn't recall lighting it at all, as though everything he'd said had happened outside of him. Still, he went right on looking at the house.

'They say he died of a broken heart,' he said.

'Who did?'

'Sir Walter Cope.'

A wind picked up. I could feel my heart aching.

'Was it a woman?' I asked him.

Robert shook his head.

'A man?'

'His brother. Within a month of his brother's death, he became ill. It was quite sudden. According to accounts at the time, he didn't want to go on living without him.'

I swallowed hard. 'Yeah, well, that's what happens.'

'Not necessarily. It's what *can* happen. Not to you. You owe her too much. You owe yourself too much.'

'I've got nothing!' I said. I wanted everyone to hear, the Italians eating ice cream, and the dogs, and the girl in the Prince T-shirt who'd asked for the time, kids in the adventure playground and the hot blue and white skies of West London, and the dusty fading pink roses, and old Sir Walter Cope with his broken heart, too. I wanted them all to know it. *I've got nothing.* And Robert didn't tell me that it wasn't true. He didn't look at me and say all the things that people say when they want to make you feel better. He just nodded, and he held out a hand, still looking straight ahead, and I took his hand in mine. He squeezed my hand tight, like I was twelve years old.

'We've got tomorrow,' he said.

I laughed right out loud because I couldn't help it. It was the unexpectedness of hearing Robert talking like Diana would have talked, like something from a Molly Ringwald movie, but spoken with such total conviction that it came out like Walt Whitman.

We went back to St Quintin Avenue together. Just before we walked through the door, I asked him what I had to ask him.

'Are you going to leave us? Are you going to leave her?'

He didn't answer. In desperation, I turned my head up to the sky.

'The point between Holland Park Avenue and Notting Hill Gate is the deepest point on the Central Line,' I said.

He turned his key in the lock, and we walked back into the house. Ann was in the kitchen. She'd poured herself a glass of red wine and she'd pulled off her shoes so that she was barefoot. Her pink nail varnish had chipped off her big toe. She looked up when she saw us.

'Ah,' she said. 'You're back.'

Robert walked up to her, took the glass from her, drank. When the glass was empty, he walked over to the sink and washed it. Dried it properly on the tea-towel with Hampton Court and Henry VIII's wives on the front, with the saffron stain on Catherine Parr's face from Theo's cooking on the weekend, and the rip through Anne Boleyn's dates. Then

Robert opened the cupboard door above the cooker and put the glass back, like it had never been taken out in the first place. He turned back to Ann.

'Just tea for now,' he said.

She looked at him, expressionless.

'Is that it?' she said. Her voice trembled.

'I think it's all we need for the time being.'

'You're still here,' said Ann.

'I am,' said Robert.

'He's going back,' blurted Ann. 'He was never going to stay.'

Robert picked up the paper and a pen and put on his glasses. He sat down, and he stared into the square of the crossword. Ann walked past him, but he reached out his hand and caught hers. She stood still, held by him, his eyes down on the printed page.

Sometimes I wonder if she's ever forgiven herself for rescuing me.

I walked up to my bedroom, with the wallpaper of the Chinese men on swings, and Kate and Yellow in the cage with their nest and their little blue eggs, and I shut the door.

32

Gone

After two weeks, one of the eggs hatched, but the baby bird inside the egg didn't live. It made it out of the nest, but it couldn't seem to feed. It was as though the effort of struggling from the shell had made it impossible for it to do anything more than that; it had taken everything, all its energy, just to break out. I took the featherless creature from Yellow and Kate, took it out of the cage, and I wrapped it in a box, and I buried it at the bottom of the garden. I didn't cry. Theo had known my sister and he hadn't told me. He was Eric's brother, and he had kept it from me. What was there left to cry for? Beside the dead bird sat the two other eggs, but when they hadn't hatched three days later, I realized they never would. I buried them too.

Maybe it had all happened too soon. Yellow, Kate, Theo. They came into my life before I was ready for them. At least, that's what I tell myself. It's a good thing he's gone. In his own way, he was part of the dust falling after Diana had gone, it was all part of the dust. You take someone into your life at your peril. You make your decision to do that thing, to think about them, to care whether they've shown up somewhere, and once you've jumped off that bridge, you've got to remember that it was you who allowed yourself to jump. I wasn't pushed. I did it because I wanted to. Peace isn't there for everyone. But when I lie in bed, and I reach for the Top 40, and I hear Bruno, I know that with Theo Farrah I'd walked like I had purpose and intent, and I'd been to the Lovelock, and I'd handed a flyer to Michael Hutchence on the King's Road. I'd got close to fooling people into thinking that there might be a chance I could make some kind of a life for myself. Now I stay safe in the bedroom with the Chinese men on swings, and I look at the birds, and I think this is it now. Ann is alive because she's right in the heart of a damn crisis. Robert's alive because he wants to rescue her. Perhaps they can get up every day because they're grown-ups. Who taught them that? The telephone and the doorbell ring, and the post drops through the letterbox, and Kelvin's dad carries on building. They're the only things I care about now. The hatching of the new flyers. I spend hours watching them, all concentration on them, because what else is there?

His imprint is on everything. When I walk upstairs, it's the first time he walked up to my bedroom, and Ann's asking him about *Little Women*. I see his white trainers just ahead of mine on every step of the pavement on St Quintin Avenue, his long fingers holding cans of Coca-Cola. In my bedroom, when I look at the canaries, I see Yellow and Kate how he saw them. It's his laughter breaking over Bruno's voice, as he punches the pause button on my stereo. Most of all, in my bedroom, with Diana's T-shirt under the bed, I ache for his body, and I wonder whether I could just go on with that alone, with borrowing him every night, and in the morning, he could vanish again into the air, and it might just be enough. I hear his voice over the sound of the Top 40. *I've never been a fan of inner beauty myself ... Do you want a Coke? It's not a fucking trick question, Tracey ... You're the deepest point on the Central Line. YOU are.* Then comes the line that I hear loudest. *I've hidden things from YOU. From beautiful YOU.* I lie here and I wonder if anyone gets through life without hiding things from people, and why the hell we always end up hiding things from the people we never wanted to hurt, and I wonder if some people will always be the hiders, and some will always be open wide up for anyone to read, who end up feeling as dumb as a box of rocks for believing in things, for believing in *something*, for believing in *anything* that might make life worth waking up for. Now here we are, Robert, Ann and I, all on a thread in St Quintin Avenue, but he's gone.

The days edge closer towards the summer holidays, and still I stay here, with Yellow and Kate, and their empty nest, and their babies buried in the bottom of the garden. Ann and Robert are quiet, they communicate gently, they ask no questions of each other, and I ask nothing of them, but I know that last Tuesday, Gregory Arrowsmith left for New York. Ann's calmer now he's gone, but I don't know if she'll ever stop aching for that night when we sat outside, and he told us how much he loved her. I wonder how Plato is, and when he and Theo are coming back, but I know that it won't matter because too much is altered now. Everyone will move on, and although there's a letter to Texas on my desk, telling people on the other side of the Atlantic that I want to join them, I don't know that I'll ever send it.

33

Pretty Yellow Things

Yesterday afternoon, Ann walked upstairs to my room and dropped *Smash Hits* on the end of my bed, and she didn't walk out again.

'Page five,' she said. She folded her arms and looked at me. There was still no sign of her pregnancy; she still looked so thin you could snap her in two. I didn't move. I felt her patting the magazine softly, like it was a sleeping dog she didn't want to wake. I kept my eyes closed, waiting for her to leave the room. 'Page five,' she said again. I kept still. 'Page *five*, Feb,' she said for a third time. Again, no reaction. If I didn't react, she would go. I was sure of it.

'Plato's being interviewed. He's in the magazine. He's being *interviewed*.' She gave a sudden explosive, delighted laugh. I took a great intake of breath and I swallowed hard. I heard Theo talking to me, that first time he'd been up to

369

my room. *He'll be in Smash Hits before the end of the summer. I promise you that much, Tracey.*

'Don't you want to see?' I heard her opening the magazine and flicking through the pages. 'Look!' Still, I gave her nothing, although my heart was leaping around like a catfish on a line.

I heard her shutting the door behind her. I straightened my legs out and I heard the magazine dropping to the floor and I felt Diana beside me.

Open it, she said. *Go on. Open it. Don't be an idiot, Feb.*

I reached down and felt the pages silky thin in my hands. *Page five. Page five. Page five.* The picture of Plato only covered a small square of the page, but it was him all right.

He's tall! He's 'mad'! He went to a snoot-school called 'Eton'! He thinks he's going to be bigger than the Stone Roses!

Who was your first best friend?
I had an imaginary friend called Lord Marmaduke Peters when I was six. He wrote to my parents and told them I'd been kidnapped and demanded a ransom of sixty pounds. I thought that was what I was worth. They never paid up. Hahahaha!

Do you believe in spontaneous combustion?
What kind of a question is that? Yes. Of course. I've combusted five times already this week. I combust all the time. Doesn't everyone?

If you had to win at something to prevent yourself from being jailed for a hundred years, what would it be?

I'm good at tennis so probably I'd play a tennis match. There's someone I need to play a game with. We agreed to play on July 8th in Notting Hill but I'm pretty sure she won't be there. She's too scared of me. She knows I'll beat her. Hahahahaha!

A 'Misfit' called 'Plato'. He's a fortnight's fun in one!

Had Theo been there when he was interviewed? Had he set this up? Had he thought of me reading this, in my bedroom, with the Chinese men on swings, after he'd promised me that it would happen? I read it again. And again. July 8th. It gave me some time. I called down the stairs to Ann.

Then slowly I stood up. I crossed the room and I glanced in at the birds.

Another egg. They were laying eggs again. Just as beautiful, just as perfect, just as fragile as the last ones had been. Same nest. Same parents. New eggs. They'd failed and they were trying again. Diana stood beside me, I felt her watching the birds. I heard her voice. *You have to play. Play again. Play again.* Shaking, I crept from the bedroom, and I opened the cupboard under the stairs and brought out the racquet that I hadn't used since the last time I'd played. It was a Head racket, and I had bought it from a girl who'd been two years above me at school, a short while before Diana had died. The racquet still had her nametape stuck on around the handle. Jacinda Hawkins. I felt it firm in my hands. I would play against Plato in a few days' time because *what was the alternative?*

I carried the racquet back to the bedroom, and I pulled my hair up off my face and looked in the mirror, holding the racquet up beside me, and when Ann walked in, she stepped back again, as though frightened.

'It's OK,' I said. 'I'm going to play him.'

'You must tell Theo, then,' said Ann. She turned away; I could see her fighting tears.

'I'm not doing it for Theo,' I said, and as I said it, I realized it was true. I wasn't doing it because I wanted him to be there. I wasn't doing it because I wanted him to see me being good at something or winning. I was doing it for me, and for my sister, and for Ann.

'Come here, Feb,' said Ann.

I followed her into her bedroom. She held out the Japanese book that she had first shown me all that time back. It looked different to me now; it looked explosive, salty.

'You once told me Plato speaks Japanese,' she said.

'Plato says a lot of things.'

'Worth a try, though, isn't it?'

I looked at her, understanding what she meant. She pushed the book into my hand.

'You want me to ask Plato what this says? To translate it?'

'I need to know. It's been on my mind for too long.'

'You could have asked anyone, at any time to translate this for you.'

'You think I don't know that?' My aunt looked at me with incredulity, so like Mama.

'Why now?' I asked her.

'Why *not* now? It's important.'

'And it wasn't important before?'

'It's always been important. It just hasn't always been necessary for me to know *why* it's important.'

I felt Diana next to me. She shrugged. She didn't know what to say any more than I did. 'But I can't just *take* it – what if he notices it's gone?' I said.

'Gone' is one of those words I can't make sound un-American. I heard Grandma Abby's voice in mine, and I almost laughed out loud at hearing her in me. *Whadif he notices it's ghan?* What was it Gregory had said to me about being from Texas? *It's in your skin, whether you want it to be or not.*

'Most private things aren't private,' said Ann. 'Every time someone picks up a pen to write, they do so imagining others reading.'

'They could never have imagined Plato,' I said.

'Robert wants me to know something now. I need to know what that is.'

I put the book into the bottom of my bag.

I guess a lot of people read *Smash Hits*, and I guess Plato had a lot of people interested in him. There was a crowd of fifty or so hanging around outside the gate of the court. I walked past them carrying my racquet and they parted for me, at speed.

'Hey!' I shouted, seeing Plato in the garden beyond. 'You ready?'

'Oh my God, he's coming over! Can you ask him to come and talk to us?' begged one of the girls.

Plato loped across the garden towards me. Seeing the crowd at the door, he stared in surprise. One of the girls waiting to come in spoke up, breathless.

'Oh my God,' she said. 'It's actually you! We read you were going to be here today. We followed you here from the station.'

'How creepy!' said Plato delightedly. He looked at me sideways. 'Tracey-July,' he said. 'I see you've come dressed for a fight.' He bent down and read the nametape on my tennis racquet.

'Jacinda Hawkins. How many names do you have, for God's sake?'

'We saw you at the Lovelock last week,' said one of the girls. 'We're coming again this weekend. We think you're amazing. You're a genius. You're like Prince.'

'I'm taller than Prince,' said Plato quickly.

'Yeah. You're the tall, London version,' said the girl breathlessly.

'You're just so *real*,' said the other girl. 'You're so *real*.'

'Very kind of you,' said Plato. 'I can only say that none of it is achieved without agony, loss, heartbreak and sacrifice, but nothing worth fighting for *is*, wouldn't you agree?'

'Are you playing tennis with her?' asked one of the girls, nodding at me.

374

'She has a name. God knows what it is, but she does. And yes. Yeah. We are. Grudge match.'

'What's the grudge?' asked the girl.

'He thinks he can beat me. I know he can't,' I said. It was the sort of joke I would have made for my friends before I had played in the past. It felt utterly disingenuous now, when I could barely imagine standing on the court, let alone winning a single point against Plato.

'Ha!' he said hotly.

'Can we watch?' asked the girl.

It was a bold question, but Plato wasn't an idiot. Having spectators on his side was what he was used to; he needed a crowd for just about everything.

'Sure thing,' he said. 'Only this is a private garden. No pissing around.'

The kids couldn't believe their luck. He opened the door for them, and they scuttled through, and Plato nodded at me. It was Alice in Wonderland time: new-mown lawns, explosions of red, pink, white and yellow roses, discreet gravel paths, a couple of terriers chasing a ball, three statues of nymphs in various stages of undress, a couple of wooden huts, all framed by those famous stucco mansions and black cast-iron railings. Planes flew low towards the west and Heathrow, and at the far end of all this fantasy, a tennis court. *We agreed to play on July 8th in Notting Hill'* he had said in *Smash Hits* and yet I couldn't ever remember agreeing to it. How had these kids known where the court was? Known where to find him? I guess if you're that obsessed, you know how to get answers. I felt my legs weaken. I couldn't do it. Plato was wearing red shorts and a red headband, and his white T-shirt was already patchy with sweat. He pulled a packet of Extra Strong Mints out of his pocket and offered me one. Tossing one into his mouth, he lit a Silk Cut.

'Menthol,' he said, sucking on the fag and the mint and nodding at me. 'I think I'm getting a cold,' he said.

'That's the chain-smoking talking,' I said.

'Theo kicked me out, you know.'

'Kicked you out?'

'Yeah. He said that I could bloody well get my own place. He thinks we'll work better if we're not living together.'

'He has a point,' I said.

'Ah no. This is how we suffer, us Eton boys. This is what I *knew* would happen if he knew about it.'

'I don't think it's the fact that you went to Eton, I think it's the fact that you hid it from him, pretended you had nothing, but kept throwing out money to people on the side,' I said.

'Yeah, well. There were things he didn't tell you, I think too, weren't there, Tracey-November?' I said nothing. How much Plato knew about everything remained a mystery to me. 'Right. I should be done with this game in about twenty minutes, if you want to book your cab home,' he said.

'Cab? Not all of us are made of money.'

'Sod off, Jacinda Hawkins.'

Plato's fan club positioned themselves down his end of the court, spread out on the grass. They immediately lit cigarettes; one of them started rolling a joint.

'Could you do something for me before we start?' I reached into the bottom of my bag and handed him the book.

'What is this?' said Plato.

'You learned Japanese at school, didn't you?'

'Yeah. What about it?'

'What does this mean? What's the writing inside this book?'

Plato frowned and looked at the spine, then at the front.

'Well. It's Mutsuo Takahashi for a start.' He looked at me as though that should make sense to me.

'Who was he?'

'Famous Japanese poet? He was a homo-eroticist.' His eyes bore into me. 'Do you even know what that means, Chris Evert Lloyd?'

'Shut up. What does the writing in the front say?'

'Christ alive,' Plato peered at the writing. 'It's not easy. I haven't exactly kept up the Japanese. Kind of hard to keep it up over here.'

'So, you don't know what it says, then?'

'No, I *didn't* say that.' He looked annoyed. He frowned at the foreign shapes, the strange drawings, the Kanji that was simultaneously as enigmatic as cave pictures and as sophisti-cated as computer coding.

'I think it translates as "I will never forget. With love from" – this is hard, give me a second – "with love from" – yes, that's it – "pretty yellow stuff".' He shook his head. 'No. no, no. "Pretty yellow *thing*." Ha. A Japanese man wrote this, and he's calling himself that. Do you think he meant that to be funny?' He was mumbling now, as though not confident in what he was saying, working through it in his head. He turned the book over in his hands again, then flipped it open once more. Mercurial as light, I could see him in a classroom at school, immersed in the learning, determined, refusing to let anyone else know more than him. *He's a thinker and an intellectual,* Gregory had said to me. I could see it now, for the first time.

'Who does it belong to?' Plato asked me, delivering curiosity as an accusation.

'I found it at home. That's all.'

I didn't trust Plato with information that he might store and use to his own advantage.

'That's right,' he nodded to himself slowly, 'the "yellow" written there probably refers to "cowardice",' said Plato.

'What do you mean?'

He sighed at me as though frustrated that I couldn't keep up with him.

'In basic terms, Tracey-November, this is one of the most famous collections of poems ever written for, to and about gay men. The great love between one man and another. Or the great heartbreak of one man when another man doesn't love him back.'

'If you were a girl, you wouldn't give this book to the man you loved?' I asked him.

'Look, Tracey-July. I *know* that this book wasn't given to anyone by a girl,' said Plato.

'How do you know?'

'It's obvious. It was given *to* a man, *by* a man.'

Given *to* a man. *By* a man. Given to Robert. I looked up. A plane, high in the sky above us, looked to me like no more than a plaything. Where was it going? To Tokyo? To Edinburgh? Or perhaps to Austin, Texas? Maybe it didn't even matter where it was going. What did anything matter, except for the action of movement itself, of flying? Plato looked up and then back to me. I thought of Robert, and I wanted to weep for him.

'Now look. Don't go around talking about me translating Japanese poetry in my spare time, will you? Get a grip, please. Aren't we here to play tennis?'

'Yes,' I said.

'Well, come on then.'

34

Court

Standing on the grass court felt dreamlike. Plato's fan club had been joined by a few of the other people who held a key to this little piece of hidden glory behind black railings in Notting Hill. Two young girls, surely sisters, helped each other off with their shoes and socks so they could run under a sprinkler.

'Hurry up!' one of them said to the other with that unmistakable impatience that came from years of waiting for another, slower sibling. Oh, Diana. What I would do to have one more afternoon of waiting for her, of showing her the right way, of helping her, of being of use to her. Plato handed me a can of tennis balls, and I opened them, and the smell knocked me out. New yellow balls, yellow balls new hatched. I shoved the balls in the pockets of my shorts, and we started to knock up, to hit balls to each other with some sort of purpose. The first ball I hit went into the net. Plato's fan club, progressively more stoned, and out for my blood, started to whoop.

I hit a ball to Plato. He hit it back, and hard. I swiped at it, and once more, into the net. I felt that familiar rise of anxiety and fury, that horror that had infected every game I had ever played. *Keep sane, keep steady.*

'Shall we start?' he asked me. I would like to say that Plato could see that this was difficult for me, and that he wanted to make sure that I was all right, but it just wasn't in him to behave like this. I had told him that I played tennis, he had challenged me, and now he wanted to win. I felt dizzy. *Diana*, I thought. *Diana.* I stared out to the left of my court, the side where she used to sit, but she wasn't there. There was no sense of her, no sense of her anywhere. I watched Plato picking up the ball and serving to me, and suddenly I felt something shift in my bones. I thought of Yellow and Kate and of Theo and me, watching the birds and laughing, with the sound of the street drifting in through the windows of a house built in 1890, a house that knew far more than it was letting on about everything. That knew far more about all of us than we would ever know. I clicked into a place that I hadn't been since Diana had died. I brought back my arm, my hand tight as all hell on Jacinda Hawkins's racquet, and I smashed it back over the net. Plato stretched to reach it, but he couldn't. But oh, dear God. It was tennis. Tennis, that moodiest of games. Tennis that had pushed me over the edge time and time again. One point won meant nothing.

One point won meant a whole load more that could be lost. I always felt like a cartoon character, running off the cliff and out into the sky beyond with confidence and concentration, and not falling until I looked down and realized I was defying the laws of gravity. You could keep going as long as you didn't look down, but once you did, you were finished. I made the mistake of looking down in that first match with Plato. I made the mistake of overthinking it.

From then onwards, it was a fight to the death. Plato was a good, good player, and he was stronger than me, and he was a man, for God's sake; he seemed double back-boned. I hadn't often played against the boys on the circuit, and when I had, I'd been too shy to play in the way that I had wanted to. Now I had to shove all of that into history; I had to play in a way that I never had before. Plato's size meant that he served like he was imitating Becker, all that weight and height and power which meant that when it worked, he was lethally difficult to return. Fortunately, it didn't work all the time, and when it didn't, I went for him. Plato had the advantage of being turned on by a crowd, and when I won the first game, he started making a lot of noise, shouting furies at himself, roaring down at his hands after every point lost, like we were on Centre Court at Wimbledon. Yet I felt it wasn't real, it was all a show. I realized, as I collected the balls to serve, that although Plato wanted to win, it was all about the performance. If that was good enough, the end result didn't especially matter. If I could stop the performance, I could stop him.

I served in the way that I always had done, as though it were the only thing that mattered on the planet, and the feelings that ran all through my body, from the top of my head right down to the ends of my toes, were the same feelings that I had felt when I used to play as a child, then as a teenager. It became life and death, it became a conductor for every single thing that was happening in my life; it became my enemy, my only friend, my nemesis, my swagger, my shame. I lost the second game, and the third, and I felt that swelling feeling inside me, the sense that if I didn't win, everything was lost. *Tennis is a moody sport.* Diana used to say she was glad she didn't play it. Glad her poor eyesight had denied her the chance to race around hitting a ball like a loon. I was glad for her too. If I struggled with my temperament where tennis was concerned, Diana would have obliterated herself, not least through an overanalysis of the language. All those words that seemed to represent so much more than just their meaning on the court. *Serve, love, fault.* It was all back with me now, and although I fought it, the feeling was in me that if I didn't win, everything would collapse. That magical thinking that had overtaken me that awful day that Diana had gone. I felt the pain in my side, the old injuries returning and edging their way out of my body again. *Woah! You're really doing that thing again?* There it was; the pain from my left ankle when I sent a backhand across the court, the swell in my right wrist as I served. Was it worth it? Who was I proving anything to, anyway? Daddy, I think. Daddy, who had watched me play from the time that I could barely hold a racquet. Daddy, who had known me for what I was, and loved me all the same.

I lost the first set. Only just, but it was a loss all the same. Plato came to the net to shake my hand.

'You're very good,' he said. 'Very, *very* good. It's always a shock when someone says they can do something, and then they actually *can*.'

'Don't patronize me,' I said.

'I'm not.' He looked at me with something he'd never looked at me with before. It was some form of respect, I suppose, although with Plato it was always hard to tell.

'I wish he was here,' I said to him.

Plato nodded at me slowly. 'He's at the pet shop. Clearing up. It's his last day.'

'He's leaving?'

'You think he still needs to be fondling gerbils when he's managing a pop star?' He snorted with laughter and looked at me sideways.

'You *are* a pop star. You're in *Smash Hits*—'

'Well, we all have to start somewhere.'

'You talked about this match in your interview.'

'Yeah. Knew you'd read it. Thought it would get you out of your bed.'

'But he's not here,' I said. I needed to say it out loud to Plato almost as much as he needed to hear it from me.

'The whole point of this was to show off in front of him,' said Plato. 'For you, and for me. For both of us. Pathetic really if you think about it.' He paused and nodded at me. 'I know what happened,' he said. 'He told me everything.'

I shrugged at the ground. 'It's been hard,' I said.

'Yeah, well. He knew you'd show up today. He wants you to win. He said to say good luck, the disloyal bastard.' He looked at me carefully.

'I told him I couldn't see him again.'

'Well, that's that then.'

'What do you mean?'

'From most people that would be the kind of overblown crap that means nothing twenty-four hours later. But it's from you, so you probably mean it.'

'What does that mean?'

'You say things like you mean them. You're a . . . serious person. So's he.'

I said nothing. I wanted to say that I'm a serious person because when you've lost all that I've lost you have no choice but to be serious about stuff, but that all I ever wanted to be doing was walking down the street and laughing with Theo. Plato read my mind.

'GRA – Mr Arrowsmith – used to go on about this at school. Tragedy is a clear ending. You know where you stand with a tragedy.'

'Comedy's harder,' I said.

'Exactly,' said Plato. 'Comedy never ends. It's bigger than us. Life is, basically, a long-form comedy.' He pushed a hand through his hair. 'I believe she's with you, you know,' he said. He looked back to me and nodded. 'You know. Your sister.

I believe in all that. Might as well believe in it, huh? Like you might as well give to the church. Nothing wrong with hedging your bets, is there, Tracey-November?'

'Thank you,' I said. I looked down at my trainers. If Plato started being nice to me then I would cry.

'Nice backhand,' I said.

When we moved into the second set, an odd, end-of-the-world party atmosphere seemed to emerge from around the court. I heard what I'd said to Plato, and I understood it for the first time. *Comedy's harder.* Maybe this was what being an adult was all about, a hot mess of half-formed plans, and mistakes and consequences and rough ideas jumped into and out of at random, essentially comic in their tone. Funny because we were mad to think that we could conquer the big things. Because we were ridiculous. Maybe there was no more to it than that. You just perfected your signature on the back of an envelope, and pretended you knew what you were doing.

Several girls who'd been in the year below me at school, along with old girls Drudge and Carter, had arrived, in bikini tops and micro-shorts, shimmering with energy that they directed in my favour.

'You're winning, Feb Kingdom!' shouted Ella Drudge, inaccurately.

'She's not!' shouted Plato's stray dogs.

Ella flicked a 'V' sign at them and came right up to the back of the court where I was standing. She was holding a stereo.

When Plato and I changed ends, I heard a loud conversation between two sixth-formers.

'I swear to God, Mrs Marlow was having a thing with Mr Arrowsmith before he left.'

'What kind of thing?'

'A sex thing.'

'Why does everything have to come down to sex?'

'Always does. Especially with him. He's a perv.'

'Sexy, though. I get why she's gone there.'

I knew how I defined sexy, I thought. Not how Theo had looked, or how he had dressed. It wasn't his Boy London cap or his trainers, or the roll of his eyes when he wanted to make a point. It wasn't his desire to make Plato successful, or even how he had brought the birds together. It wasn't even how much he made me laugh. It was that he had been kind to me. He had seen something in me. Affection, done well, outclasses everything else. Who had said that? I couldn't remember.

I fell apart in the second set. I won the first game, then lost the next four. It was all but over. Plato's fan club were half-cut, dancing around. They had a stereo, blasting 808 State. I lost another game. It had gone to deuce, then to my advantage, to deuce and then back to my advantage five times, then finally Plato had won. I felt that surge of anger, those hot tears waiting under starter's orders and between every point. I closed my eyes again, willing Diana to come. *Surely*, she would come. Plato only had to win one more game, and he would have beaten me. I clenched my fingers around the racquet. I was dead tired. Wasn't this the moment when I should have been able to feel my twin sister more than ever? This, of all occasions, was when I needed rescuing the most. What good was any of this, if Diana couldn't tell me that I was doing OK? If she couldn't tell me that it was good, and she was *proud* of me?

Plato stepped up to the net.

'You're better than this,' he said. 'Come on.'

'I can't do it,' I said. 'You win.'

'No,' said Plato. 'That's not how it works.'

I saw him before Plato saw him, and he came to me across the shimmering heat, like a mirage. He was walking across the garden, in his white trainers; I'd have known the way he walked anywhere. And he walked next to a girl, a girl wearing gingham shorts, her hair up in plaits; she'd kicked off her sandals and carried them in one hand; her feet were bare. He was walking next to her, and she was smiling as she walked, smiling as she walked towards me. *Model: Diana Kingdom at Hicks Models.* They walked towards the court, and they stood watching us. She said something to him, and he laughed, and she put her sandals onto the grass, and she sat down. He stayed standing up, he kept on watching us. Watching me. Theo Farrah. Boy, London. Next to my sister. Next to Diana. It might have been the heat, or the spent energy, or the shock of holding a racquet with intent for the first time since the day of the accident, but I swear this time she was there. It looked to me like she was there.

So, I served to Plato. I served to stay in the game. I served to win one point, to make the next point possible, to make the next game possible, to make the next match possible. As we played, the girl watched. She sat apart from everyone else, she sat like she didn't need anyone else beside her. I fought back. I fought back like everything depended on it. I shut everything out, all of them, every one of Plato's followers, and the trees and the blue sky and the children and the garden and the world beyond. *Slam. Backhand. Forehand. Slice. Ace.* I felt every ounce of energy running from the soles of my feet into the end of the racquet like I was hot-wired. With the power of each stroke came the power of knowing that this had been mine all along. I'd chosen to lose it for a while, but it was still there, and it could be mine again. The sound of the ball on the strings was a heartbeat, a certainty, an opening chord of the best song I'd ever heard. I won the next set.

When we changed ends again, Theo had stepped back, but Plato stopped me at the net.

'He's here,' he said to me.

I nodded. 'He's here,' I said right back to him.

'Walking up here, all on his own, like a fucking cowboy,' said Plato.

'On his own?' I said.

But Plato hadn't heard. He picked up a ball and threw it into the crowd. Several girls scrambled for it. He laughed out loud.

I just have the one set to win now. Just the one left. I used to talk to myself like that back in Austin, Texas, like it was the easiest thing in the world to win, just a matter of time. Now, under my breath, I talked myself through every shot. Plato was growing tired, but the force of him remained there. When I aced him in the fourth game, Theo clapped, but the girl stayed right there on the grass, in her gingham shorts, smiling. There was a Walkman in her hands just like mine. As I served for the set, I knew she was listening to Bruno.

I guess I won without really knowing how I did it, like all the best games. If anyone had asked me how, I wouldn't rightly have been able to answer them. Plato's fans didn't care; they would have loved him if he'd showed up with a ping-pong bat and a golf ball. He shook my hand over the net.

'You did it,' he said to me.

'You made it very hard,' I said.

As I walked off the court, I thought that maybe none of this had happened, that I would wake up and find myself nine years old again, in Austin, Texas, with Grandma Abby, and Mama and Daddy and Diana beside me, and Theo Farrah, and A Misfit Called Plato and Ann and Robert and Gregory no more than scrambled up pieces of a dream I was trying to recall.

'You showed up,' I said to Theo.

'I couldn't miss it,' he said. There was a pause. His face was so familiar, so completely open.

'Can I walk back with you?' he said.

I nodded. Suddenly the weight of the game overwhelmed me. His hand touched my back, wet with sweat.

'I came to say sorry,' he said, 'sorry for everything.'

'You can't be sorry for everything. You don't need to be.'

'Do you forgive us?'

Did I? I turned around to ask her, to see what she thought, but she'd gone.

'Nothing to forgive,' I said. 'You rescued me, you great idiot.'

35

The Driver's Seat

When we arrived back at St Quintin Avenue, Ann was standing in the doorway, looking out into the street like she was expecting us.

'Theo,' she said. Her face cracked into a smile. 'Oh, Feb. Did you win?' she asked, but before we could answer, she fell forward, stumbling out into the street and collapsing onto the ground just in front of the doorstep. She was out cold. I dropped my tennis racquet and crouched down. 'Get her water!' I said to Theo. He pushed past us into the house. Plato, crouching next to me, had the sense to put Ann into the recovery position; I guess they taught you that kind of thing at Eton. Ann's eyes were sliding around in her head.

'She's fainted,' said Plato. 'Cut her hand, too.'

A minute later, Ann sat up on the doorstep, her head between her legs.

'We should get her to a doctor,' said Theo. He looked at me. 'Feb?'

'I've been bleeding,' Ann mumbled into the pavement.

'The baby?'

'Yes. A little. Not much, but – you know – a bit. The baby—'

Theo looked at the car parked outside. 'That's your car?' Ann nodded, seasick. 'Get in, then. We're going to hospital. I'll drive.'

'No!' She tried to stand up. 'I'll be fine, I just need to lie down—'

'Where are your car keys?' Theo asked.

'She never locks it,' I said. 'Glove compartment.'

Theo took out the keys and started the car, and Plato helped Ann into the back where she sat between Plato and me, her head on Plato's shoulder. Plato's huge feet were planted on a crumpled, coffee-stained A–Z and a squashed, half-empty packet of Hula Hoops. The smell of sweat from his T-shirt was a strange comfort.

'I like a woman who treats a car like shit,' he said.

Ann smiled at him faintly. 'Robert doesn't,' she muttered.

Plato had picked up the A–Z. 'I'll direct,' he said.

'I know where I'm going,' said Theo from the front.

'He's gone,' Ann said. 'Robert. He's gone.'

'Where?' My heart pounded against my ribs.

'Had his bag packed an hour ago. He's left.'

'Where's he gone? He *can't* go for long, what about school?'

'He's appointed Will Gibbons to take over until the end of

term. He won't tell me where he's going or when he's back.' She was in shock.

'He'll be back,' I said. I said it hoping to God it was true. Robert couldn't leave her, not now. Ann couldn't talk anymore. She closed her eyes, her hand resting over her stomach.

'St Mary's?' said Theo from the front.

'That's the closest,' said Plato.

'No,' I said faintly. I closed my eyes. No. *Not there. Not there.*

Theo glanced at me in the rear-view mirror and nodded at me. *He knew.* He knew where we were going, and what we were going to do. He was driving to the hospital they'd taken Diana to. *I couldn't go.* I read the time on Plato's watch: 6.38pm. On Sunday. The last few records of the charts were being played right now. Reading my mind, Ann spoke.

'You can turn on the radio, Theo,' said Ann quietly. I reached forward and did it for him.

We took a route through the back streets of Queensway, past Whiteleys, the Victorian department store that had reopened as a shopping mall last year. I had watched *Dead Poets Society* in the cinema at Whiteleys, with some of the more emotionally unhinged girls in my English A level class. Afterwards, a scene had broken out next to the salty popcorn counter when Ella Drudge had been seen coming out of *Batman* on the opposite screen, with a man who looked like – or most likely *was* – Ian Brown of the Stone Roses.

'William Whiteley came to London with just ten pounds in his pocket in 1852,' I recited under my breath. This story was another one of Robert's favourites. 'He ended his life a multi-millionaire businessman, murdered in his office by his illegitimate son.'

'In my family, if you're *not* murdered by your illegitimate son, then you've failed as a human being,' said Plato. 'Simple and as straightforward as that.'

Ann leaned forward again. 'I don't want to go,' she said.

Neither do I. I held onto the sound of Bruno's voice.

'And it's a faller of two places, for Thunderbirds are Go! Featuring MC Parker!'

'Can we turn back?' Ann said again. She looked up at me. 'Please, Feb. If we go in, then it's over. That's it. I'll just know it for certain. I don't want to know.'

'Nothing's over,' said Plato.

Theo indicated left and swung down a one-way street.

'Fuck,' he said, crunching the car into reverse.

'If we go to hospital, they'll try to scan me, they'll try to check on me—'

'That's the idea,' I said. My heart was thumping, I felt like I was standing in my bedroom, watching all of this play out below me. I was aching from playing tennis, aching from knowing Theo had seen me play, aching from being so sure that Diana had been there too.

'They'll tell me it's over,' said Ann again. 'I don't want them to tell me it's over. I don't *want* it to be over.'

'What's over?' asked Plato. 'Your life? I can tell you right now that you're not dying. My mother used to faint all the time.' Plato hadn't caught up.

'Can we tell him?' I asked Ann. She nodded.

'She's pregnant,' said Theo and I at the same time.

Plato didn't miss a beat.

'Right,' he said. 'Makes sense.'

Ann laughed softly. 'The one thing it doesn't make, is sense. Not at my age. But the body's very efficient at ridding itself of unhealthy pregnancies,' said Ann. 'That's what's happening now.' She was talking fast now, as though in a fever. 'I just didn't want to have it spelled out to me just yet. I wanted a bit more time. Just a bit more time.' Still leaning forward, I could see her shoulders starting to shake. Plato put a huge arm around her.

'Please don't leave me in there on my own,' she said to him.

I leaned back and closed my eyes. I could feel the Trench Effect waiting for me, all the goblins lining up ready to take me down and it didn't matter that Theo was with me, it didn't matter that I'd won. It was still there, it could still do this to me. It still had the power.

Easy! I could hear them shouting to each other. *She's missing the end of the Top 40 and she's walking into the very hospital where her sister died!*

We parked the car as the record at number 3 started up. 'Mona' by Craig McLachlan. The cheerfulness of the chorus felt sinister, and Plato started slapping his hands onto his thighs in rhythm with the guitar. I *had* to stay for the countdown. *I had to.* I could see a man in a wheelchair lolling all over the place, being pushed in the direction of A&E. Ann sat up slowly.

'You OK?' asked Theo turning around. 'Right. What do you want to do?'

Ann took my hand in hers. 'Feb should stay in the car,' she said. 'Don't make her go in there. It's too difficult. Diana was brought here, the day of the accident.'

Plato said nothing, but he opened the passenger door and climbed out of the car, helping Ann out behind him. Theo turned around and handed me the car keys.

'We'll wait with Ann,' he said. 'We'll be back as soon as we can.'

'Thank you,' I whispered. My whole body was trembling; I screwed up my fingers into a fist and sat on my hands.

'Haven't been to A&E since I was a boy,' he said. 'I came in with Eric. He'd broken his arm in a fight. He was seventeen.' I looked straight ahead at the radio. 'He was sticking up for me, like,' said Theo. 'We were walking down the street, and some older kids started shouting at me for no good reason. The usual shite, calling me names and stuff, jokes about how I look, that sort of thing. Eric didn't like it, so he went for them, good and proper.'

'Did they mess up his hair?'

'Yeah. They did. I thought he was the greatest thing on earth that afternoon.' He smiled, but it wasn't a smile for me, it was for the memory of it. It was for his big brother. It was for Eric.

He closed the car door, and I watched as he, Plato and Ann walked towards the entrance of the hospital. I sat back and turned the keys in the car so that I could fire up the radio, leaning back and breathing. *Breathe. Breathe. Breathe.* Only one record to go, then I could hear the whole Top 40 read out, loud and clear, and I could keep the Trench Effect away from me. If I could just do that . . . .

'*And at number 2, it's "Nessun Dorma" from Luciano Pavarotti . . .*'

None shall sleep.

The ache in my muscle, the pull in my bones from the tennis match was easing over me, druggish. I opened the back door of the car, walked around the other side and climbed into the driver's seat so I could control the radio. I turned it up. Then, just as I thought I would, I heard the sound of the passenger door opening and shutting, and I knew that Diana was sitting next to me. Funny that she used the door.

What are you doing?

What do you think? Listening to the Top 40. Like we always do.

Yeah, I can see that. But don't.

What do you mean, don't?

Don't stay in here. Go after Ann. You've let her walk into the hospital with those two! You should be with her.

I can't do it. It's where you—

Who cares! What does that matter now?

I have to listen to the countdown. I have to hear it. I always do.

Go after them. Be there for her. She's been there for you!

I can't. I just can't.

Where are you sitting?

What do you mean, where am I sitting?

Where are you sitting right now?

In Ann's car!

Yeah. Which seat?

The driving seat.

I rest my case.

I can't walk in there. Why did you have to leave me? And why did you have to fall in love with Eric and make everything so difficult?

Shut up. Go and find Ann. Walk in. You'll go past the Lindo Wing!

Why should that be relevant?

It's where the Princess of Wales gave birth to William and Harry of course. Got to be worth it, even if just to walk past the steps—

I can't do it.

You can. You have to do it. This afternoon. Today. This could be everything.

This could be everything?

Yeah, that's what I said. Think about what Robert said about Sir Walter Cope.

What of it?

He died of a broken heart.

What's that got to do with this?

His brother died, and he didn't want to go on without him.

So, you're saying I'm Sir Walter Cope in this?

Yeah. You're Sir Walter Cope without the classic house. And one more thing.

What thing?

The boy Plato. Gay. Doesn't want anyone to know, because he thinks it'll ruin his career. But it's obvious, isn't it?

And I suppose you're going to tell me he's always been in love with Theo?

Yeah. That too. Just in case you hadn't realized, pet.

You can't use that word. You're not from Sunderland.

No. But you're from Austin, Texas. Texan girls are brave. Go on . . .

36

Signals from the Deep

I opened my eyes. I opened my eyes and I turned off the radio and I turned it back on. Turned it off. Turned it on. Turned it off. *Off.* Then I switched off the ignition, put the keys in my pocket and stepped out of the car, and I ran towards them, to Ann, and to Theo and Plato. And as I ran, I saw what I saw, and I swear I saw it. You might not have seen it at all if you'd been running with me. Doesn't mean they weren't there.

Because I ran past a man and a woman on the steps of the Lindo Wing, a shell-shocked mother in a green and white polka-dot dress holding a baby swaddled in a blanket, standing next to her husband on the steps, while the world's photographers blinded them with flashes. I ran past Kelvin's dad, shouting *pray for the sister* at me, and waving his arms. I ran past the man in the wheelchair, out of the corner of my eye, and when he looked up at me, he had Eric's eyes. I ran past Kate Moss, laughing, wearing just her bra and knickers, fairy lights framing the window, smoking a cigarette and winking at me, and I ran past Bruno Brookes in his studio, headphones on, gesturing at me in shock. I ran past old Walter Cope, holding in his hands paper plans for his big house in West London, and I ran past Daddy holding up a beer and a bible, and telling me I was brave and good, and that I'd *always* been brave and good, and I ran past Mama, cigarette in hand, holding Thomasina and nodding at me with approval as I pushed through the heavy swing doors to find my aunt. I felt Yellow and all the little flyers, bursting on ahead of me, singing to me, singing to me for their freedom, for my freedom, for escape.

I stood still in the entrance, and I inhaled disinfectant and anxiety and bravery and terror, hardship and hope, and I looked right ahead to where they'd hurried me along to Diana, white faces, knowing what they had to tell me would never leave me. There at the end of the wide corridor, I could see Ann, Plato and Theo going into a room, and I started to run. Theo turned and saw me. He held out his hand.

'Good,' he said. That was all he needed to say. *Good.*

'You've had some bleeding and you fainted?' the nurse asked Ann. Ann nodded. She was whiter than the sheet that covered the bed she was lying on. *Please dear God, can Ann be all right?* I hadn't thought beyond this. *Just let her be OK.* The nurse squeezed jelly onto the head of the scanner; Plato's eyebrows rose.

'We're just going to take a look and see if we can see baby's heartbeat,' said the nurse.

'You won't be able to see a thing,' said Ann. 'I'm forty-five. I've been bleeding. It's over.'

The nurse glanced at Plato.

'And how many weeks along are you?'

'Eleven.' She said the word like it was everything.

'Well. Now just relax, if you can.'

Ann clutched my hand and she looked away, her eyes as far from the screen as they could be. Plato leaned forward, his trainers squeaking on the floor. Theo lowered his eyes. I could see his lips moving. *Please, please, please.*

The nurse stared at the screen. On the other side of the door, I could hear a man laughing and saying goodbye to someone. *'Tell Sunita happy birthday from me,'* he said. Who was Sunita? How old was she today? Who was her mother, who had given birth to her, who had the date of that birth etched into her bones forever? *Happy birthday, Sunita. Happy birthday.* I hummed the tune in my head. *Happy birthday to you . . . Happy birthday to you . . .*

'All right, give me a moment,' said the nurse. I watched her hand move the scanner over Ann's tummy, searching for clues. The screen was black and green, incomprehensible.

'There's the placenta,' she said. 'Let's just see if we can find – ah. Yes. There it is. Can you see? There's the heartbeat, right there. Nice and strong. You see?'

Slowly, we moved our eyes to the screen. There it was. The heartbeat. A little signal from the deep, a submarine signal from a dark, half-understood land, a flashing cursor of new life. Utterly in control. Unmistakably *alive*. In that moment, the flickering movement on that screen felt to me like it knew all the secrets. Everything to know in the whole universe pulsed there. Ann drew in her breath.

'Of course, you'll be back here for your scan at twelve weeks, but I would say all signs point to a healthy baby at this stage. You were right. Eleven weeks exactly. Keep an eye on everything at home of course, but a little bleeding at this stage isn't uncommon.' The nurse turned to the three of us.

'You take care of her,' she said to Plato.

'My wife is a wonderful woman,' said Plato sincerely.

The nurse smiled at him and swept out of the room leaving Ann to wipe the jelly from her stomach. Plato looked at me and winked. When he grinned, he looked thirteen years old. Theo looked at me and rolled his eyes.

We walked back out to the car and Plato took Ann's arm to steady her. He was a good man, I realized. A good man. I thought of all the things he'd tried to tell me, the half-finished cryptic sentences about burning houses and smoke, and I knew Diana had been right about him. Theo walked next to me.

'You did a brilliant thing, Tracey,' he said. 'Didn't think you could leave Bruno on a Sunday.'

That evening I handed Ann the poetry book. How to tell her what Plato had told me? Ann took it from me and shook her head.

'I know what it is. I – I've always known. I think I just

wanted you to know too. I wanted you to hear it from some-one else, not me. I've – I've let him down. We've let each other down.'

'You always knew?'

'I always knew that he'd loved someone before he met me. Always. He was terrified of it. Terrified of everything about it. I believed he loved me enough to make a life together. I thought it would be enough. Turns out that it's not enough. Not for either of us. But maybe that's all right. Maybe it always has been.'

You can shut the doors in the burning house, but the smoke will always find another way to get out.

I didn't want this for Plato. He couldn't live like Robert had done.

Please, please can things change.

It was two days later that I looked into the canary's cage, and found the first of the new eggs was hatching. A bald, weak little baby bird lay featherless, helpless in the nest, while either side, three more little aliens were struggling out of their eggs and onto the soft, weird intricacy of the nest made of our hair: my hair, Diana's hair and Ann's hair, all threaded together and used for a purpose far more complex, yet far simpler than any of us could have understood. Pieces of the beautiful blue shell lay shed, their purpose served. What had grown in them, the skeletons and skin, beating hearts and veins, was ready. The shells were no longer needed. They were alive. This time, I knew they would be all right.

'Oh!' I breathed.

A great lump came to my throat, same as how I felt when I had watched Grandma Abby dancing on her own in the kitchen back in Austin when I was a little girl. I watched them, barely breathing, feeling fine as cream gravy and torn apart at the same time, just like I had back then when I'd watched Mama and Daddy laughing together when they thought I couldn't see them. The baby birds were beautiful and grotesque, they were unformed little dinosaurs, primitive as all hell, eyes unopened, barely able to hold up their own necks, yet they were *alive*. They had done it. *I* had done it. Theo and I had done it. And I stood there, quite still, because if you move too fast, or make too much noise, the joy gets frightened and won't stick around for long, but I knew then, as I saw the birds take their first breaths outside the eggs, I knew then that I would play tennis again, that I had permission from my soul to do it. Despite *everything*. What Gregory had said was true.

Later that day, Theo stood in my bedroom, and we looked at the baby birds reaching out with their scrawny necks for food, blindly. *Blindly.* Seeking strength through instinct and chance. Theo held my hand tight as tight, and I saw myself as I was before, and as I would be again, in all my splintered pieces, and even though I don't know which way is up, I don't mind February Kingdom nearly as much as I used to. I like the version of February Kingdom who looked after Yellow and made sure the babies happened. We made that happen. Me and Theo Farrah. No. Let me get it right. We *helped* it to happen. The truth of it is that something way bigger did the real work for us. The real work – feathers, claws, beating hearts in little chests and wings – happened as the best kind of magic happens. No sleight of hand, no tricks, but in good old ignorance, sunlight and real time, right before your eyes, hiding nothing.

'A couple of weeks, and they'll fly,' he said. 'Until then, we have to look after them. You and me. Together.'

I stood next to him, and I put my arms around him, not knowing how the birds had the power to do what they had done, but understanding that something had changed, irreversibly altered, that couldn't be changed back, only we didn't quite know what yet. They couldn't go back inside the eggs. Not one of us could. It was out, and once you were out nothing could be put back. You just need to make the best of it, with all that movement, with being hurtled along.

Eventually, Theo sat down on the floor, with his back to the wall as he always did.

'If I'm here, and you want me here, then we have to move on,' he said. 'We move on like we did today. We move on from you listening to the Top 40 every week like it's an exam that you mustn't fail. We move on from the magical thinking stuff. We hit forehands like Agassi, and we believe in maniac liars like Plato, and fuck it, maybe it'll be all right. But you have to understand me, Tracey, you just *have* to. It's unputdownable stuff.'

I nodded at him. Unputdownable stuff, like Ann telling Robert that he didn't have to lie anymore. That she didn't have to. Unputdownable stuff like sadness and freedom.

'And you have to *talk* to me, Tracey. Yeah, I should have told you earlier about Eric. I know I should have. I just didn't want to – to ruin it.' I looked at his hands. I think I might have loved his hands more than anything else about him, their elegance and their grace and the odd feeling I had when I looked at them, that everything would be all right.

'Ruin what?' I asked.

'Ruin how I felt when I was around you. I didn't want you to go. Not ever. Not from the second you walked into the pet shop. I *never* wanted you to go.'

'Where have you been since the hospital?' I asked him.

He hesitated.

'I went to see Lisa,' he said. 'And Charlie.'

'How is he?'

'Huge. Happy as anything. Smiles all the time.'

'He's the best baby in the world,' I said.

'Lisa thinks he might have a problem with his sight,' said Theo. 'She doesn't know for sure, but he's had a few tests. They think he can't see very much out of his right eye.'

I stared at him.

'He can't *see*?'

'Well, they can't tell for sure. He's certainly got problems with his vision.'

I let his words sit between us. *He's certainly got problems with his vision.*

Theo looked at me. 'Yeah,' he said. 'Just like—'

'Like Diana,' I said.

That thing that I'd felt itching away at me, this strange

certainty that was deep in me, seemed to sigh inside me deeply then let go. I saw myself as a little girl, standing next to Diana in old Abby's backyard, letting go of helium balloons. I opened my fist, and the balloon floated away, into the blue sky. Theo looked down at his hands.

'It's bad luck,' he said, 'but there are things that they can do, in time. He'll have the best mother, won't he, and he won't want for anything. And Eric'll step up to the mark, you watch.'

'He was always hers,' I said.

For the first time, I pulled the *Evening Standard* out from under the bed. I pulled it out, and I unfolded it, and I handed it to him.

'This is what they wrote about her,' I said.

He hesitated.

'Would you read it to me?' he said. 'Go on, Tracey. It's all right. Read it out to me.'

I cleared my throat.

Fresh Tragedy for Family
Already Affected by Disaster

The victim of a fatal car accident in North London last Monday has been named as nineteen-year-old Diana Kingdom. The driver of the car, Lisa Hicks, was unhurt. Diana, who was visually impaired, was a successful teenage model and appeared

on the cover of numerous magazines
including *Just Seventeen*, *SKY* and *Elle*.
Her parents, Joseph and Lily Kingdom,
were killed in the King's Cross fire in
November 1987. Diana leaves behind her
twin sister, February.

'Diana leaves behind her twin sister, February,' repeated Theo.

Quiet as quiet, the radio played 'Perfect' by Fairground Attraction.

We lay together in silence. I closed my eyes and thought about Charlie. I ached for him. I ached for the babies that never got as far as him, for the rollercoaster hope-train of Ann and Gregory's baby, and for Mama and for Daddy never able to hold their grandchildren. I ached to open every single one of Lisa's letters, and to tell her that everything was all right, and I knew now that I would.

As Theo spoke, I looked up, and I saw Diana in the mirror, and I knew that I was seeing her there for the last time. She smiled at me, and when I looked into her eyes, they were clear and bright, but unremarkable, just the eyes of an ordinary pretty girl, and they looked right back at me, and I know that she could see me properly for the first time, and I knew that it was all right, and that she didn't need me any longer. When I was alone in my room, when I was walking down the street, when I was working for my exams, I would only feel myself. She had let go of my hand for the first time. The stereo clicked off, but I didn't turn the tape

410

over. I looked back into the mirror, in the silence, in the bedroom with the blue wallpaper of the Chinese men on swings
and the writing desk. In the silence. The bird called Yellow
looked at me. In the silence. In the silence and in the mirror.

And in the mirror, there was just me.

Just me.

Epilogue

Plato got his record deal. He's going to play Reading Festival, then he's going out on tour with a band called the Farm. Theo's going too. He's done it, just like he said he would. When they read my paper on canaries, Texas said my place was still there if I wanted it. But I don't know yet. Maybe. Maybe Ann and her baby will come with me. She and Robert agreed to sell the house in St Quintin Avenue, but Ann can't forget Gregory telling her she should hold onto it. Maybe he's right. Maybe it *will* be worth two million pounds in twenty years' time. I wouldn't put anything past this crazy bit of town. Robert's given some money to the building of a Japanese garden in Holland Park. He said he'd take me there when it's open, to look at the cherry trees and remember the boy he lost when he was nineteen.

The baby birds fledged and flew from the nest. We gave two of them to Lisa and Charlie, and Lisa called them Rifat and Ozbek.

I wrote all of this down because I couldn't not. I mean,

once you start thinking about how things started, you have to keep on till you get to the bit where you catch up with yourself. I suppose all I'm saying is don't give up. Pull up a chair for Hope. You never know, you might just find that she slinks up to you one day, when you're not expecting her. She's a bird, she's a boy from Sunderland in a Boy London cap, she's a pop star outside a record shop, she's a faint line on a test and she's advantage from deuce. But she's always hanging around.

You just have to know where to look for her. That's all.

Afterword

They say you should never meet your heroes, but I'll never regret introducing myself to Michael Hutchence outside Our Price on the King's Road that afternoon. He died in Sydney, Australia, in November 1997. He was thirty-seven years old.

Diana, Princess of Wales, was killed in a car accident in Paris the same year, three months earlier. She was just thirty-six.

Acknowledgements

Bouquets and copies of *Now 17* to: Claire Conrad (agent supreme), Clare Hey (editor supreme), Arzu Tahsin, Tamsin Shelton, Clare Wallis, Louise Davies, Sabah Khan, Justine Gold, ALL at Simon & Schuster UK, Lucinda Prain, Marie Florio for the Kazantzakis estate, Samantha Evans (Petrol Records) and Andrew Farriss for INXS, Alison Clarkson, Kate Weinberg, Lucinda Labes, Vince Power for talking to me on the phone in lockdown about running venues in the 90s, Luca Balbo, Alice Compton, Fay Rawlinson, Lucy Rawlinson, Gareth Belsey, Willie Dowling, my brother Donald Rice for reading and noting, Mum, Dad, Martha, Billy and Kit Hobbs and Pluto. Always remembering Melanie Richardson, Joe Haddon and Roddy Dart who represented nothing but fun times in the early–mid 90s, Galaxy bars to all of my boarding-school friends of this decade who knew what good pop could do for a girl. Thank you to Hugh Smith who helped me with my canaries.

And, of course, thank you to PB. Spot on, as usual.

A note about quoted lyrics

Feb is a pop music obsessive, just like me (or at least I used to be, back when chart positions really mattered). I knew that to illustrate the grip that the Top 40 has on my narrator, I would need to quote lyrics from some of the songs that were ubiquitous in 1990. Early drafts of this novel had three times the number of lyrics quoted, before I encountered the tricky business of getting permission from music publishers to include their artists' songs in a book. I decided to keep in the lyrics where not to include them would have seriously compromised the scene where they occur. As Michael Hutchence appears in my story as a real-life character, it felt imperative to me to be able to quote lines from INXS. The lyrics to 'New Sensation' are perfect for Feb and her story. Whenever I listened to this song – still amazingly fresh thirty-six years after it was written – I could imagine Feb, pushing her way out of darkness towards a new day accompanied by that unmistakable riff from Andrew Farriss. I was also lucky enough to get permission to use the lyrics of the brilliant, completely uplifting 'Doin' the Do' by Betty

Boo – aka Alison Clarkson – who allowed me to use one of her lines for free. I was determined to quote from the melodramatic lyrics to 'Drama!' by Erasure that is playing on the radio when Feb and Theo learn the truth about one another. Transvision Vamp was a band with a front-woman who was so cool even her lipstick had frosted over; Wendy James deserves to be better recognized as the force of nature she was at this time and the inclusion of a lyric from 'I Want Your Love' felt perfect. Ted Hughes and the beautiful Nikos Kazantzakis poetry included in *This Could Be Everything* sit alongside these pop mavericks in a way that might have bewildered them both. Or perhaps delighted them. *Smash Hits* and *Just Seventeen* are long-gone now, but for a number of years these magazines were culturally crucial to a teenager like me with a fixation with pop statistics and an interest in affordable denim and lipgloss. I didn't manage to gain permission to quote 'Edie (Ciao Baby)' by the Cult which Feb hears in her head when she is outside Our Price. If you have the time, you can play this when you reach this chapter.

Credits:

Epigraph: Lines from 'God's Prayer: St Francis of Assisi' by kind permission of Niki Stavrou on behalf of the Kazantzakis estate.